VIZ GRAPHIC NOVEL
RANMA 1/2™

12

This volume contains
RANMA 1/2 PART SIX #12 through #14 and PART SEVEN #1 through
#3 (first half) in their entirety.

Story & Art by Rumiko Takahashi

English Adaptation by Gerard Jones & Toshifumi Yoshida

*

Touch-Up Art & Lettering/Wayne Truman
Cover Design/Hidemi Sahara
Editor/Trish Ledoux
Assistant Editor/Bill Flanagan

*

Managing Editor/Hyoe Narita
Editor-in-Chief/Satoru Fujii
Publisher/Seiji Horibuchi

*

First published by Shogakukan, Inc. in Japan

*

Printed in Canada

*

Published by Viz Communications, Inc.
P.O. Box 77010
San Francisco, CA 94107

*

10 9 8 7 6 5 4 3 2 1
First printing, January 1999

Vizit us at our World Wide Web site at www.viz.com,
our Internet magazine, j-pop.com, at www.j-pop.com,
and *Animerica, Anime & Manga Monthly* at
www.animerica-mag.com

VIZ GRAPHIC NOVEL

RANMA 1/2™

STORY & ART BY
RUMIKO TAKAHASHI

CONTENTS

PART 1
THE ROAR OF HEAVEN

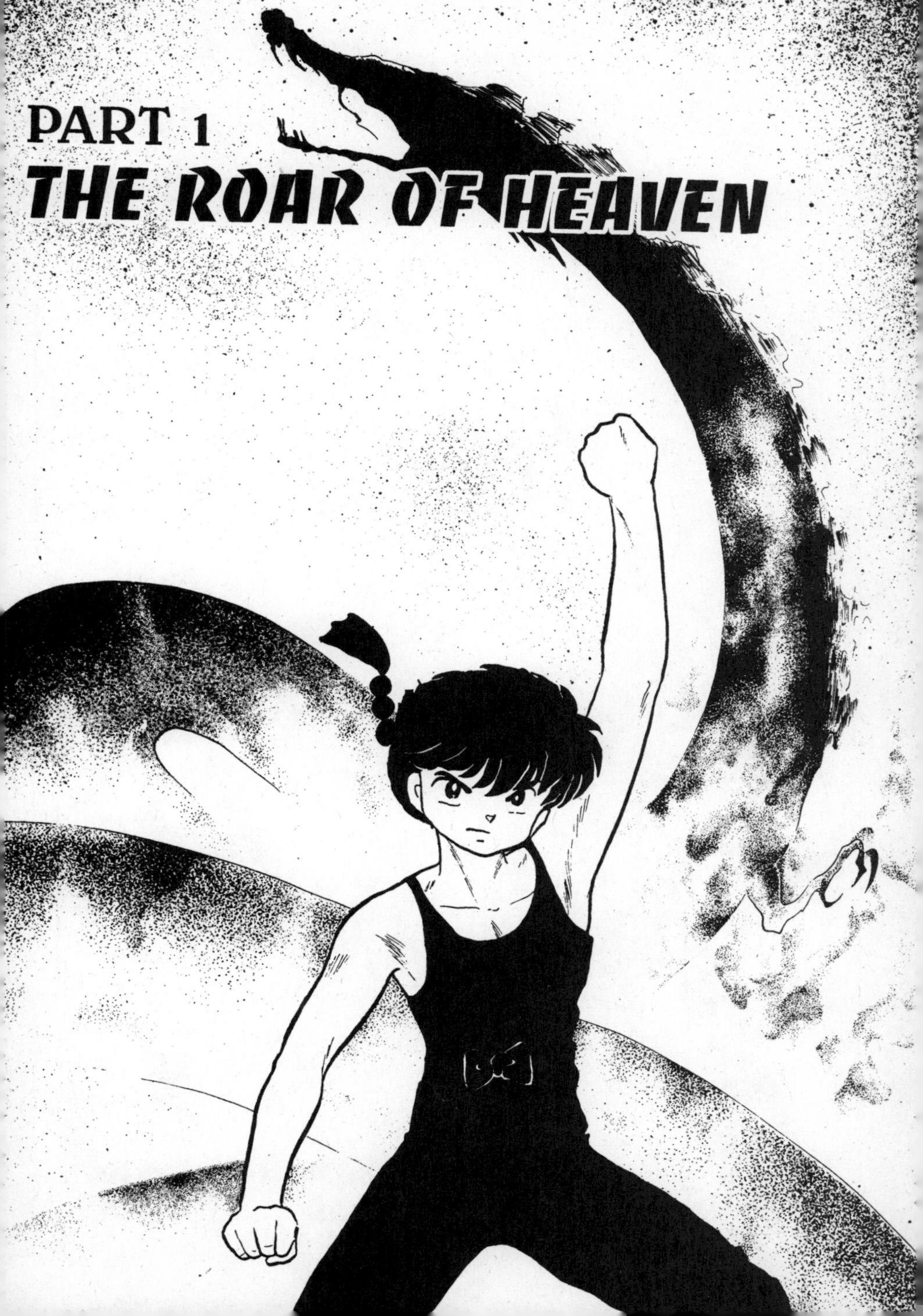

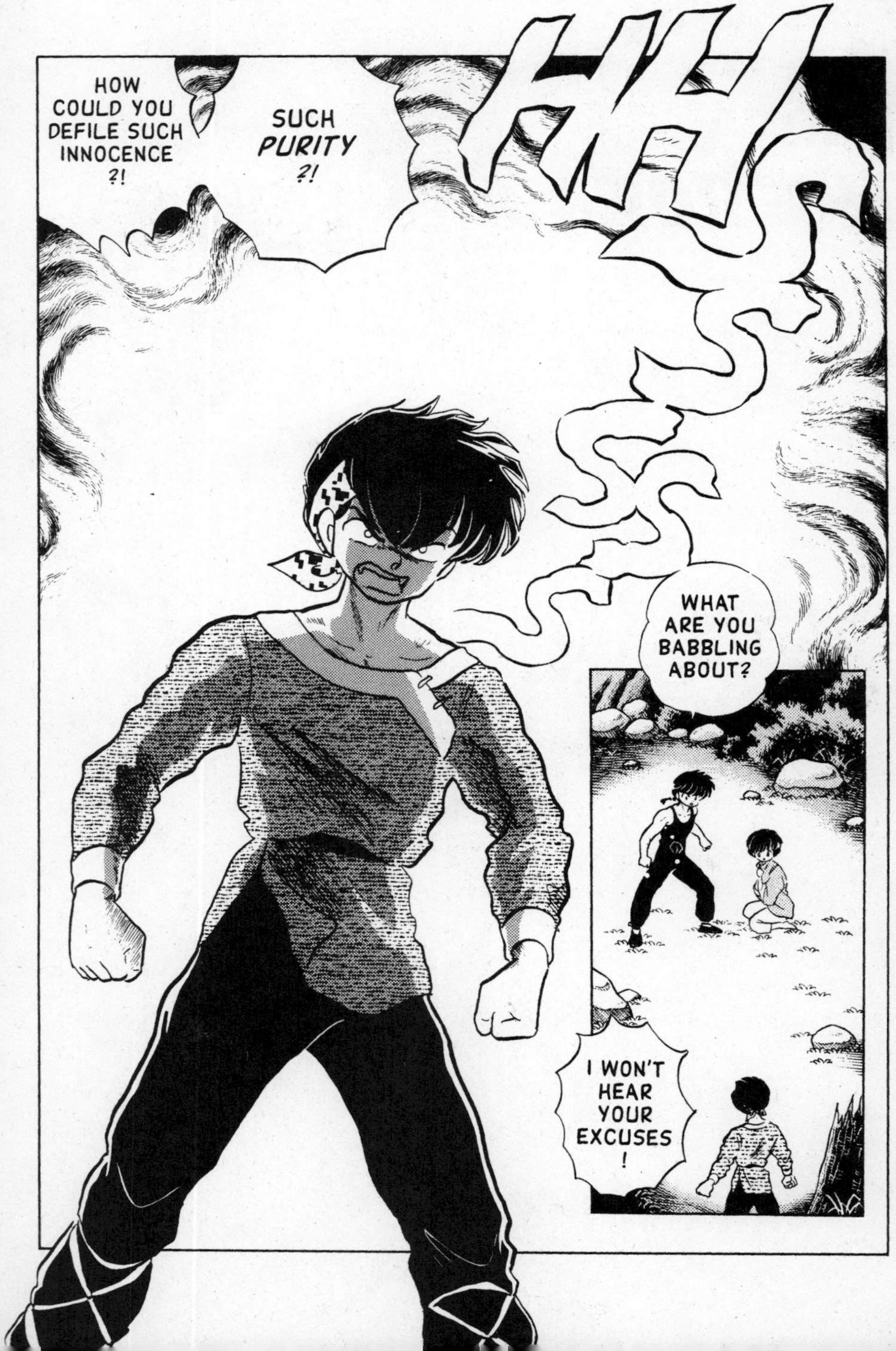
HOW COULD YOU DEFILE SUCH INNOCENCE ?!
SUCH PURITY ?!
WHAT ARE YOU BABBLING ABOUT?
I WON'T HEAR YOUR EXCUSES !

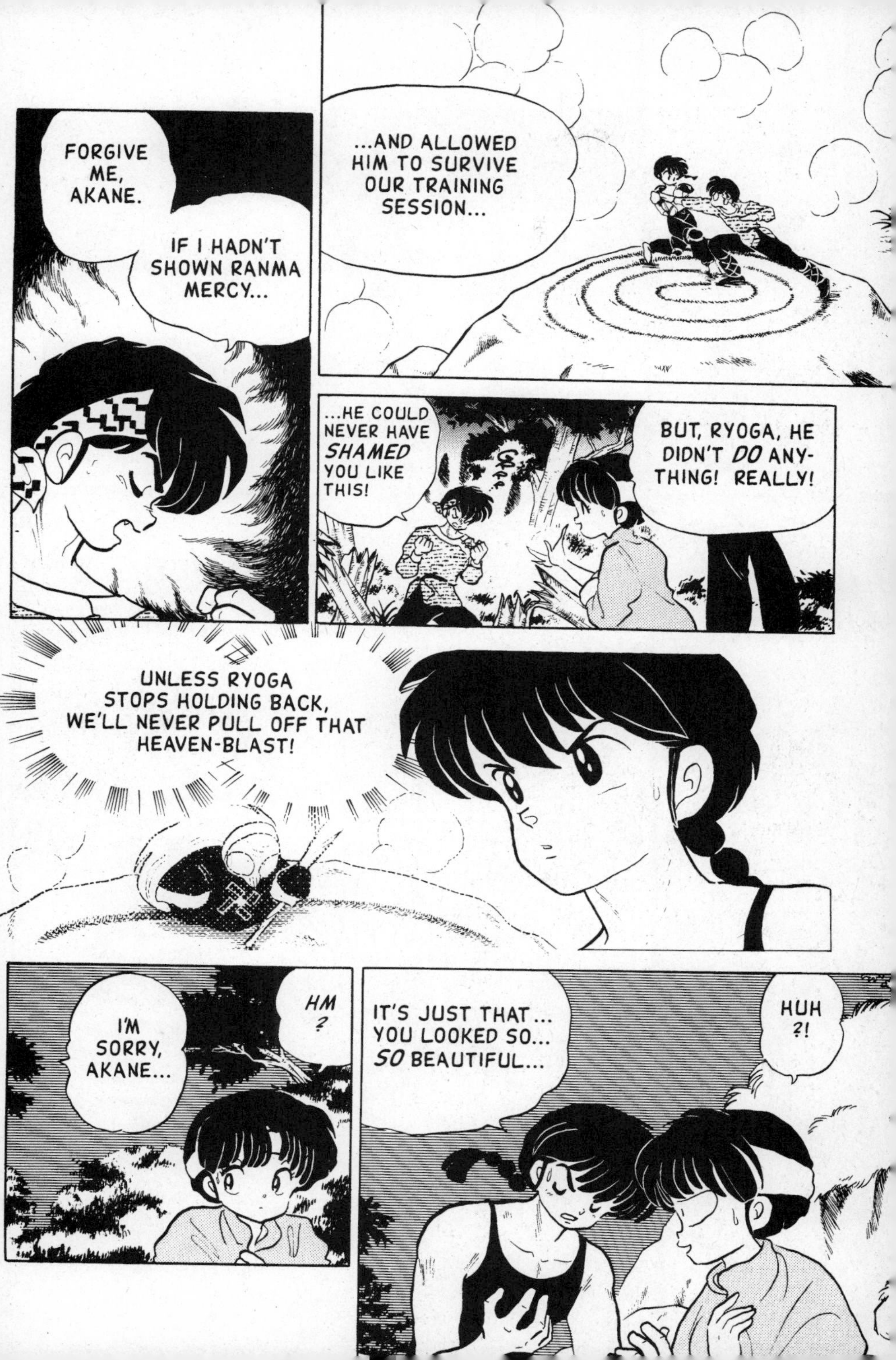
FORGIVE ME, AKANE.
IF I HADN'T SHOWN RANMA MERCY...
...AND ALLOWED HIM TO SURVIVE OUR TRAINING SESSION...
...HE COULD NEVER HAVE SHAMED YOU LIKE THIS!
BUT, RYOGA, HE DIDN'T DO ANY-THING! REALLY!
UNLESS RYOGA STOPS HOLDING BACK, WE'LL NEVER PULL OFF THAT HEAVEN-BLAST!
I'M SORRY, AKANE...
HM ?
IT'S JUST THAT... YOU LOOKED SO... SO BEAUTIFUL...
HUH ?!

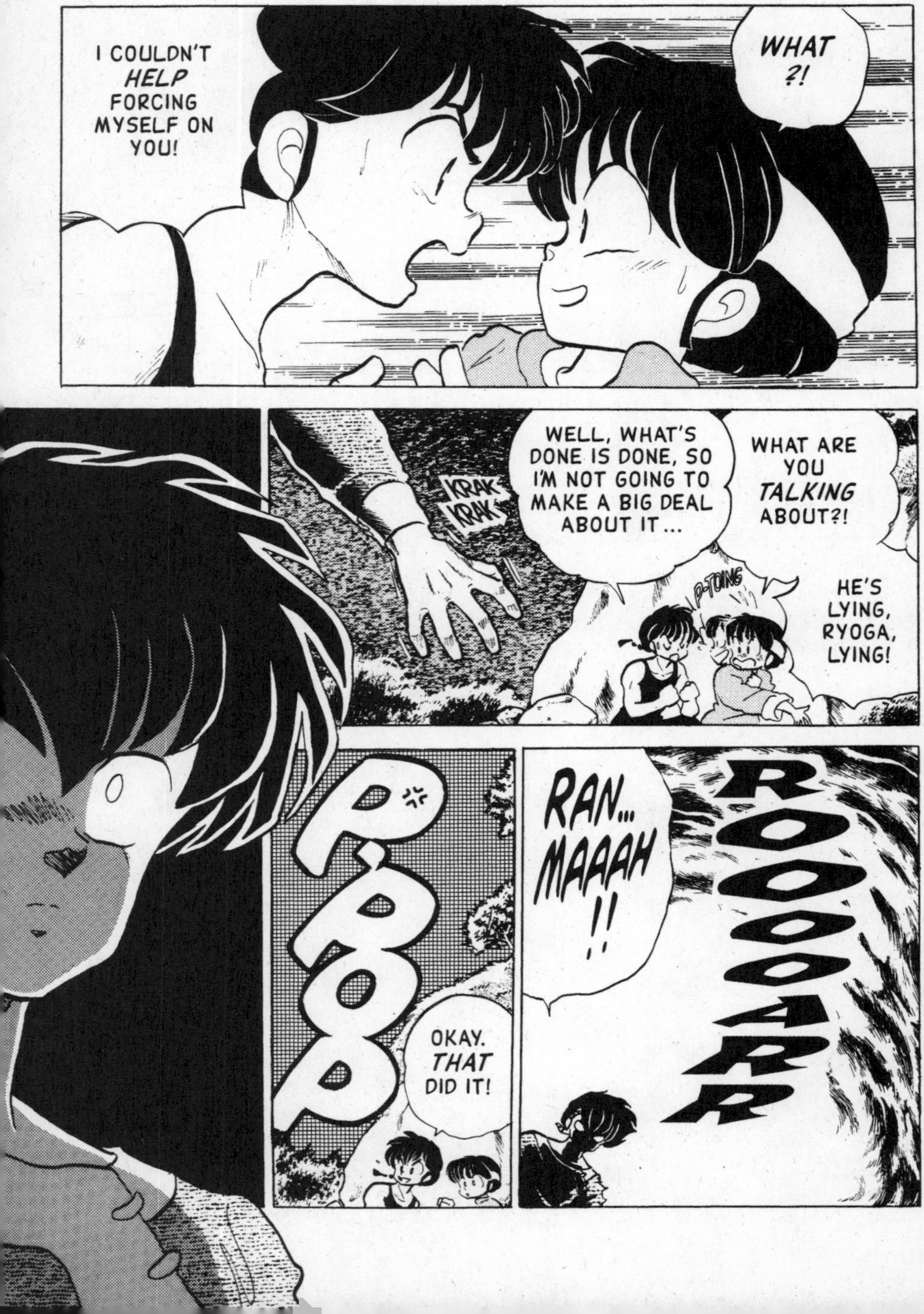
I COULDN'T HELP FORCING MYSELF ON YOU!
WHAT ?!
KRAK KRAK
WELL, WHAT'S DONE IS DONE, SO I'M NOT GOING TO MAKE A BIG DEAL ABOUT IT...
WHAT ARE YOU TALKING ABOUT?!
P-TOING
HE'S LYING, RYOGA, LYING!
PPOP
OKAY. THAT DID IT!
RAN... MAAAH !!
ROOOOARR

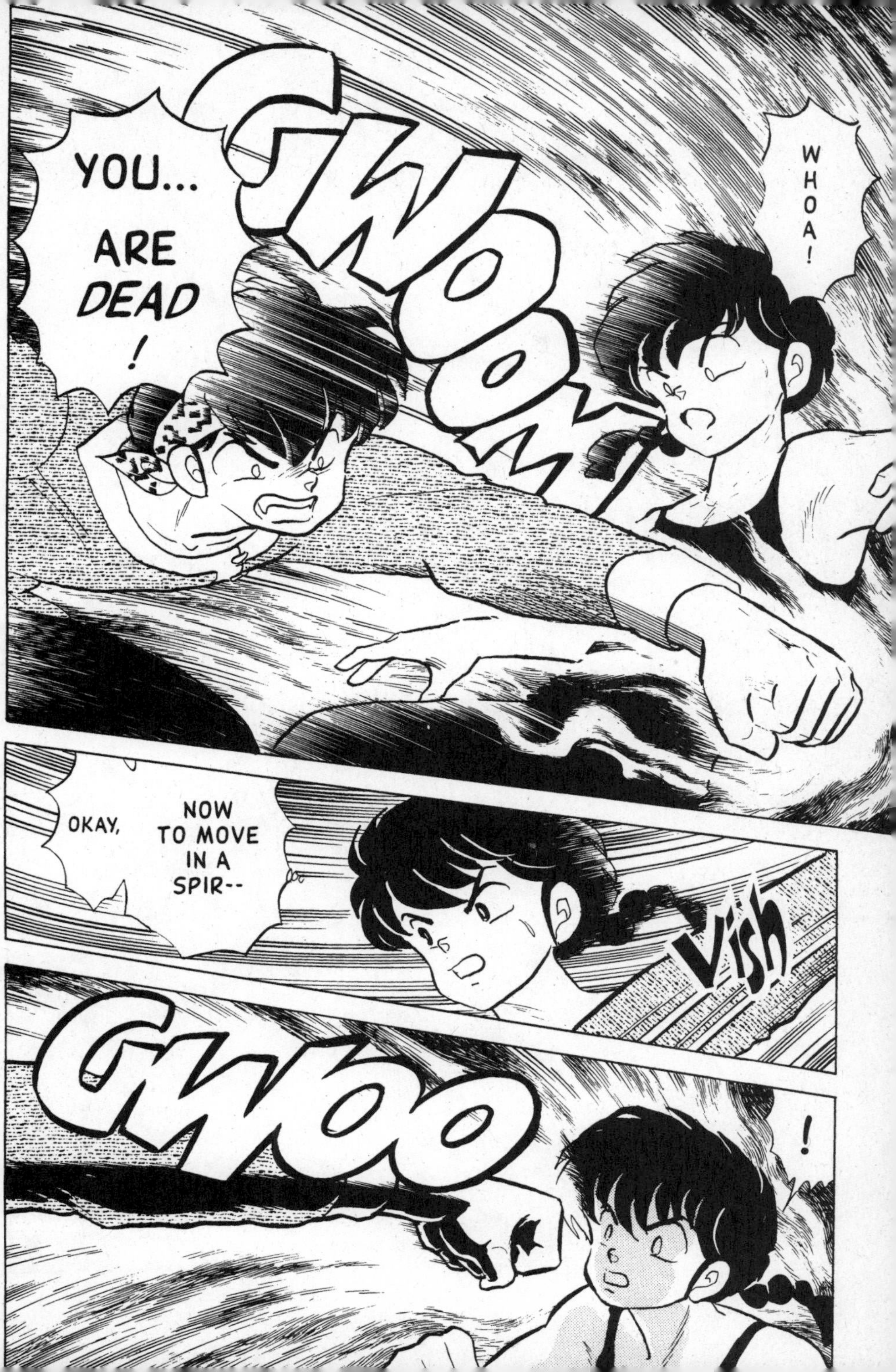
YOU... ARE DEAD!
GWOOM
WHOA!
OKAY,
NOW TO MOVE IN A SPIR--
VISH
GWOO
!

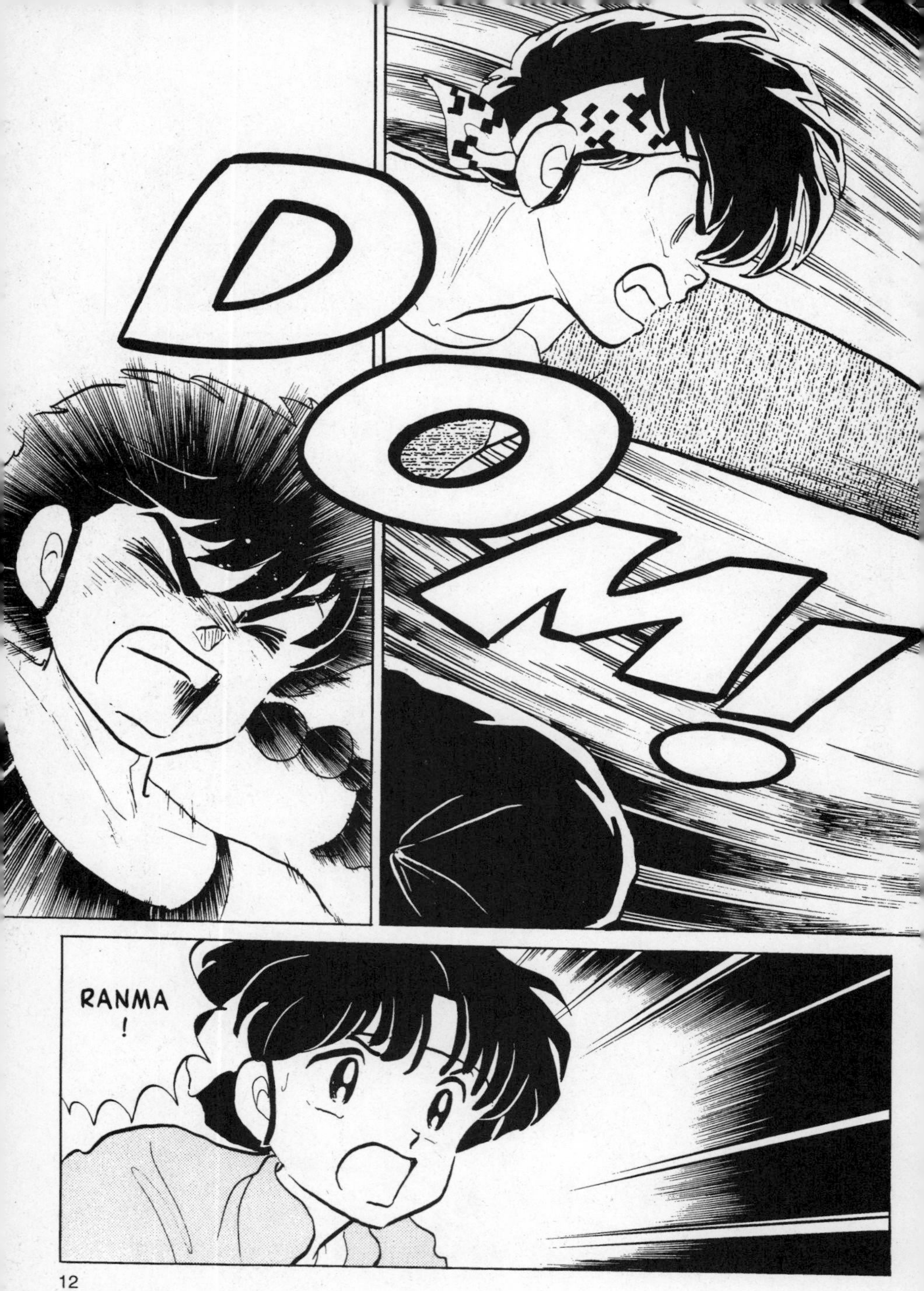
DOM!
RANMA
!

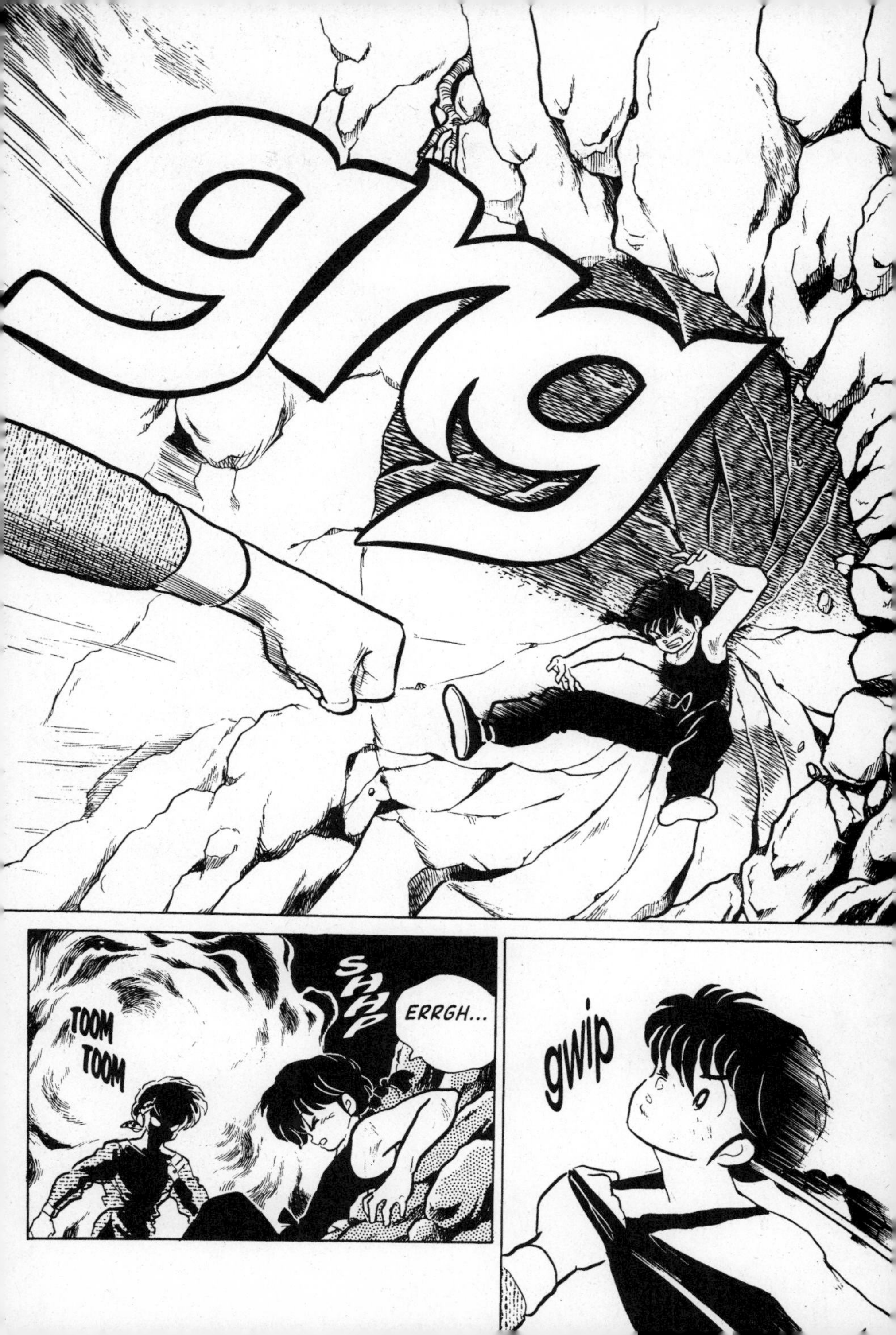
TOOM TOOM
ERRGH...
gwip

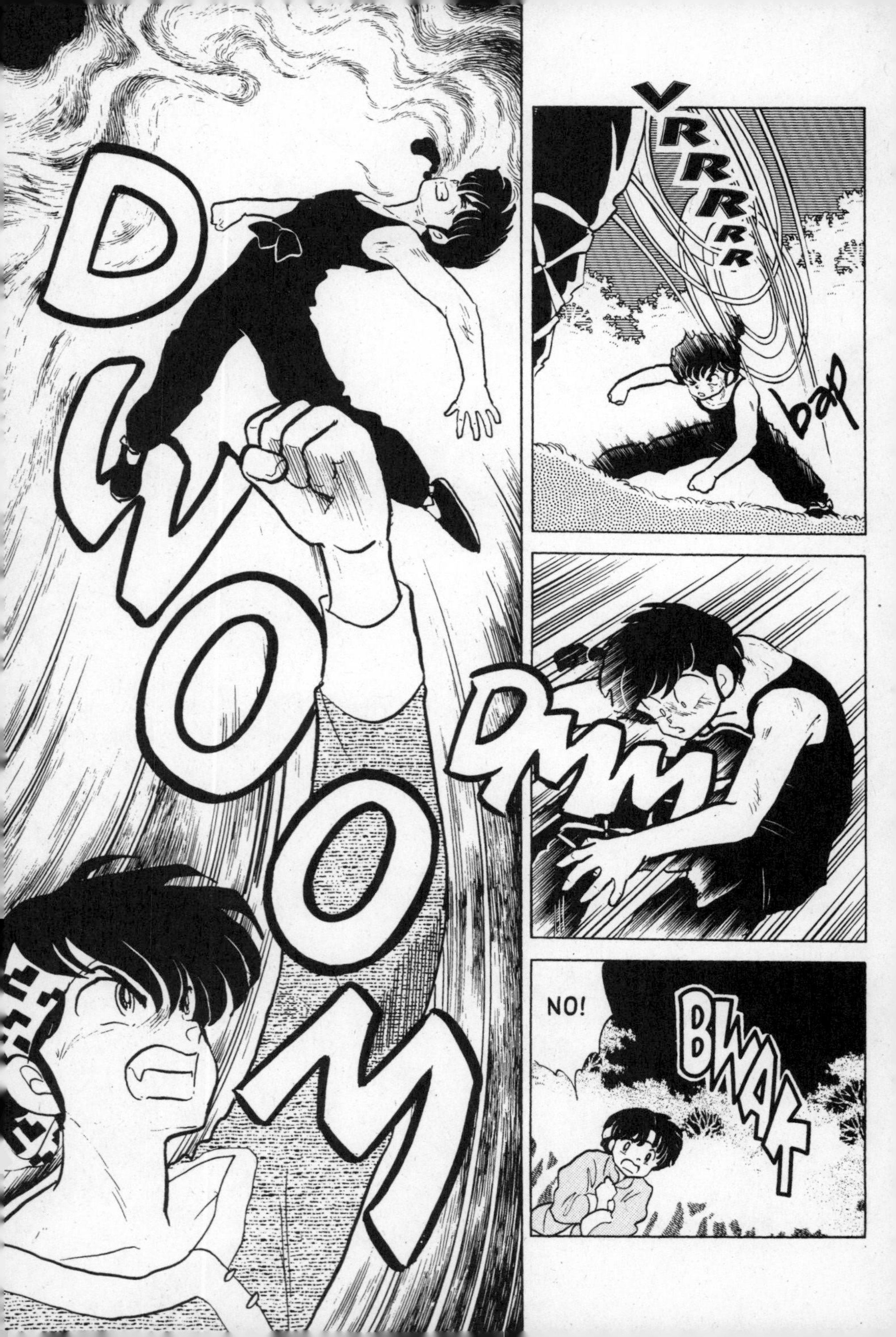
DWOOOM
VRRRRR
bap
DMMM
NO!
BWAK

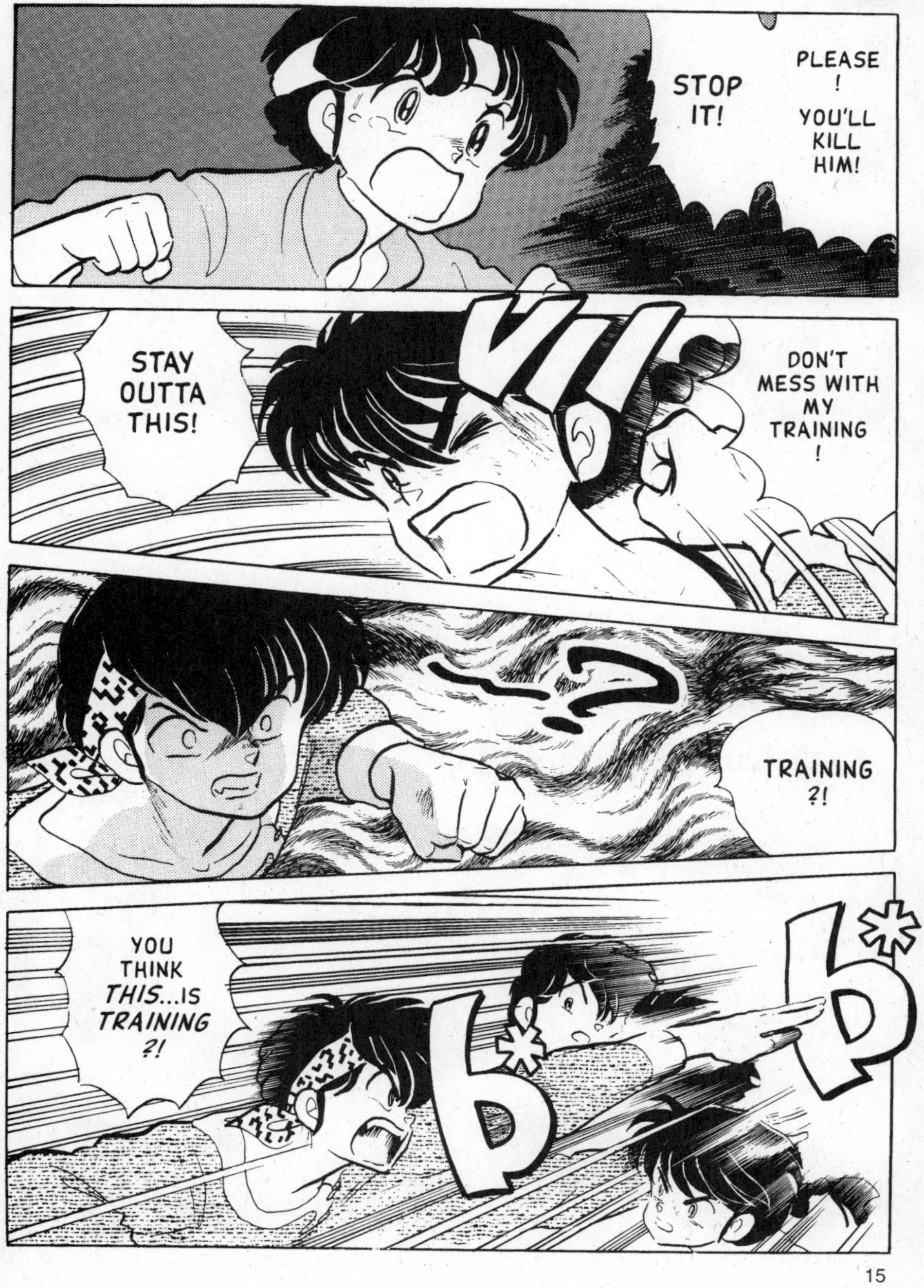
STOP IT!
PLEASE! YOU'LL KILL HIM!
STAY OUTTA THIS!
DON'T MESS WITH MY TRAINING!
--?
TRAINING?!
YOU THINK *THIS*...IS *TRAINING*?!

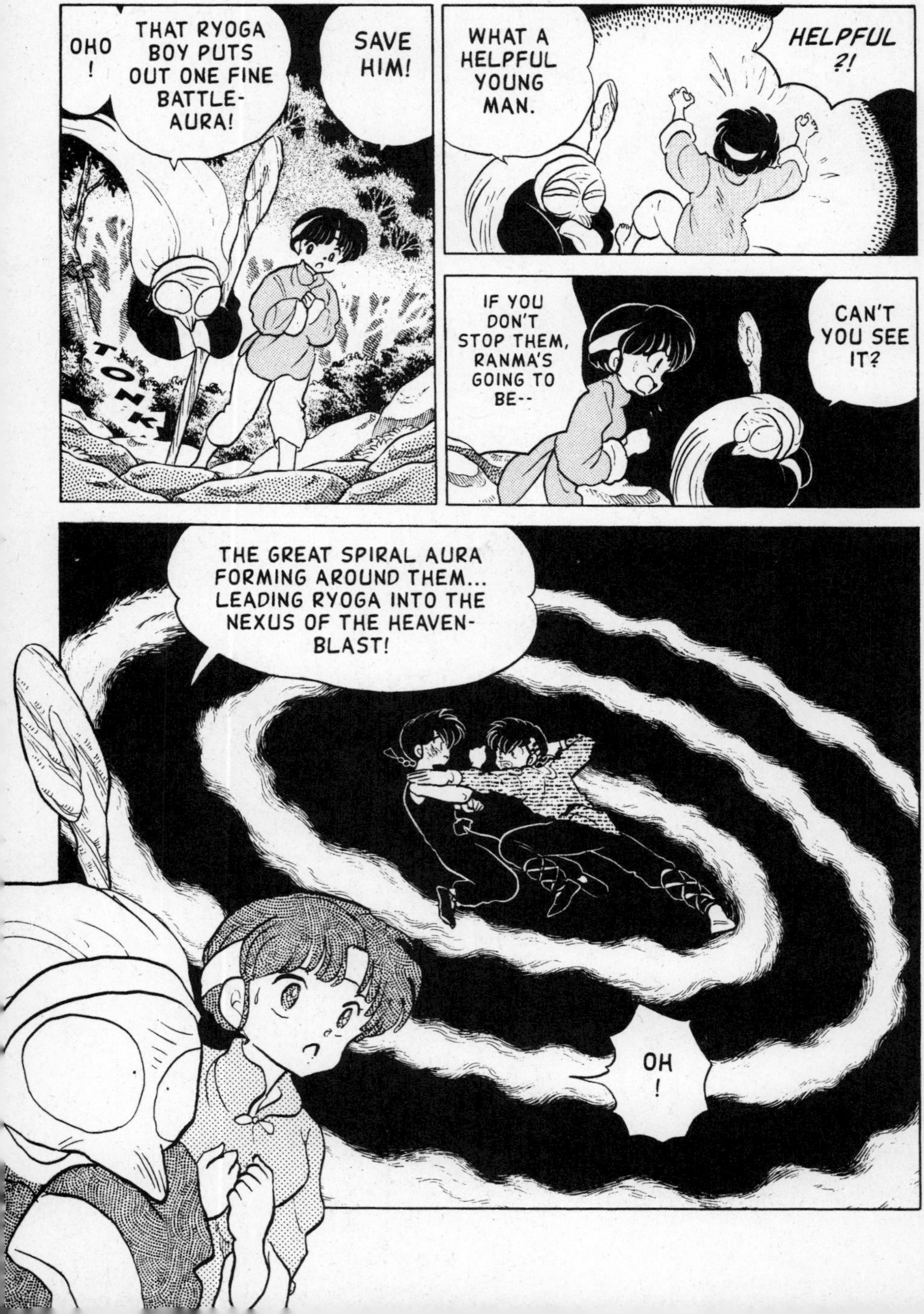
OHO!
THAT RYOGA BOY PUTS OUT ONE FINE BATTLE-AURA!
SAVE HIM!
TONK
WHAT A HELPFUL YOUNG MAN.
HELPFUL?!
IF YOU DON'T STOP THEM, RANMA'S GOING TO BE--
CAN'T YOU SEE IT?
THE GREAT SPIRAL AURA FORMING AROUND THEM... LEADING RYOGA INTO THE NEXUS OF THE HEAVEN-BLAST!
OH!

GWOM

FIVE MORE STEPS...TO THE CENTER OF THE SPIRAL!

AND ONCE IN THE CENTER, HE'LL WAKE THE DRAGON...

...LETTING LOOSE THE BLAST OF HEAVEN...

...WITH ONE FINAL MOVE!

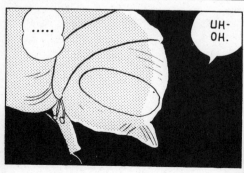

.....

UH-OH.

I SUPPOSE I SHOULD HAVE TAUGHT HIM THE FINAL MOVE...

WHAT ?!

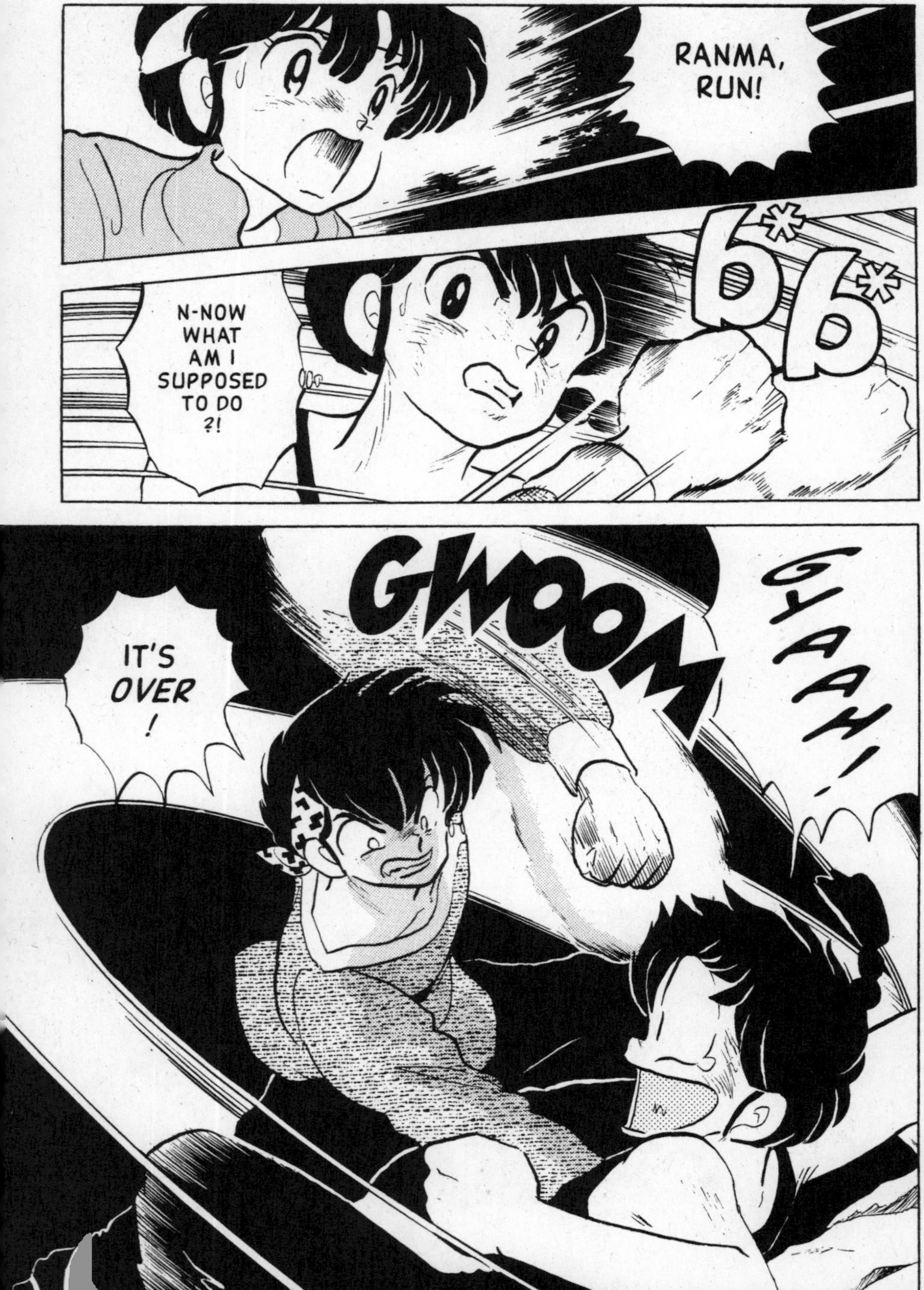
RANMA, RUN!
N-NOW WHAT AM I SUPPOSED TO DO ?!
6*6*
GWOOM
IT'S OVER !
GYAAH!!

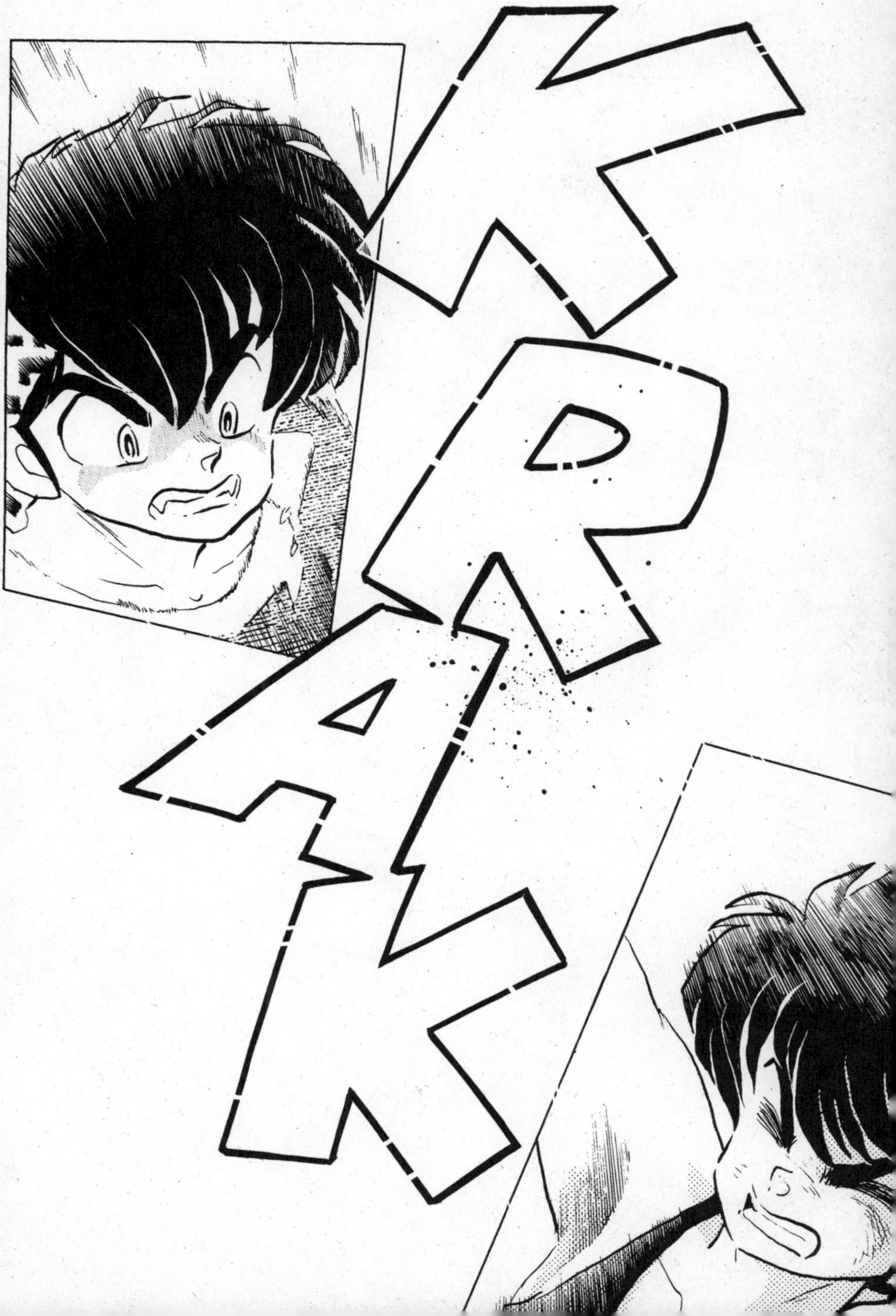
WHAK!

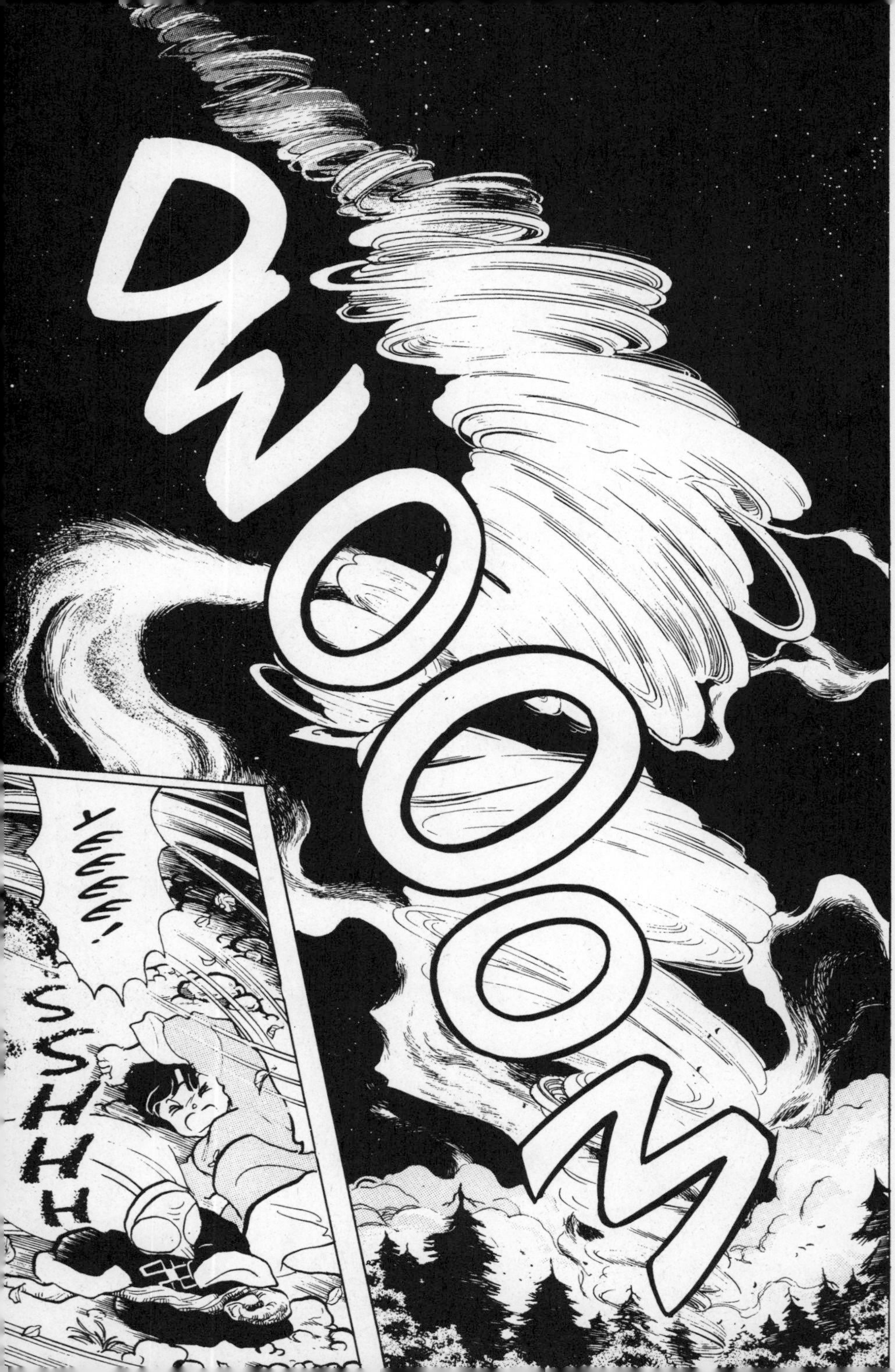
DWOOOOM
YEEEEEE!
SSHHH

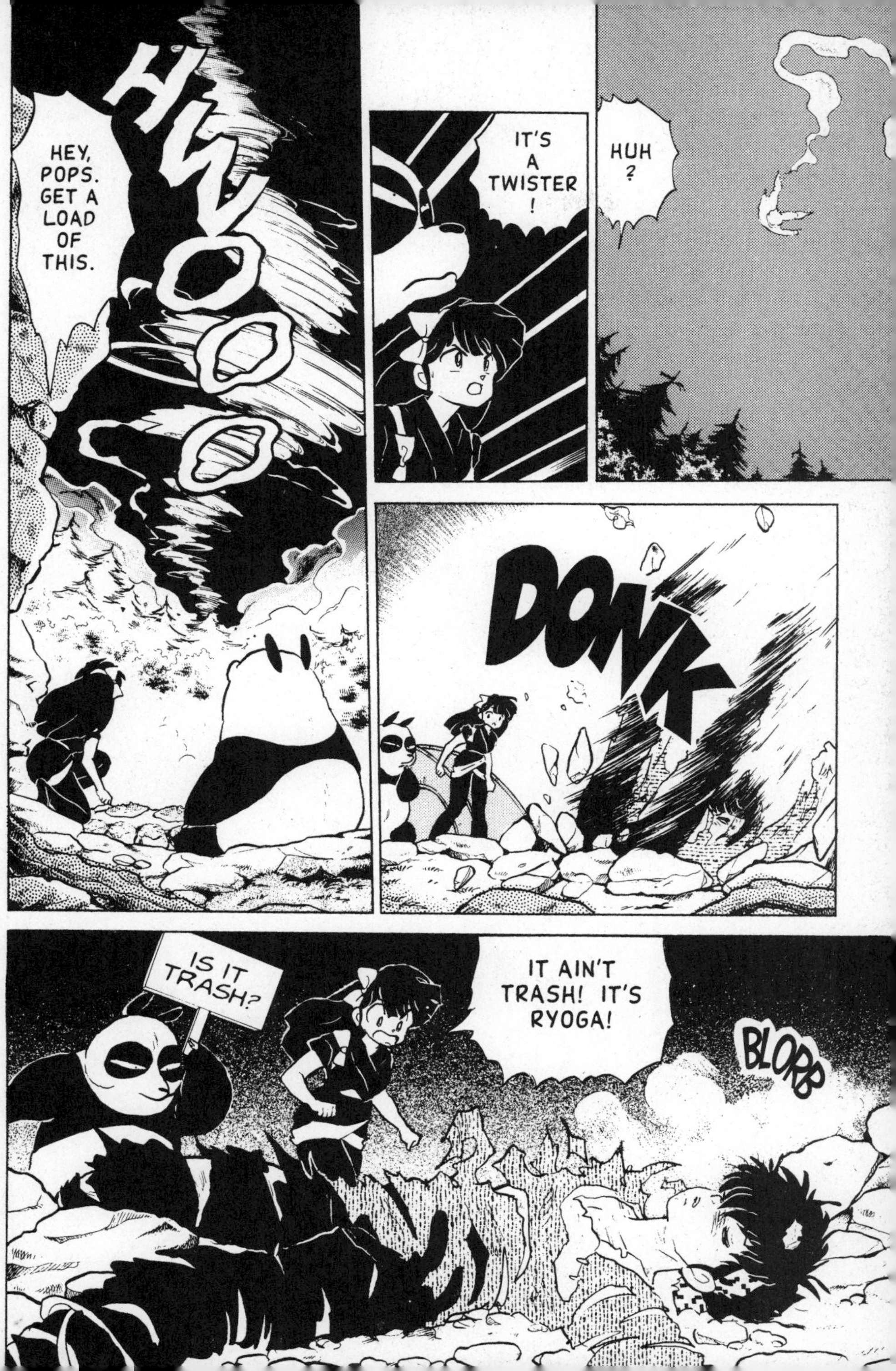
HWOOO
HEY, POPS. GET A LOAD OF THIS.
IT'S A TWISTER!
HUH?
DONK
IS IT TRASH?
IT AIN'T TRASH! IT'S RYOGA!
BLORB

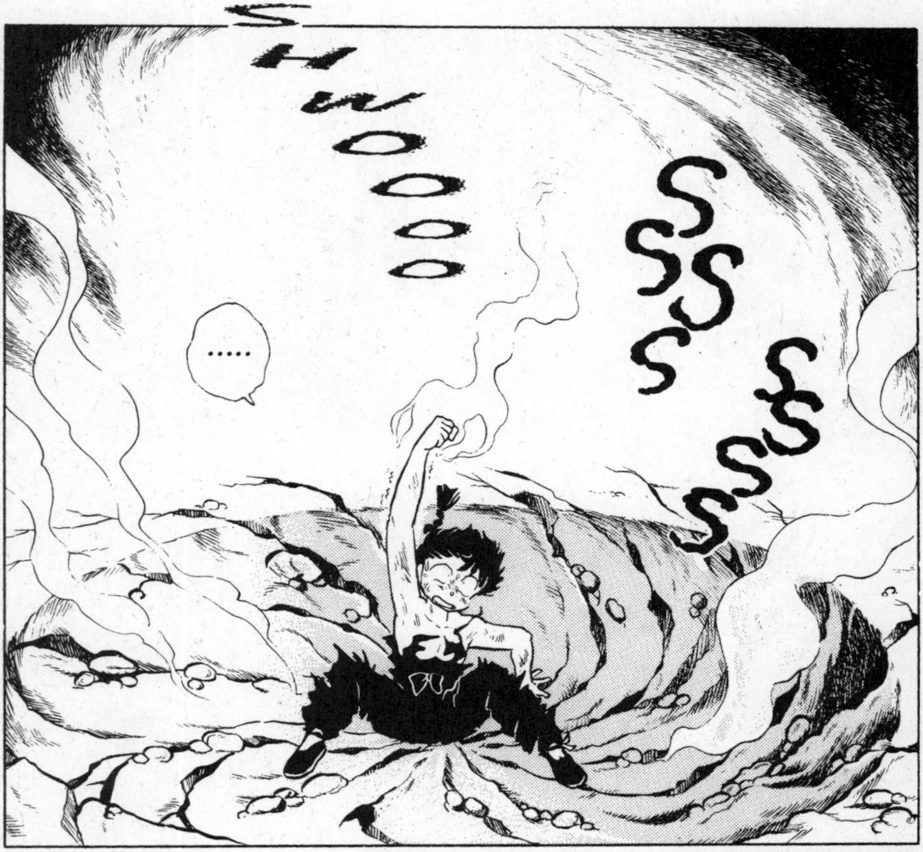
SHWOOOOO
......
SSSSSSSS

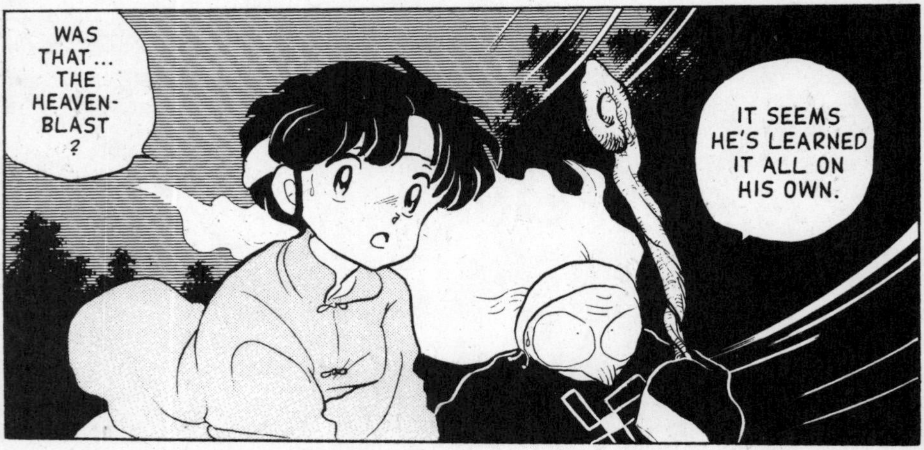
WAS THAT... THE HEAVEN-BLAST?
IT SEEMS HE'S LEARNED IT ALL ON HIS OWN.

PART 2
THE GREAT REMATCH

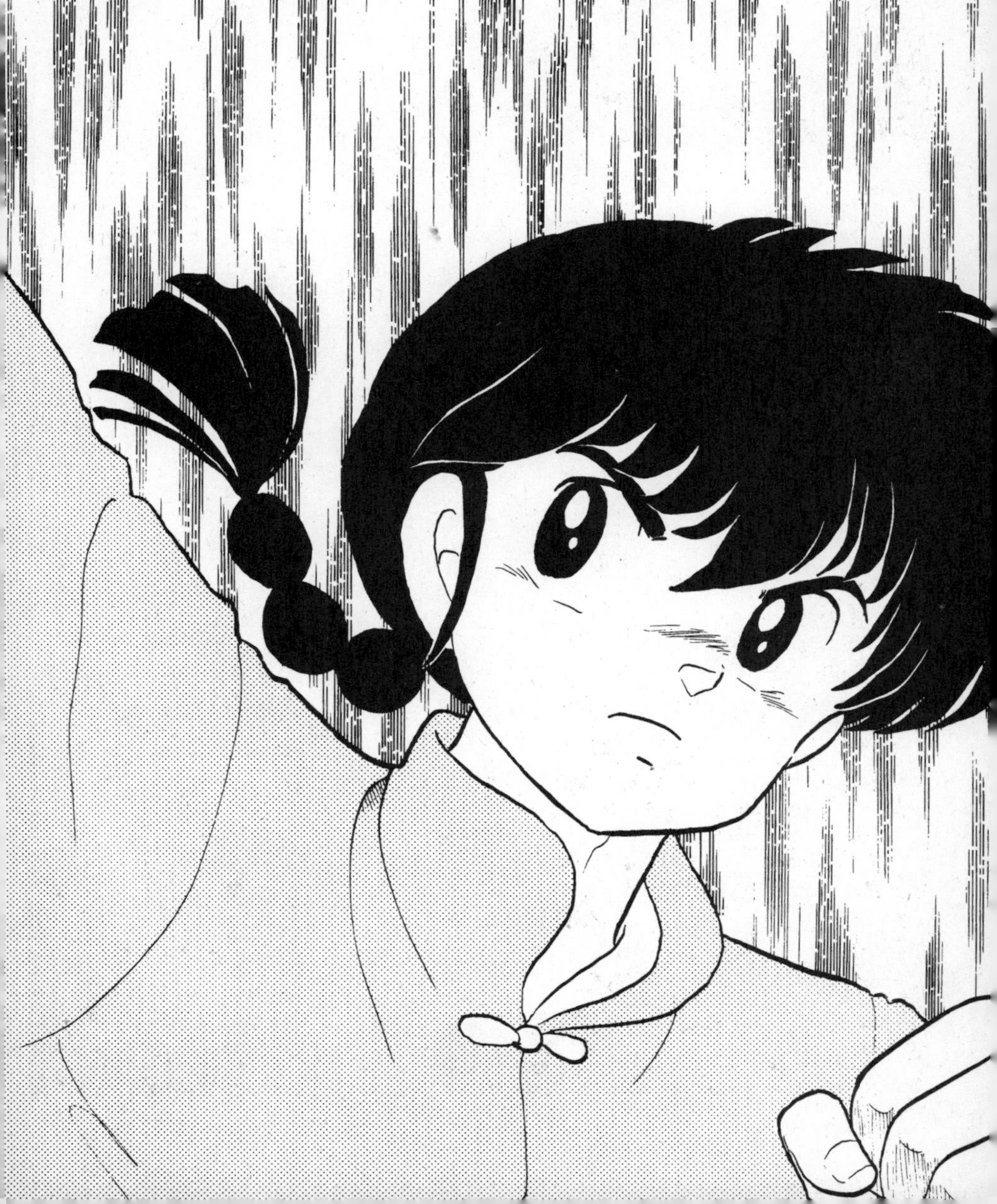

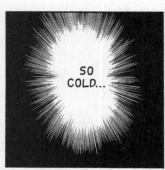

SO
COLD...

AN ICY
WALL OF
POWER COMING
AT ME...

NNGH! UGHH!
UNGH! NNNH!

SOUNDS
LIKE HE'S
HAVING
A NIGHT-
MARE...

UNKH!
GNKH!
HNNK!

POOR
GUY.

GET SOME SLEEP?

HE'S FINALLY QUIETED DOWN.

WHAT HAPPENED, ANYWAY?

FIRST RYOGA COMES CRASHING DOWN IN A CRUMPLED MESS...

DONG

THEN, RANMA-HONEY...

HE'S JUST A BIT BATTERED.

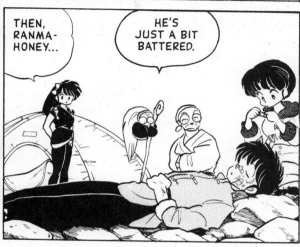

YOU MADE YOUR POINT ABOUT THAT "HEAVEN-BLAST OF THE DRAGON." *BRRR.*

YES.

AND THE SECRET BEHIND IT...

...IS REALLY ONLY...

...A CLASH OF *TEMPERATURES*!

TEMPERATURES?

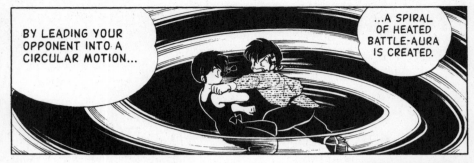

BY LEADING YOUR OPPONENT INTO A CIRCULAR MOTION...

...A SPIRAL OF HEATED BATTLE-AURA IS CREATED.

AS FOR WHAT HAPPENS WHEN IT STRIKES PURE *COLD*...

THE COLLISION OF HOT AND COLD FORCES THE HEATED AURA TO RISE INTO THE AIR...

COLD

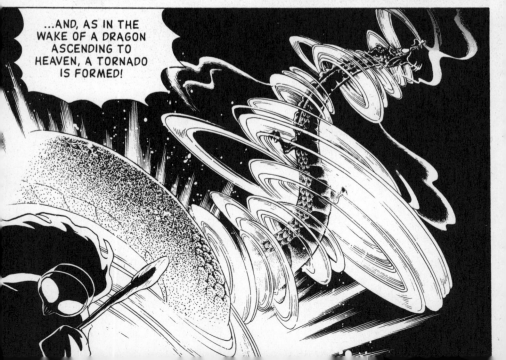

...AND, AS IN THE WAKE OF A DRAGON ASCENDING TO HEAVEN, A TORNADO IS FORMED!

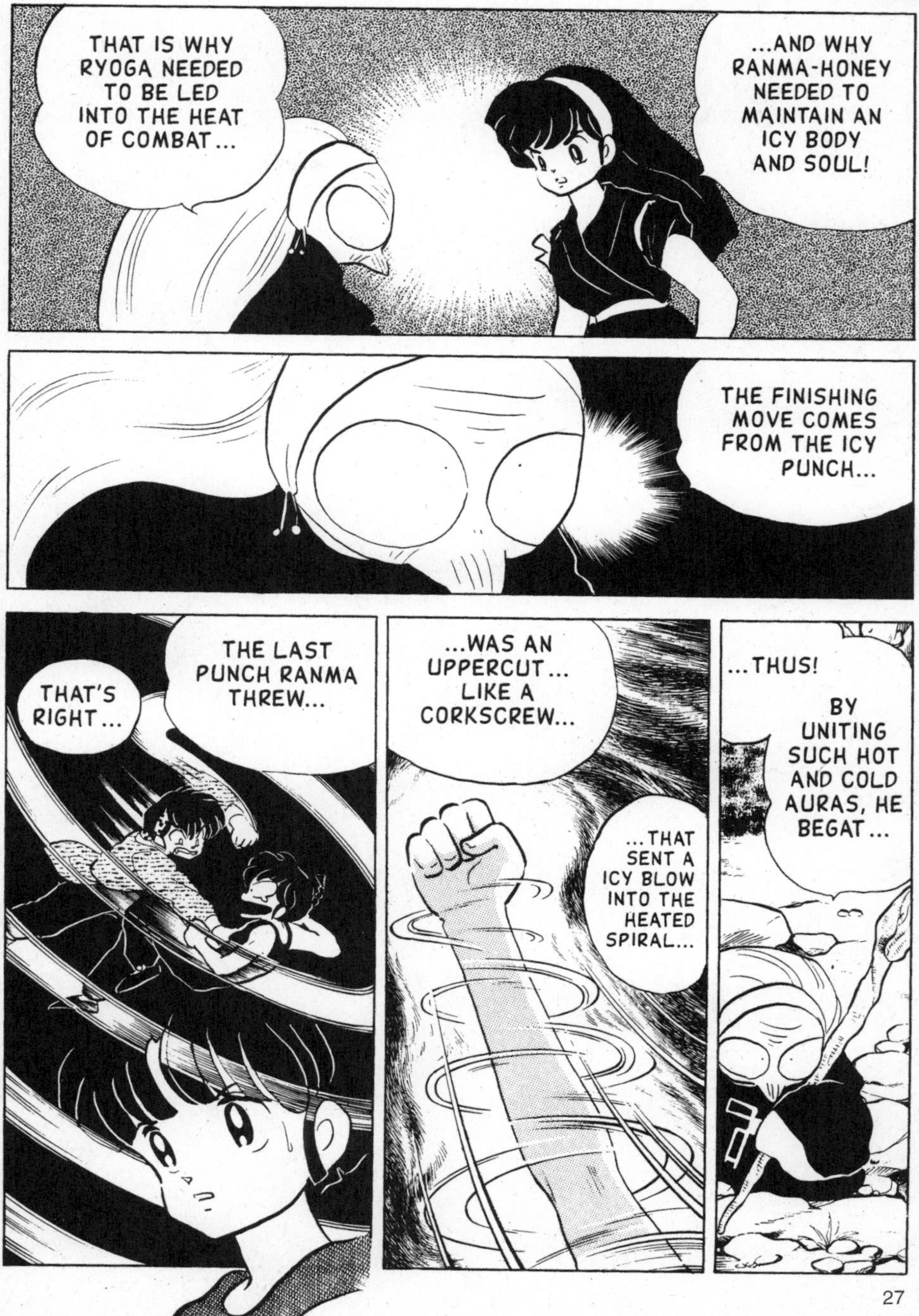
THAT IS WHY RYOGA NEEDED TO BE LED INTO THE HEAT OF COMBAT...
...AND WHY RANMA-HONEY NEEDED TO MAINTAIN AN ICY BODY AND SOUL!
THE FINISHING MOVE COMES FROM THE ICY PUNCH...
THE LAST PUNCH RANMA THREW...
THAT'S RIGHT...
...WAS AN UPPERCUT... LIKE A CORKSCREW...
...THAT SENT A ICY BLOW INTO THE HEATED SPIRAL...
...THUS!
BY UNITING SUCH HOT AND COLD AURAS, HE BEGAT...

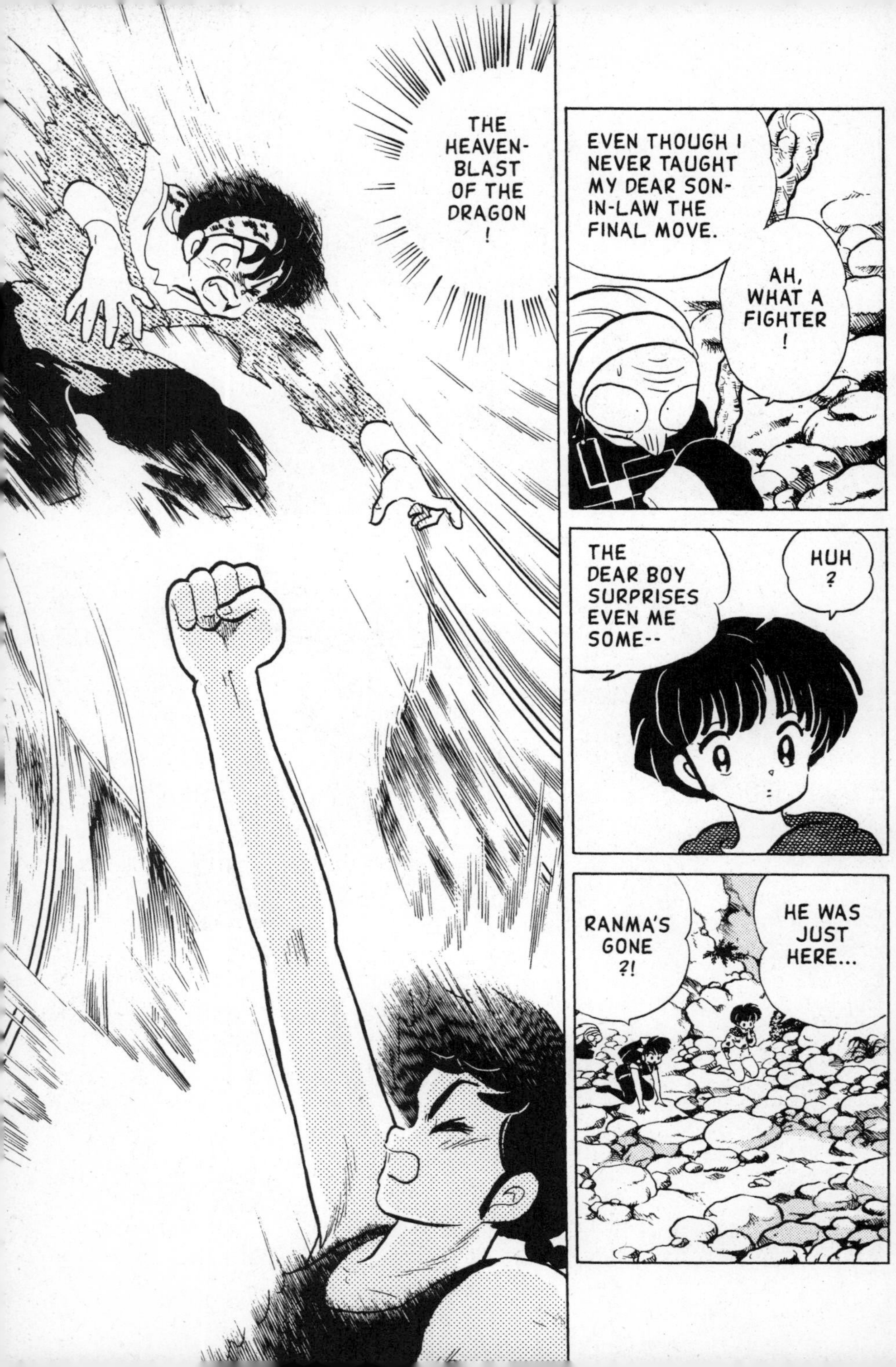
THE HEAVEN-BLAST OF THE DRAGON!
EVEN THOUGH I NEVER TAUGHT MY DEAR SON-IN-LAW THE FINAL MOVE.
AH, WHAT A FIGHTER!
THE DEAR BOY SURPRISES EVEN ME SOME--
HUH?
RANMA'S GONE?!
HE WAS JUST HERE...

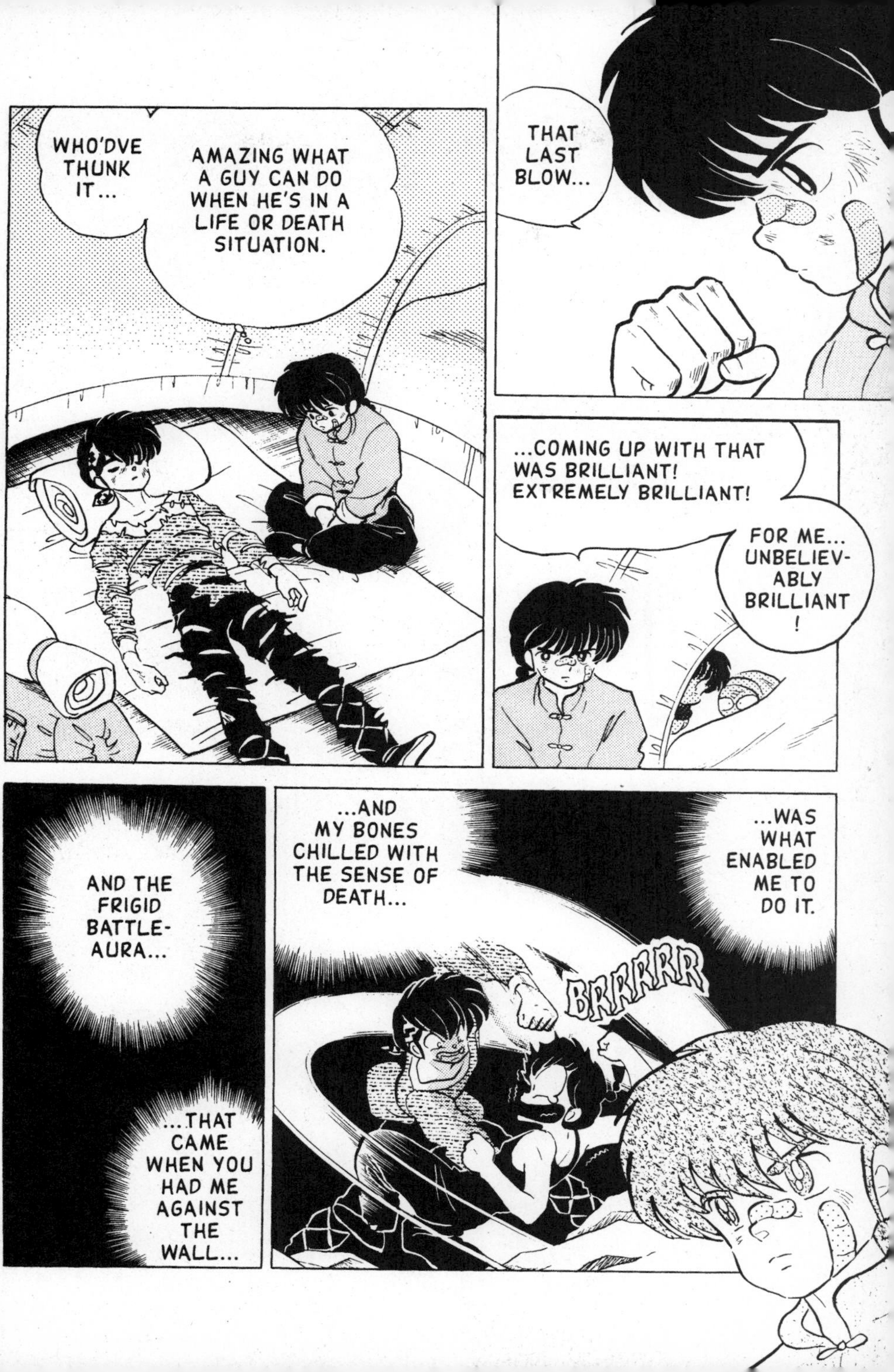
WHO'DVE THUNK IT...
AMAZING WHAT A GUY CAN DO WHEN HE'S IN A LIFE OR DEATH SITUATION.
THAT LAST BLOW...
...COMING UP WITH THAT WAS BRILLIANT! EXTREMELY BRILLIANT!
FOR ME... UNBELIEV-ABLY BRILLIANT!
AND THE FRIGID BATTLE-AURA...
...THAT CAME WHEN YOU HAD ME AGAINST THE WALL...
...AND MY BONES CHILLED WITH THE SENSE OF DEATH...
...WAS WHAT ENABLED ME TO DO IT.
BRRRRR

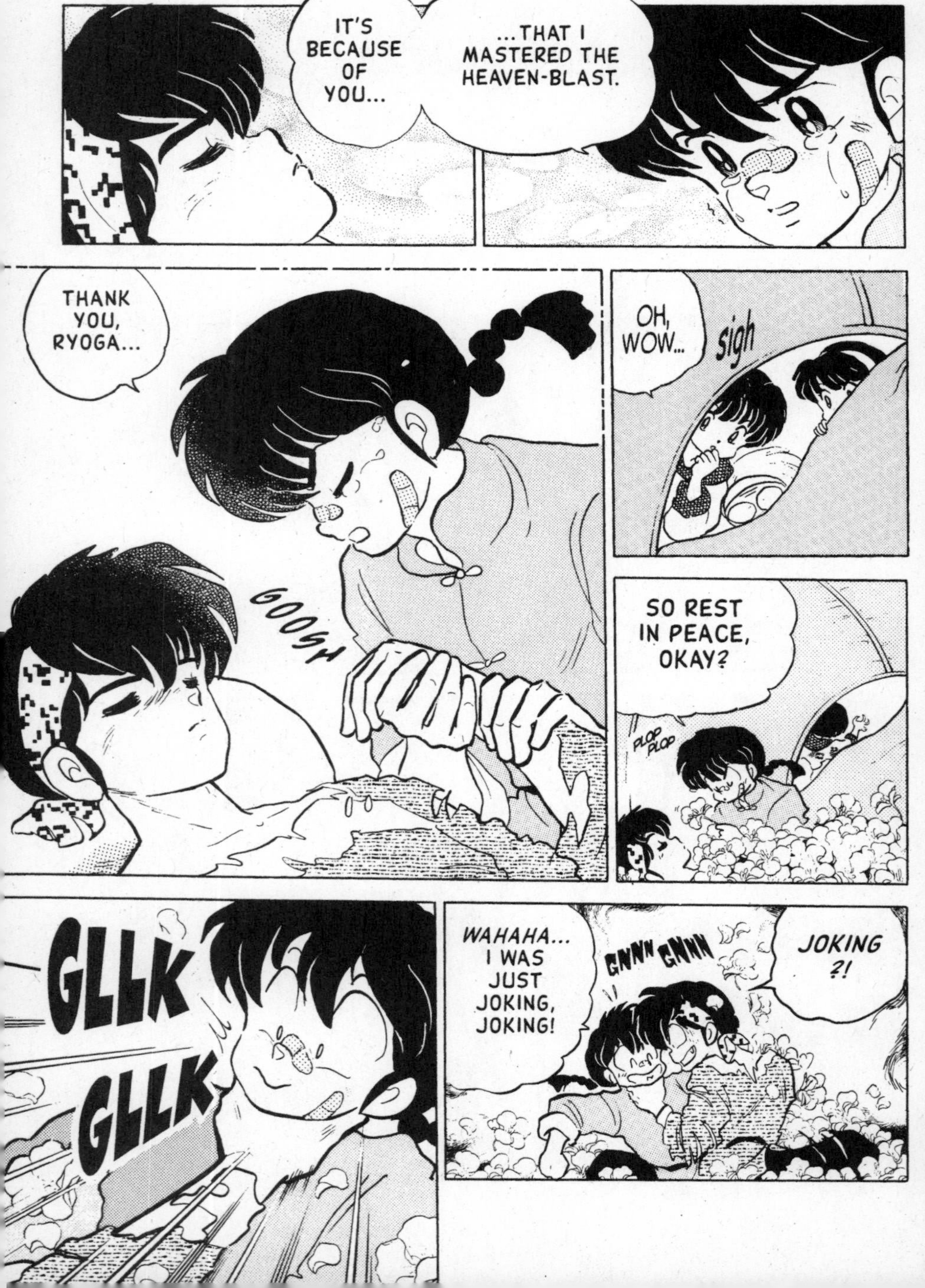
IT'S BECAUSE OF YOU...
...THAT I MASTERED THE HEAVEN-BLAST.
THANK YOU, RYOGA...
GOOSH
OH, WOW...
sigh
SO REST IN PEACE, OKAY?
PLOP PLOP
GLLK
GLLK
WAHAHA... I WAS JUST JOKING, JOKING!
GNNN GNNN
JOKING ?!

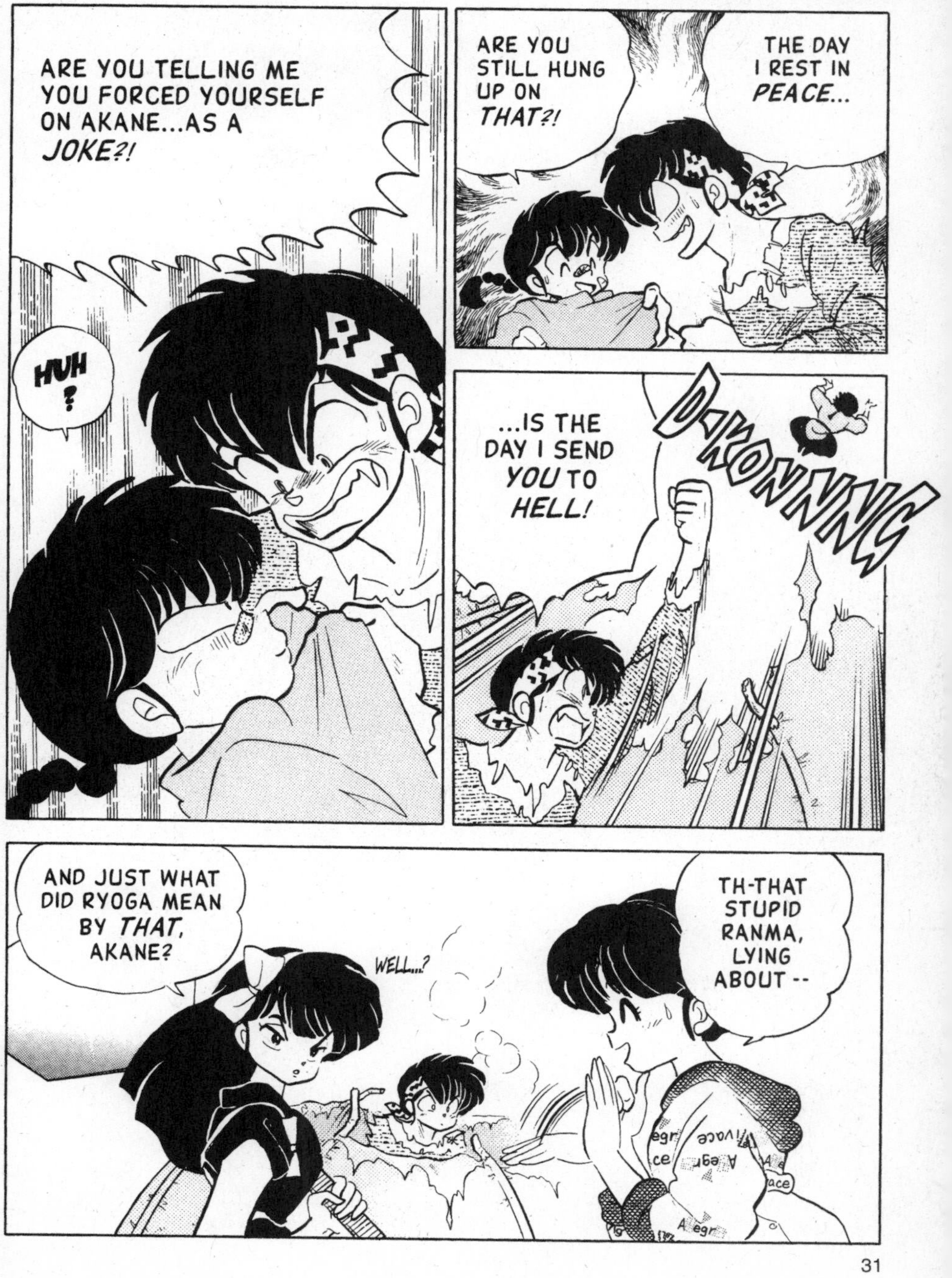
ARE YOU TELLING ME YOU FORCED YOURSELF ON AKANE...AS A JOKE?!
HUH ?
ARE YOU STILL HUNG UP ON THAT?!
THE DAY I REST IN PEACE...
...IS THE DAY I SEND YOU TO HELL!
D-KONNNNG
AND JUST WHAT DID RYOGA MEAN BY THAT, AKANE?
WELL...?
TH-THAT STUPID RANMA, LYING ABOUT --

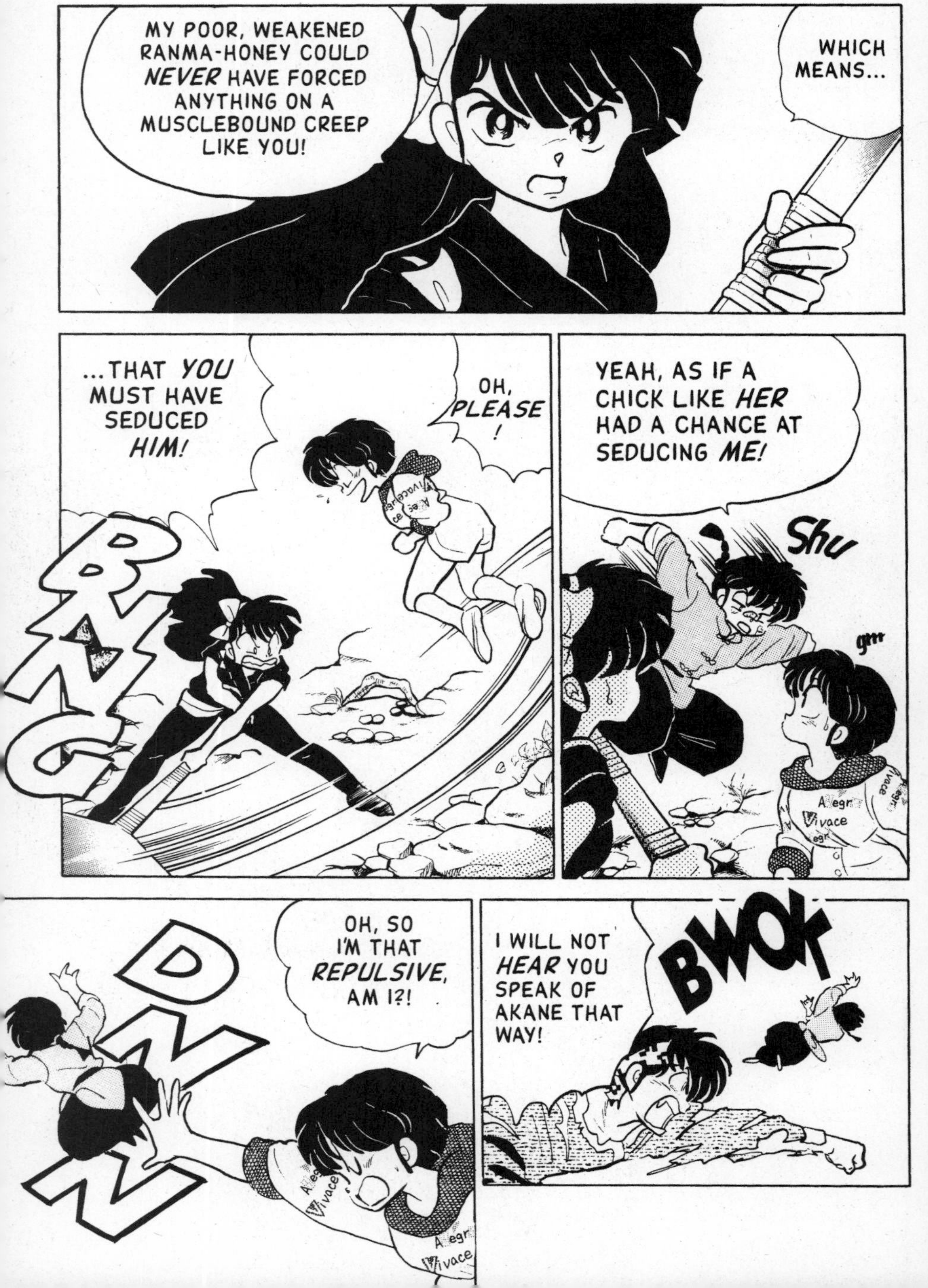
MY POOR, WEAKENED RANMA-HONEY COULD NEVER HAVE FORCED ANYTHING ON A MUSCLEBOUND CREEP LIKE YOU!
WHICH MEANS...
...THAT YOU MUST HAVE SEDUCED HIM!
OH, PLEASE!
YEAH, AS IF A CHICK LIKE HER HAD A CHANCE AT SEDUCING ME!
Shu
grrr
OH, SO I'M THAT REPULSIVE, AM I?!
I WILL NOT HEAR YOU SPEAK OF AKANE THAT WAY!
BWOK

SO, SHALL WE GO HOME?

SO WE SHALL.

WE MUST RETURN TO THE CITY...

biff
BAM
POW

...TO HELP CURE RANMA OF THAT STRENGTH-SAPPING MOXIBUSTION...

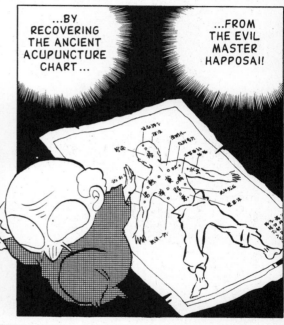

...BY RECOVERING THE ANCIENT ACUPUNCTURE CHART...

...FROM THE EVIL MASTER HAPPOSAI!

ONCE WE DO THAT, RANMA-HONEY WILL BE STRONG AGAIN, RIGHT?

THERE'S NO TIME TO WASTE.

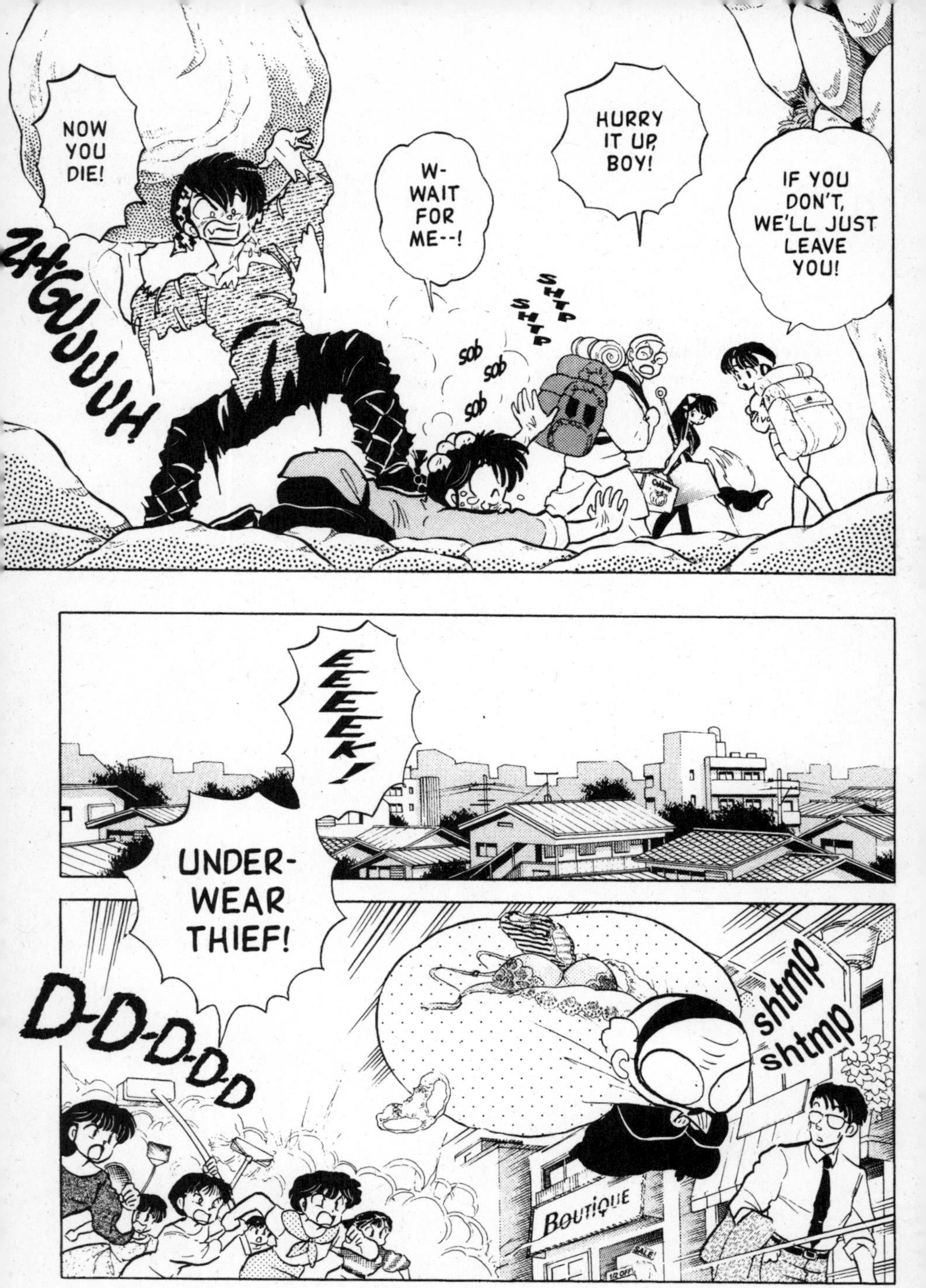
NOW YOU DIE!
ZHGUUUUH!
W-WAIT FOR ME--!
sob sob sob
SHTP SHTP
HURRY IT UP, BOY!
IF YOU DON'T, WE'LL JUST LEAVE YOU!
EEEEEK!
UNDER-WEAR THIEF!
D-D-D-D-D
shtmp shtmp
BOUTIQUE

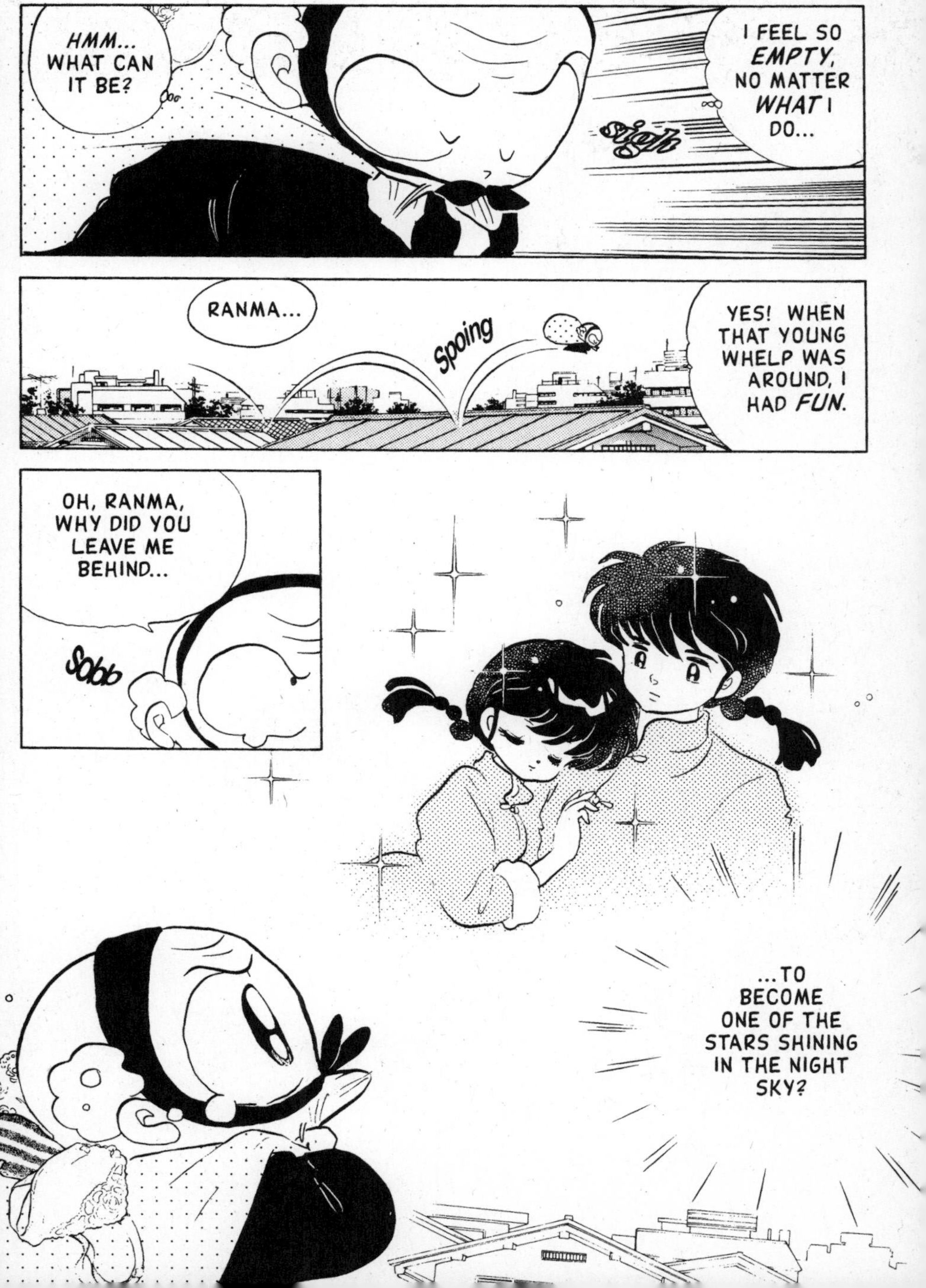
HMM... WHAT CAN IT BE?
sigh
I FEEL SO EMPTY, NO MATTER WHAT I DO...
RANMA...
Spoing
YES! WHEN THAT YOUNG WHELP WAS AROUND, I HAD FUN.
OH, RANMA, WHY DID YOU LEAVE ME BEHIND...
Sobb
...TO BECOME ONE OF THE STARS SHINING IN THE NIGHT SKY?

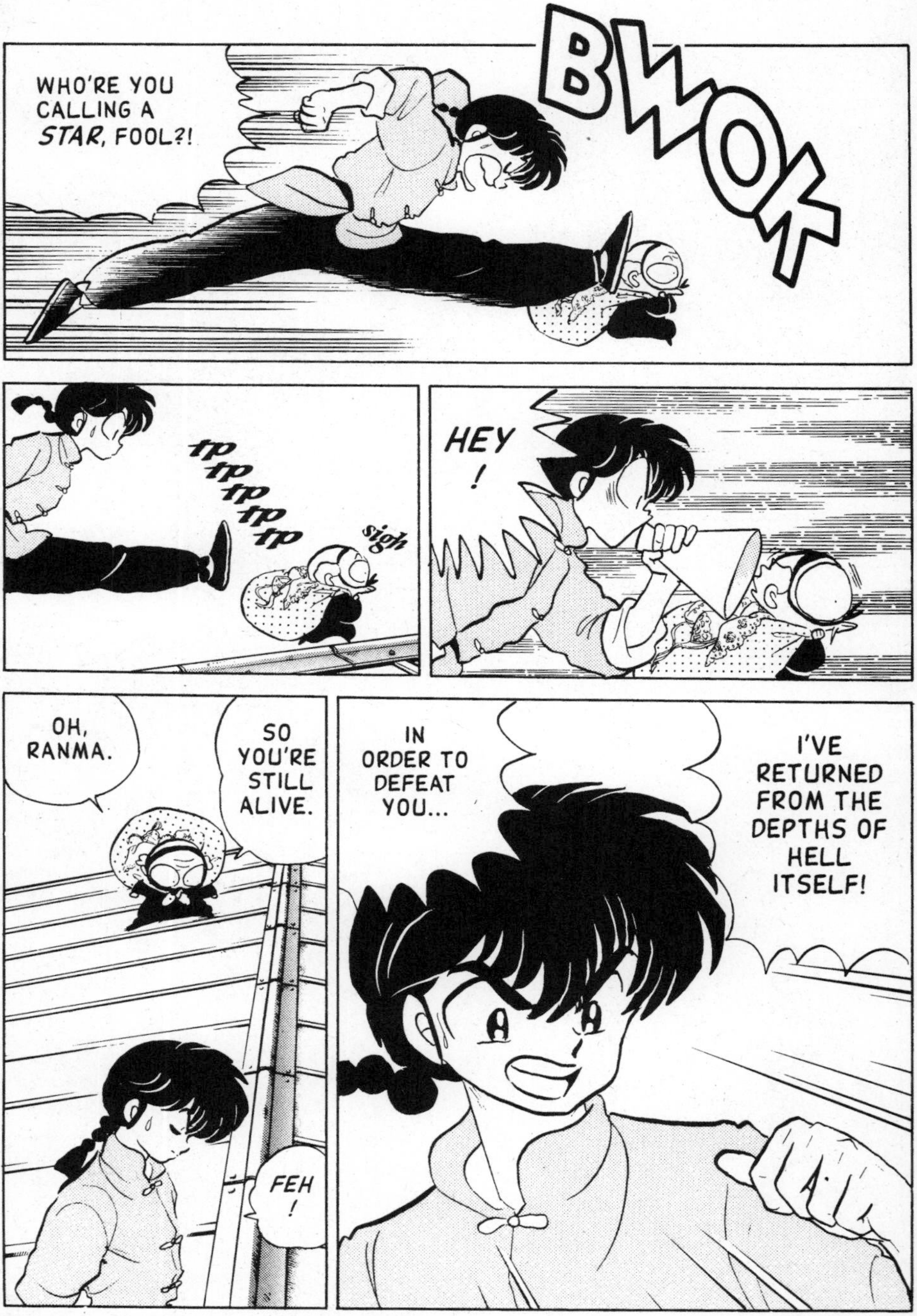
WHO'RE YOU CALLING A STAR, FOOL?!
BWOK
tp tp tp tp tp tp
sigh
HEY!
OH, RANMA.
SO YOU'RE STILL ALIVE.
FEH!
IN ORDER TO DEFEAT YOU...
I'VE RETURNED FROM THE DEPTHS OF HELL ITSELF!

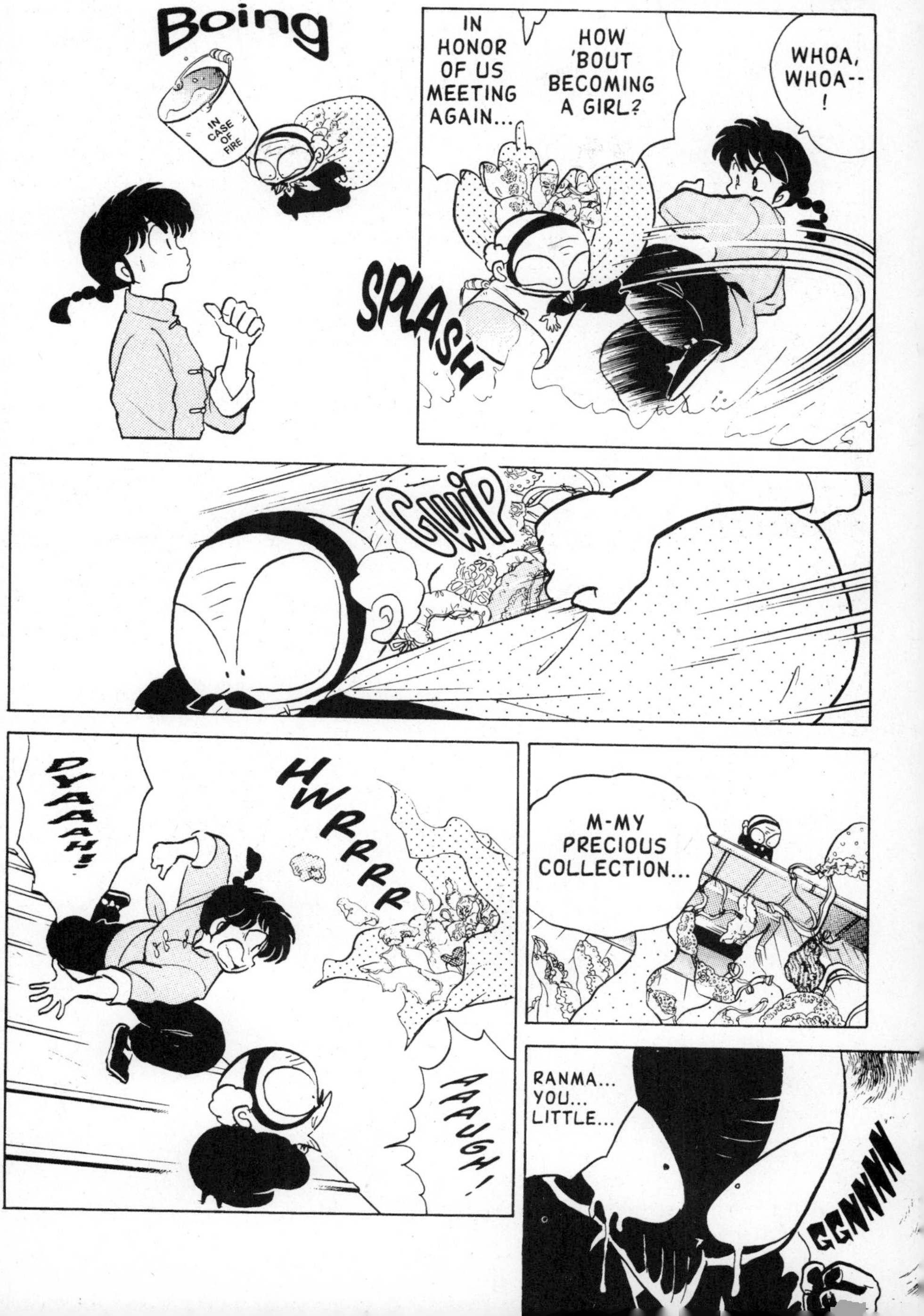
Boing
IN CASE OF FIRE
IN HONOR OF US MEETING AGAIN...
HOW 'BOUT BECOMING A GIRL?
WHOA, WHOA--!
SPLASH
GWIP
DYAAAAH!
HWRRRR
AAAAUGH!
M-MY PRECIOUS COLLECTION...
RANMA... YOU... LITTLE...
GGNNNN

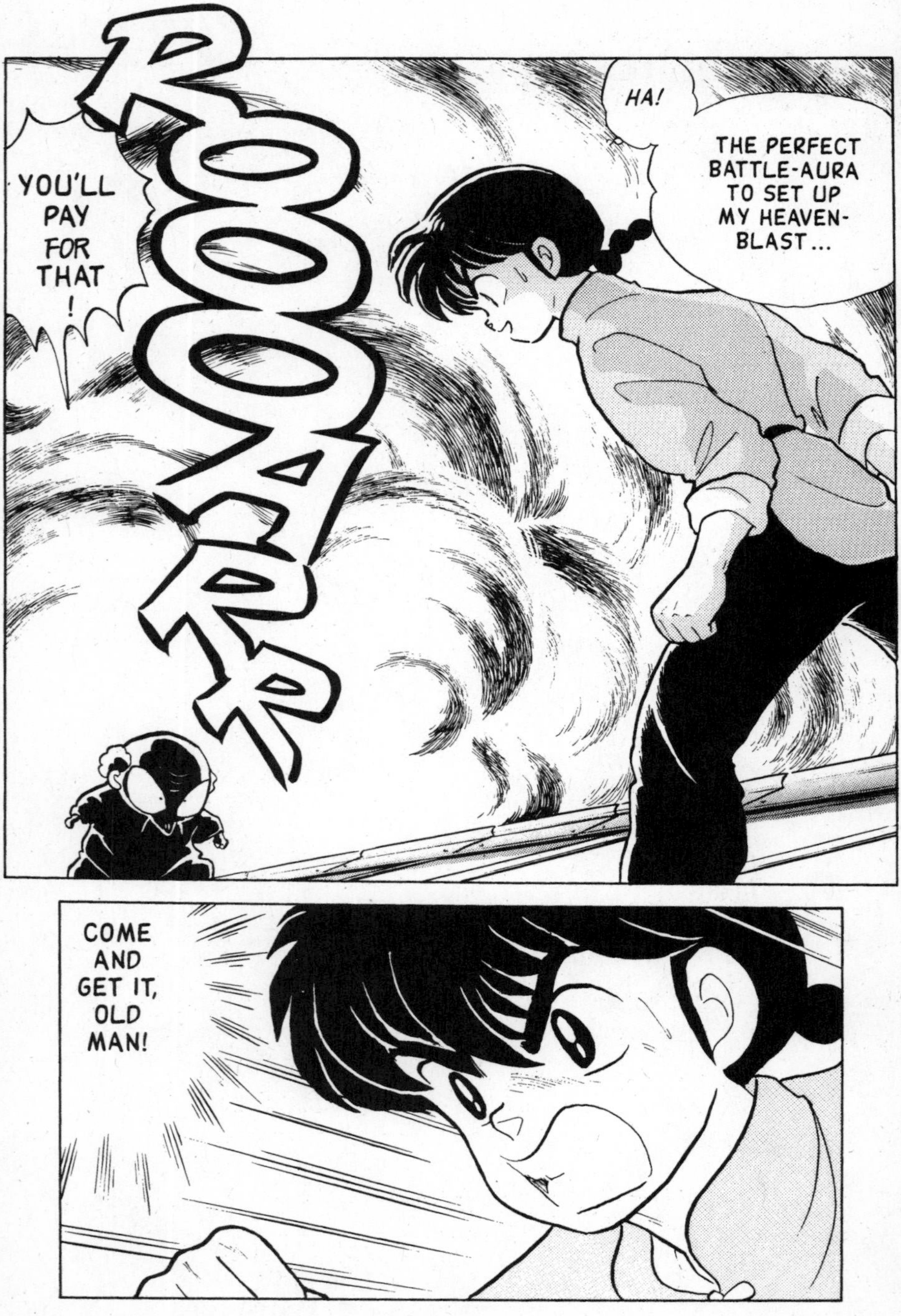
YOU'LL PAY FOR THAT!
ROOOARR
HA!
THE PERFECT BATTLE-AURA TO SET UP MY HEAVEN-BLAST...
COME AND GET IT, OLD MAN!

PART 3
ST. HAPPOSAI

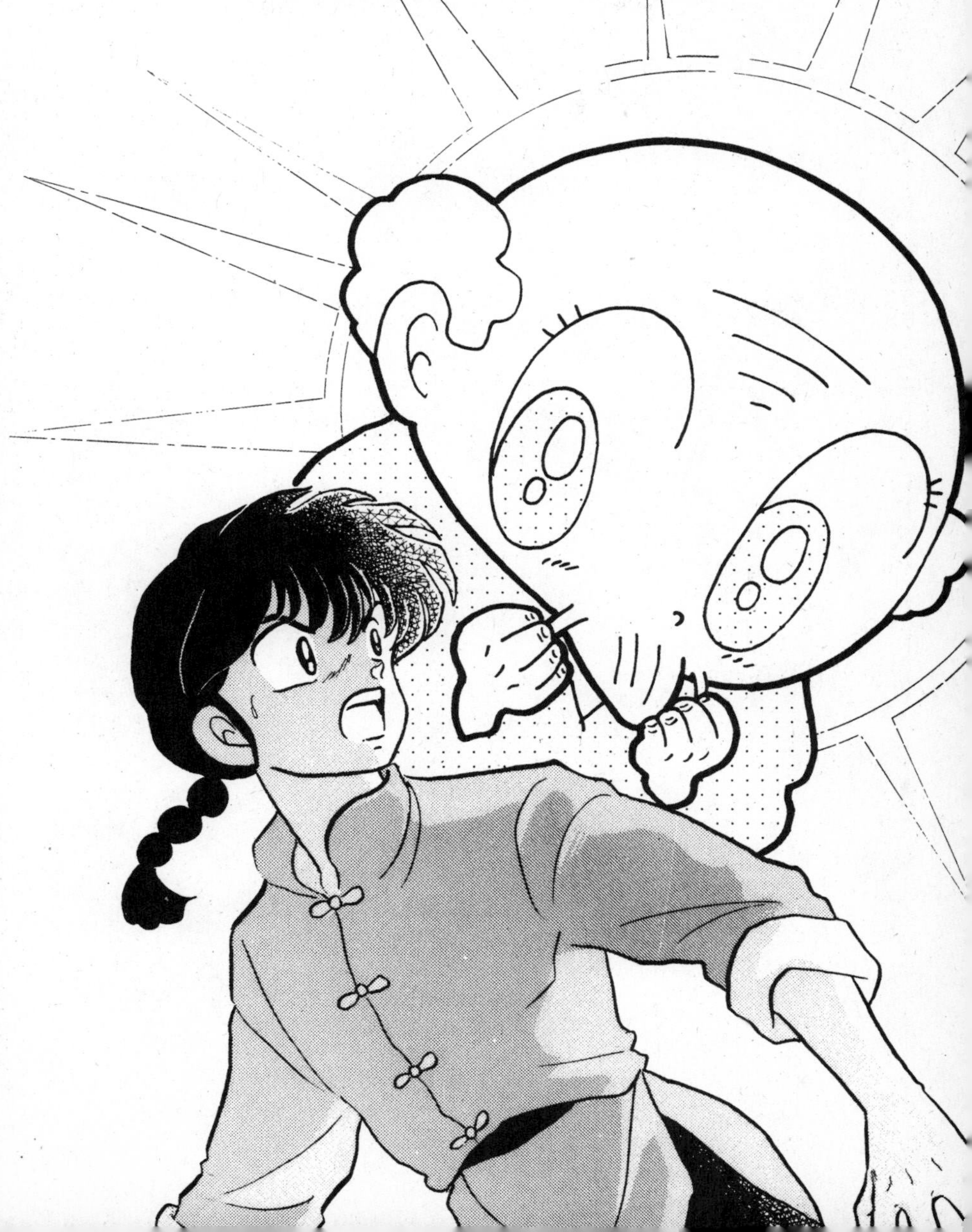

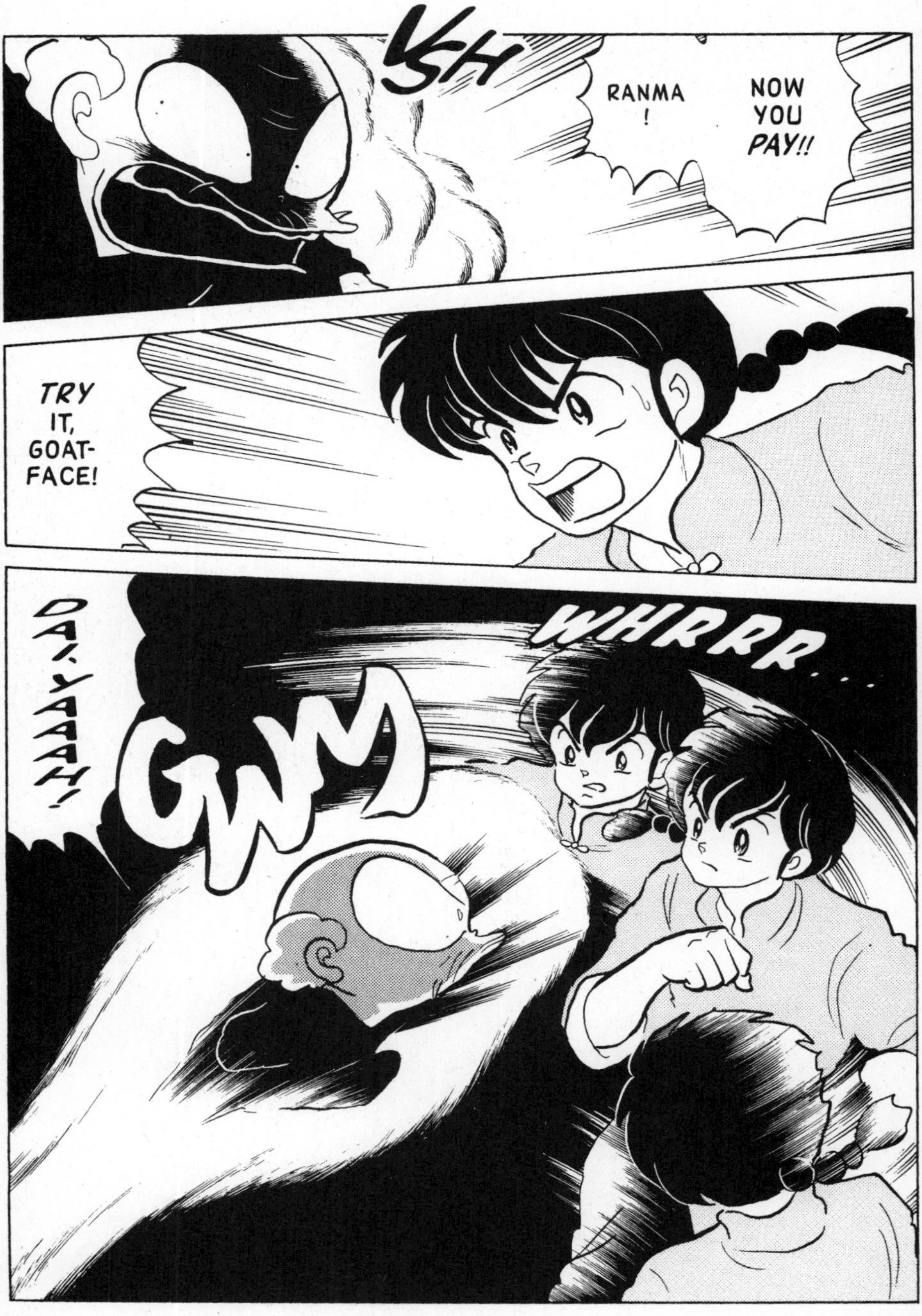
VSH
RANMA!
NOW YOU PAY!!
TRY IT, GOAT-FACE!
DAI YAAAAH!
WHRRRR...
GWM

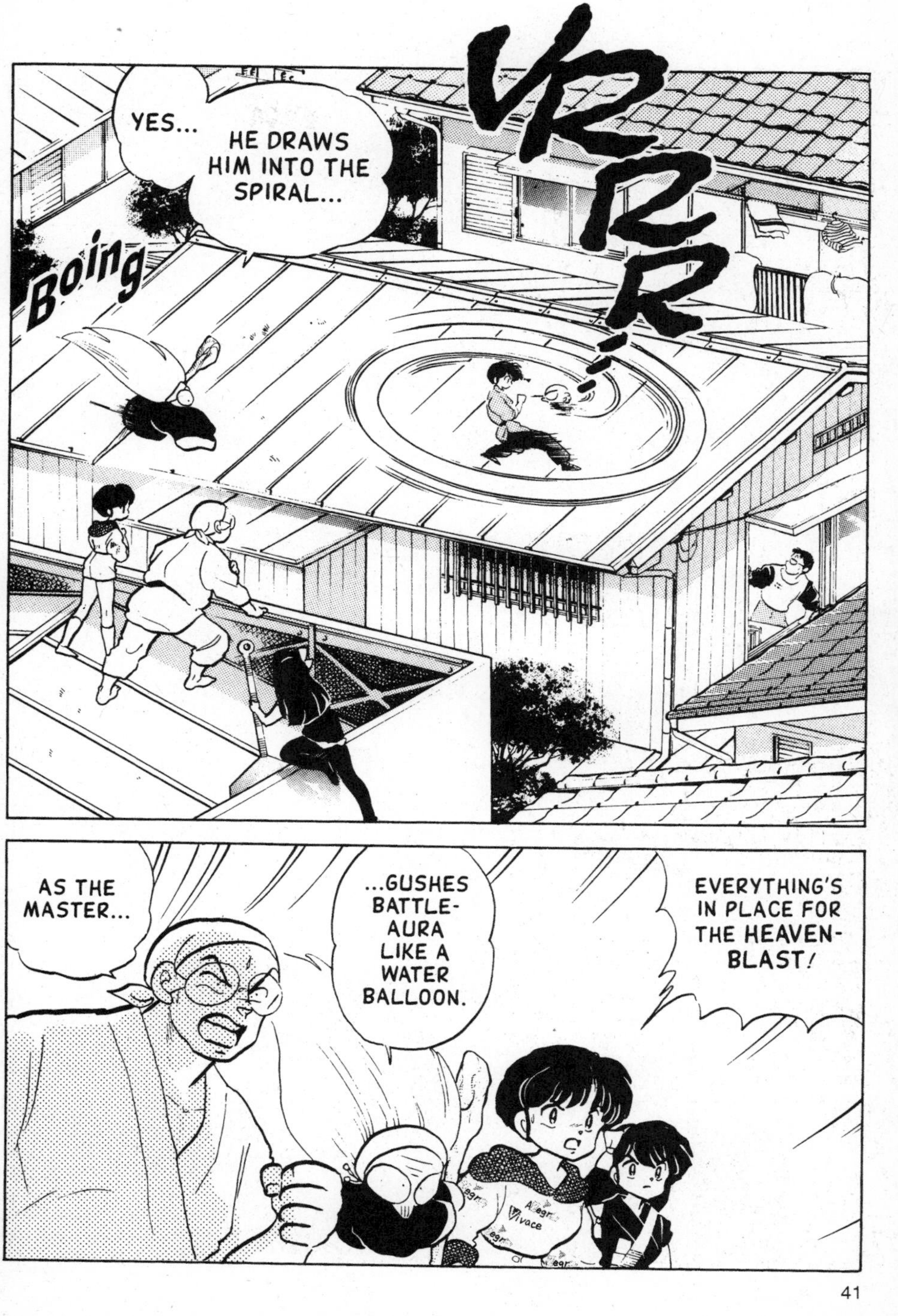
YES...
HE DRAWS HIM INTO THE SPIRAL...
VRR!
Boing
AS THE MASTER...
...GUSHES BATTLE-AURA LIKE A WATER BALLOON.
EVERYTHING'S IN PLACE FOR THE HEAVEN-BLAST!

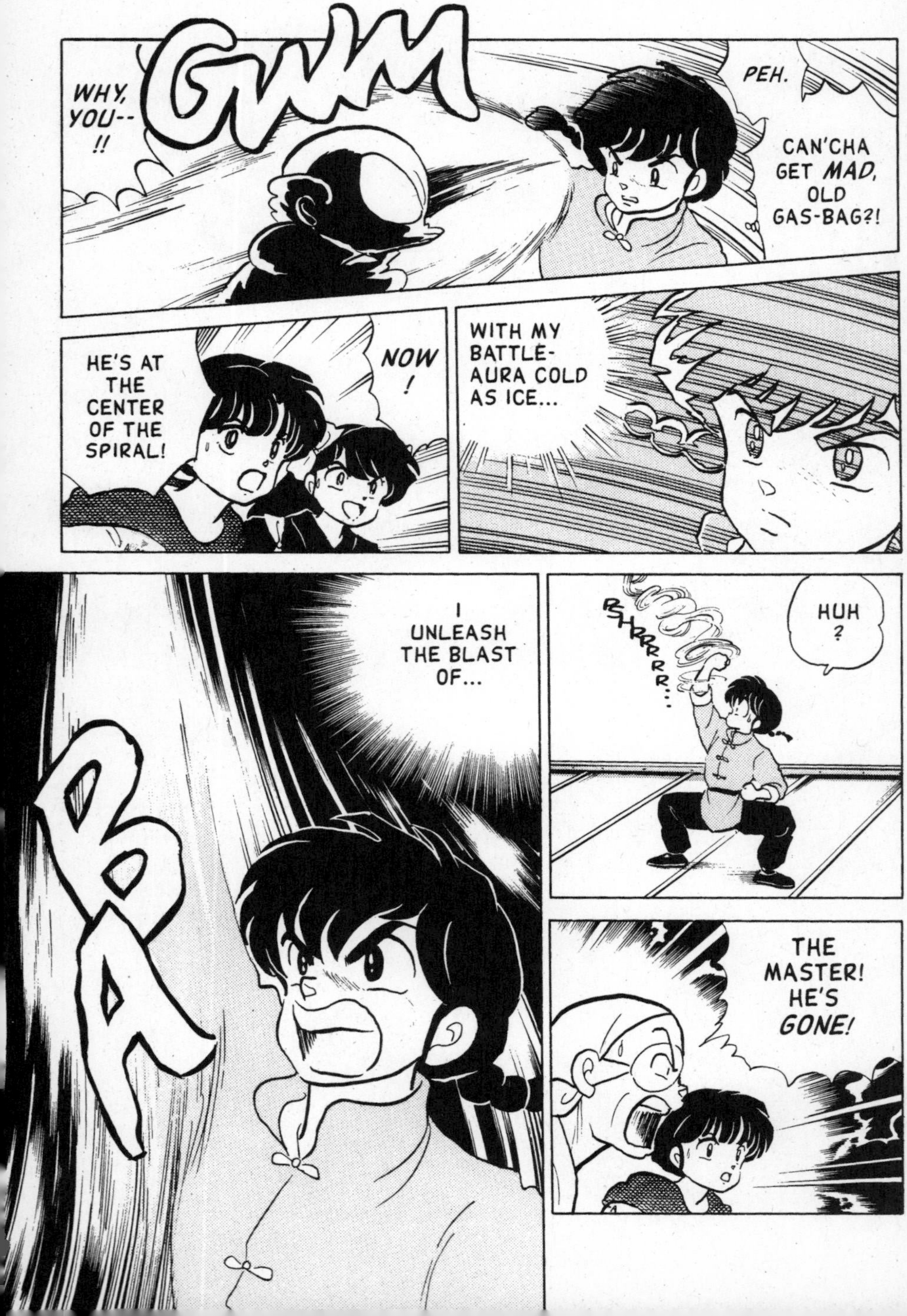
WHY, YOU-- !!
GWM
PEH.
CAN'CHA GET MAD, OLD GAS-BAG?!
HE'S AT THE CENTER OF THE SPIRAL!
NOW !
WITH MY BATTLE-AURA COLD AS ICE...
I UNLEASH THE BLAST OF...
BA
PSHRRRRR...
HUH ?
THE MASTER! HE'S GONE!

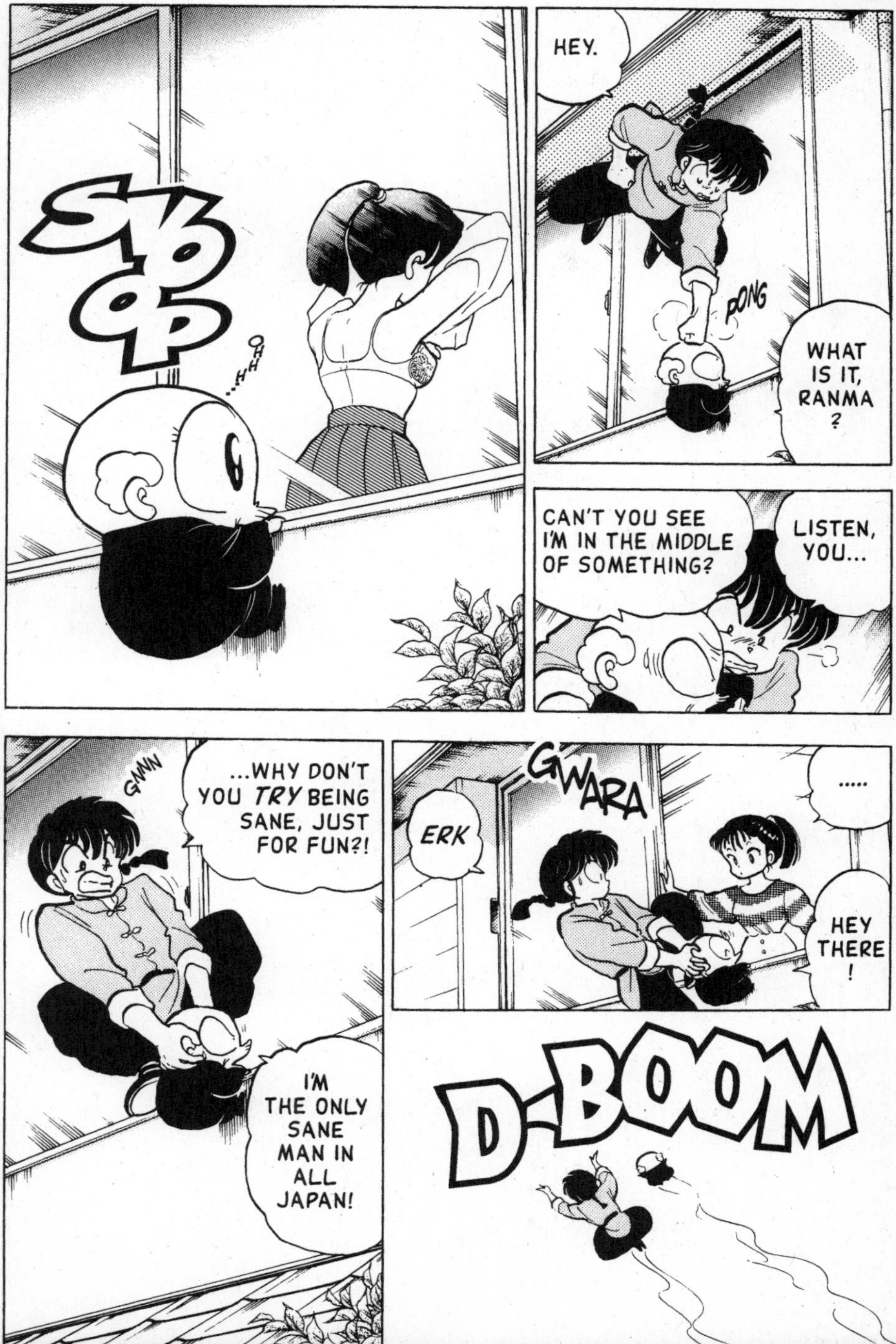
SKOOP
OHHH...
HEY.
PONG
WHAT IS IT, RANMA?
CAN'T YOU SEE I'M IN THE MIDDLE OF SOMETHING?
LISTEN, YOU...
GNNN
...WHY DON'T YOU TRY BEING SANE, JUST FOR FUN?!
I'M THE ONLY SANE MAN IN ALL JAPAN!
GWARA
ERK
.....
HEY THERE!
D-BOOM

OH, CRUEL, CRUEL YOUTH!

TO ROB A POOR OLD MAN OF HIS FEW WANING JOYS!

HAH!

MADE YOU MAD, EH...?

FONG

THEN COME *AT* ME!

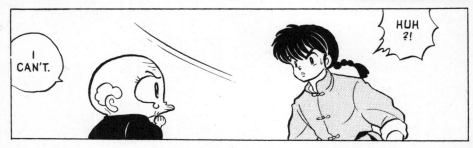

I CAN'T.

HUH ?!

TO ATTACK YOU IN YOUR WEAKENED STATE...

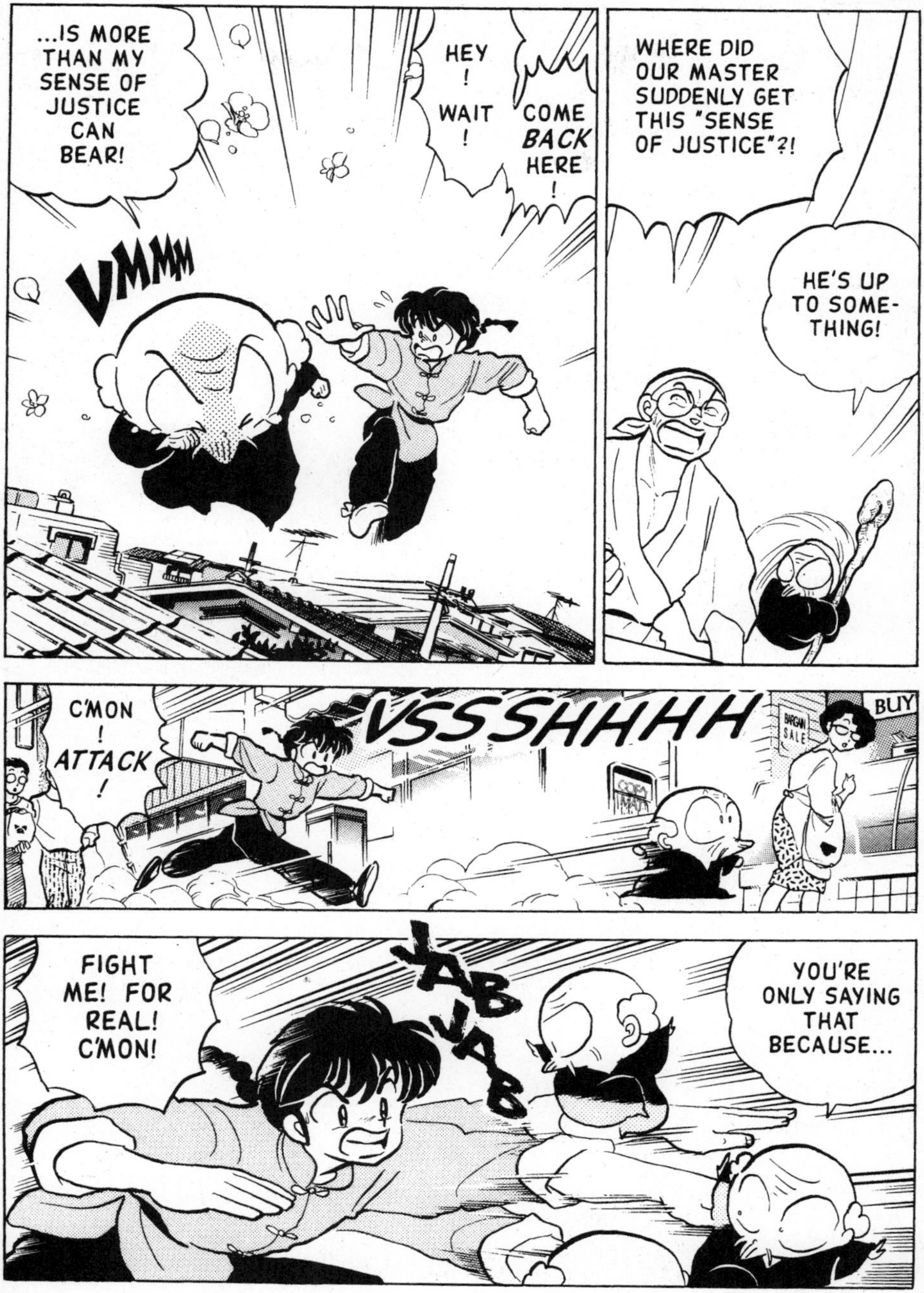
...IS MORE THAN MY SENSE OF JUSTICE CAN BEAR!
HEY! WAIT!
COME BACK HERE!
VMMM
WHERE DID OUR MASTER SUDDENLY GET THIS "SENSE OF JUSTICE"?!
HE'S UP TO SOME-THING!
C'MON! ATTACK!
VSSSHHHH
BARGAIN SALE
BUY
FIGHT ME! FOR REAL! C'MON!
JAB JAB
YOU'RE ONLY SAYING THAT BECAUSE...

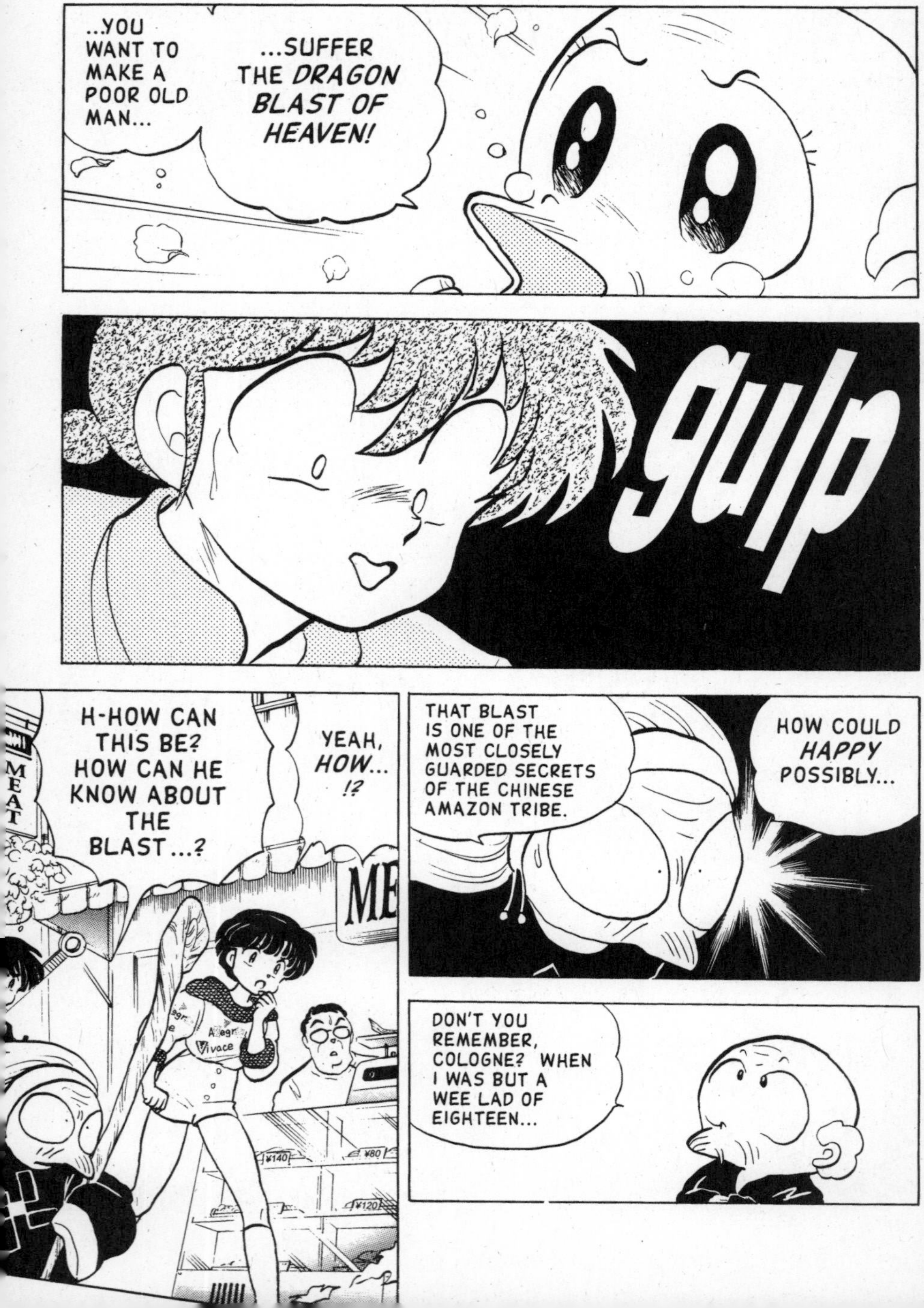
...YOU WANT TO MAKE A POOR OLD MAN...
...SUFFER THE *DRAGON BLAST OF HEAVEN!*
gulp
H-HOW CAN THIS BE? HOW CAN HE KNOW ABOUT THE BLAST...?
YEAH, *HOW...* !?
MEAT
ME
Vivace
¥140
¥80
¥120
THAT BLAST IS ONE OF THE MOST CLOSELY GUARDED SECRETS OF THE CHINESE AMAZON TRIBE.
HOW COULD *HAPPY* POSSIBLY...
DON'T YOU REMEMBER, COLOGNE? WHEN I WAS BUT A WEE LAD OF EIGHTEEN...

THE VILLAGE OF THE CHINESE AMAZONS

GRRRRR

HOW *DARE* YOU, COLOGNE?!

SSSSIZZLE!

HOW *DARE* YOU STAND ME UP ON A DATE?!

VIP

COLOGNE AS A ☞ YOUNG GIRL...

...AND...UM...NOW. ☜

D-GWOOOOOOOMM

DRAGON'S HEAVEN-BLAST!

HWOOOOOOOO...

COULDN'T YOU HAVE *MENTIONED* THIS?

AHH, THE BITTER-SWEET MEMORIES...

SCRITCH SCRITCH

47

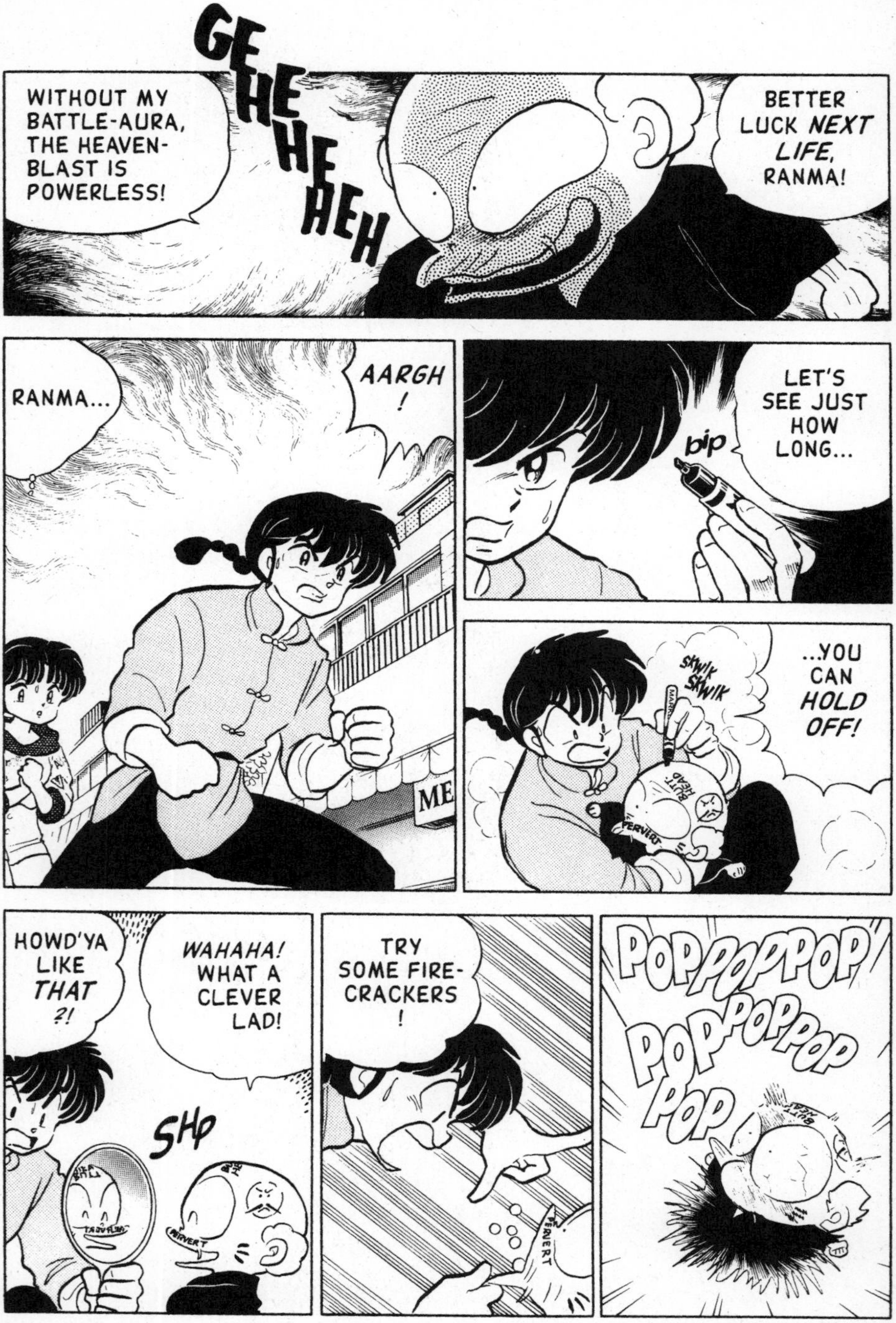
GEHEHEHEH
WITHOUT MY BATTLE-AURA, THE HEAVEN-BLAST IS POWERLESS!
BETTER LUCK NEXT LIFE, RANMA!
RANMA...
AARGH!
LET'S SEE JUST HOW LONG...
bip
...YOU CAN HOLD OFF!
SKWIK SKWIK
BUTT-HEAD
PERVERT
HOWD'YA LIKE THAT?!
WAHAHA! WHAT A CLEVER LAD!
SHP
PERVERT
TRY SOME FIRE-CRACKERS!
PERVERT
POPPOPPOP POPPOPPOPPOP POP

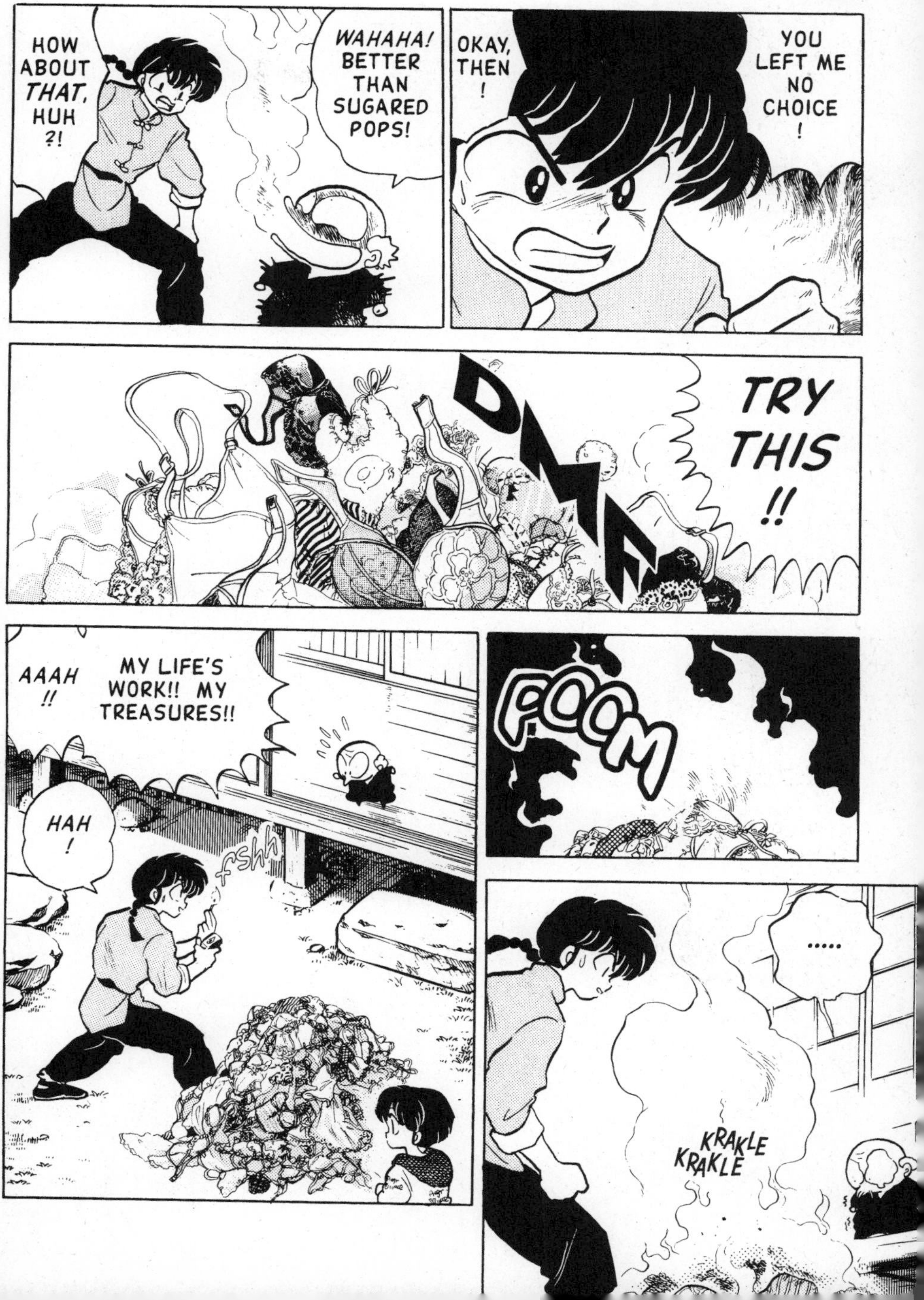
HOW ABOUT THAT, HUH ?!
WAHAHA! BETTER THAN SUGARED POPS!
OKAY, THEN !
YOU LEFT ME NO CHOICE !
DMAF
TRY THIS !!
AAAH !!
MY LIFE'S WORK!! MY TREASURES!!
HAH !
fshh
FOOM
......
KRAKLE KRAKLE

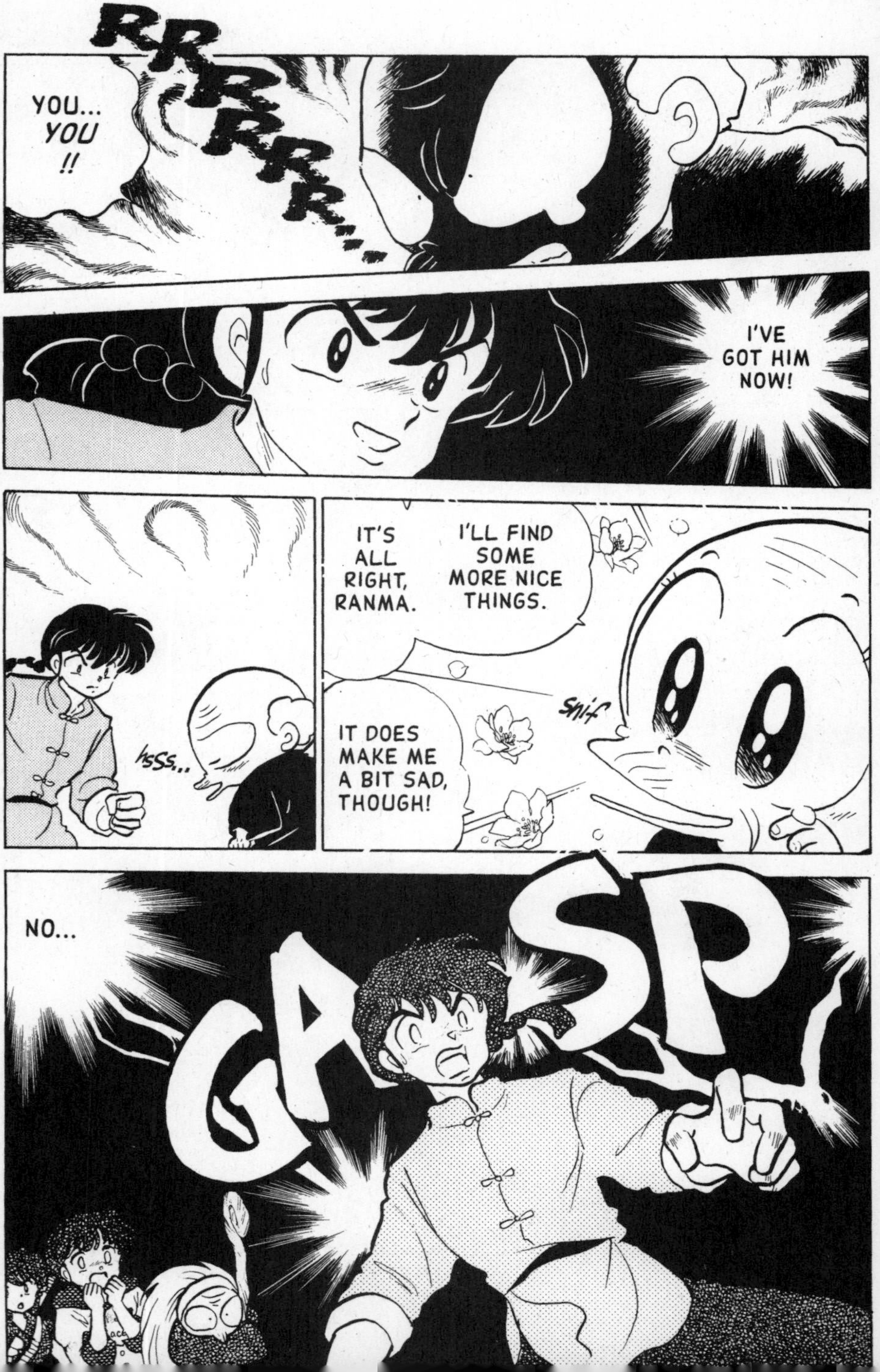
RRRRRR...
YOU... YOU !!
I'VE GOT HIM NOW!
IT'S ALL RIGHT, RANMA.
I'LL FIND SOME MORE NICE THINGS.
IT DOES MAKE ME A BIT SAD, THOUGH!
hsss...
snif
NO...
GASP!

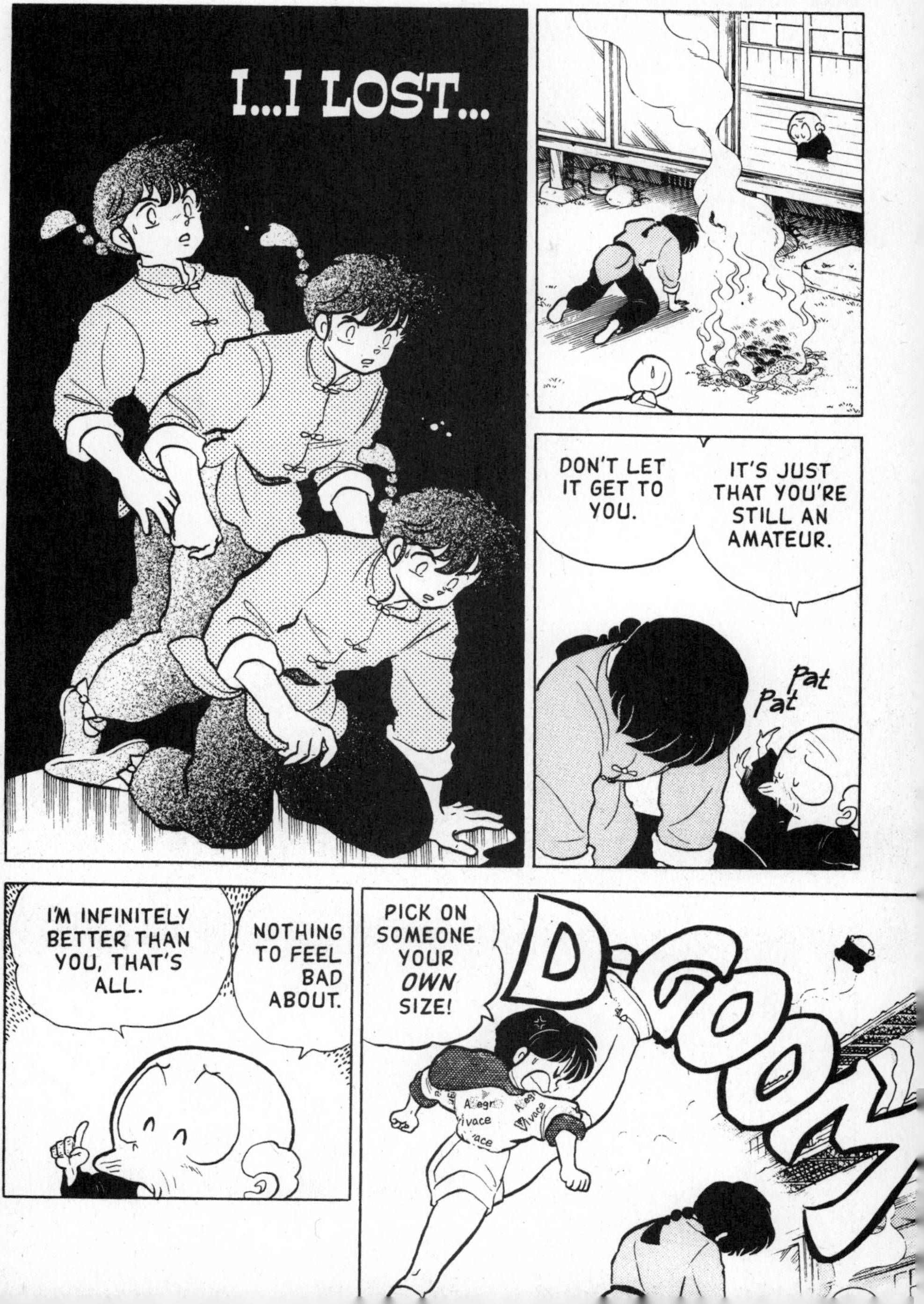
I...I LOST...
DON'T LET IT GET TO YOU.
IT'S JUST THAT YOU'RE STILL AN AMATEUR.
Pat Pat
I'M INFINITELY BETTER THAN YOU, THAT'S ALL.
NOTHING TO FEEL BAD ABOUT.
PICK ON SOMEONE YOUR *OWN* SIZE!
D-GOOOM

OH, THE HUMANITY!

SOBBB!!

AND HE WENT THROUGH ALL THAT TRAINING, TOO...

I WONDER IF RANMA-HONEY WILL EVER GET HIS STRENGTH BACK.

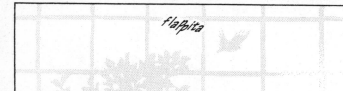

flappita

.....

IF I COULDN'T MAKE THE OLD PERVERT MAD WITH *THAT*...

AUGH.

ALL THAT TRAINING...FOR NOTHING... FOR...

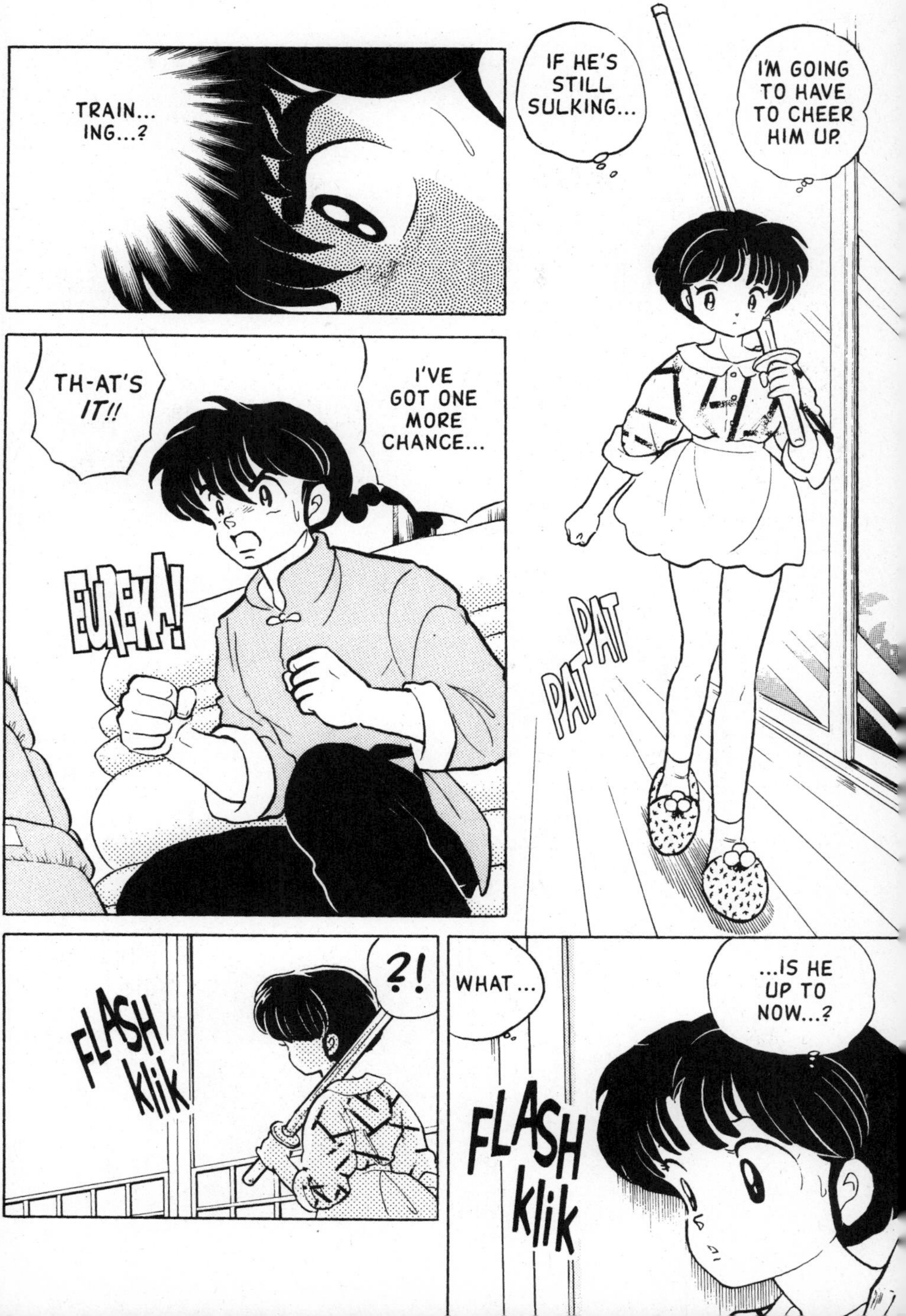
TRAIN... ING...?
TH-AT'S IT!!
I'VE GOT ONE MORE CHANCE...
EUREKA!
IF HE'S STILL SULKING...
I'M GOING TO HAVE TO CHEER HIM UP.
PAT PAT
FLASH klik
?!
WHAT...
...IS HE UP TO NOW...?
FLASH klik

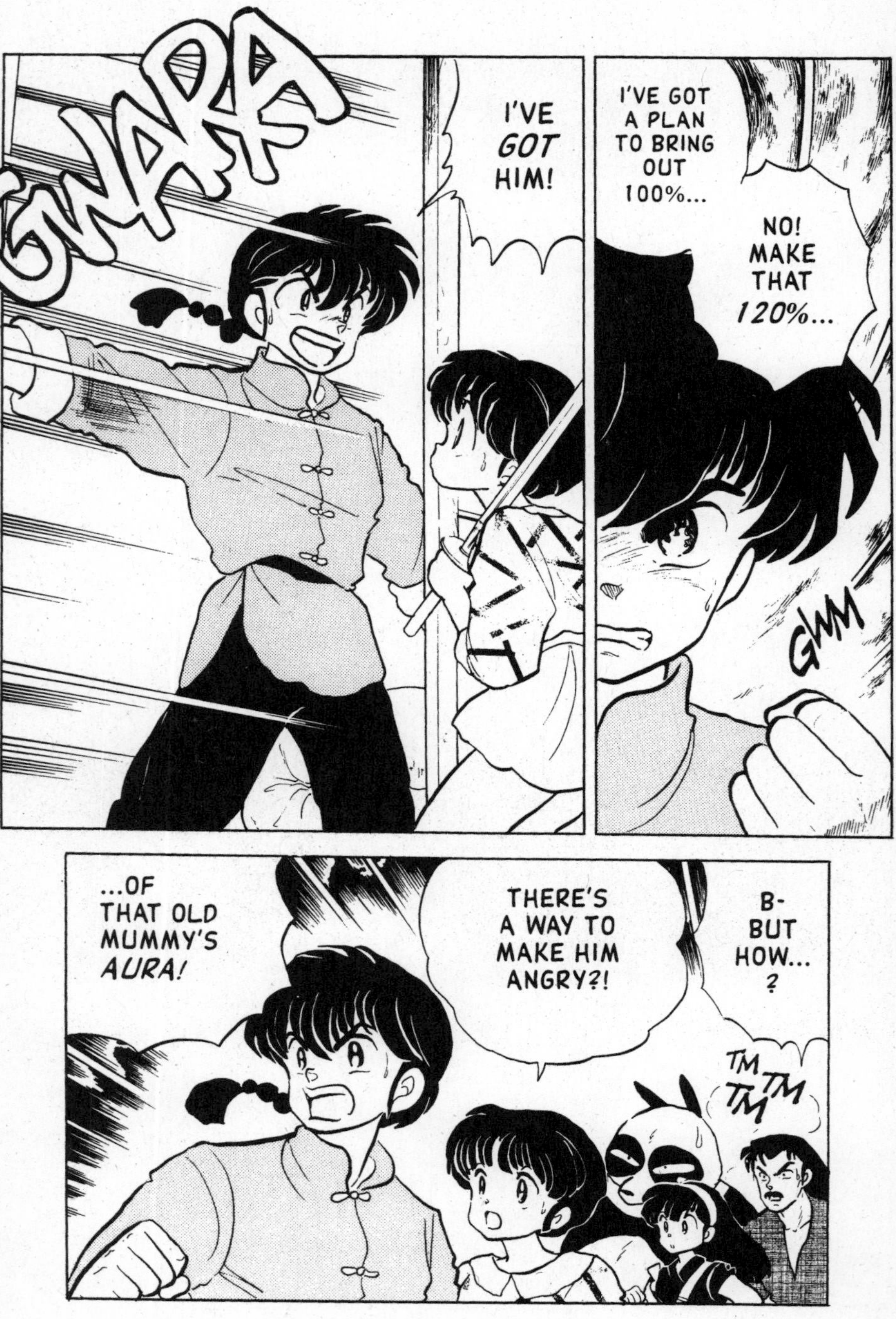
GWARA
I'VE *GOT* HIM!
I'VE GOT A PLAN TO BRING OUT 100%...
NO! MAKE THAT *120%*...
GWM
...OF THAT OLD MUMMY'S *AURA*!
THERE'S A WAY TO MAKE HIM ANGRY?!
B-BUT HOW...?
TM TM TM

PART 4
BURN, HAPPY, BURN

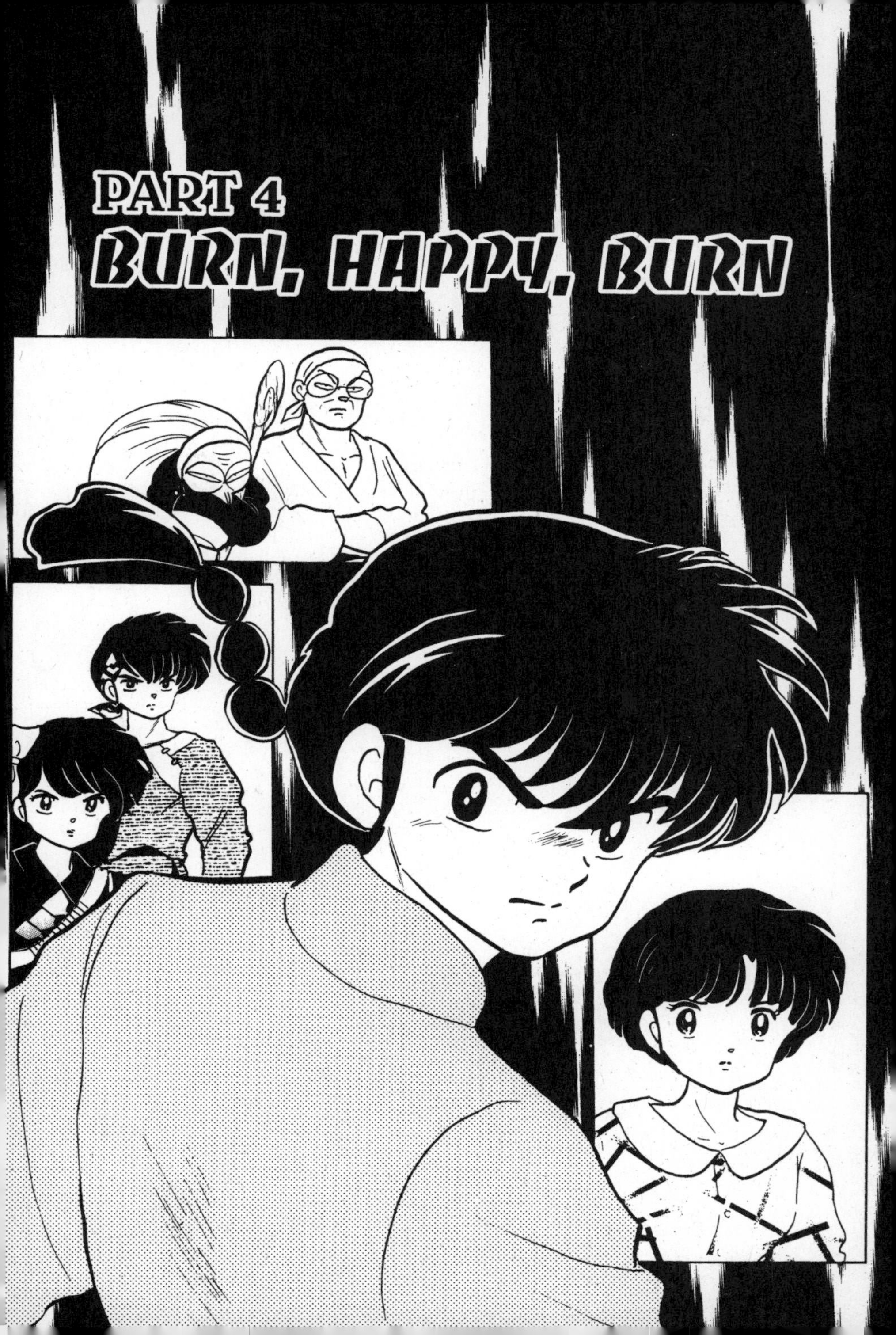

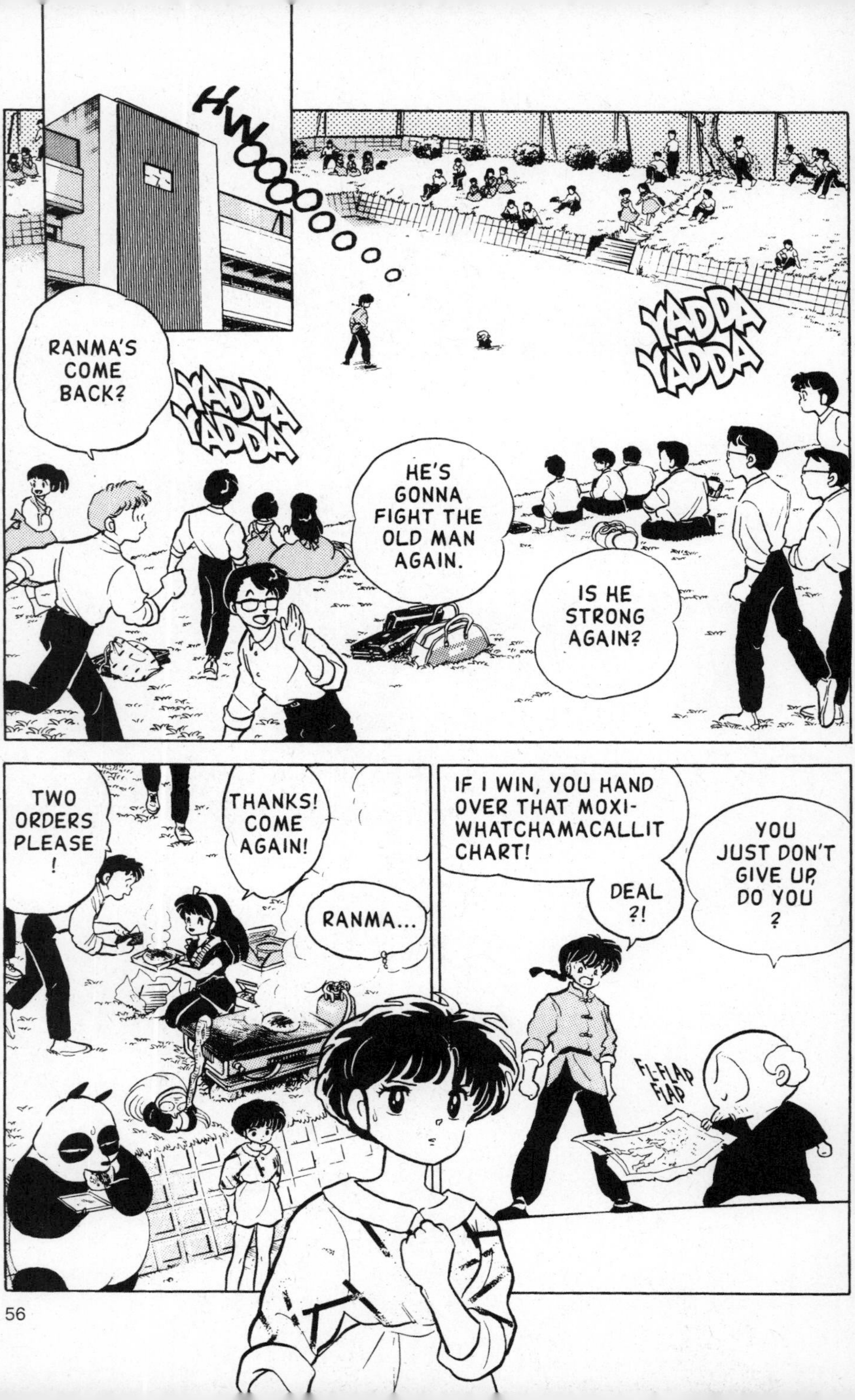
HWOOOOOOOOO
RANMA'S COME BACK?
YADDA YADDA
HE'S GONNA FIGHT THE OLD MAN AGAIN.
YADDA YADDA
IS HE STRONG AGAIN?
TWO ORDERS PLEASE!
THANKS! COME AGAIN!
RANMA...
IF I WIN, YOU HAND OVER THAT MOXI-WHATCHAMACALLIT CHART!
DEAL?!
YOU JUST DON'T GIVE UP, DO YOU?
FL-FLAP FLAP

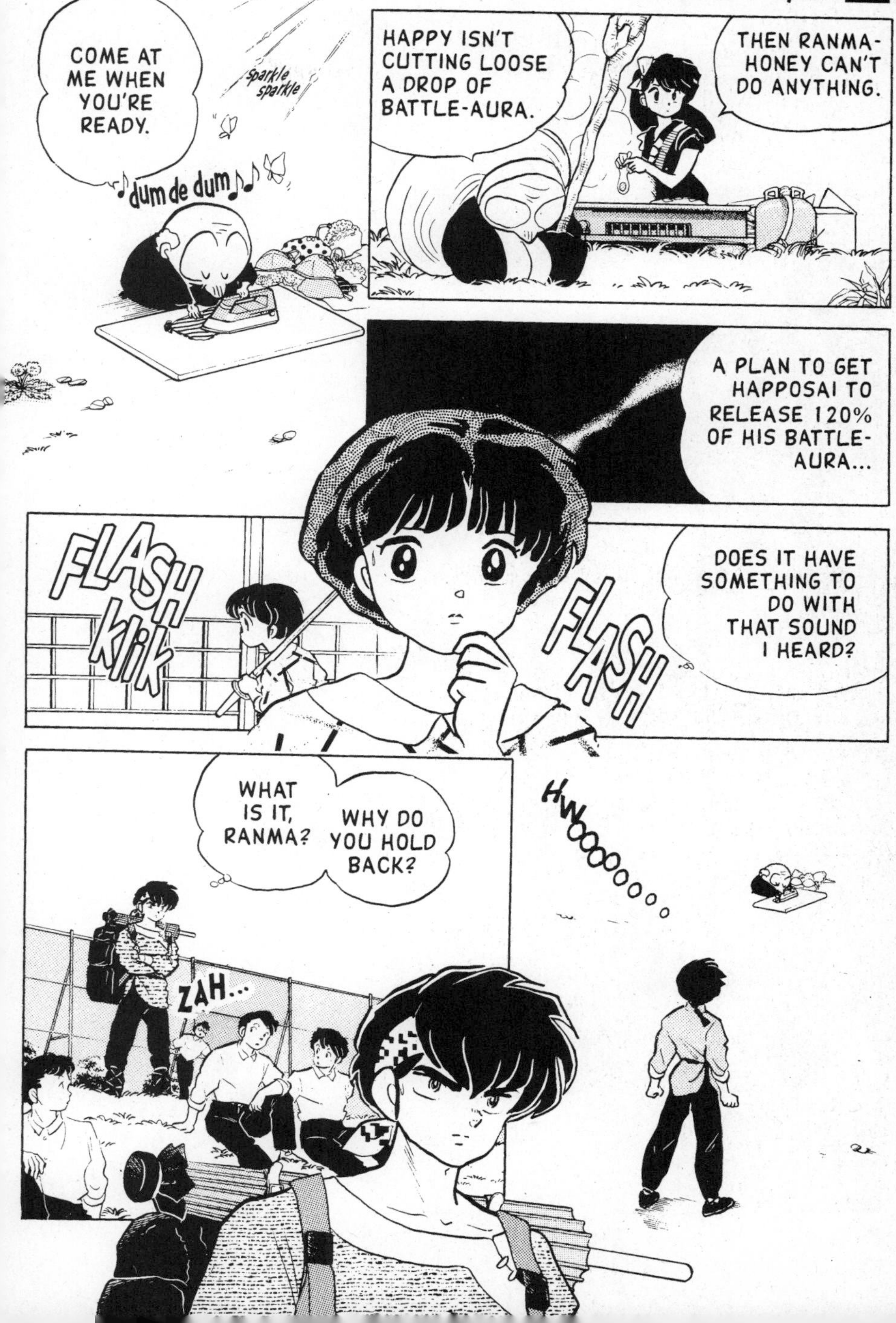
COME AT ME WHEN YOU'RE READY.
sparkle sparkle
dum de dum
HAPPY ISN'T CUTTING LOOSE A DROP OF BATTLE-AURA.
THEN RANMA-HONEY CAN'T DO ANYTHING.
A PLAN TO GET HAPPOSAI TO RELEASE 120% OF HIS BATTLE-AURA...
FLASH
klik
FLASH
DOES IT HAVE SOMETHING TO DO WITH THAT SOUND I HEARD?
WHAT IS IT, RANMA?
WHY DO YOU HOLD BACK?
HWOOOOOOOOO
ZAH...

I'D NEVER HAVE RESORTED TO THIS IF IT COULD'VE BEEN HELPED...

WITH THIS...

GNNN

...I CAST AWAY THE LAST OF MY PRIDE.

AND YET...

GLITTER

...IF IT'S TO REGAIN MY STRENGTH...

SHFF

I'LL DO ANYTHING !

TAKE A *LOOK*, FREAK!

FWA

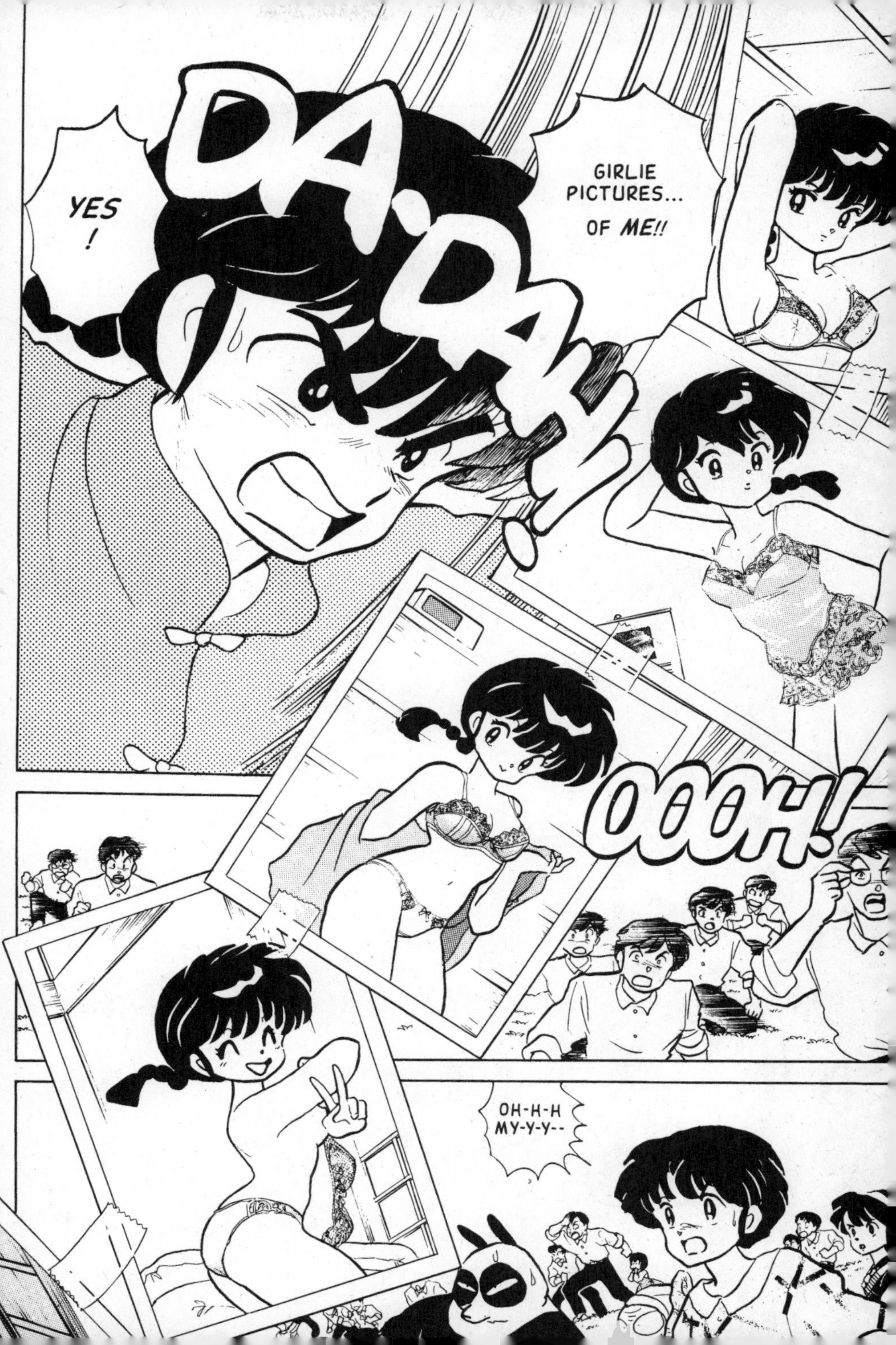
YES!
DA DA DA!!
GIRLIE PICTURES... OF ME!!
OOOH!
OH-H-H MY-Y-Y--

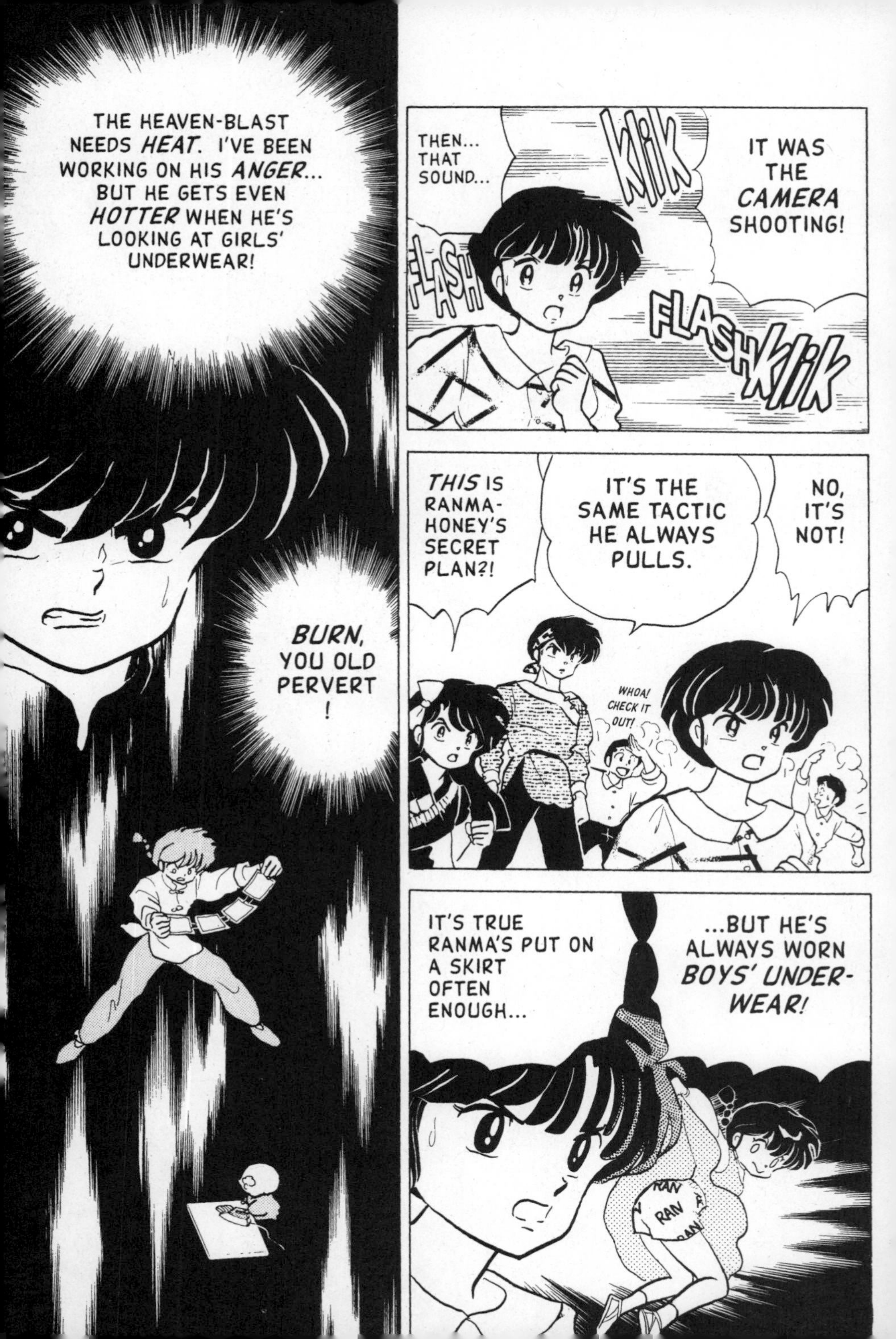
THE HEAVEN-BLAST NEEDS *HEAT*. I'VE BEEN WORKING ON HIS *ANGER*... BUT HE GETS EVEN *HOTTER* WHEN HE'S LOOKING AT GIRLS' UNDERWEAR!
BURN, YOU OLD PERVERT!
THEN... THAT SOUND...
klik
IT WAS THE *CAMERA* SHOOTING!
FLASH
FLASH klik
THIS IS RANMA-HONEY'S SECRET PLAN?!
IT'S THE SAME TACTIC HE ALWAYS PULLS.
NO, IT'S NOT!
WHOA! CHECK IT OUT!
IT'S TRUE RANMA'S PUT ON A SKIRT OFTEN ENOUGH...
...BUT HE'S ALWAYS WORN *BOYS' UNDER-WEAR!*

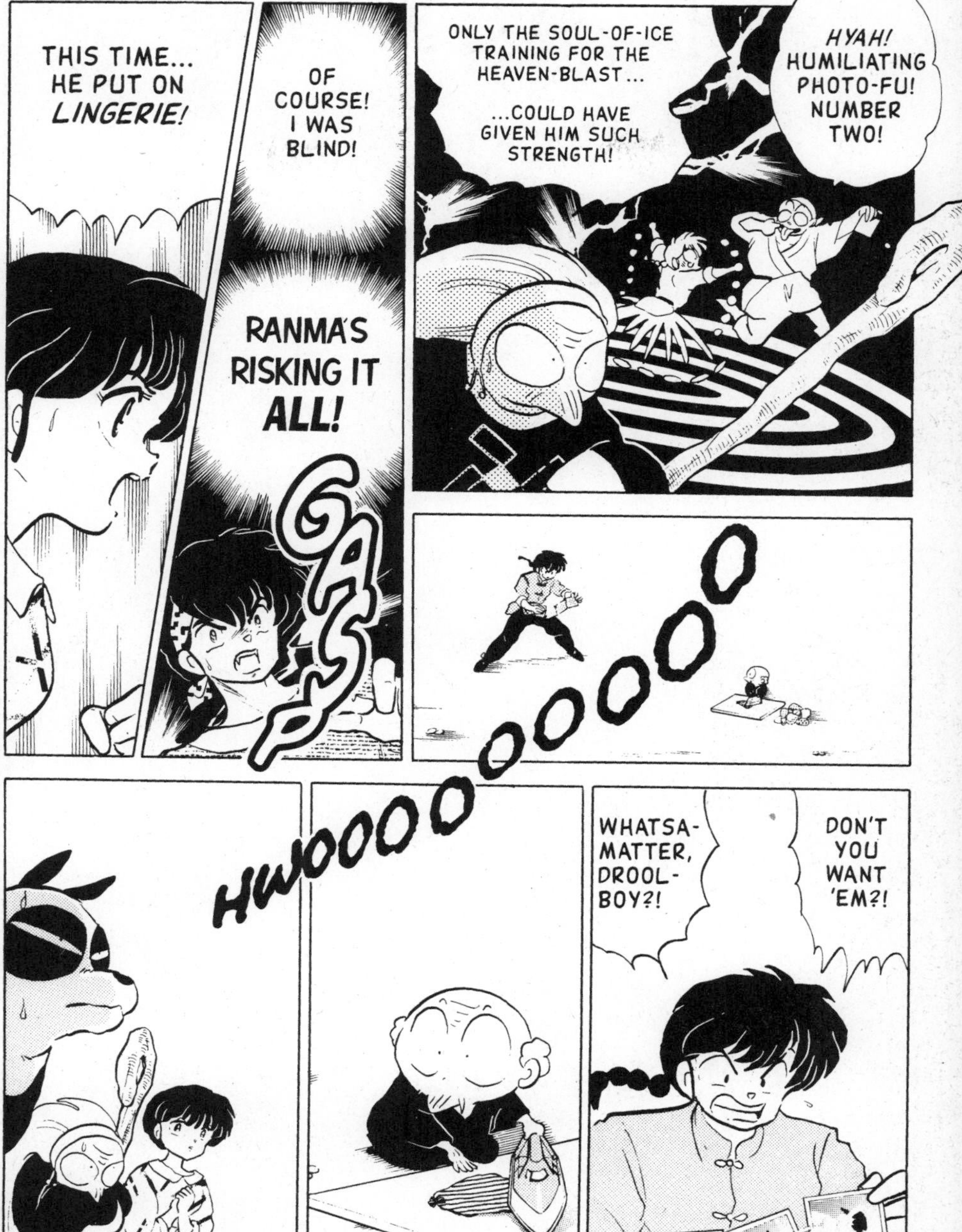
THIS TIME... HE PUT ON *LINGERIE!*
OF COURSE! I WAS BLIND!
RANMA'S RISKING IT **ALL!**
GASP
ONLY THE SOUL-OF-ICE TRAINING FOR THE HEAVEN-BLAST...
...COULD HAVE GIVEN HIM SUCH STRENGTH!
HYAH! HUMILIATING PHOTO-FU! NUMBER TWO!
HWOOOOOOOOOOOOO
WHATSA-MATTER, DROOL-BOY?!
DON'T YOU WANT 'EM?!

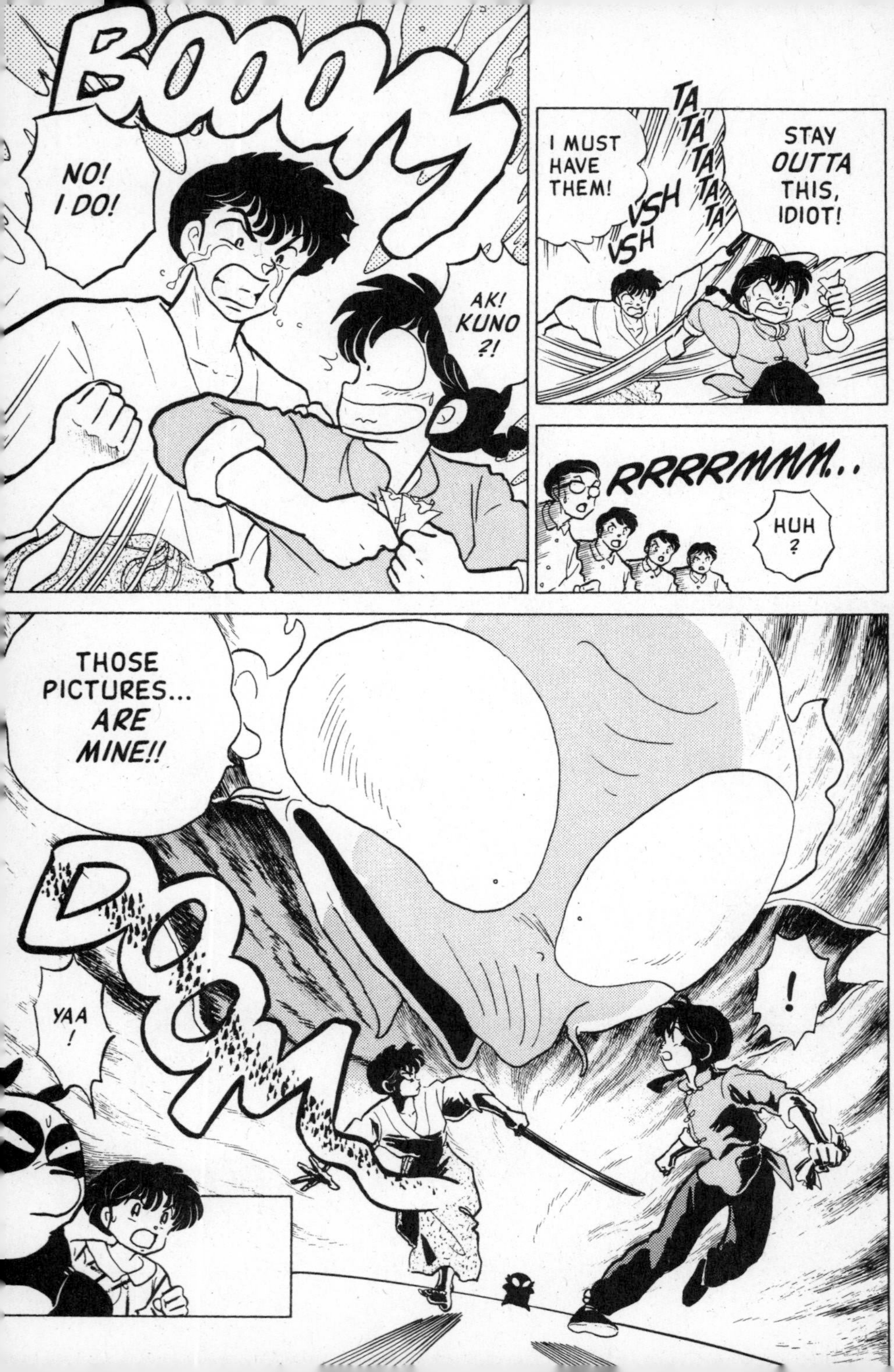
BOOOM
NO! I DO!
AK! KUNO?!
I MUST HAVE THEM!
TATATATATATA
VSH VSH
STAY OUTTA THIS, IDIOT!
RRRRMMM...
HUH?
THOSE PICTURES... ARE MINE!!
DOOM
YAA!
!

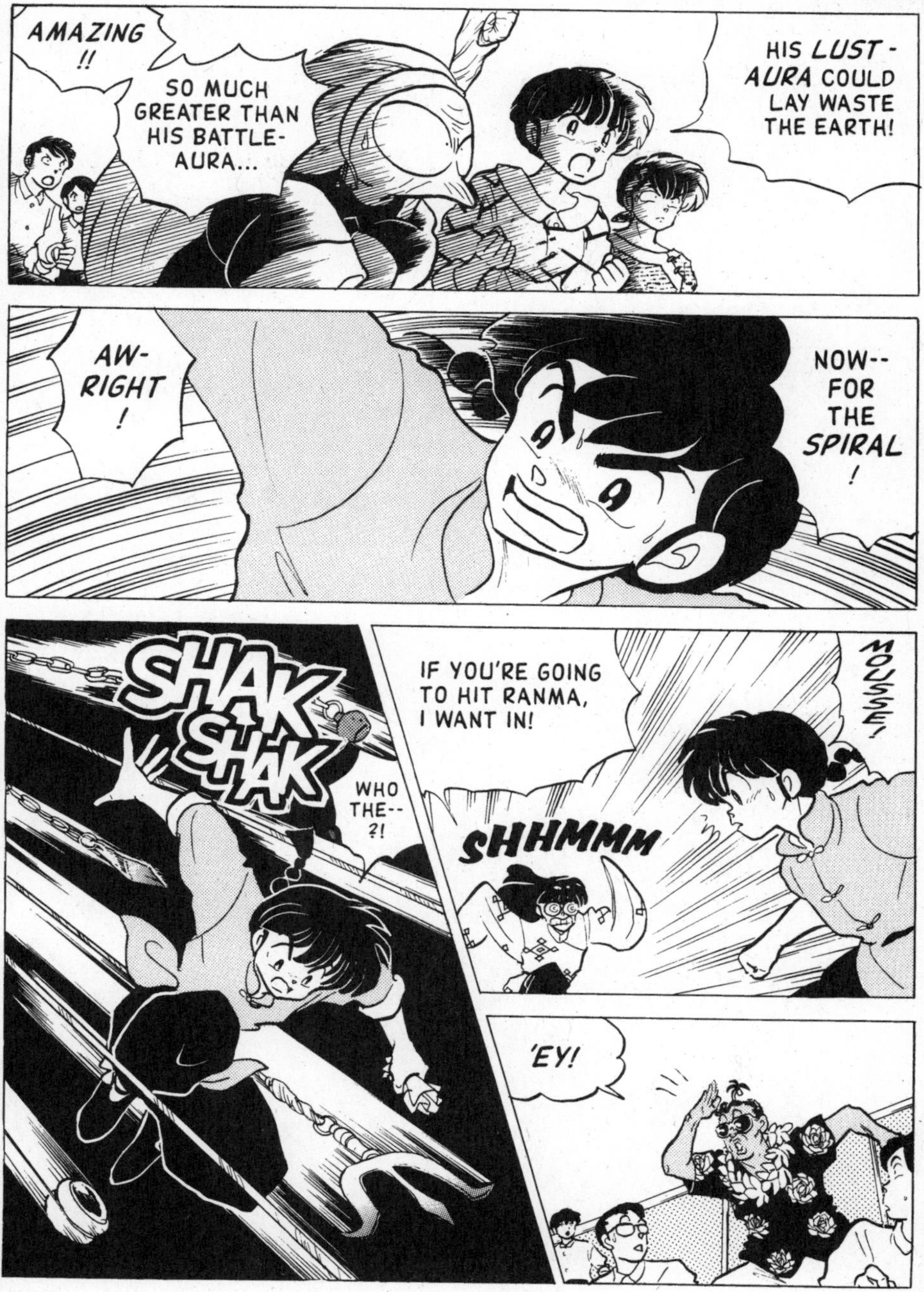
AMAZING !!
SO MUCH GREATER THAN HIS BATTLE-AURA...
HIS LUST-AURA COULD LAY WASTE THE EARTH!
AW-RIGHT !
NOW-- FOR THE SPIRAL !
SHAK SHAK SHAK
WHO THE--?!
IF YOU'RE GOING TO HIT RANMA, I WANT IN!
MOUSSE!
SHHMMM
'EY!

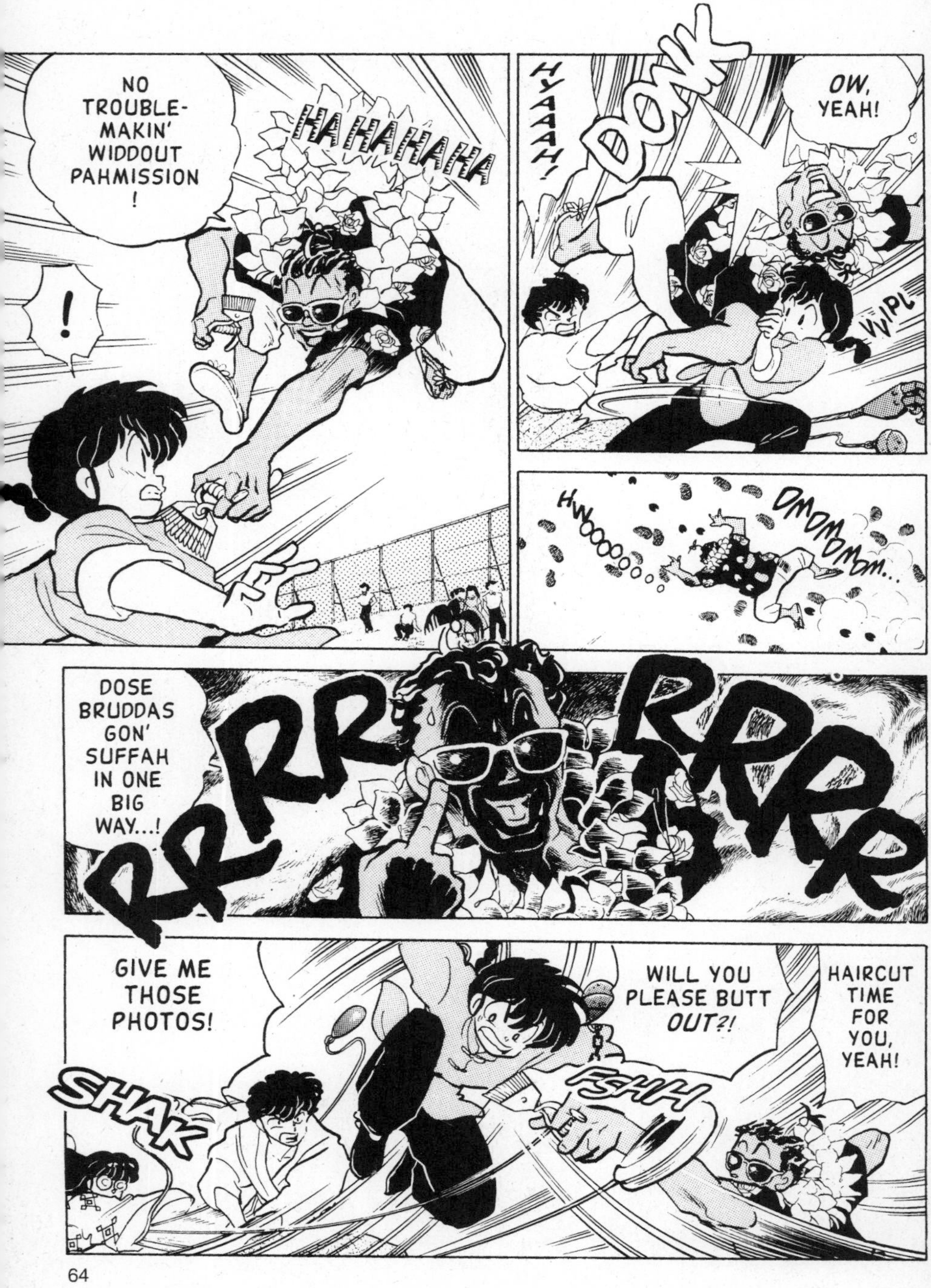
NO TROUBLE-MAKIN' WIDDOUT PAHMISSION!
HAHAHAHAHA
!
HYAAAAH!
DONK
OW, YEAH!
WIPL
HWOOOOOOoo
OMOMOMOMOM...
DOSE BRUDDAS GON' SUFFAH IN ONE BIG WAY...!
RRRRRRRRRRRR
GIVE ME THOSE PHOTOS!
WILL YOU PLEASE BUTT OUT?!
HAIRCUT TIME FOR YOU, YEAH!
SHAK
FSHH

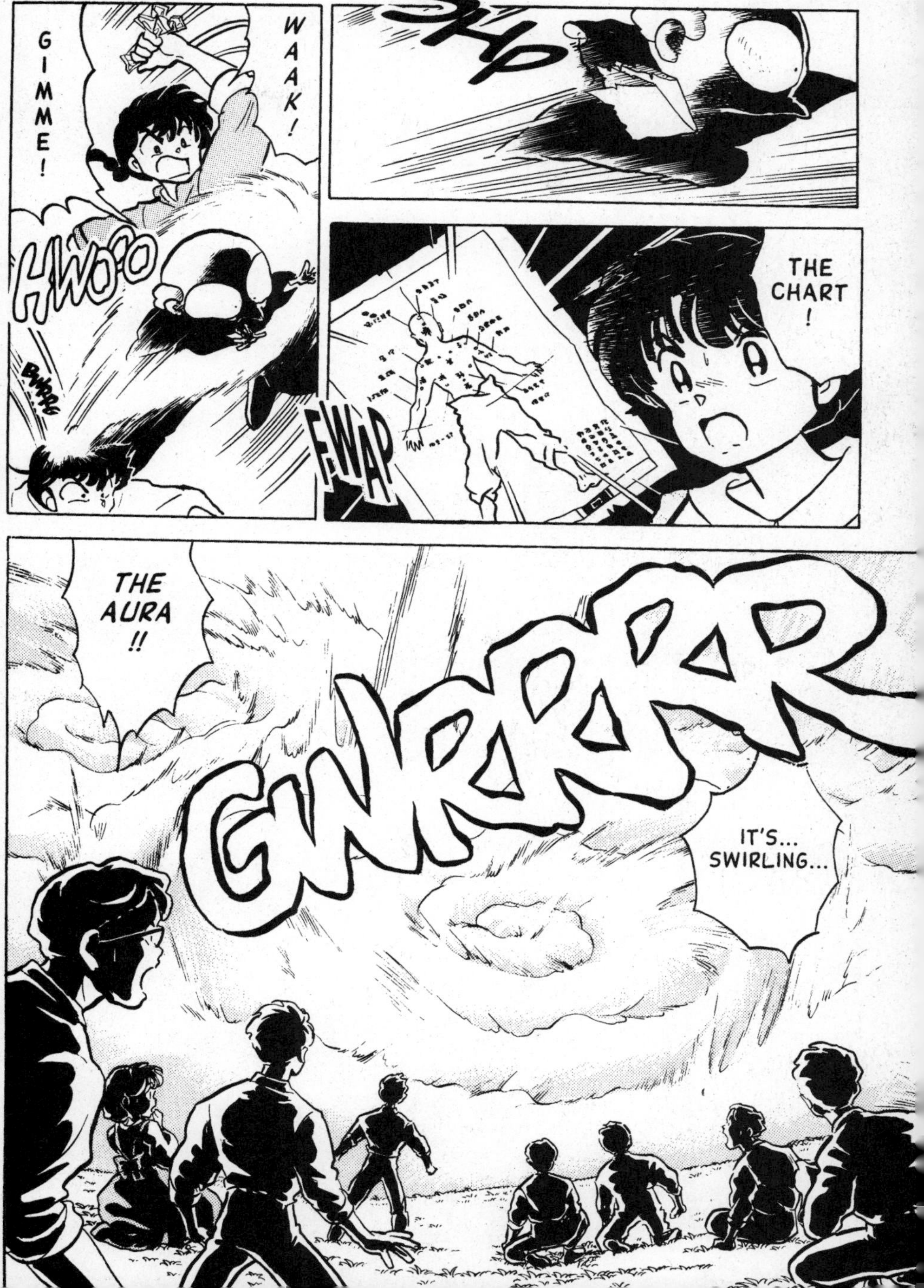
GIMME!
WAAK!
HWOOO
SHP
FWAP
THE CHART!
THE AURA!!
GWRRRR
IT'S... SWIRLING...

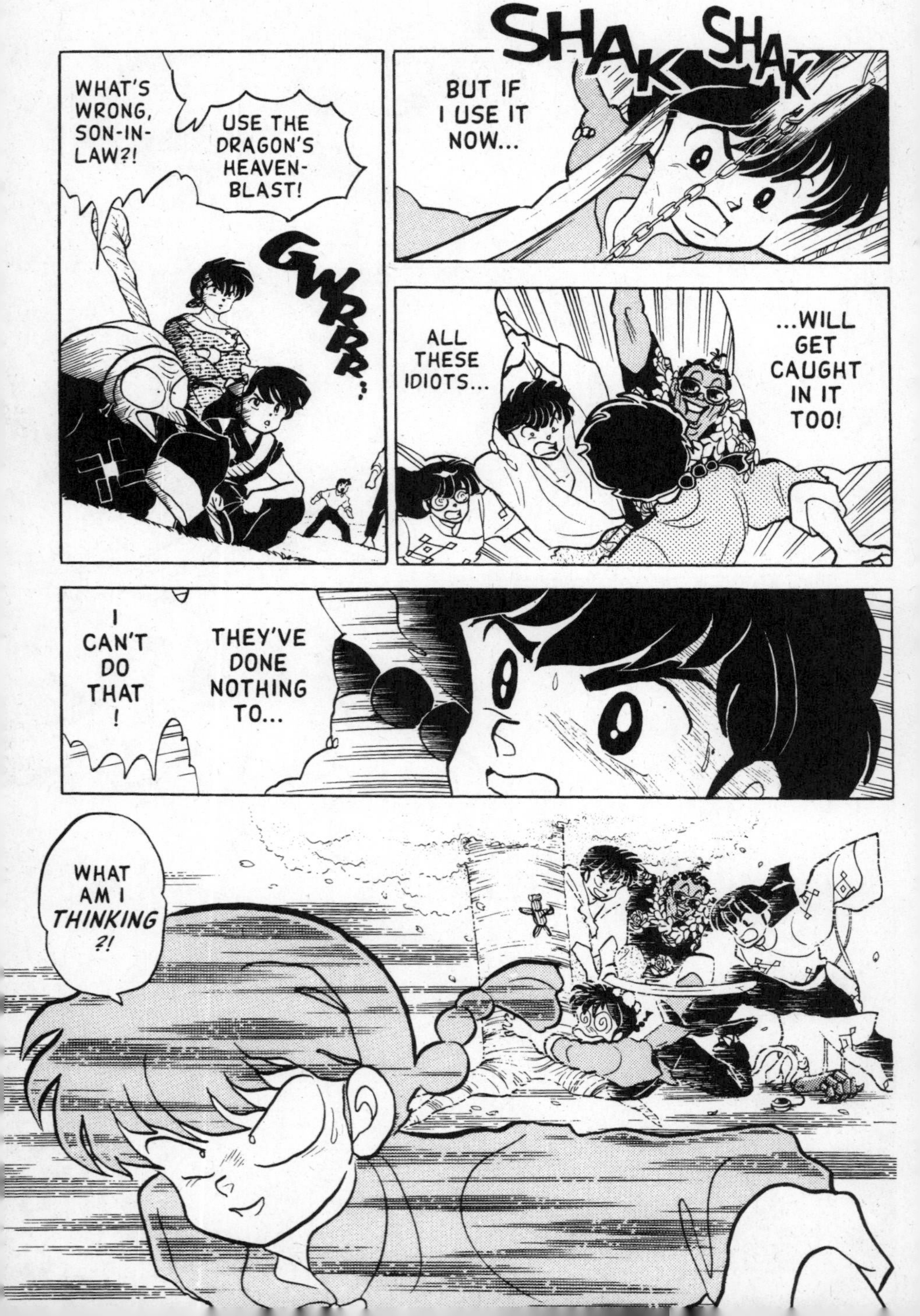
WHAT'S WRONG, SON-IN-LAW?!
USE THE DRAGON'S HEAVEN-BLAST!
GWRRR
SHAK SHAK
BUT IF I USE IT NOW...
ALL THESE IDIOTS...
...WILL GET CAUGHT IN IT TOO!
I CAN'T DO THAT!
THEY'VE DONE NOTHING TO...
WHAT AM I *THINKING*?!

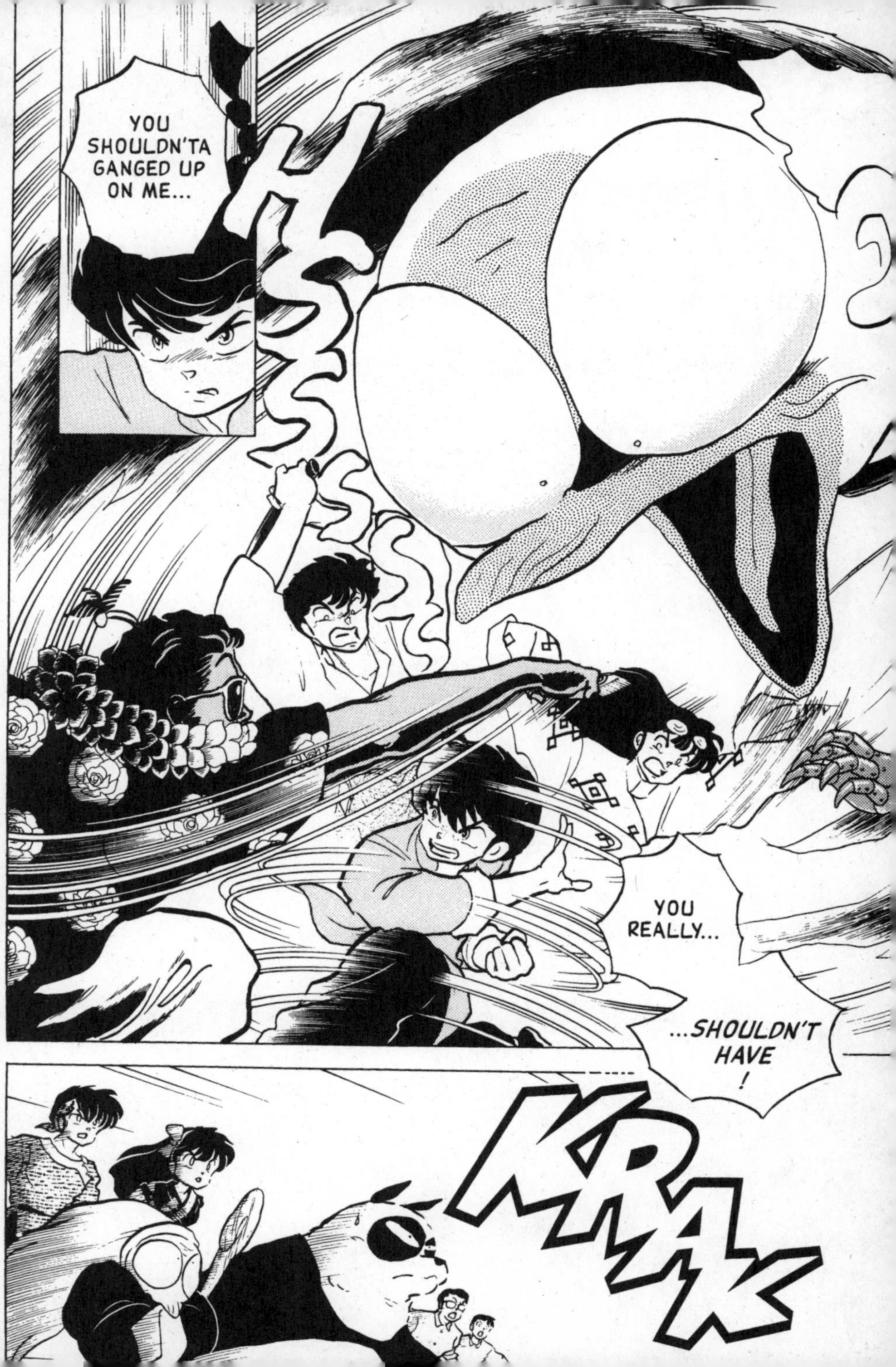
YOU SHOULDN'TA GANGED UP ON ME...
YOU REALLY...
...SHOULDN'T HAVE!
KRAK

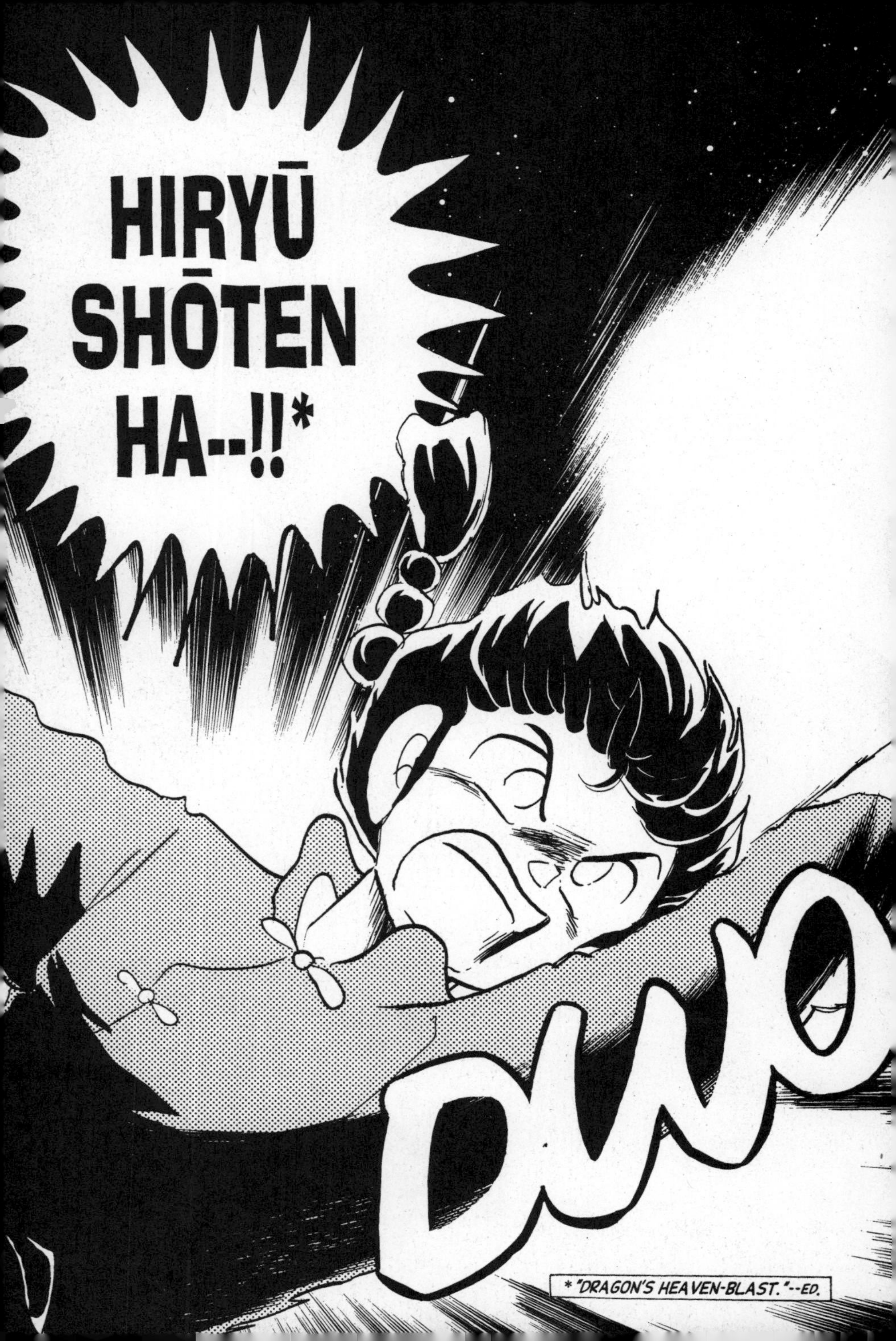
HIRYŪ SHŌTEN HA--!!*
DUO
* "DRAGON'S HEAVEN-BLAST." --ED.

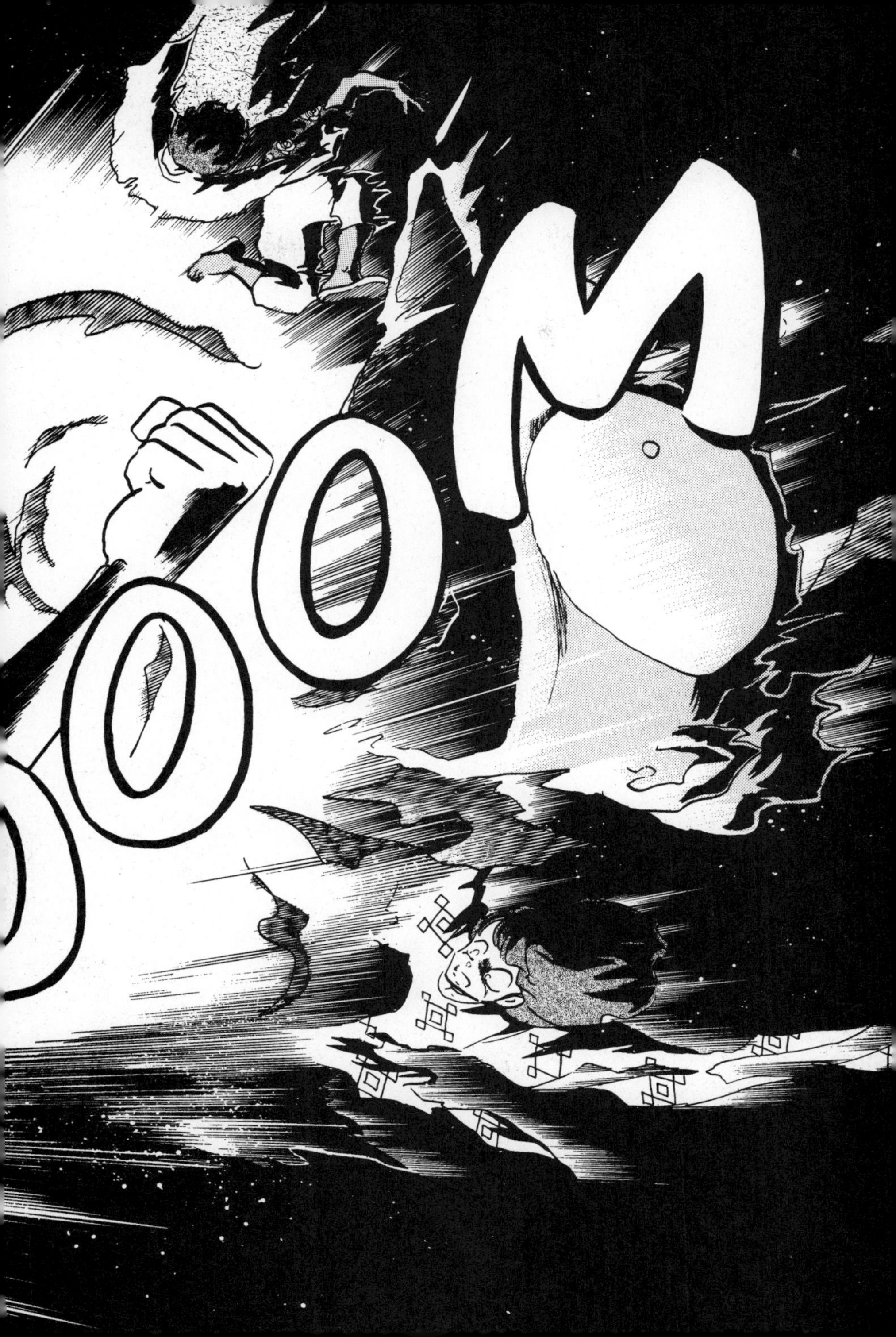
OOOM

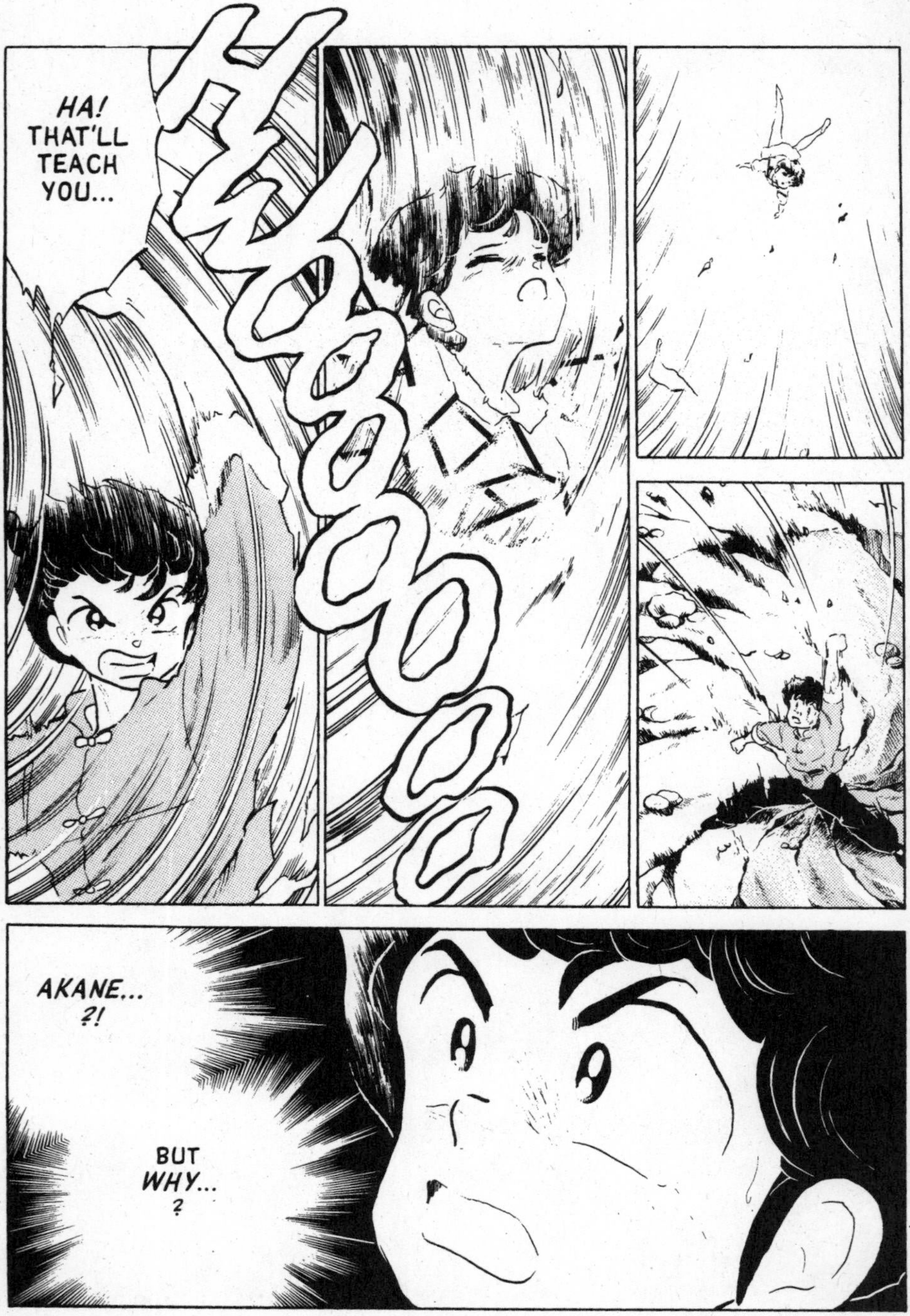
HA! THAT'LL TEACH YOU...
FWOOOOOOOOOO
AKANE... ?!
BUT WHY... ?

PART 5
THE PAPER CHASE

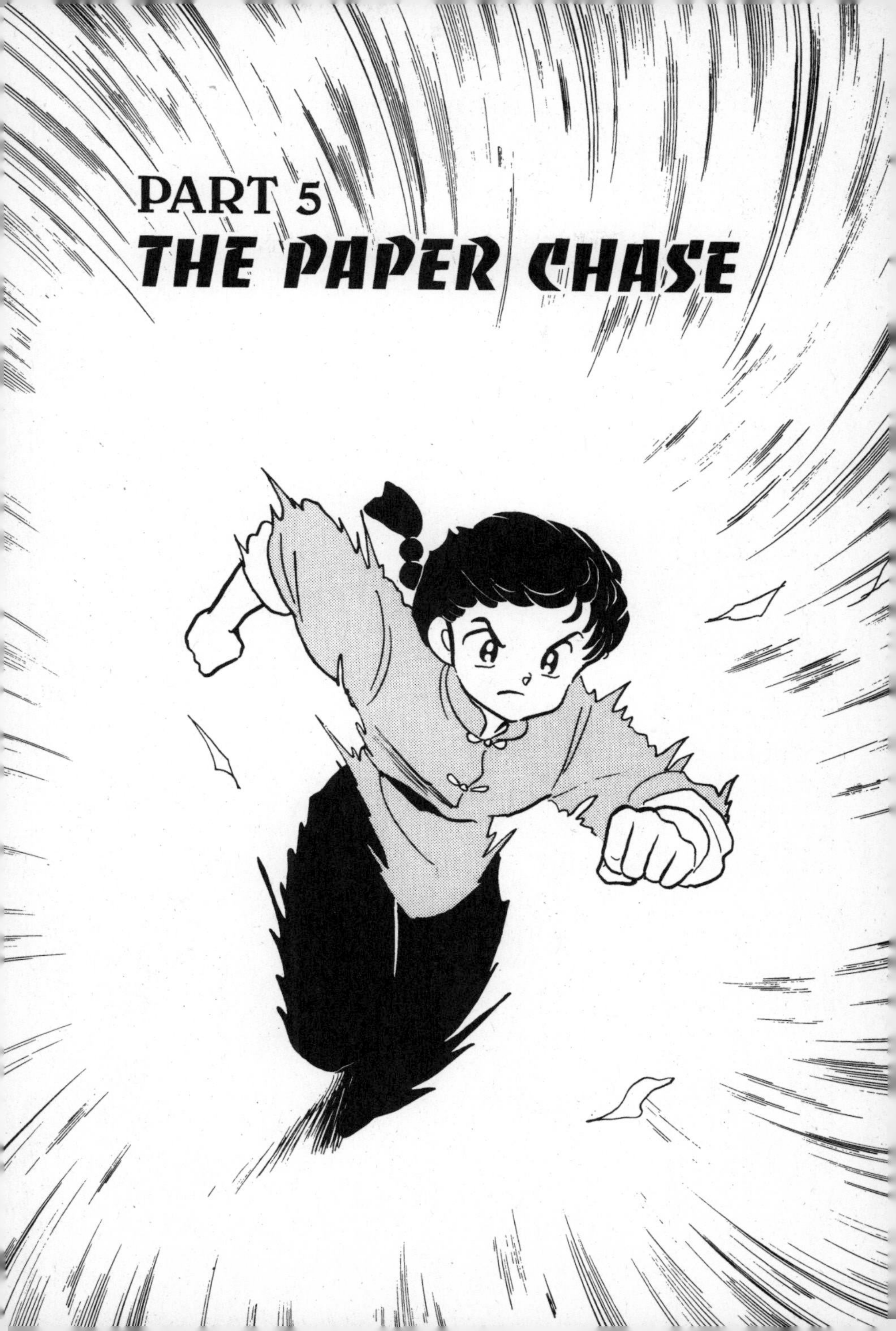

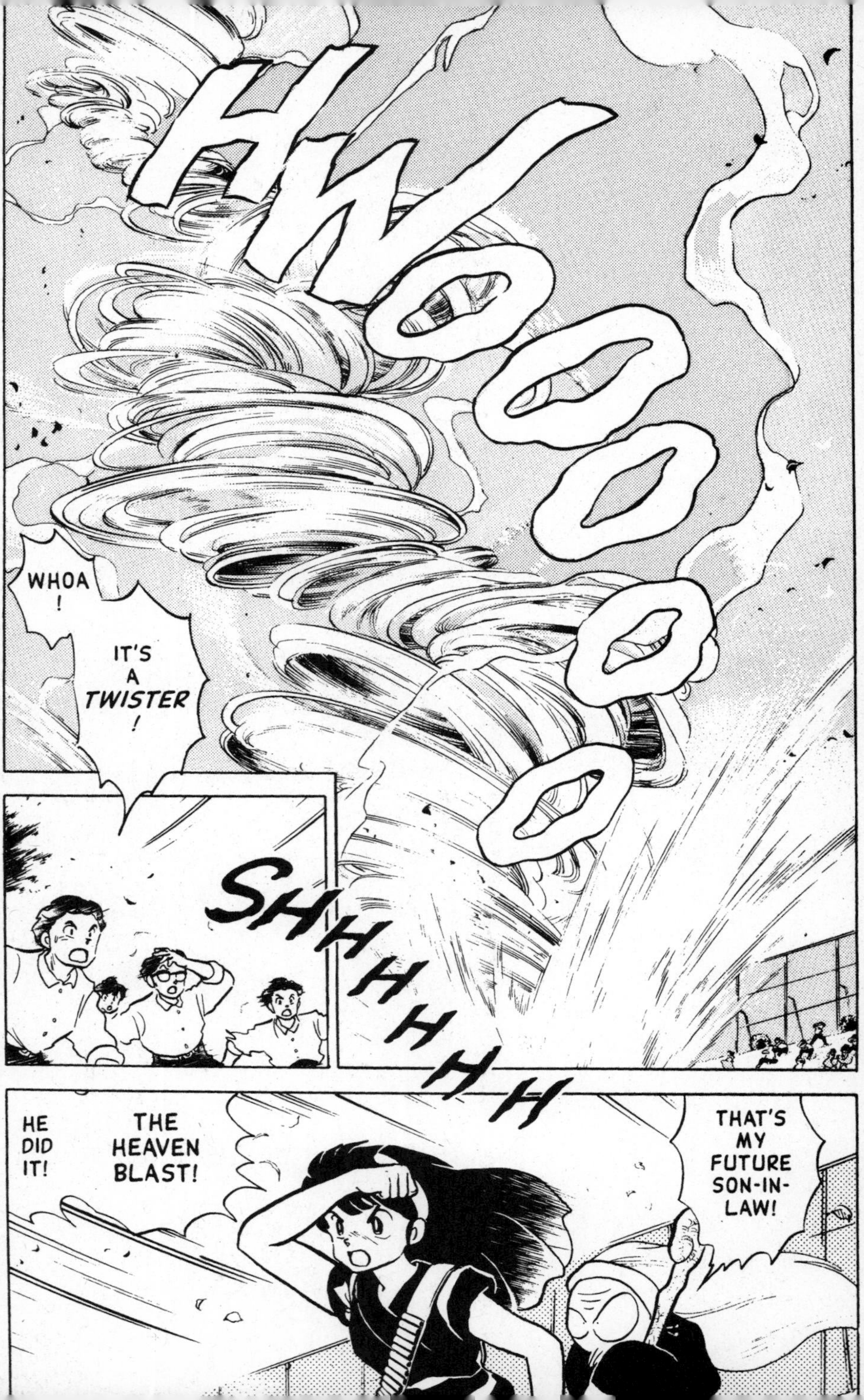

HWOOOOOOO
WHOA!
IT'S A TWISTER!
SHHHHHHH
HE DID IT!
THE HEAVEN BLAST!
THAT'S MY FUTURE SON-IN-LAW!

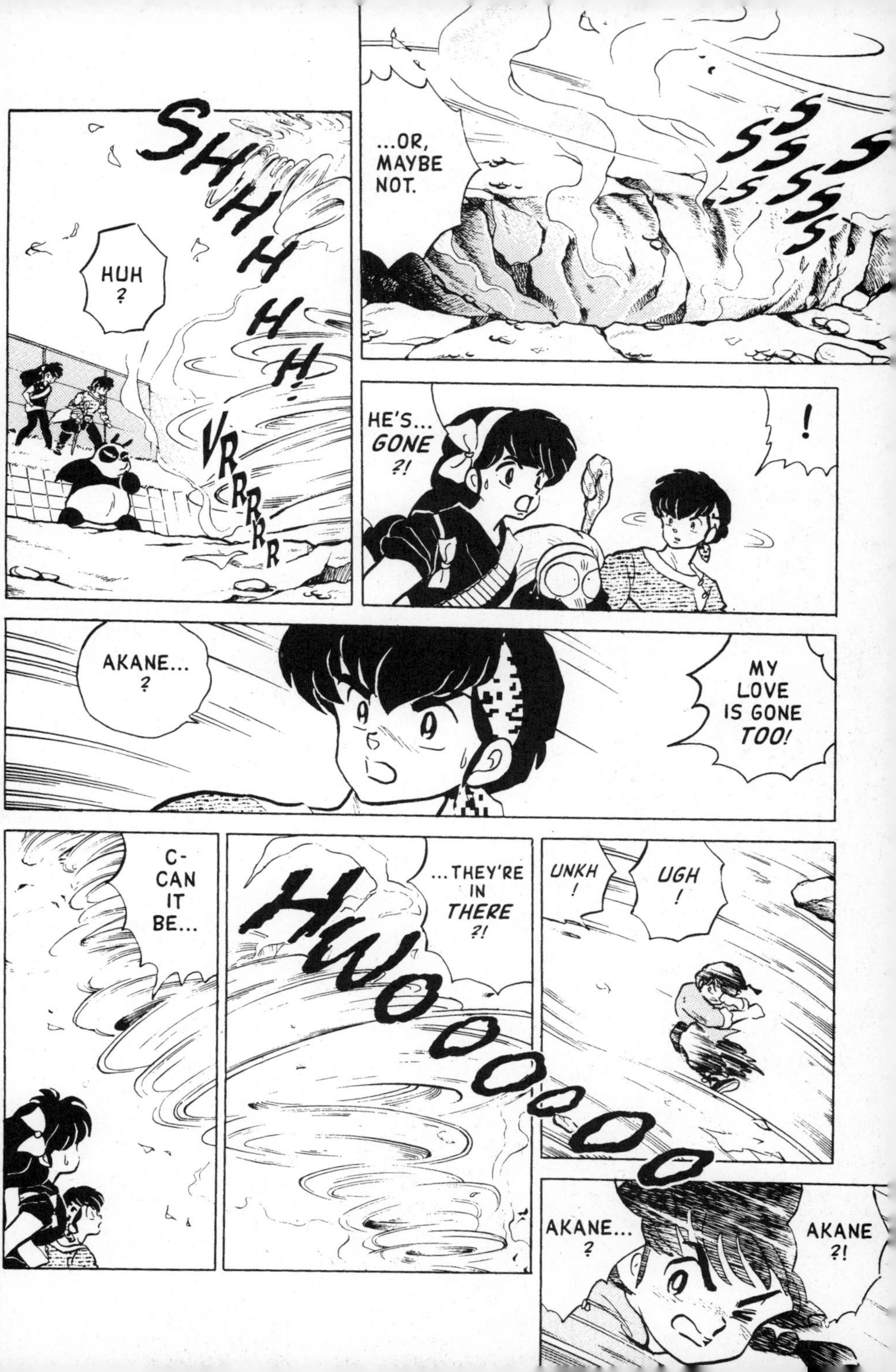
SHHHHHH!
HUH ?
VRRRRRR
...OR, MAYBE NOT.
SSSSSSSSSSSSS
HE'S... GONE ?!
!
AKANE... ?
MY LOVE IS GONE TOO!
C-CAN IT BE...
...THEY'RE IN THERE ?!
HWOOOOOOOOO
UNKH !
UGH !
AKANE... ?
AKANE ?!

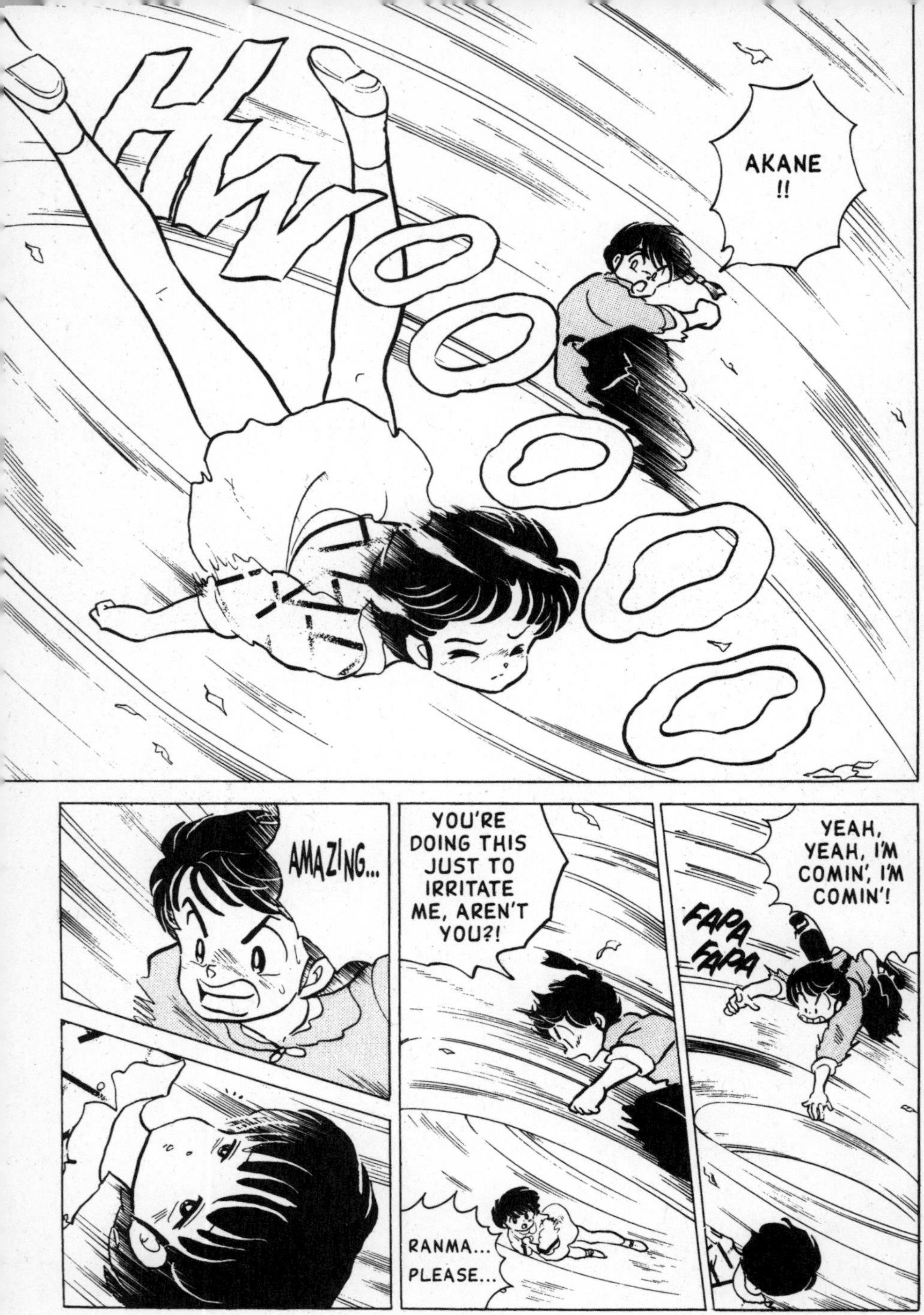
AKANE !!
AMAZING...
YOU'RE DOING THIS JUST TO IRRITATE ME, AREN'T YOU?!
RANMA... PLEASE...
YEAH, YEAH, I'M COMIN', I'M COMIN'!
FAPA FAPA

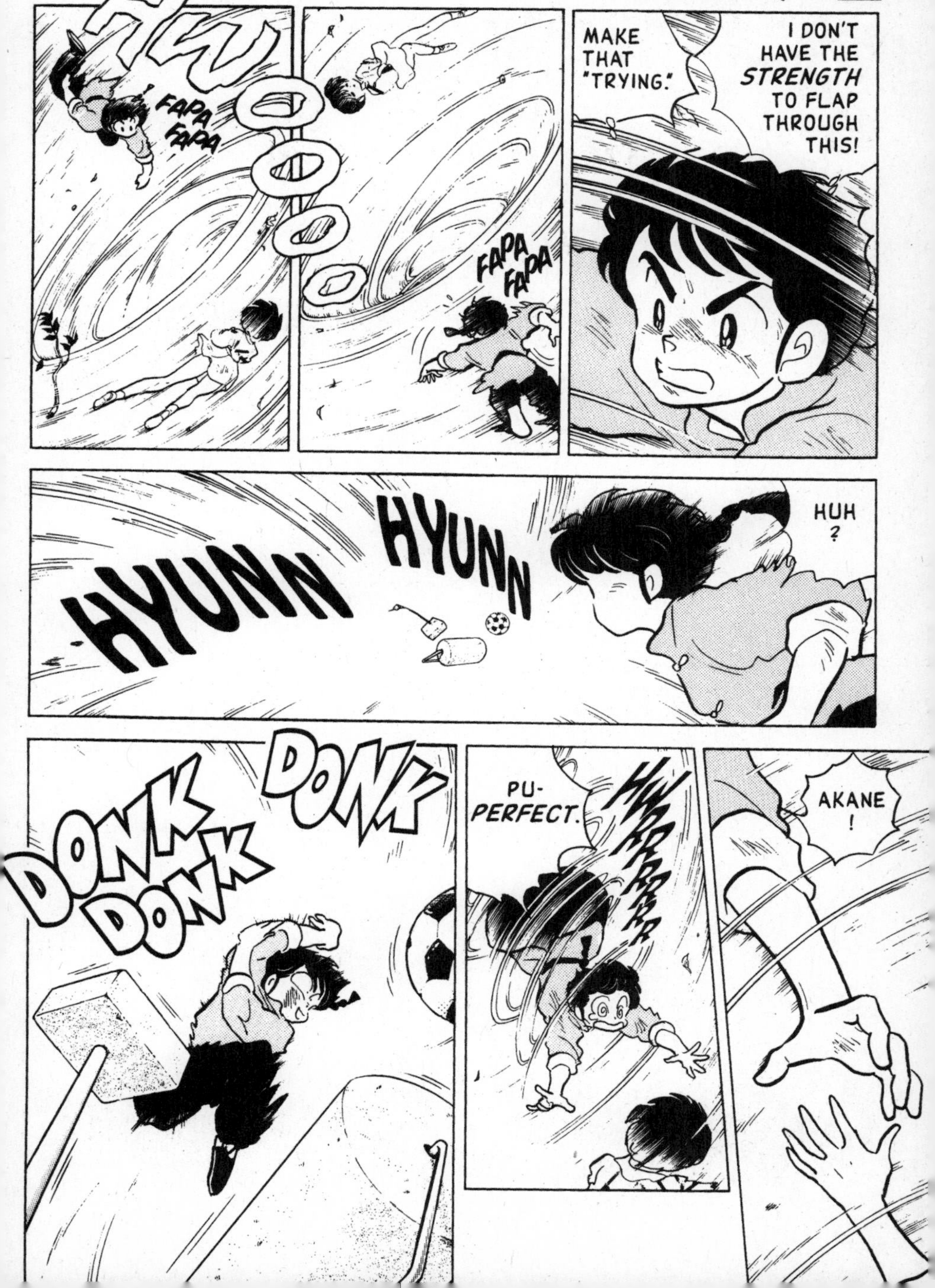
HWOOOOO
FAPA FAPA
FAPA FAPA
I DON'T HAVE THE *STRENGTH* TO FLAP THROUGH THIS!
MAKE THAT "TRYING."
HYUNN
HYUNN
HUH ?
DONK
DONK
DONK
DONK
PU- PERFECT.
AKANE !

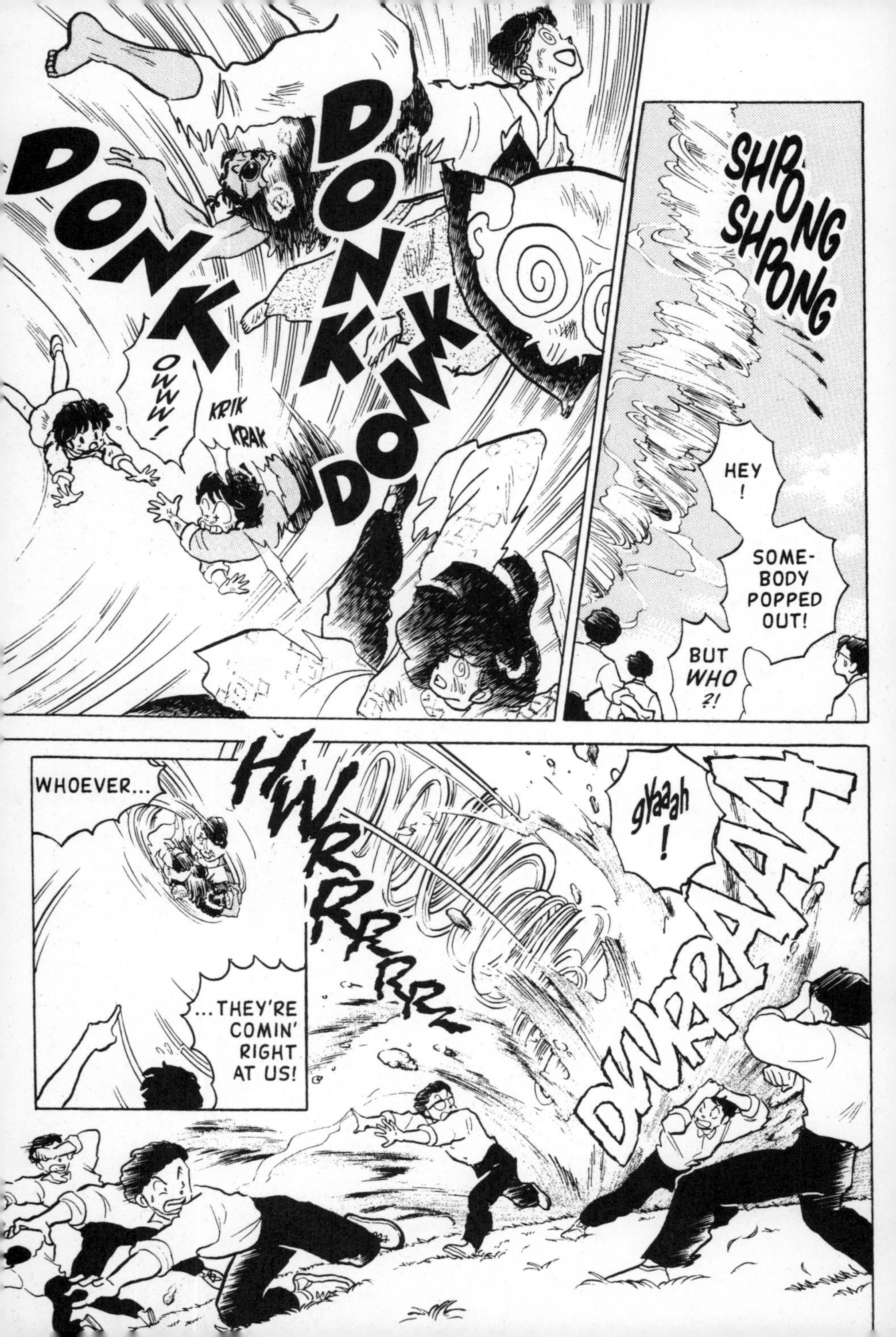
DONK
DON K'K DON
OWWW!
KRIK KRAK
SHPONG SHPONG
HEY!
SOME-BODY POPPED OUT!
BUT WHO?!
WHOEVER...
...THEY'RE COMIN' RIGHT AT US!
HWRRRRRR
gYaaah!
DWAPAAA

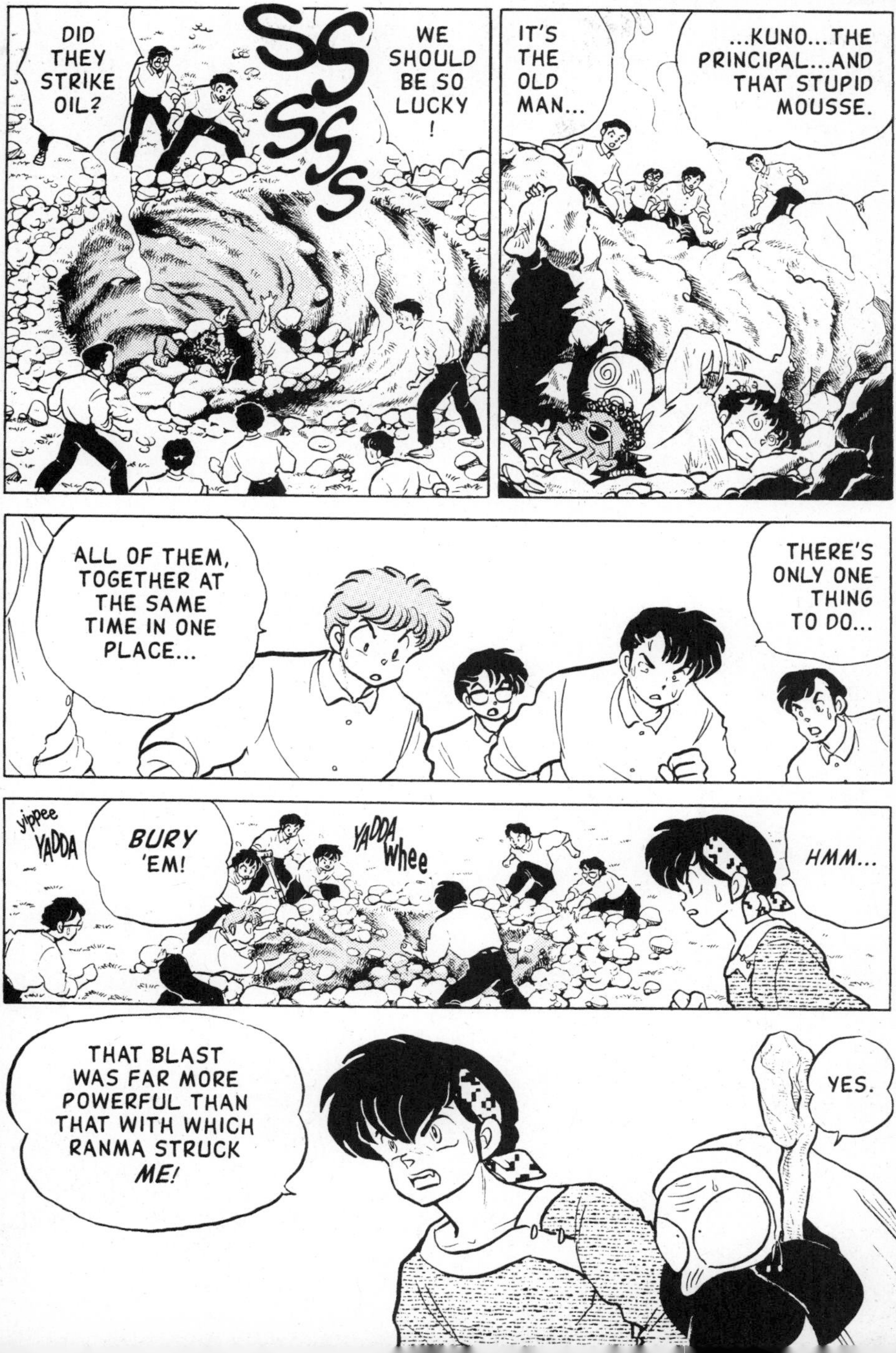
DID THEY STRIKE OIL?
SSSSS
WE SHOULD BE SO LUCKY!
IT'S THE OLD MAN...
...KUNO...THE PRINCIPAL...AND THAT STUPID MOUSSE.
ALL OF THEM, TOGETHER AT THE SAME TIME IN ONE PLACE...
THERE'S ONLY ONE THING TO DO...
yippee YADDA
BURY 'EM!
YADDA whee
HMM...
THAT BLAST WAS FAR MORE POWERFUL THAN THAT WITH WHICH RANMA STRUCK ME!
YES.

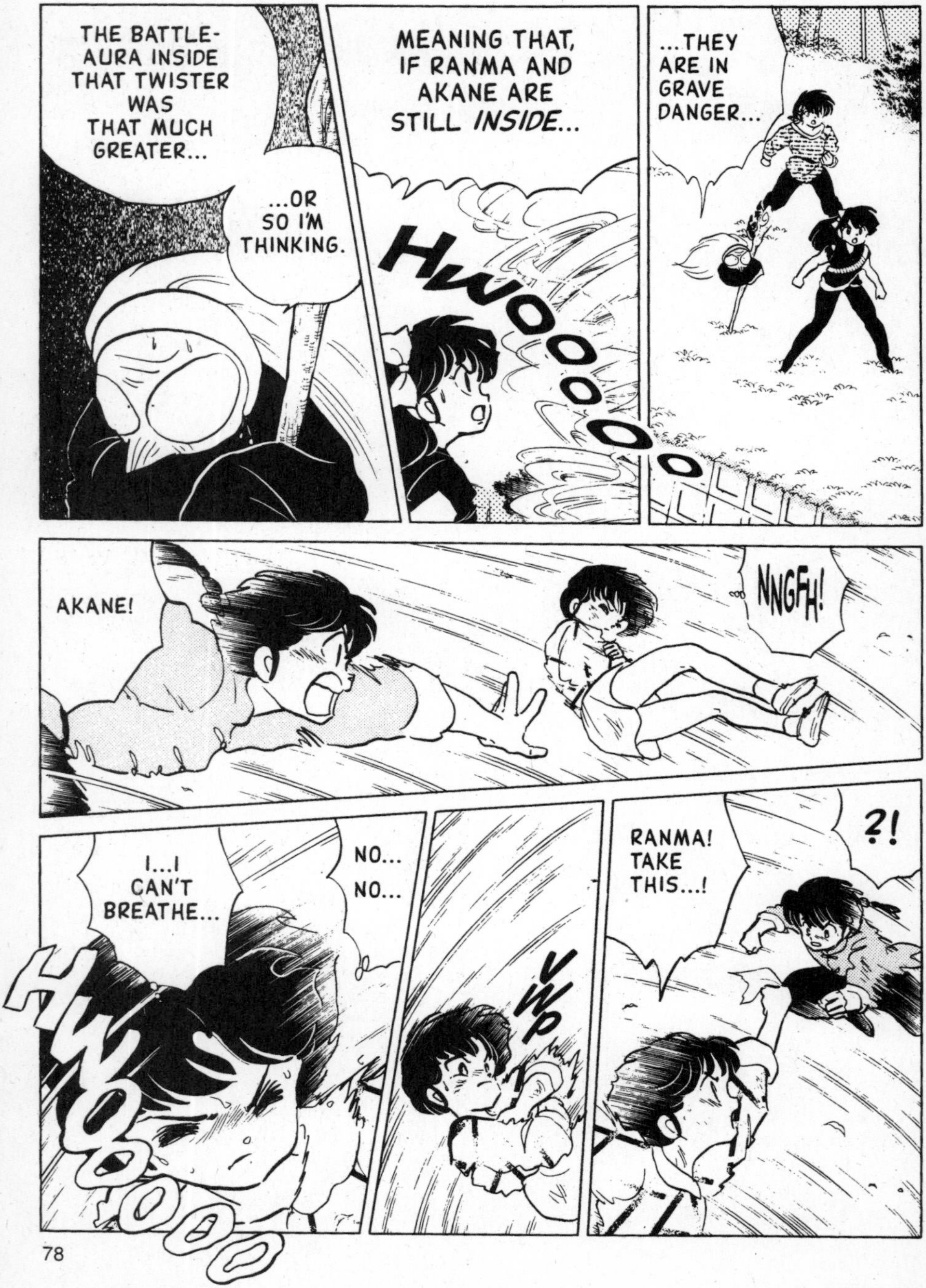
THE BATTLE-AURA INSIDE THAT TWISTER WAS THAT MUCH GREATER...
...OR SO I'M THINKING.
MEANING THAT, IF RANMA AND AKANE ARE STILL *INSIDE*...
HWOOOOOO
...THEY ARE IN GRAVE DANGER...
AKANE!
NNGFH!
I...I CAN'T BREATHE...
HWOOOOOO
NO... NO...
VWP
RANMA! TAKE THIS...!
?!

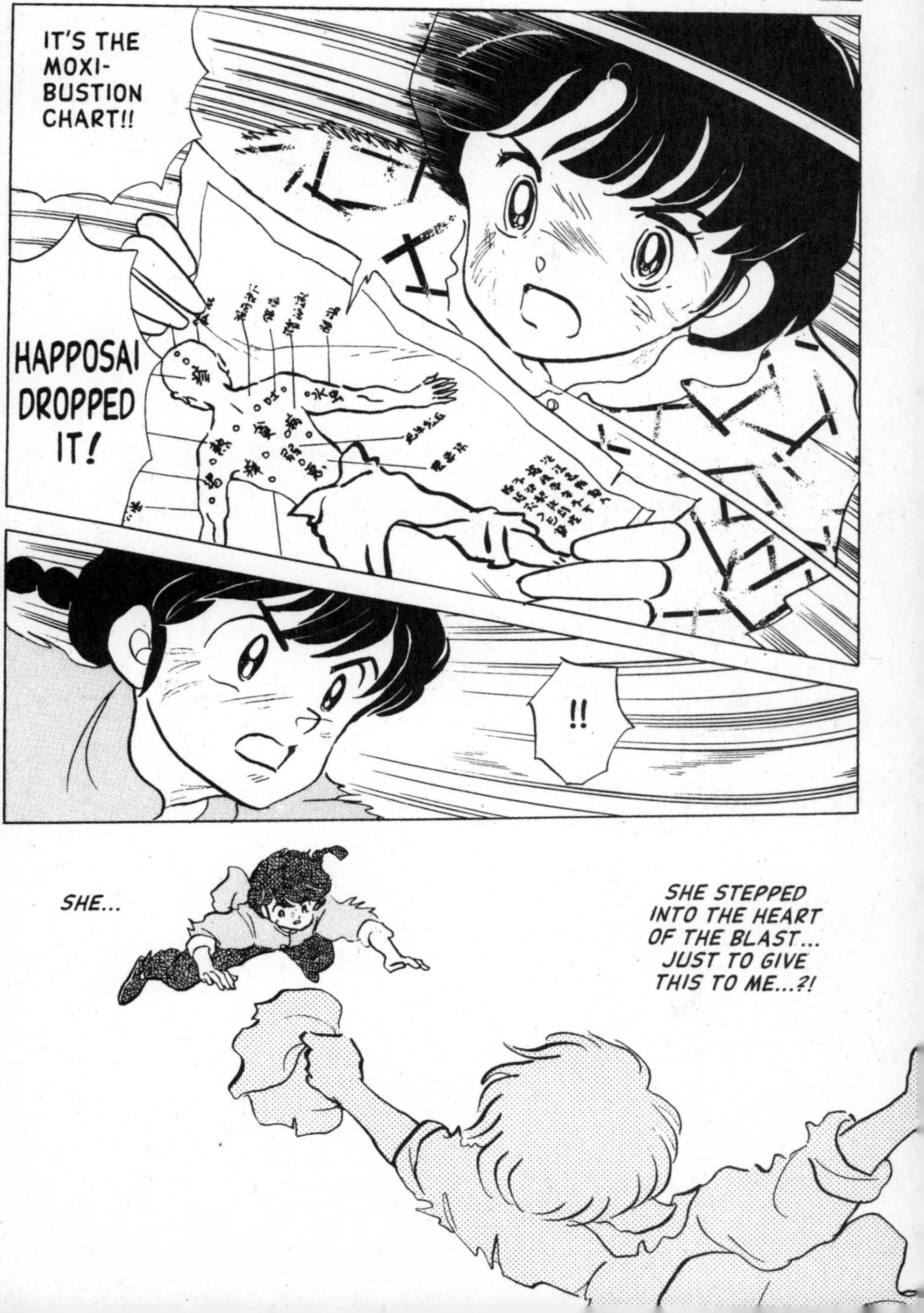
IT'S THE MOXI-BUSTION CHART!!
HAPPOSAI DROPPED IT!
!!
SHE...
SHE STEPPED INTO THE HEART OF THE BLAST... JUST TO GIVE THIS TO ME...?!

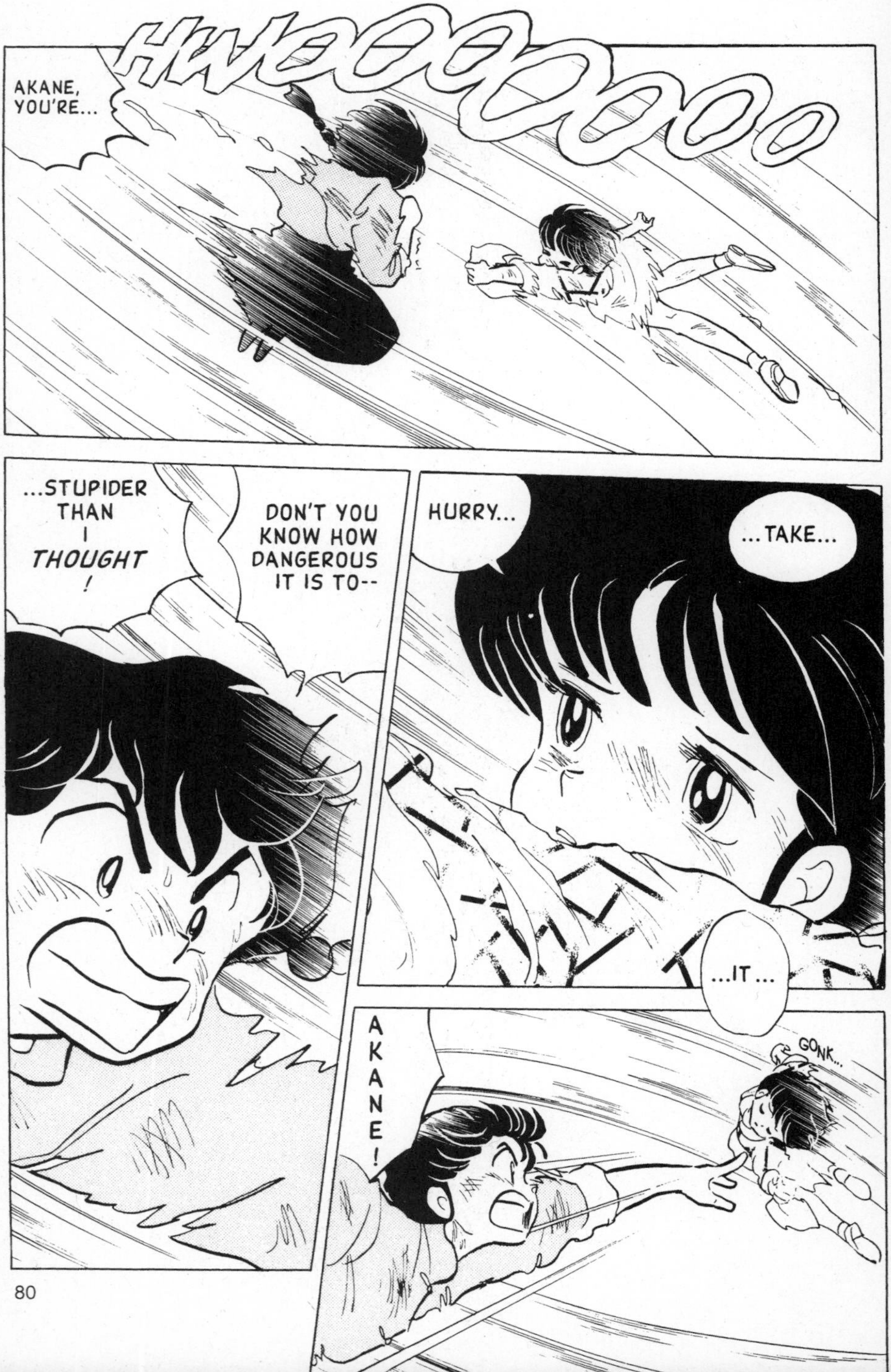
HWOOOOOOOO
AKANE, YOU'RE...
...STUPIDER THAN I *THOUGHT*!
DON'T YOU KNOW HOW DANGEROUS IT IS TO--
HURRY...
...TAKE...
...IT...
AKANE!
GONK...

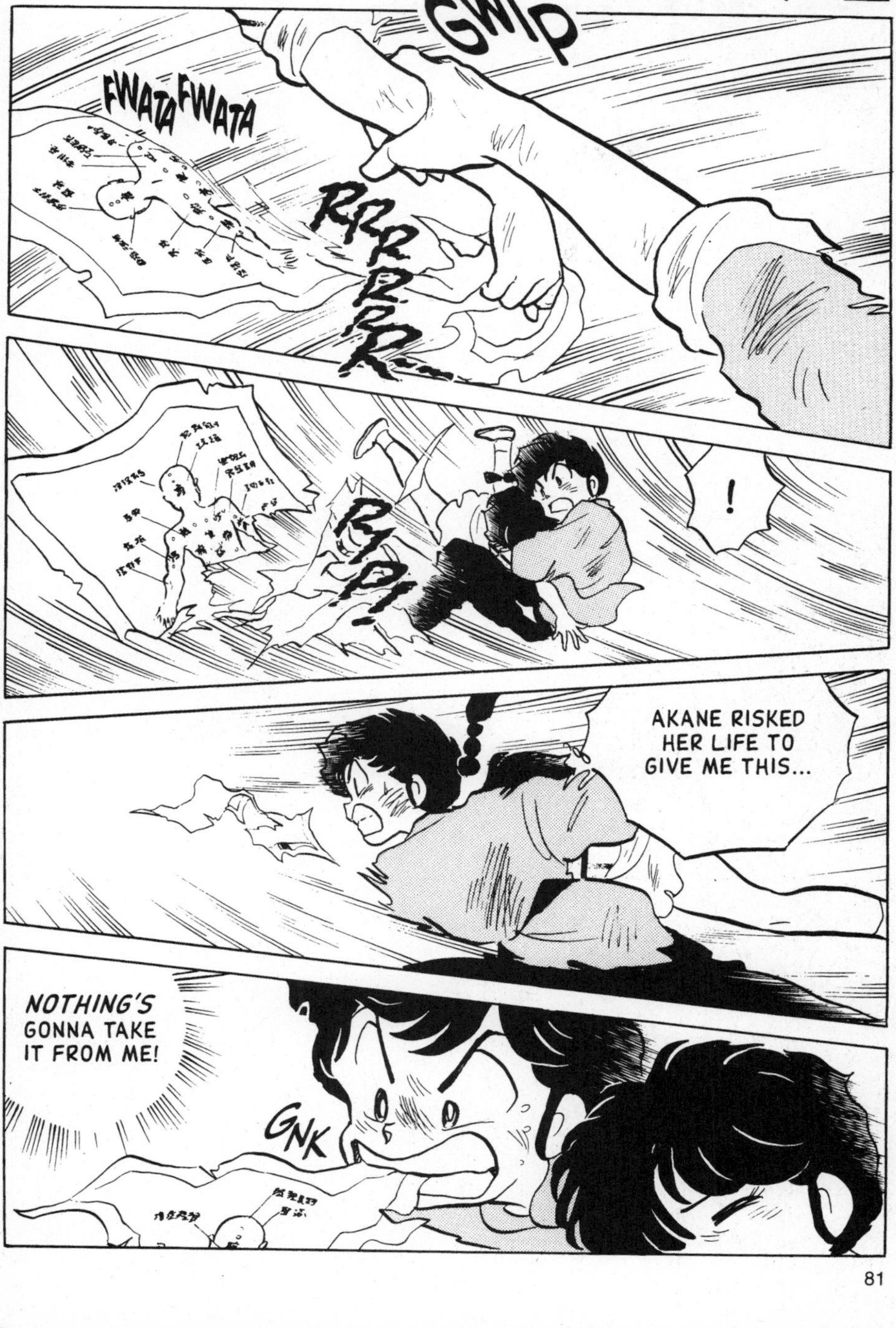
GWIP
FWATA FWATA
RRRRR...
!
RIP!
AKANE RISKED HER LIFE TO GIVE ME THIS...
NOTHING'S GONNA TAKE IT FROM ME!
GNK

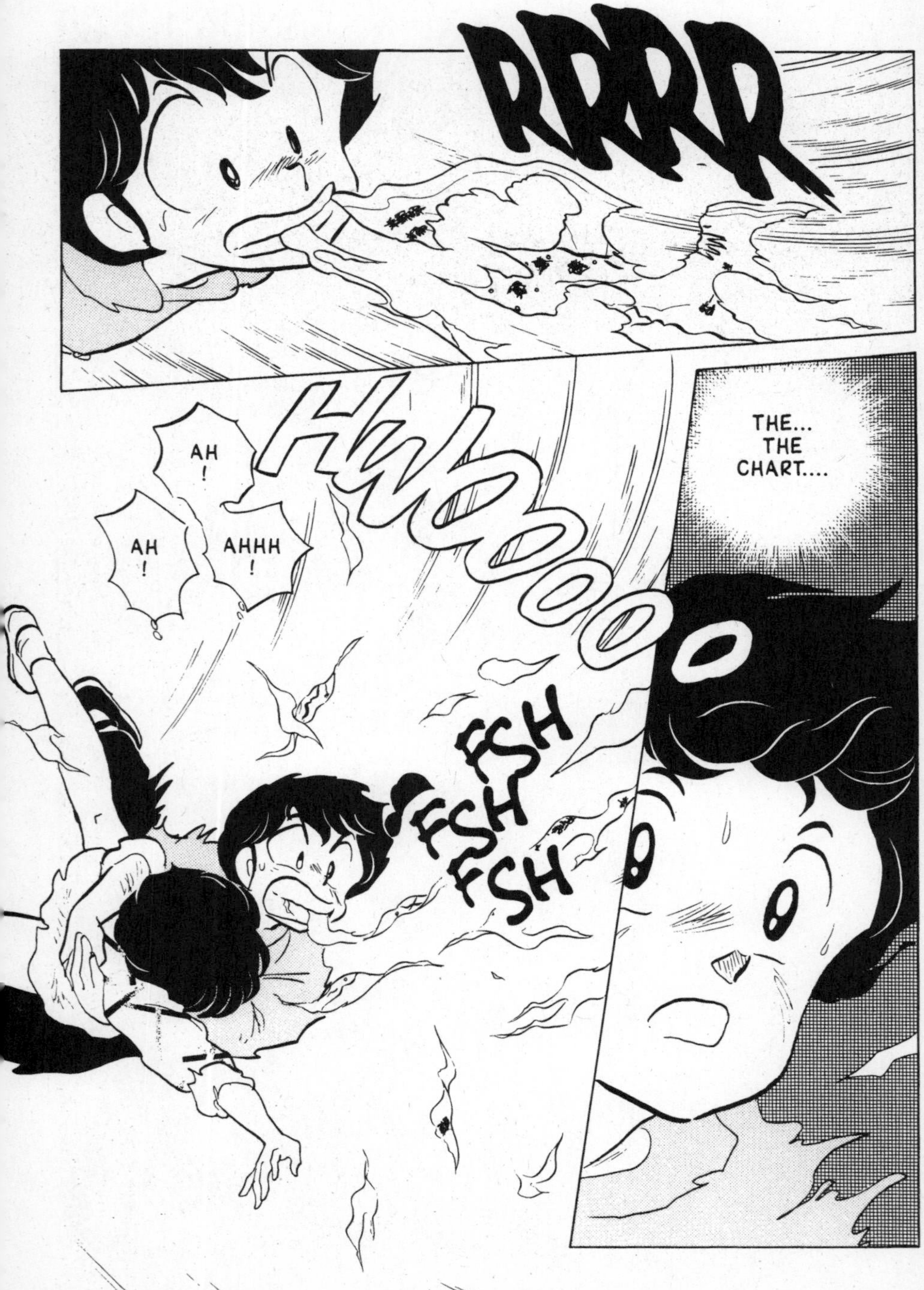
RRRR
AH!
AH!
AHHH!
HWOOOOOO
FSH
FSH
FSH
THE... THE CHART....

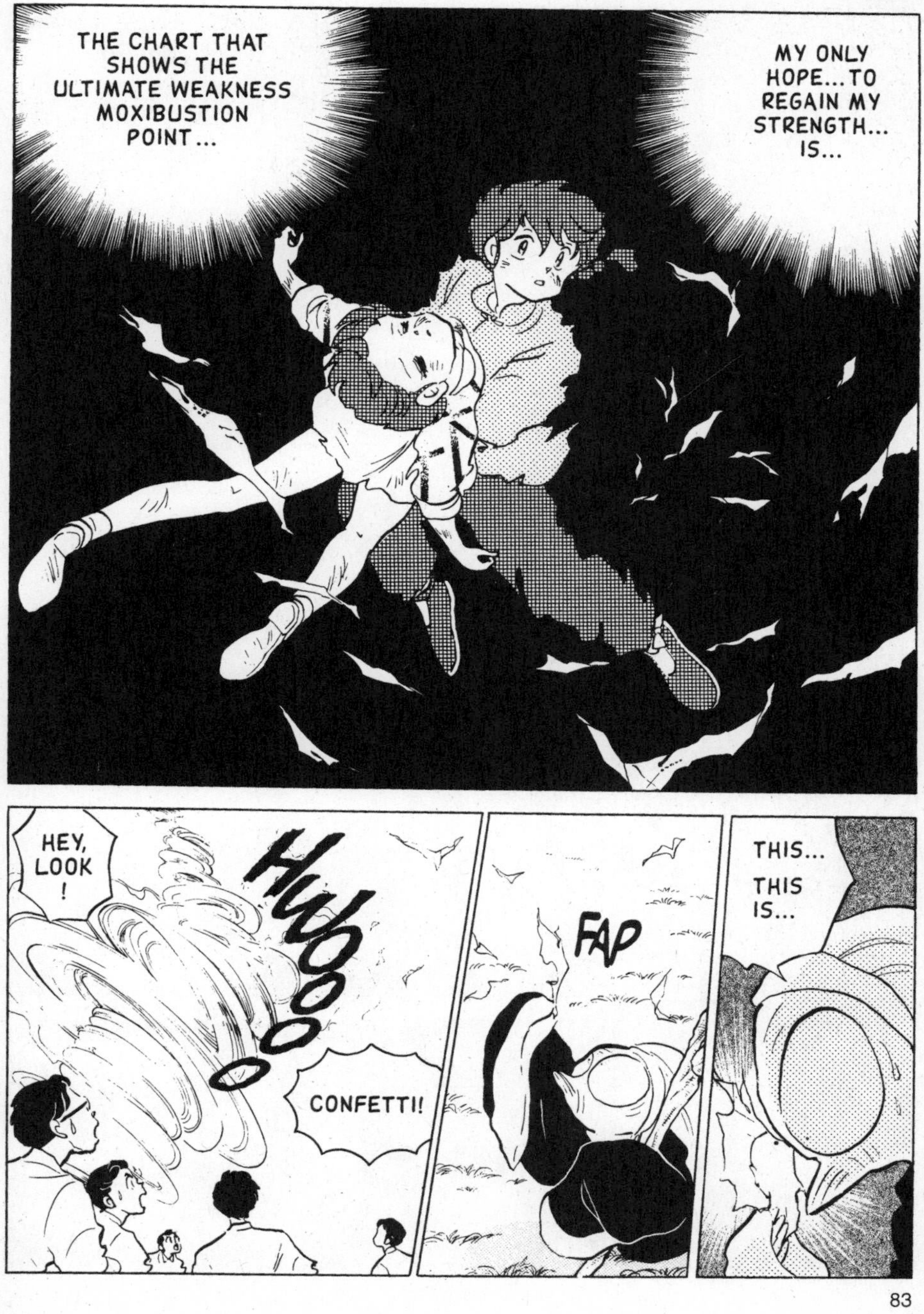
THE CHART THAT SHOWS THE ULTIMATE WEAKNESS MOXIBUSTION POINT...
MY ONLY HOPE...TO REGAIN MY STRENGTH... IS...
HEY, LOOK !
HUWOOOOO
CONFETTI!
FAP
THIS... THIS IS...

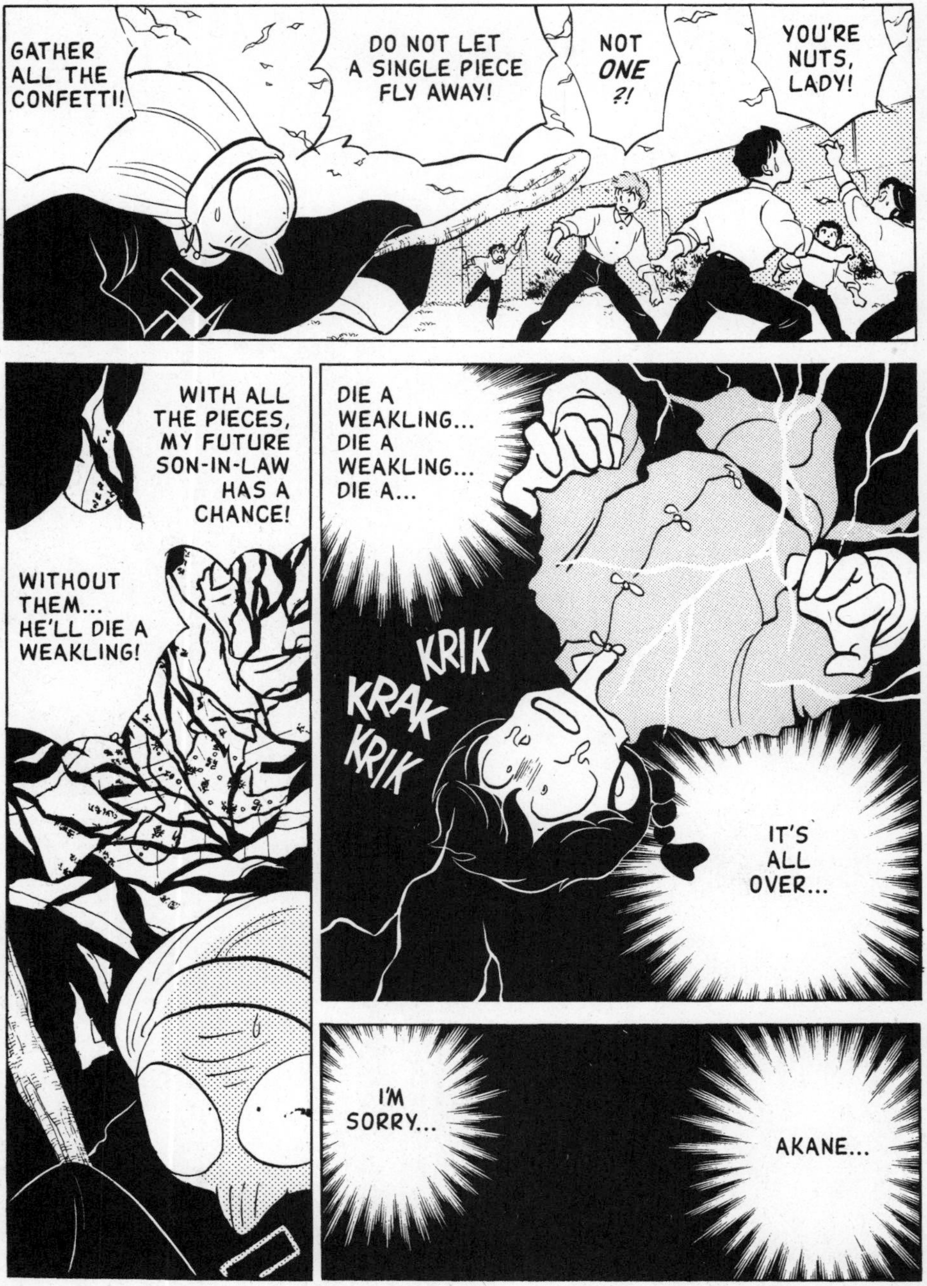
GATHER ALL THE CONFETTI!
DO NOT LET A SINGLE PIECE FLY AWAY!
NOT ONE ?!
YOU'RE NUTS, LADY!
WITH ALL THE PIECES, MY FUTURE SON-IN-LAW HAS A CHANCE!
WITHOUT THEM... HE'LL DIE A WEAKLING!
DIE A WEAKLING... DIE A WEAKLING... DIE A...
KRIK
KRAK
KRIK
IT'S ALL OVER...
I'M SORRY...
AKANE...

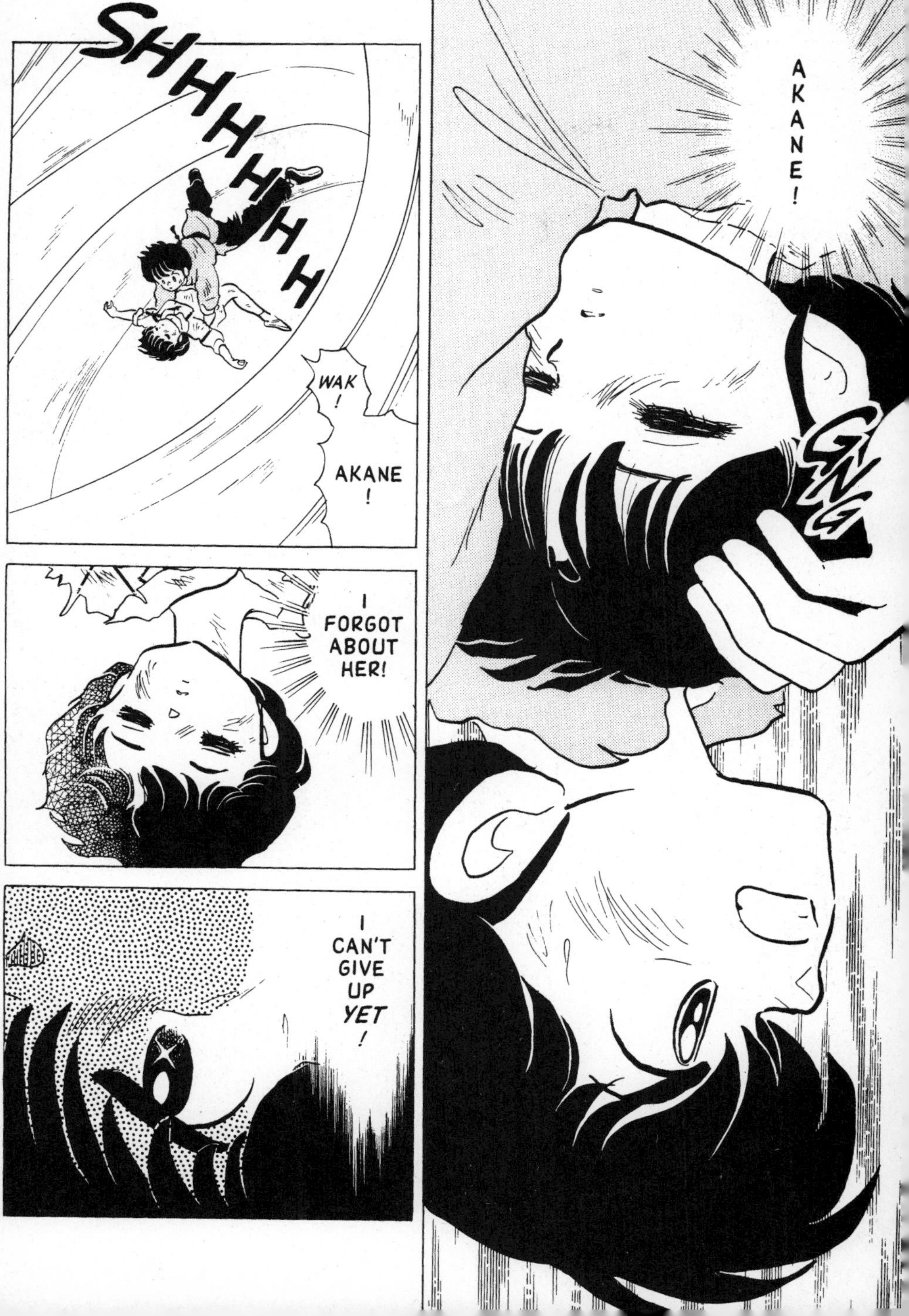
SHHHHHHH
WAK!
AKANE!
I FORGOT ABOUT HER!
I CAN'T GIVE UP YET!
AKANE!
GNG

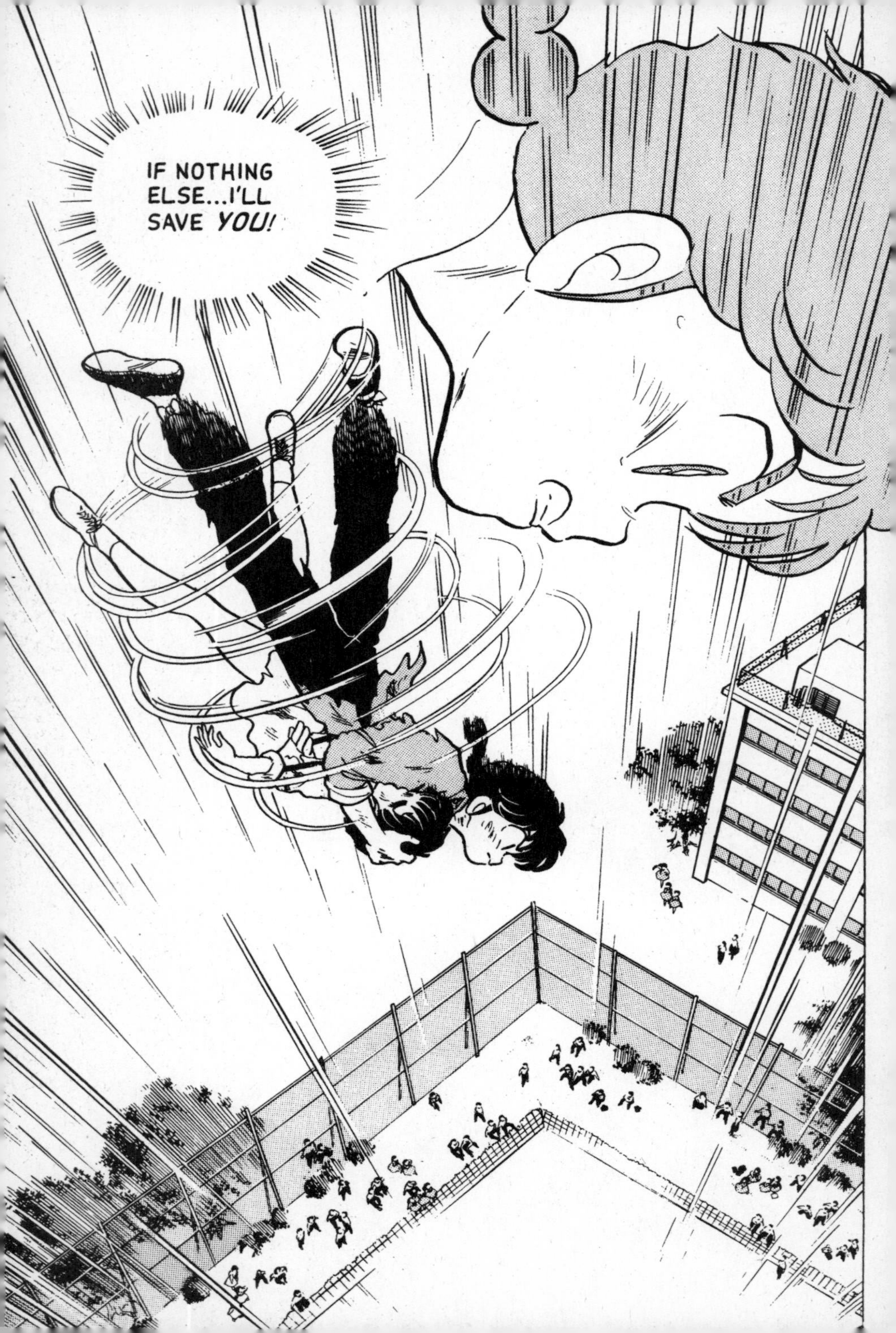
IF NOTHING ELSE...I'LL SAVE *YOU!*

PART 6
RANMA REBORN

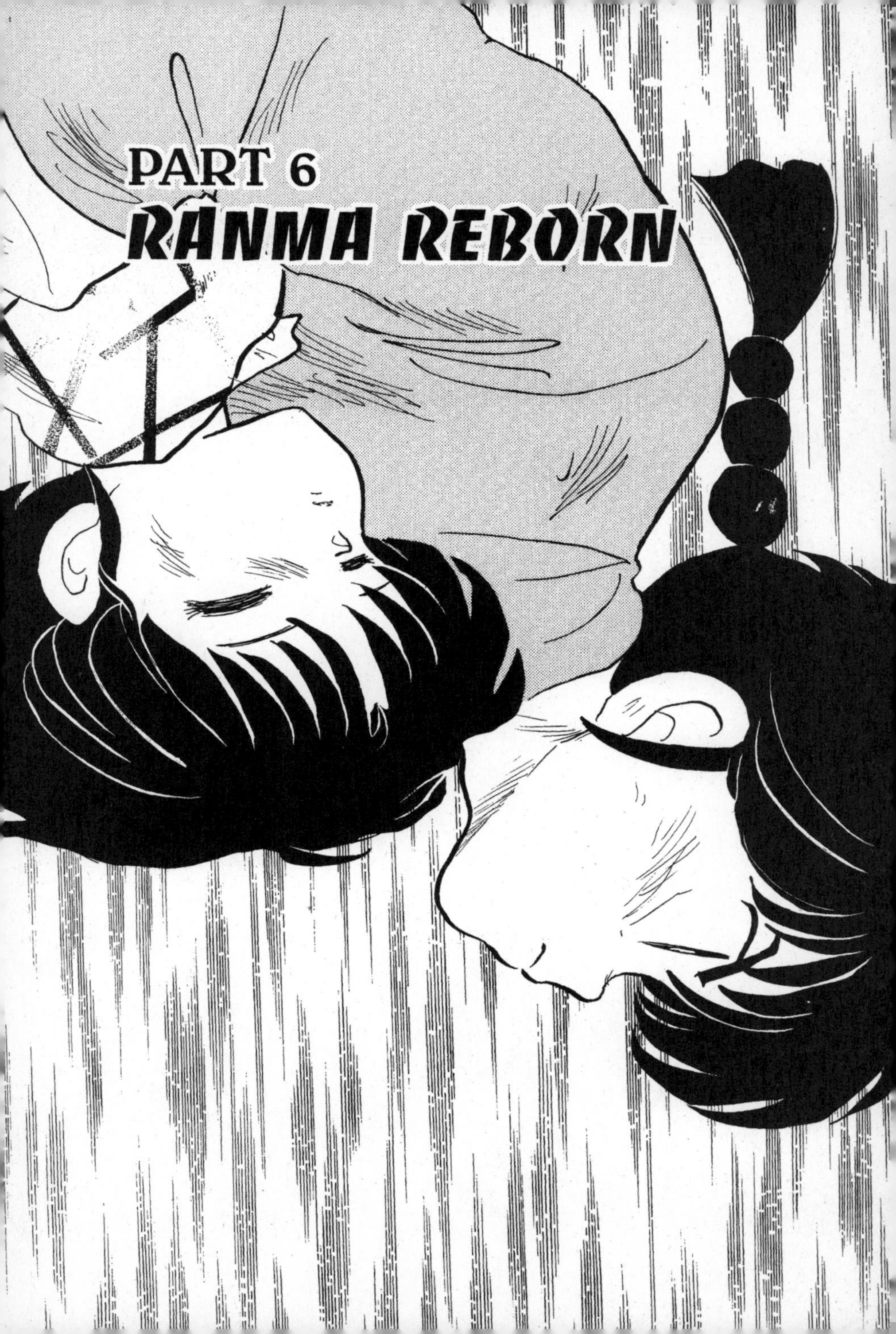

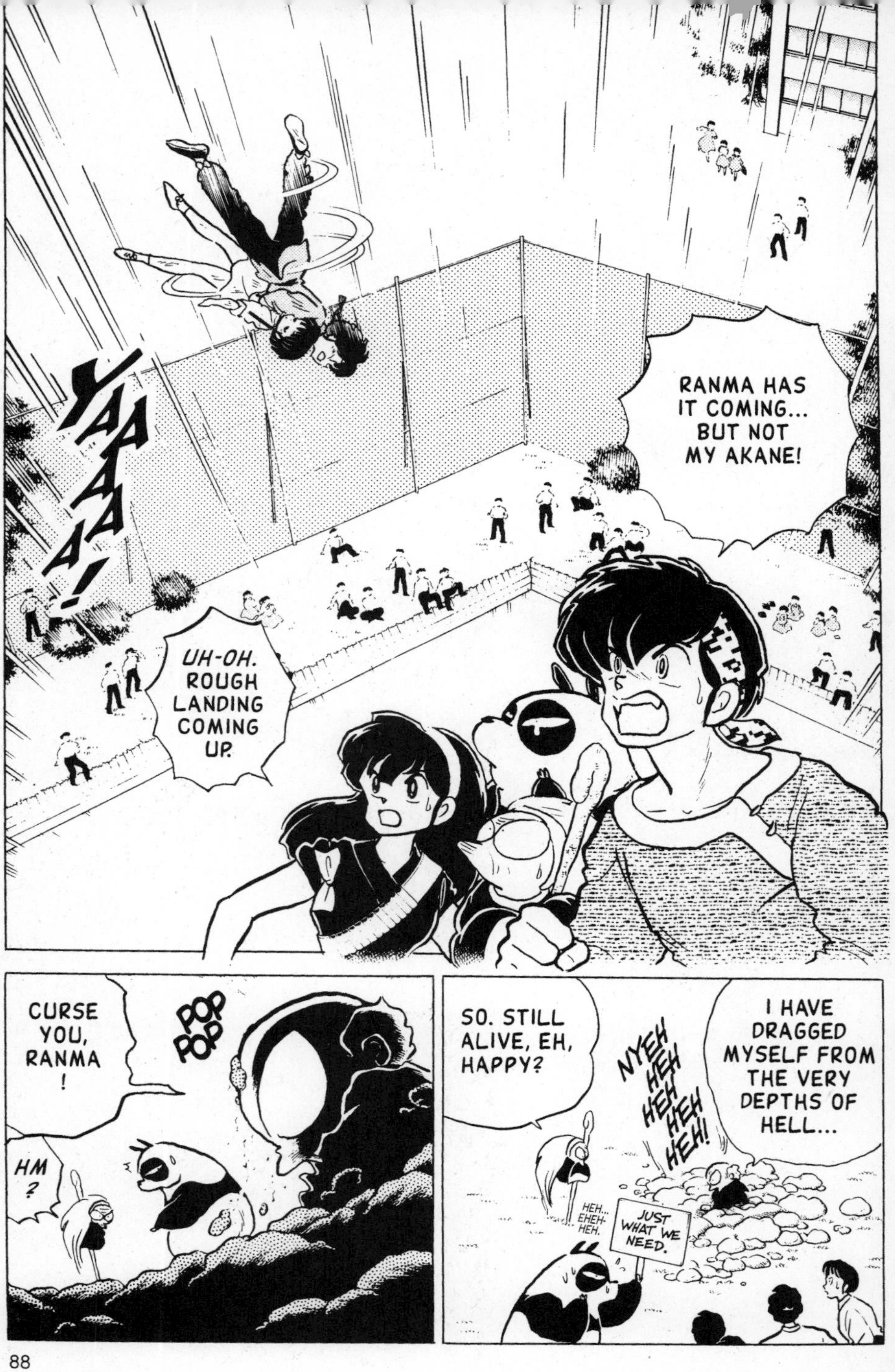
YAAAAA!
RANMA HAS IT COMING... BUT NOT MY AKANE!
UH-OH. ROUGH LANDING COMING UP.
CURSE YOU, RANMA!
POP POP
HM?
SO. STILL ALIVE, EH, HAPPY?
NYEH HEH HEH HEH HEH HEH!
I HAVE DRAGGED MYSELF FROM THE VERY DEPTHS OF HELL...
HEH... EHEH-HEH.
JUST WHAT WE NEED.

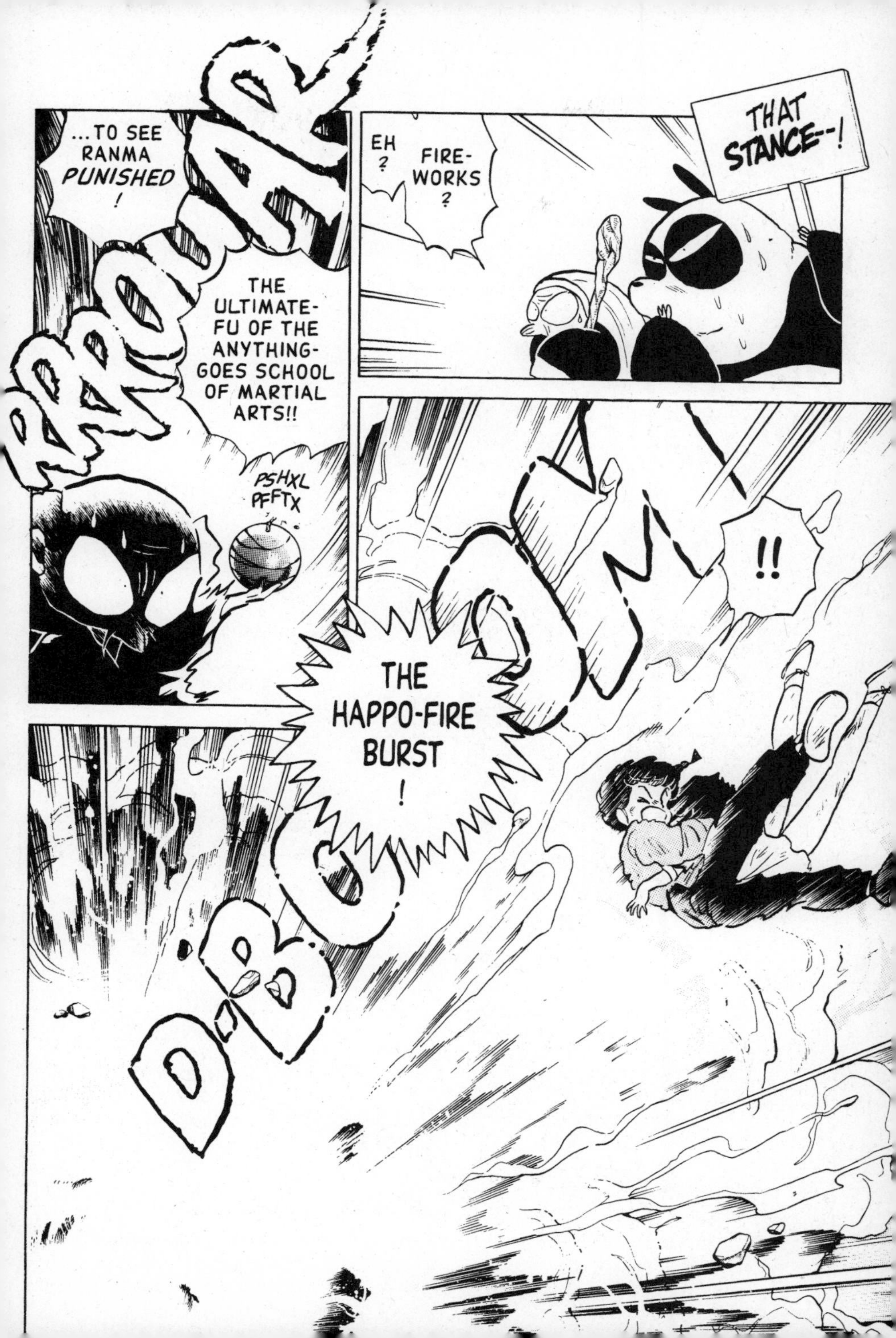
...TO SEE RANMA PUNISHED!
THE ULTIMATE-FU OF THE ANYTHING-GOES SCHOOL OF MARTIAL ARTS!!
PSHXL PFFTX
EH?
FIRE-WORKS?
THAT STANCE--!
!!
THE HAPPO-FIRE BURST!

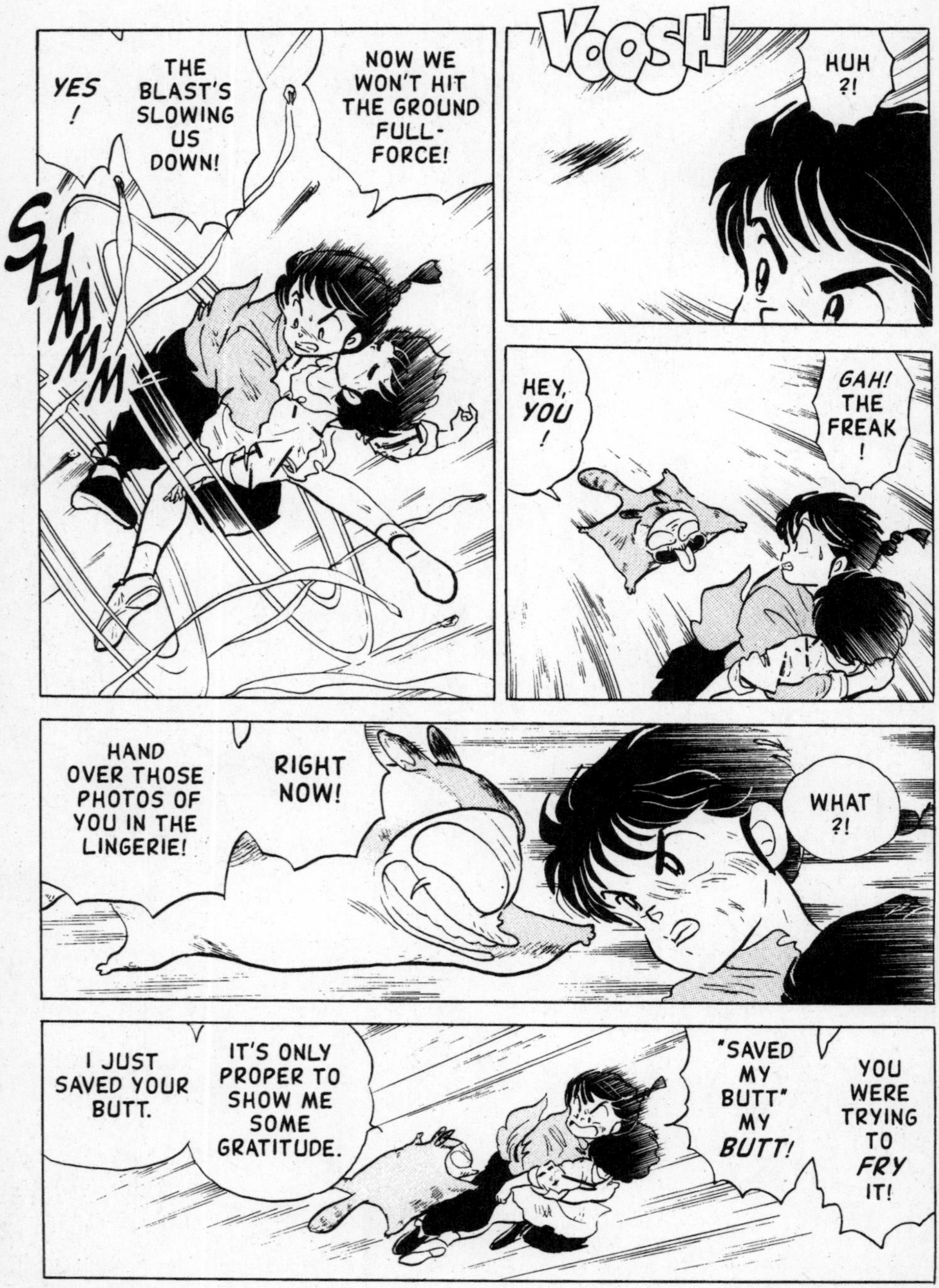
YES!
THE BLAST'S SLOWING US DOWN!
NOW WE WON'T HIT THE GROUND FULL-FORCE!
SHMMMM
VOOSH
HUH?!
HEY, YOU!
GAH! THE FREAK!
HAND OVER THOSE PHOTOS OF YOU IN THE LINGERIE!
RIGHT NOW!
WHAT?!
I JUST SAVED YOUR BUTT.
IT'S ONLY PROPER TO SHOW ME SOME GRATITUDE.
"SAVED MY BUTT" MY BUTT!
YOU WERE TRYING TO FRY IT!

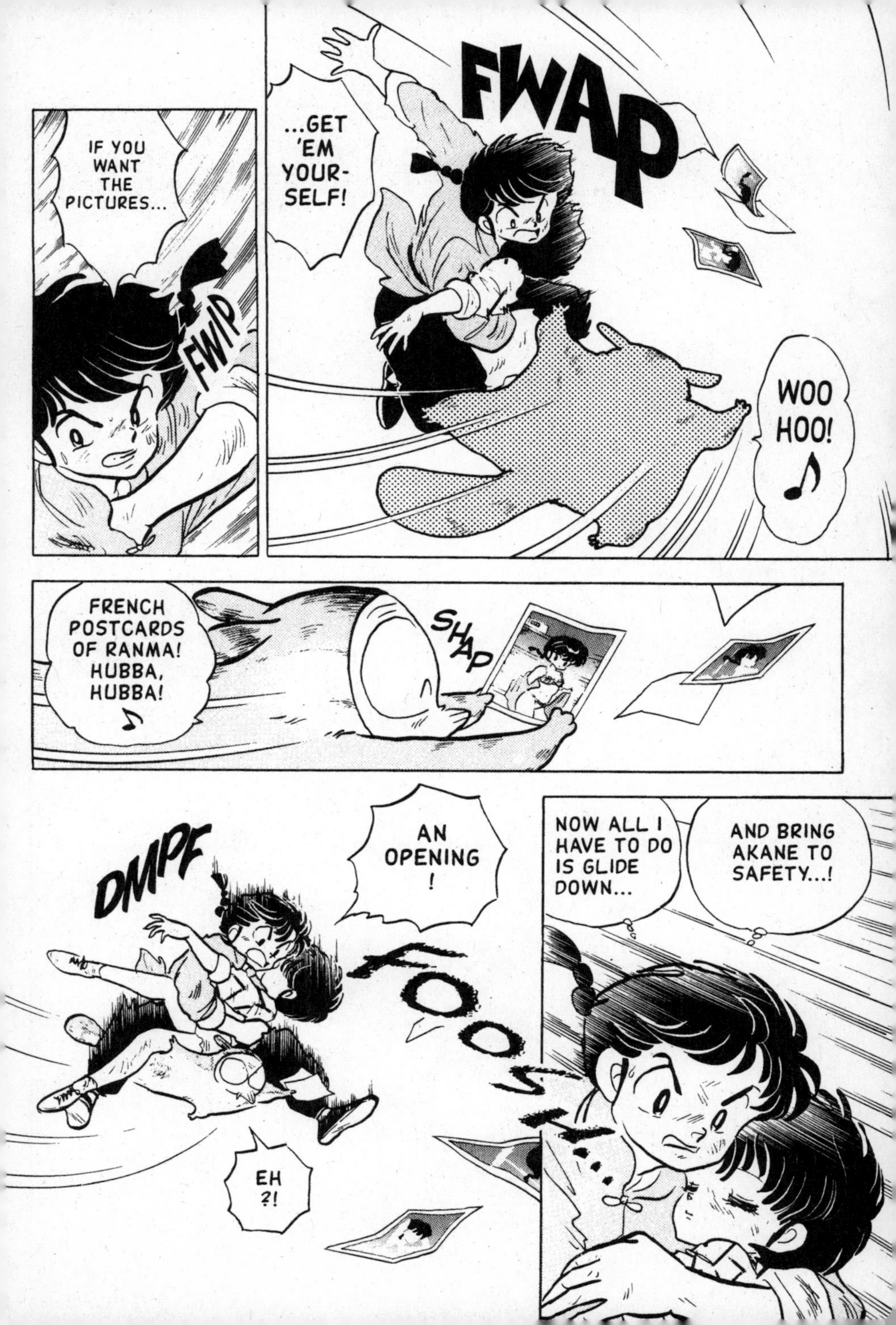
IF YOU WANT THE PICTURES...
FWIP
...GET 'EM YOURSELF!
FWAP
WOO HOO! ♪
FRENCH POSTCARDS OF RANMA! HUBBA, HUBBA! ♪
SHAP
DMPF
AN OPENING!
EH ?!
FOOSH...
NOW ALL I HAVE TO DO IS GLIDE DOWN...
AND BRING AKANE TO SAFETY...!

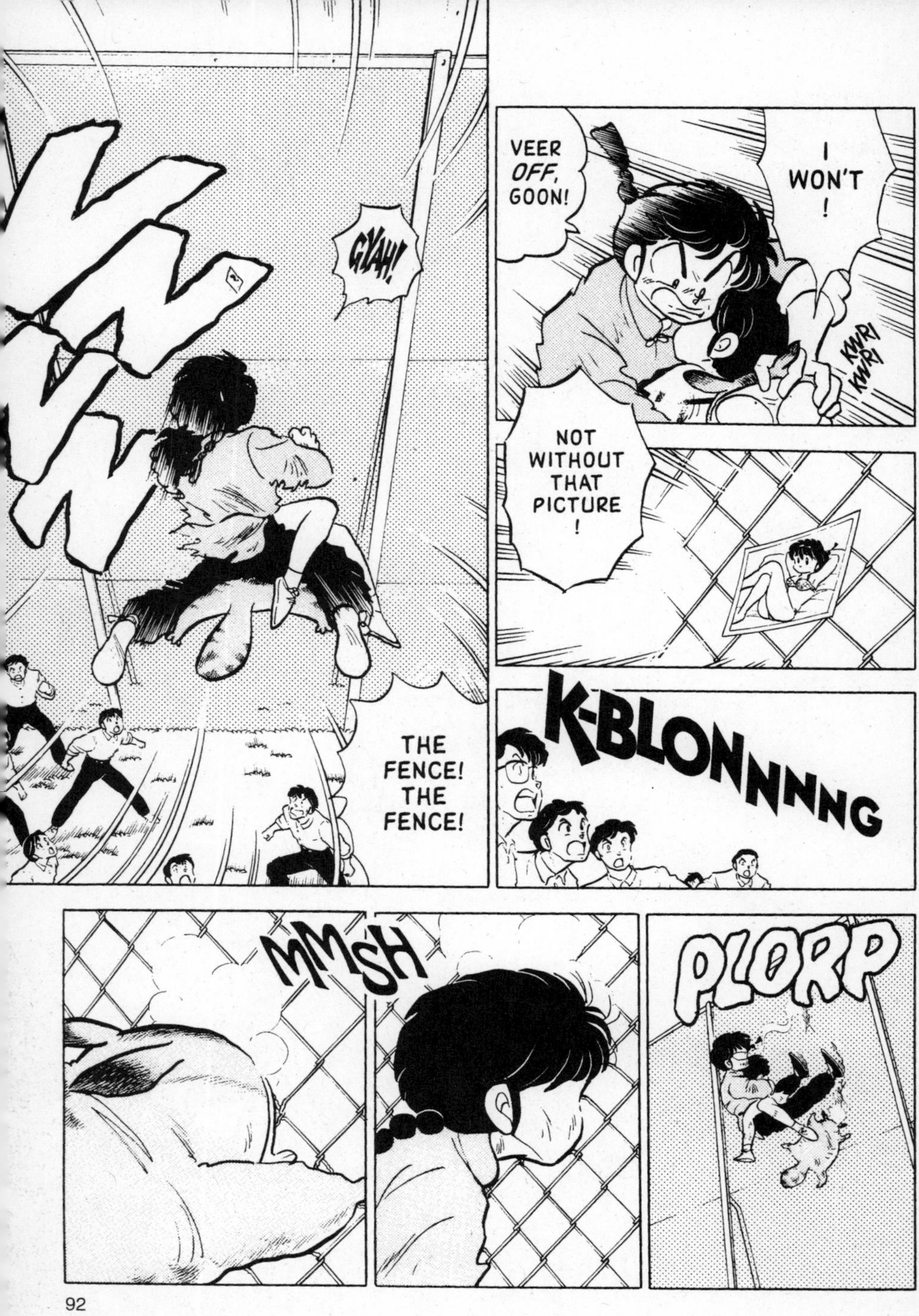
GYAH!
THE FENCE! THE FENCE!
VEER *OFF*, GOON!
I WON'T!
KWRI KWRI
NOT WITHOUT THAT PICTURE!
K-BLONNNNG
MMSH
PLORP

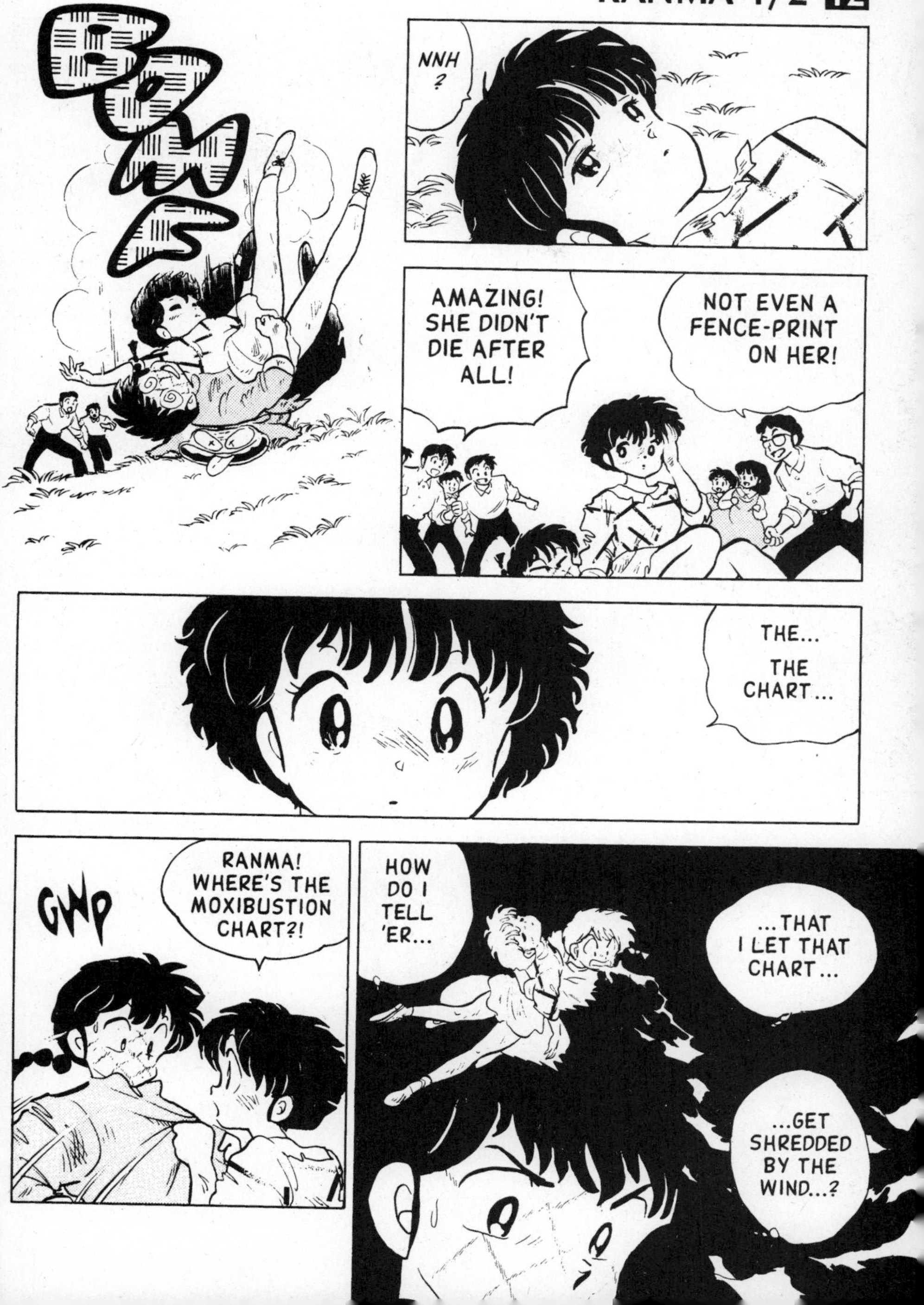
BOWS
NNH ?
AMAZING! SHE DIDN'T DIE AFTER ALL!
NOT EVEN A FENCE-PRINT ON HER!
THE...
THE CHART...
GWP
RANMA! WHERE'S THE MOXIBUSTION CHART?!
HOW DO I TELL 'ER...
...THAT I LET THAT CHART...
...GET SHREDDED BY THE WIND...?

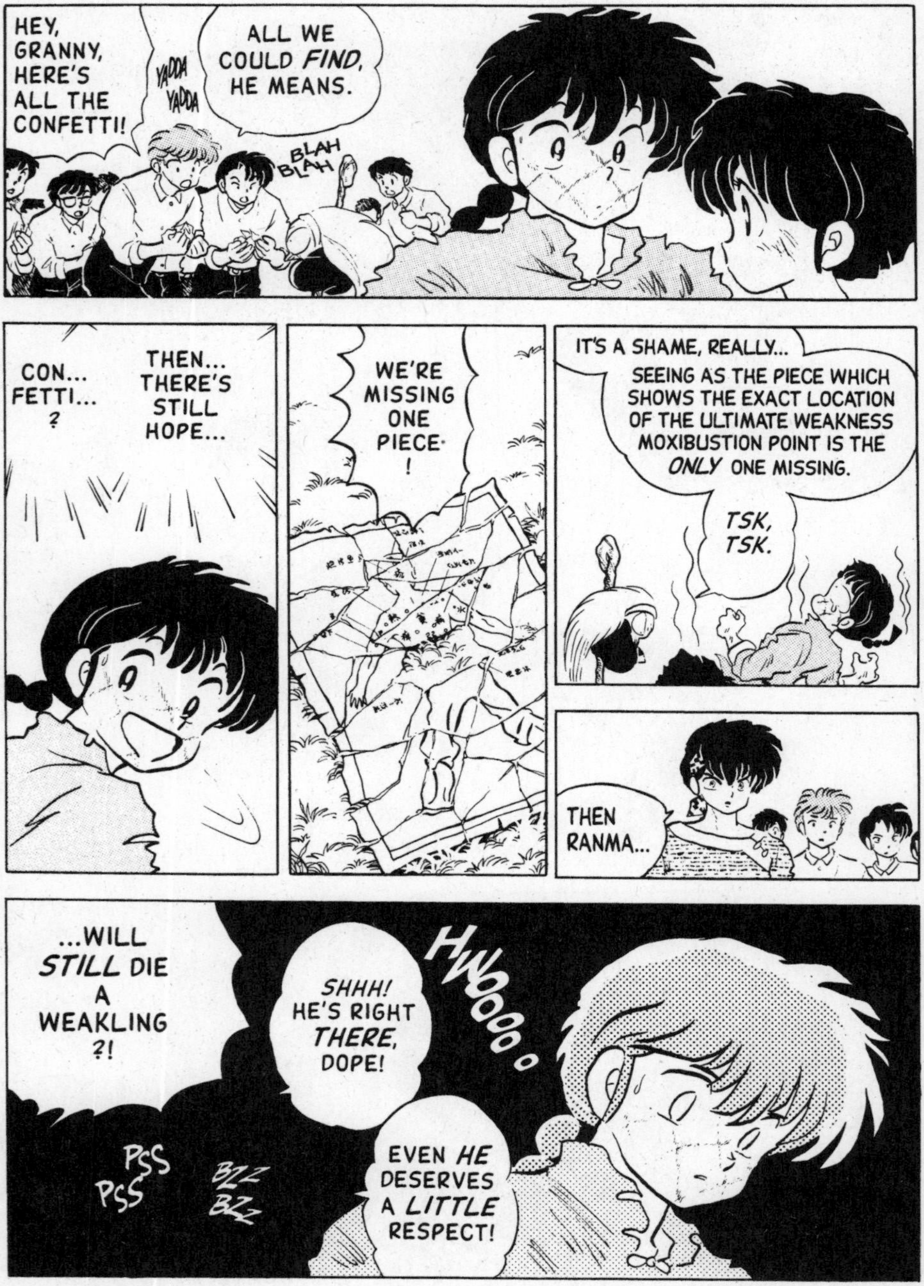
HEY, GRANNY, HERE'S ALL THE CONFETTI!
YADDA YADDA
ALL WE COULD FIND, HE MEANS.
BLAH BLAH
CON... FETTI...?
THEN... THERE'S STILL HOPE...
WE'RE MISSING ONE PIECE!
IT'S A SHAME, REALLY...
SEEING AS THE PIECE WHICH SHOWS THE EXACT LOCATION OF THE ULTIMATE WEAKNESS MOXIBUSTION POINT IS THE ONLY ONE MISSING.
TSK, TSK.
THEN RANMA...
...WILL STILL DIE A WEAKLING?!
HWOOOOO
SHHH! HE'S RIGHT THERE, DOPE!
EVEN HE DESERVES A LITTLE RESPECT!
PSS PSS
BZZ BZZ

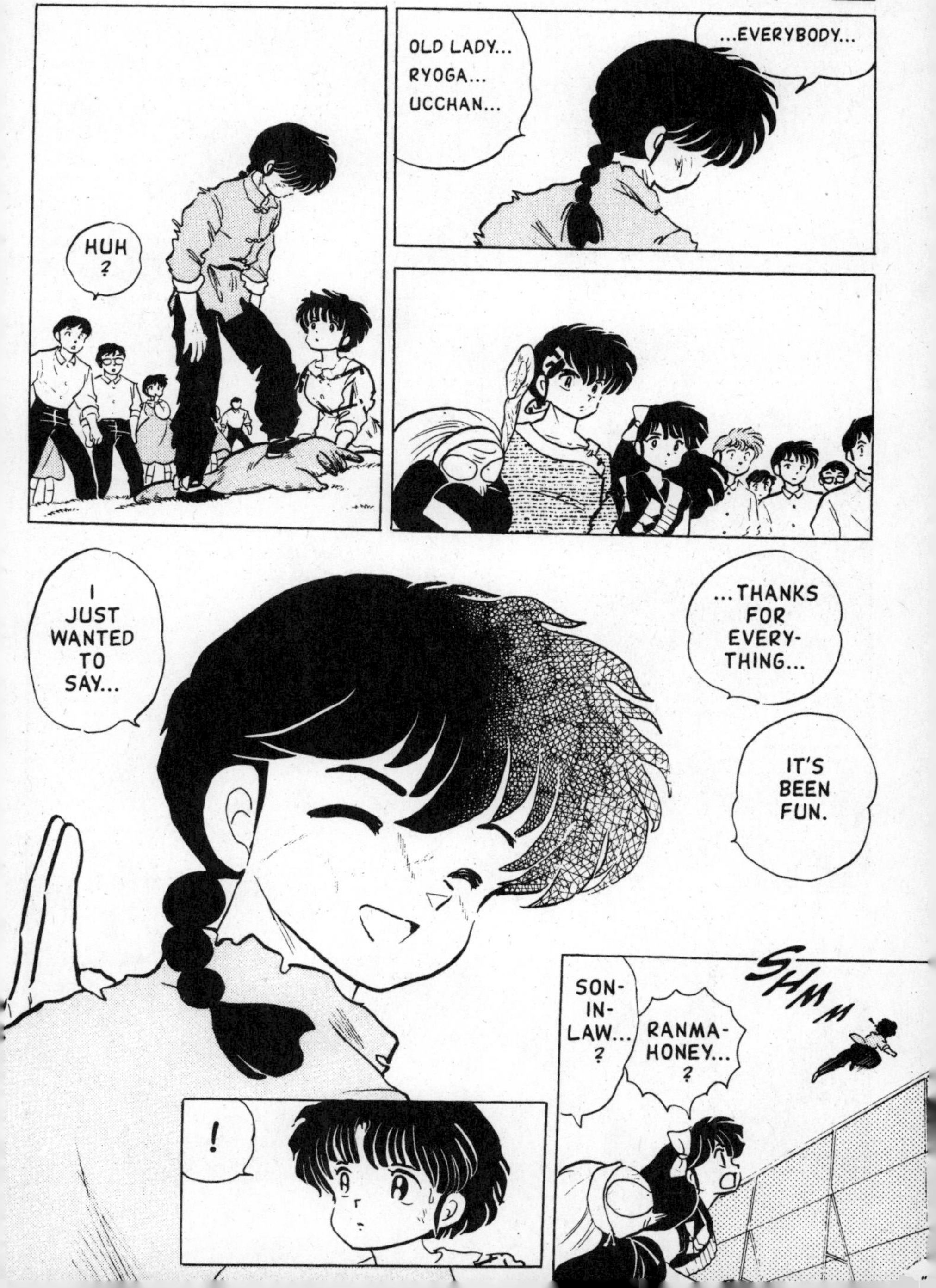
HUH ?
OLD LADY... RYOGA... UCCHAN...
...EVERYBODY...
I JUST WANTED TO SAY...
...THANKS FOR EVERY- THING...
IT'S BEEN FUN.
!
SON- IN- LAW... ?
RANMA- HONEY... ?
SHMM

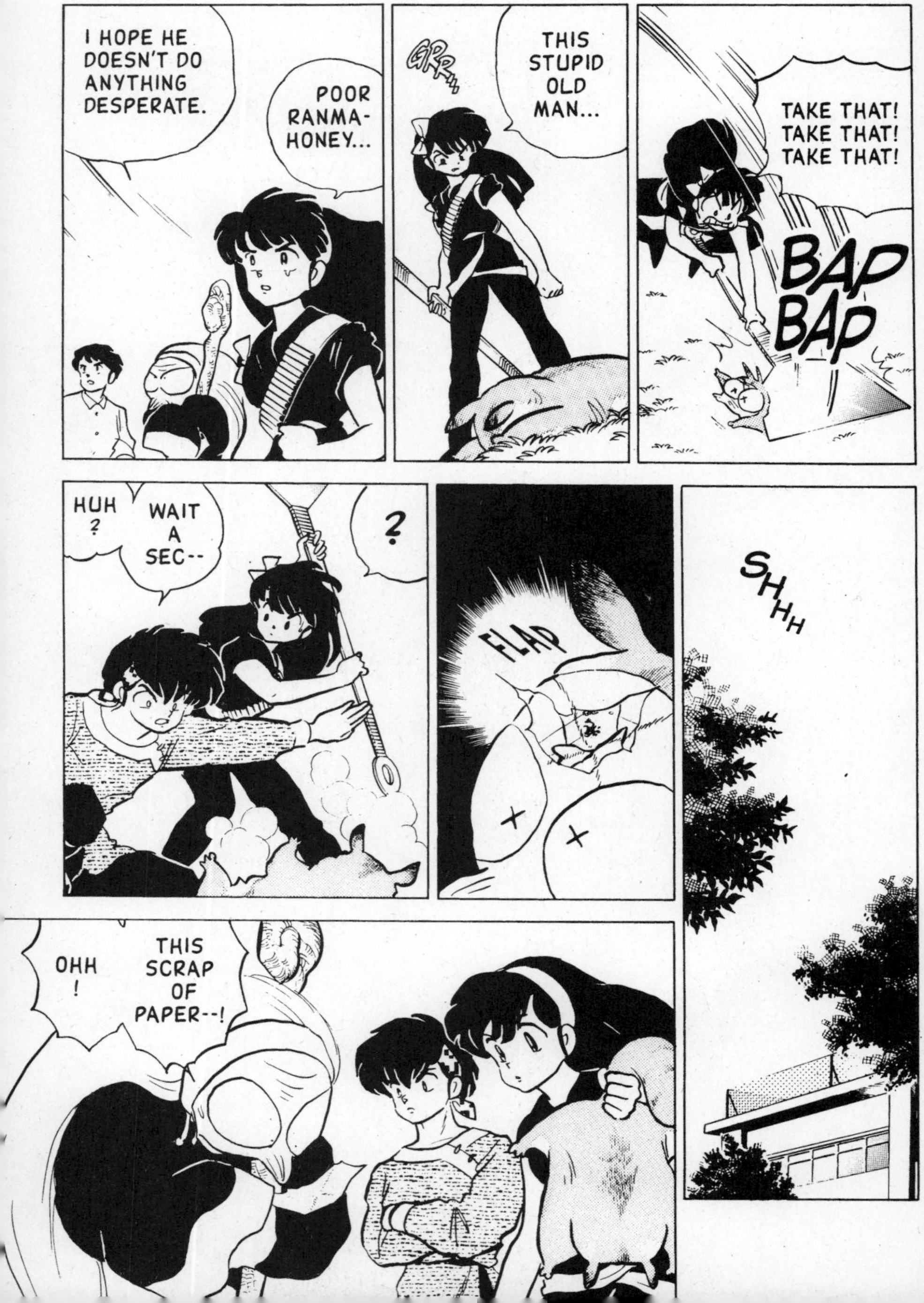
I HOPE HE DOESN'T DO ANYTHING DESPERATE.
POOR RANMA-HONEY...
GRR
THIS STUPID OLD MAN...
TAKE THAT! TAKE THAT! TAKE THAT!
BAP BAP
HUH ?
WAIT A SEC--
?
FLAP
SHHH
OHH !
THIS SCRAP OF PAPER--!

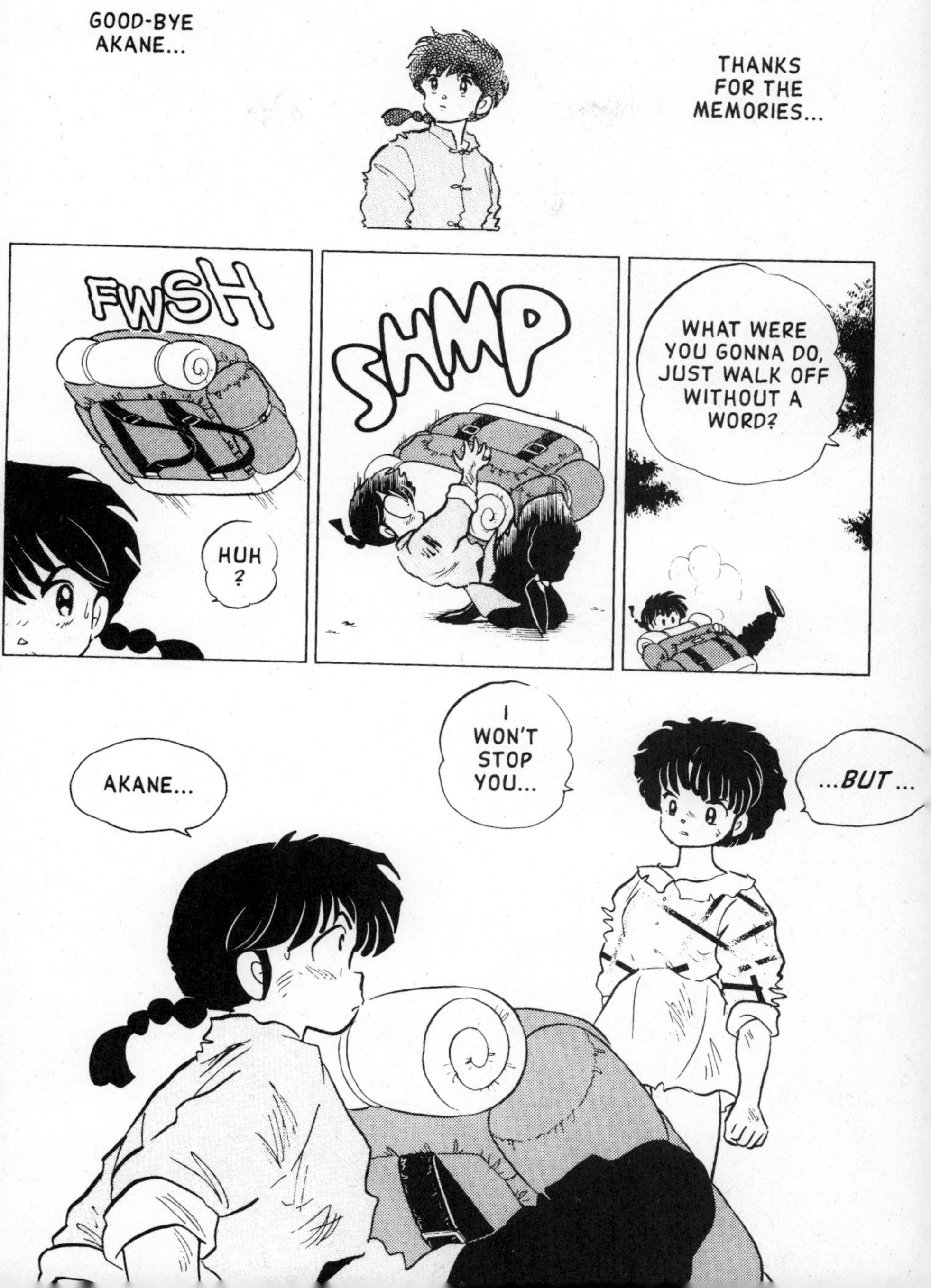
GOOD-BYE AKANE...
THANKS FOR THE MEMORIES...
FWSH
HUH?
SHMP
WHAT WERE YOU GONNA DO, JUST WALK OFF WITHOUT A WORD?
AKANE...
I WON'T STOP YOU...
...BUT...

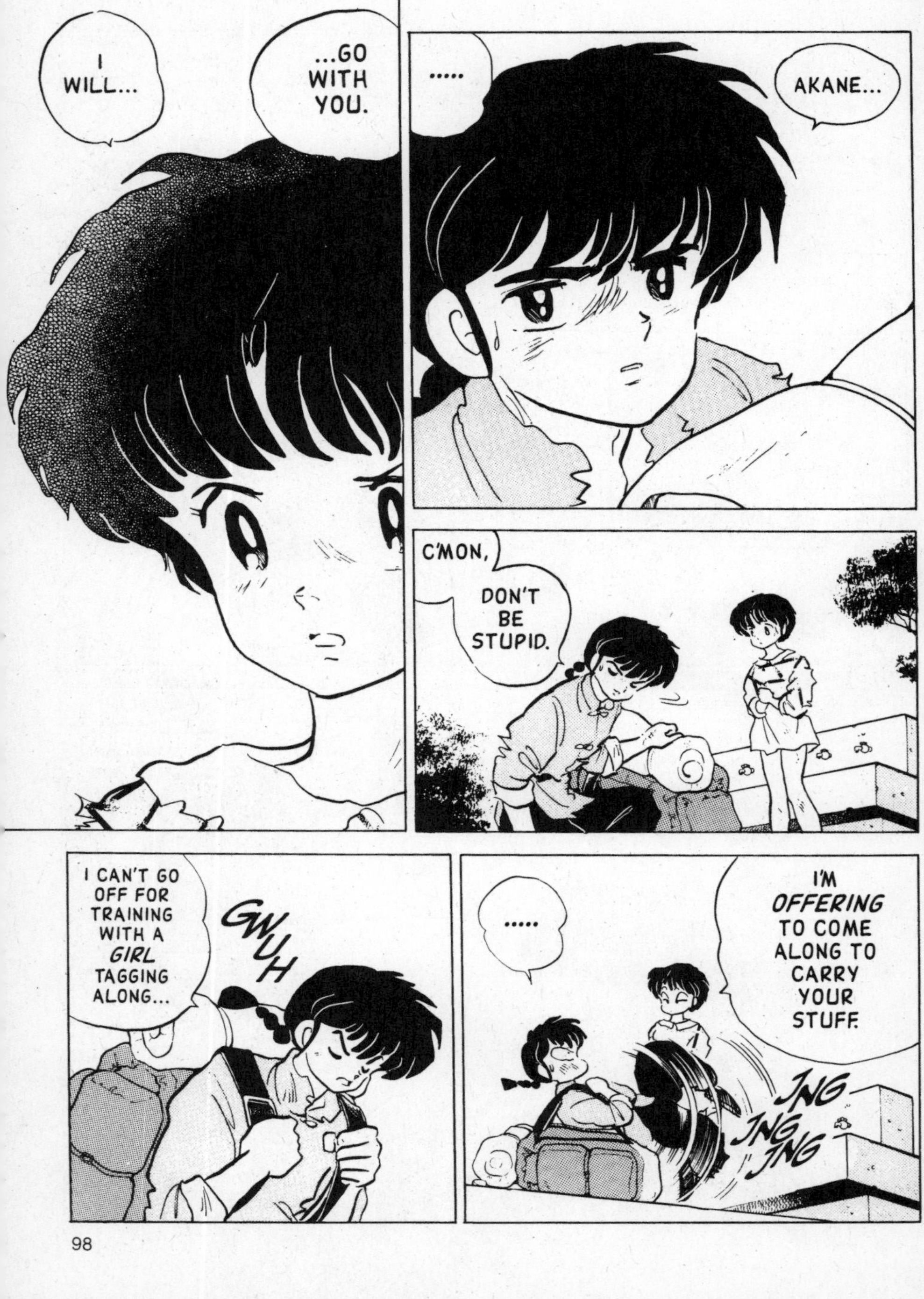
I WILL...
...GO WITH YOU.
.....
AKANE...
C'MON,
DON'T BE STUPID.
I CAN'T GO OFF FOR TRAINING WITH A *GIRL* TAGGING ALONG...
GWUH
.....
I'M *OFFERING* TO COME ALONG TO CARRY YOUR STUFF.
JNG JNG JNG

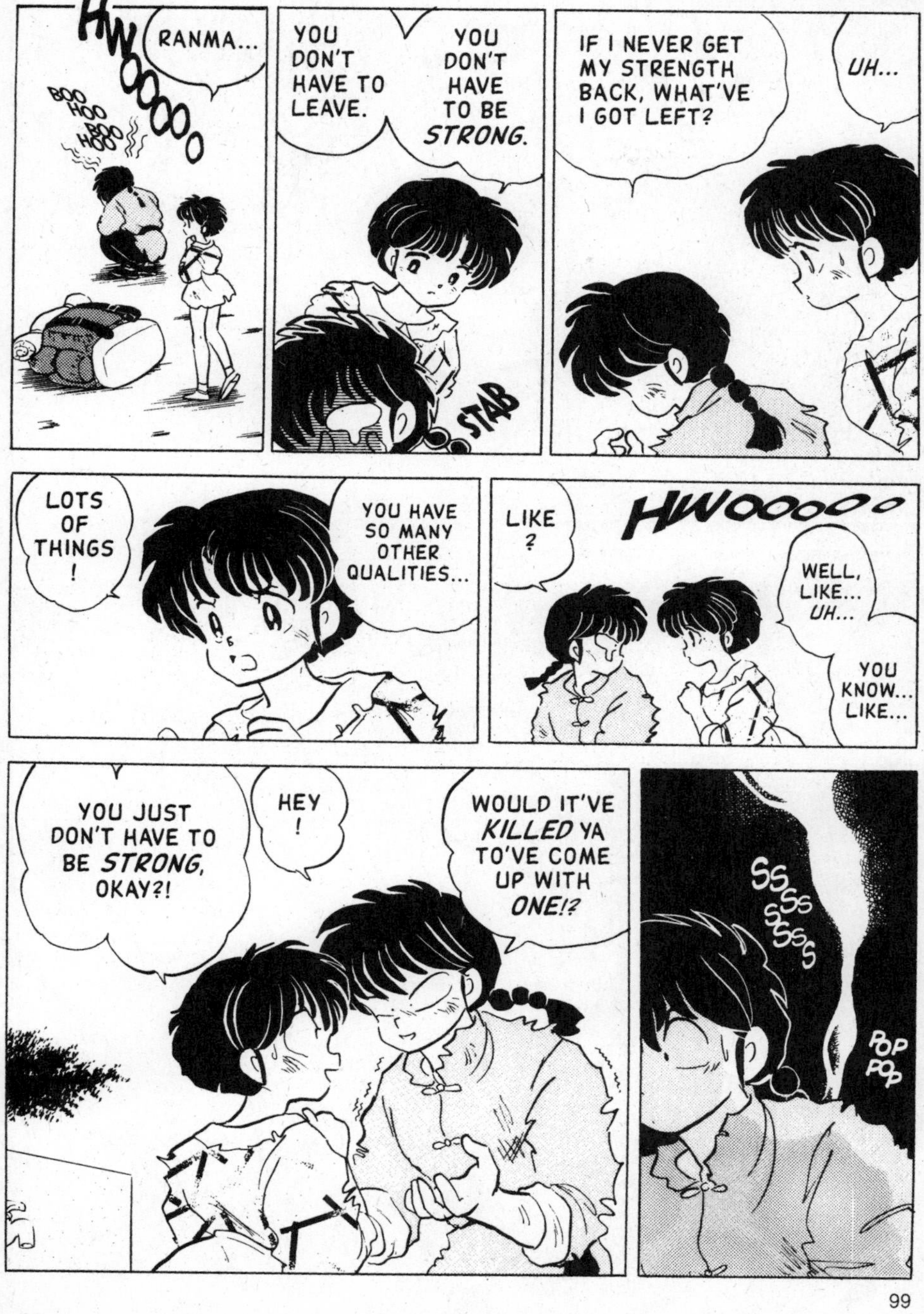
HWOOOOOO
RANMA...
BOO HOO BOO HOO
YOU DON'T HAVE TO LEAVE.
YOU DON'T HAVE TO BE *STRONG*.
STAB
IF I NEVER GET MY STRENGTH BACK, WHAT'VE I GOT LEFT?
UH...
LOTS OF THINGS!
YOU HAVE SO MANY OTHER QUALITIES...
LIKE?
HWOOOOOO
WELL, LIKE... *UH...*
YOU KNOW... LIKE...
YOU JUST DON'T HAVE TO BE *STRONG*, OKAY?!
HEY!
WOULD IT'VE *KILLED* YA TO'VE COME UP WITH *ONE!?*
SSSSSSSS
POP POP

EEEEYOW! THAT'S HOT!!!!

SSSSS

WHAT'D YOU DO THAT FOR?! LEMME ALONE!

VVMM

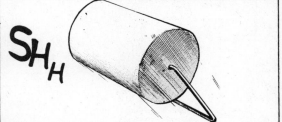

SHH

DONK

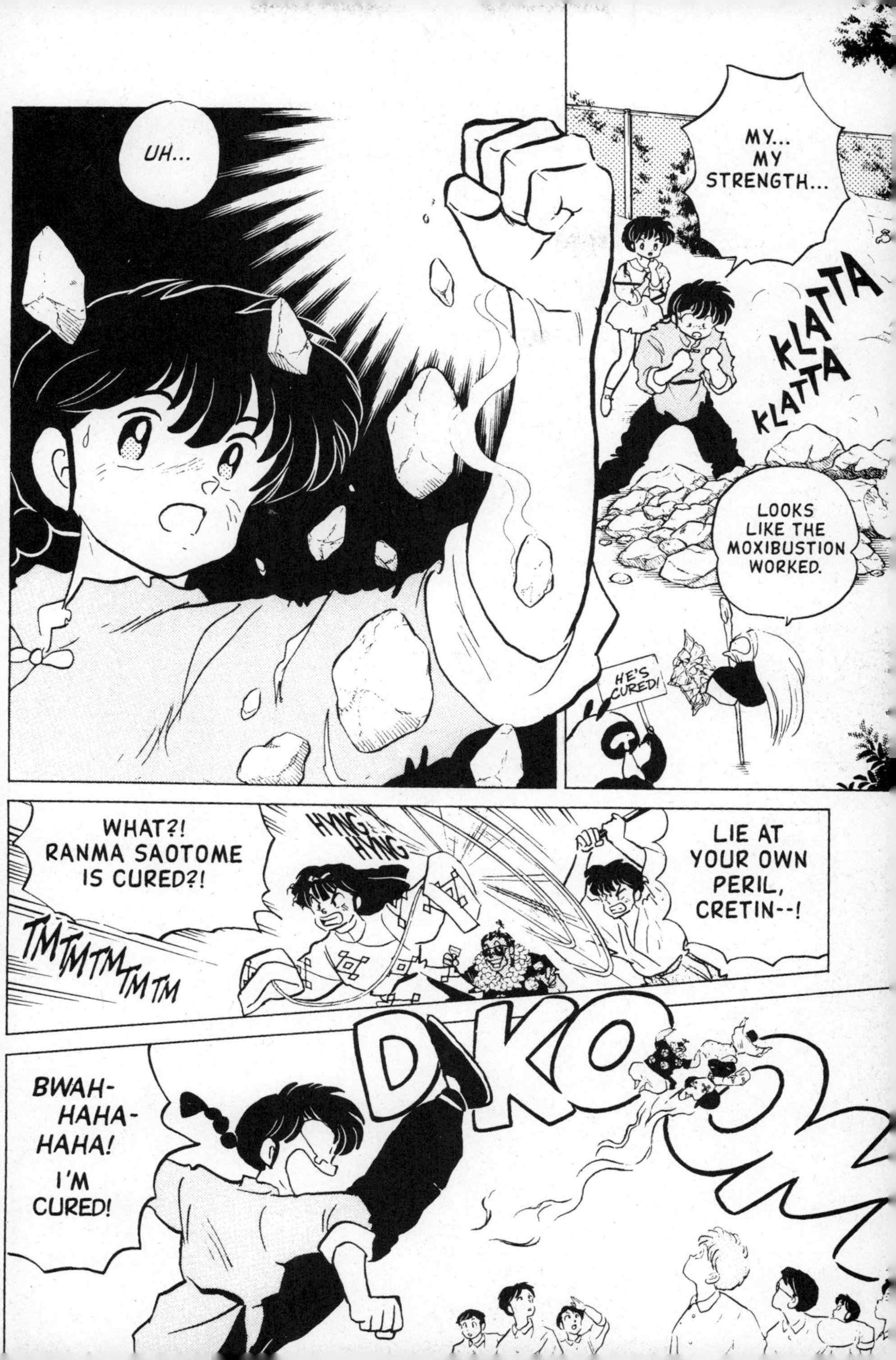
UH...
MY... MY STRENGTH...
KLATTA KLATTA
LOOKS LIKE THE MOXIBUSTION WORKED.
HE'S CURED!
WHAT?! RANMA SAOTOME IS CURED?!
HYNG HYNG
TMTMTMTMTMTM
LIE AT YOUR OWN PERIL, CRETIN--!
BWAH-HAHA-HAHA! I'M CURED!
DKOOM

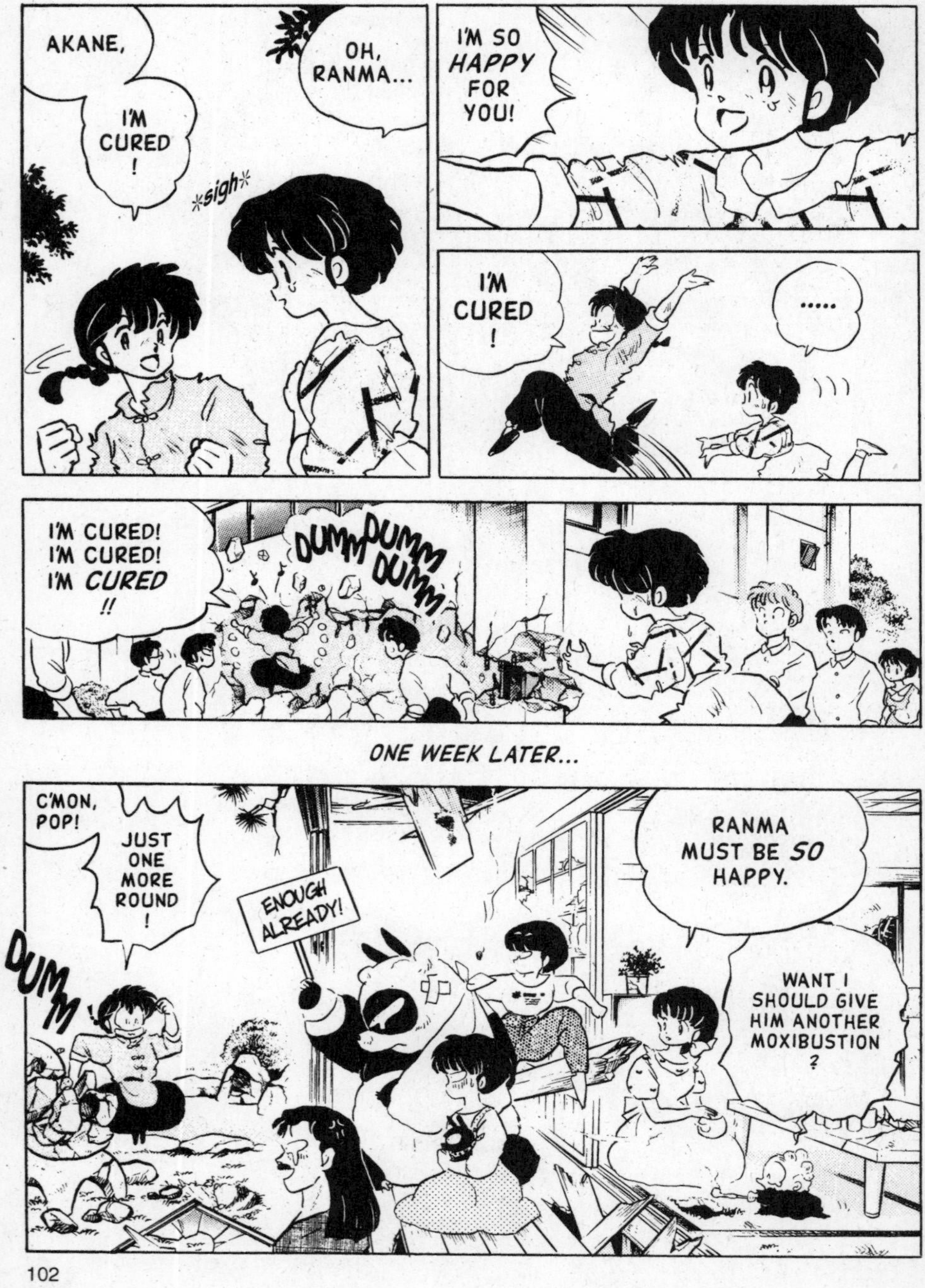
AKANE,
I'M CURED !
OH, RANMA...
sigh
I'M SO HAPPY FOR YOU!
I'M CURED !
.....
I'M CURED! I'M CURED! I'M CURED !!
DUMM DUMM DUMM DUMM
ONE WEEK LATER...
C'MON, POP!
JUST ONE MORE ROUND !
DUMM
ENOUGH ALREADY!
RANMA MUST BE SO HAPPY.
WANT I SHOULD GIVE HIM ANOTHER MOXIBUSTION ?

PART 7
WHO WILL BELL THE CAT?

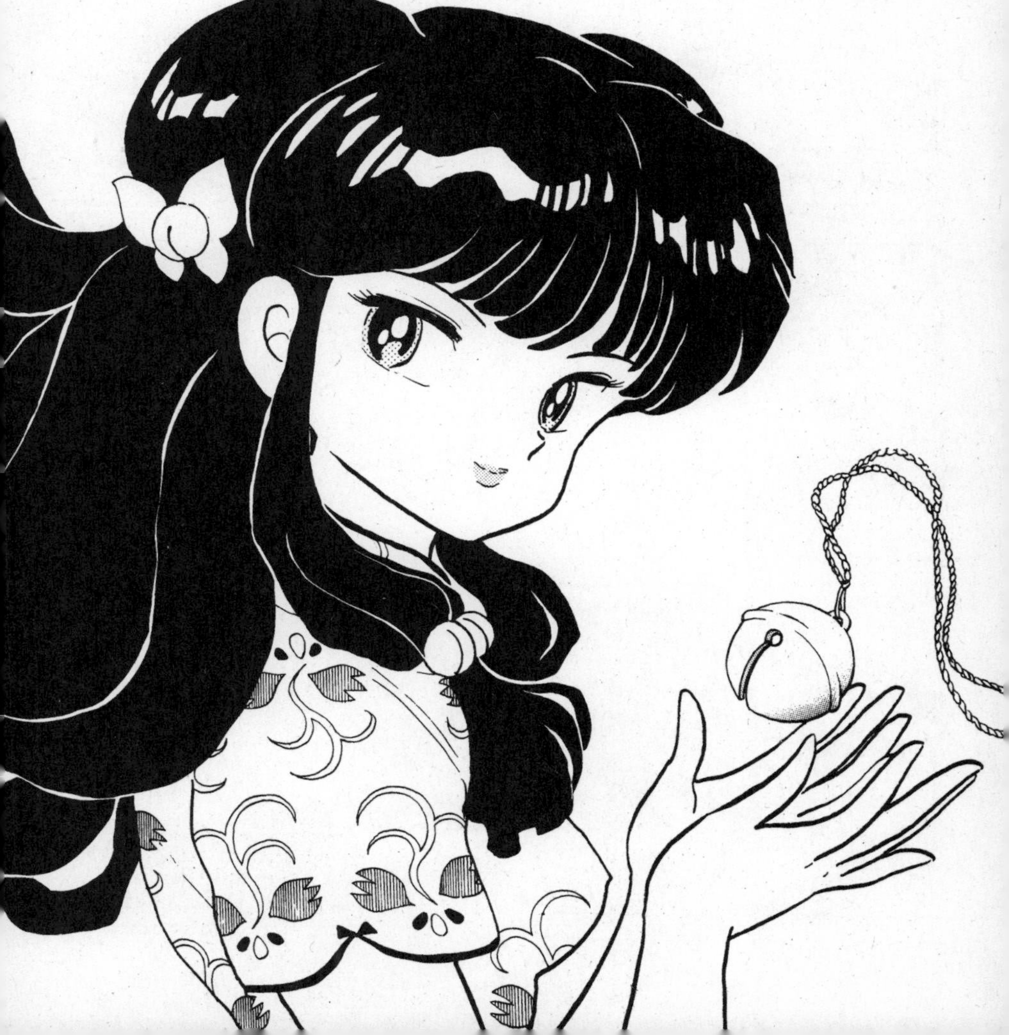

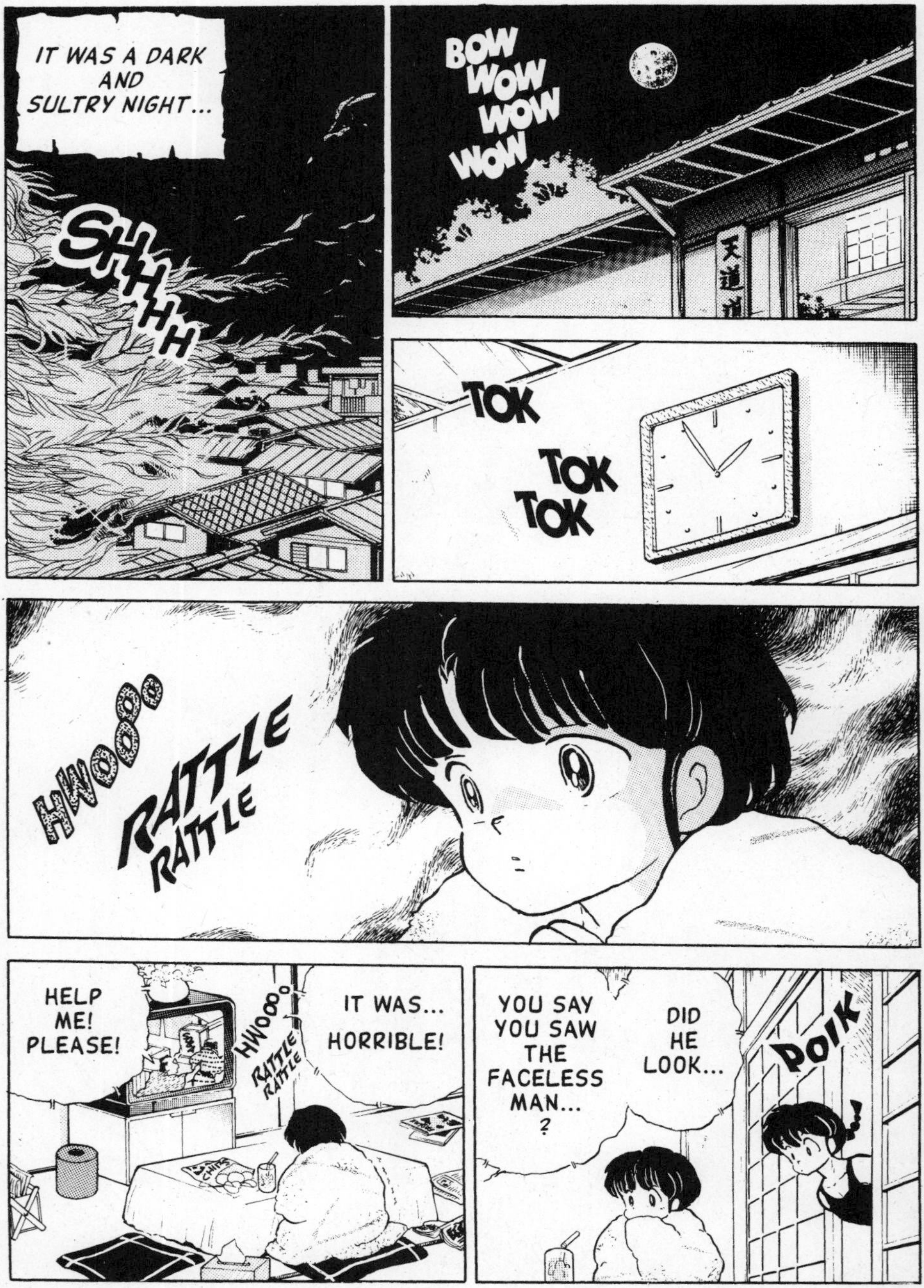
IT WAS A DARK AND SULTRY NIGHT...
SHHHHH
BOW WOW WOW WOW
TOK
TOK TOK
HWOOOO
RATTLE RATTLE
HELP ME! PLEASE!
HWOOOO
RATTLE RATTLE
IT WAS... HORRIBLE!
YOU SAY YOU SAW THE FACELESS MAN...?
DID HE LOOK...
POIK

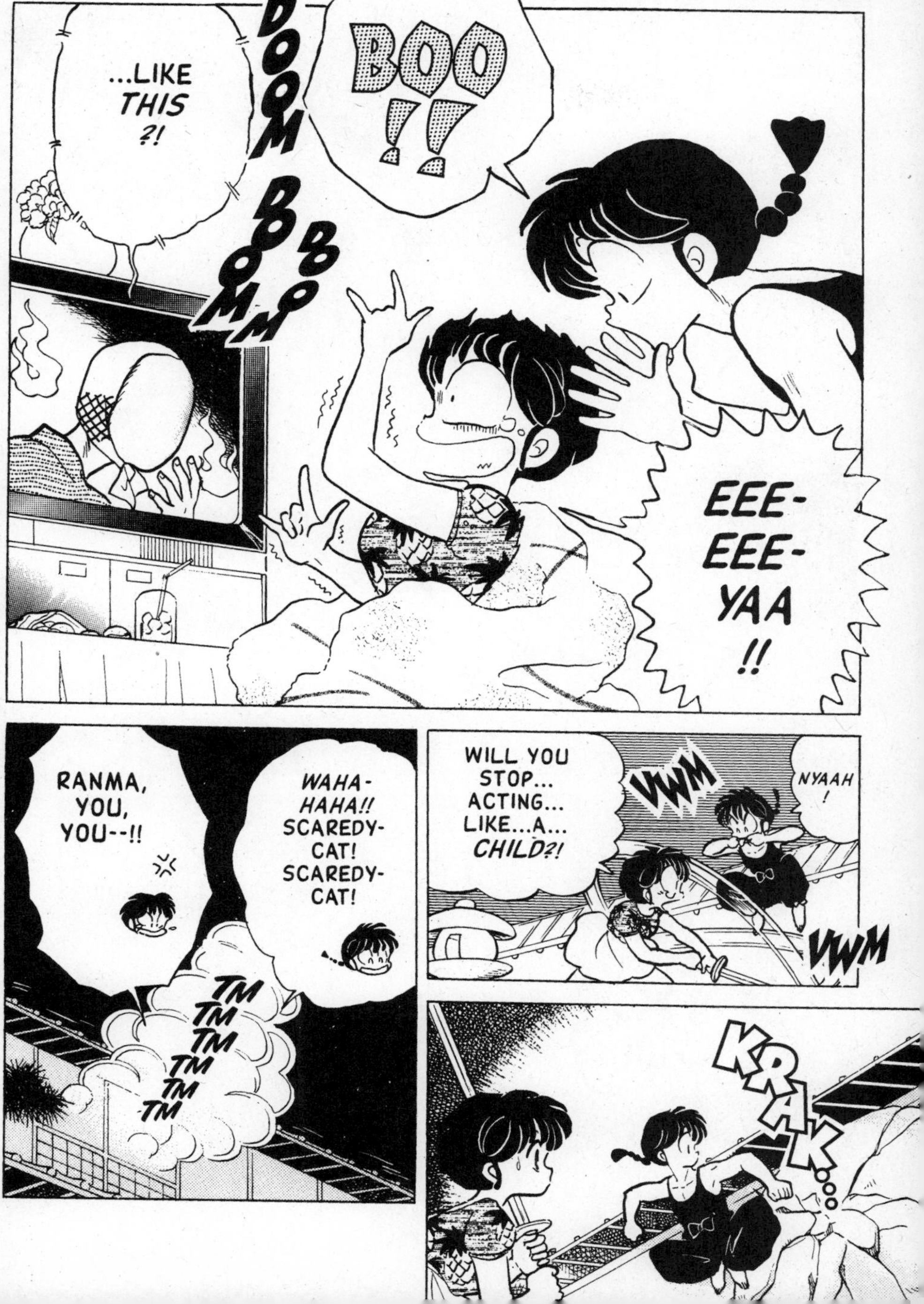
...LIKE THIS ?!
DOOM DOOM DOOM
BOO !!
EEE- EEE- YAA !!
RANMA, YOU, YOU--!!
WAHA- HAHA!! SCAREDY- CAT! SCAREDY- CAT!
TM TM TM TM TM TM
WILL YOU STOP... ACTING... LIKE...A... CHILD?!
VWM
NYAAH !
VWM
KRAK...

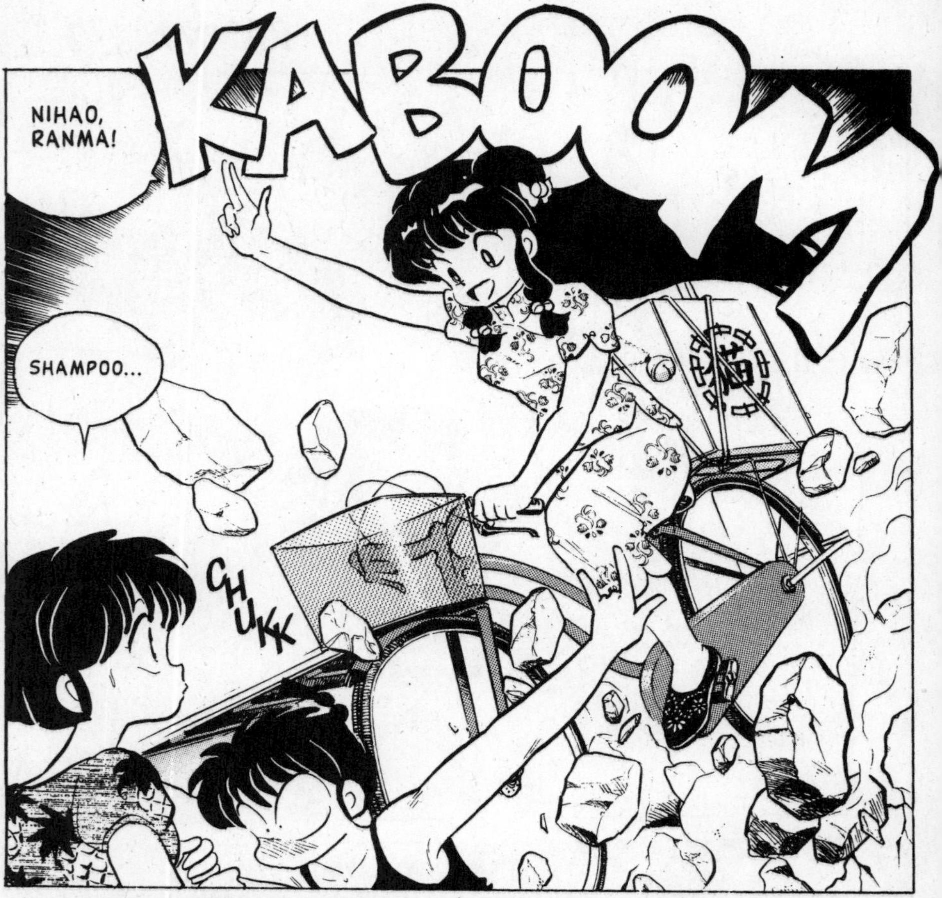
KABOOM
NIHAO, RANMA!
SHAMPOO...
CHUKK
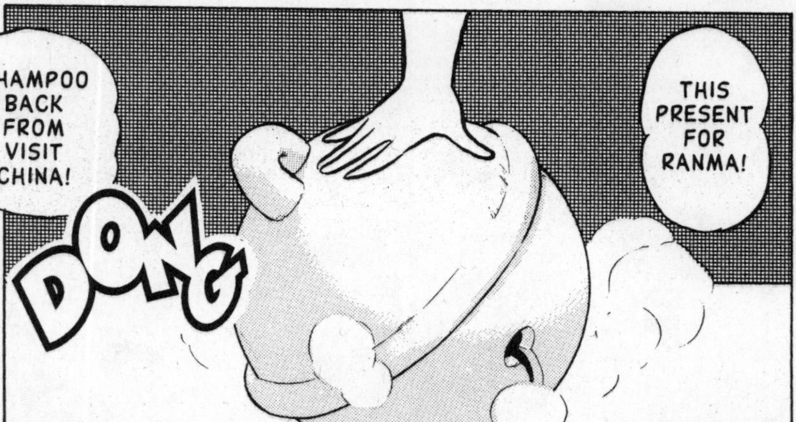
SHAMPOO BACK FROM VISIT CHINA!
THIS PRESENT FOR RANMA!
DONG

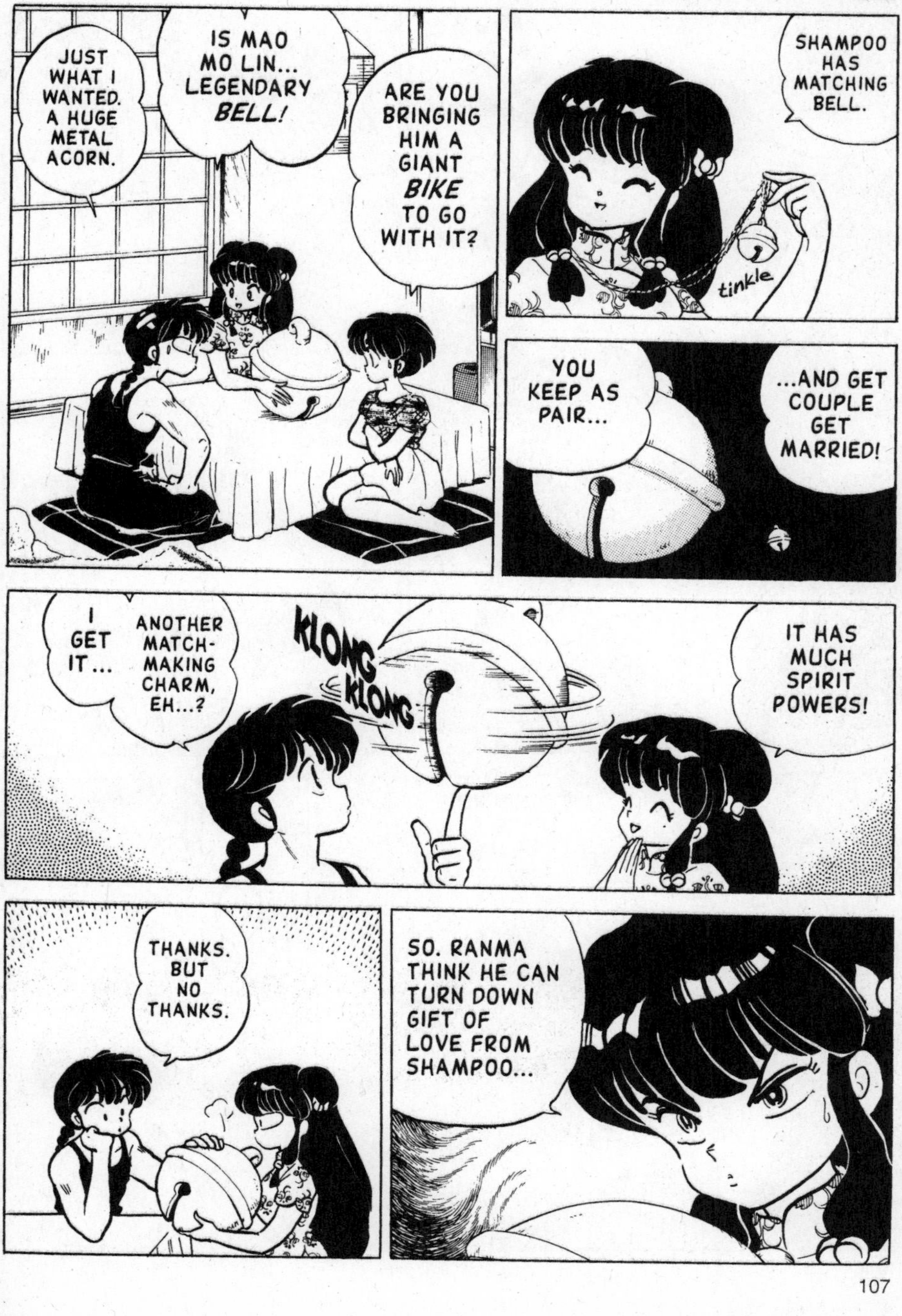
JUST WHAT I WANTED. A HUGE METAL ACORN.
IS MAO MO LIN... LEGENDARY BELL!
ARE YOU BRINGING HIM A GIANT BIKE TO GO WITH IT?
SHAMPOO HAS MATCHING BELL.
tinkle
YOU KEEP AS PAIR...
...AND GET COUPLE GET MARRIED!
I GET IT...
ANOTHER MATCH-MAKING CHARM, EH...?
KLONG KLONG
IT HAS MUCH SPIRIT POWERS!
THANKS. BUT NO THANKS.
SO. RANMA THINK HE CAN TURN DOWN GIFT OF LOVE FROM SHAMPOO...

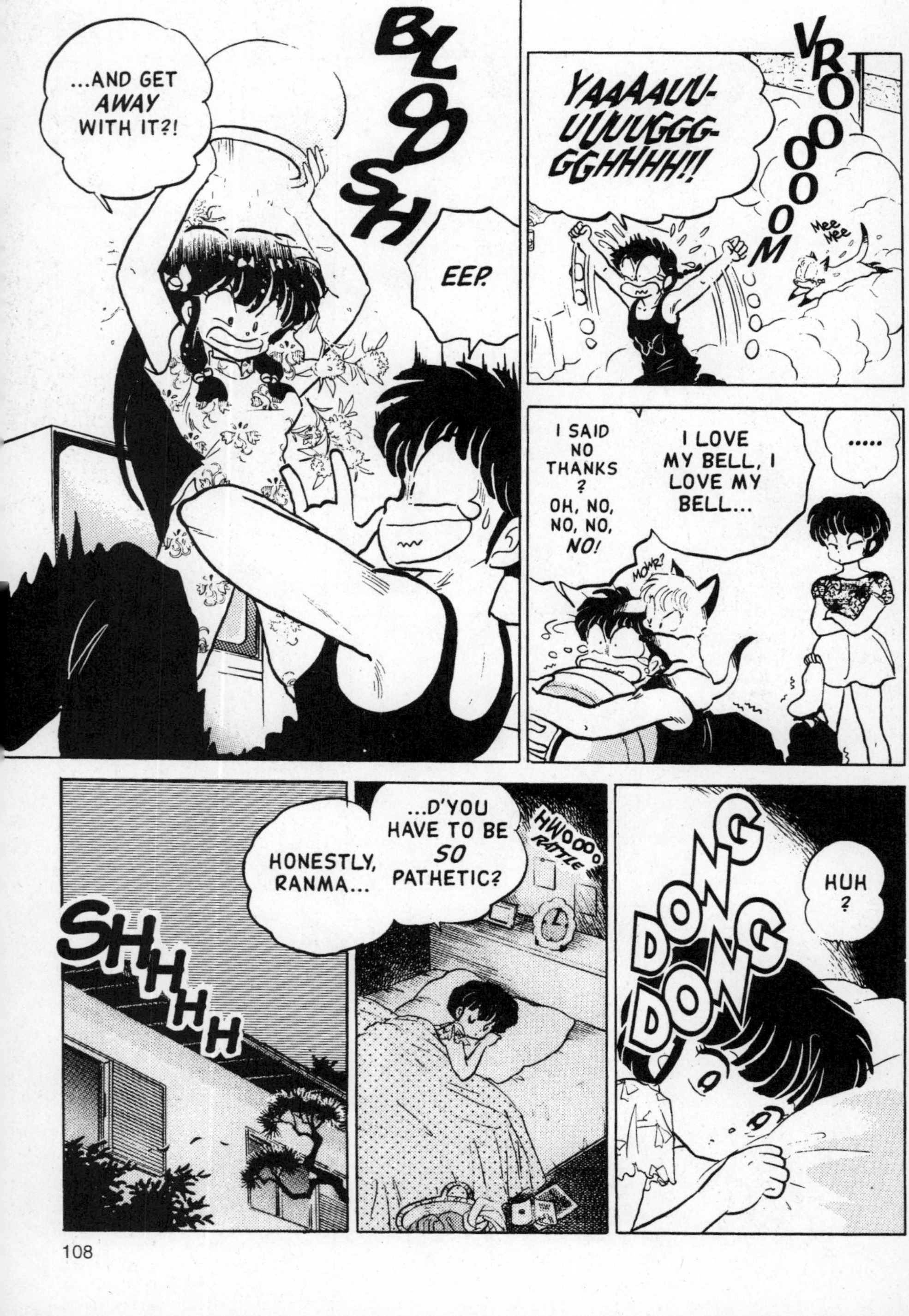
...AND GET AWAY WITH IT?!
BLOOSH
EEP?
YAAAAUU-UUUUGGG-GGHHHH!!
VROOOOOOM
Mee Mee
I SAID NO THANKS? OH, NO, NO, NO, NO!
I LOVE MY BELL, I LOVE MY BELL...
MOWR?
.....
SHHHHH
HONESTLY, RANMA...
...D'YOU HAVE TO BE SO PATHETIC?
HWOOOO
RATTLE
DONG DONG DONG DONG
HUH?

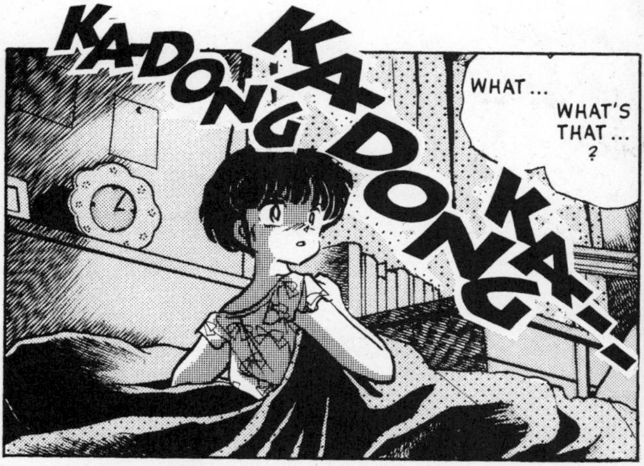
KADONG
KADONG
KADONG KA!!
WHAT... WHAT'S THAT...?

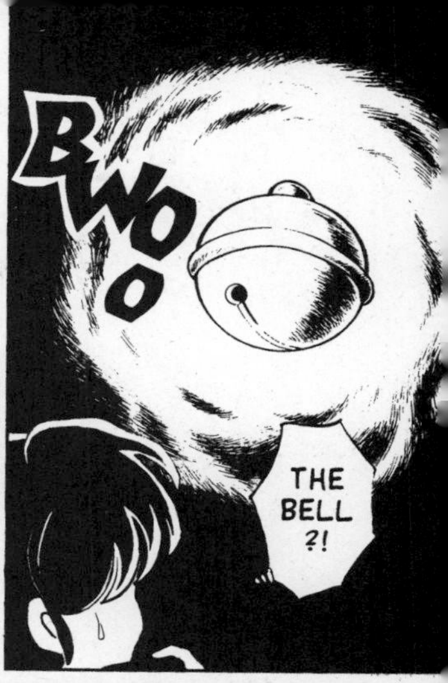
BWOOO
THE BELL ?!

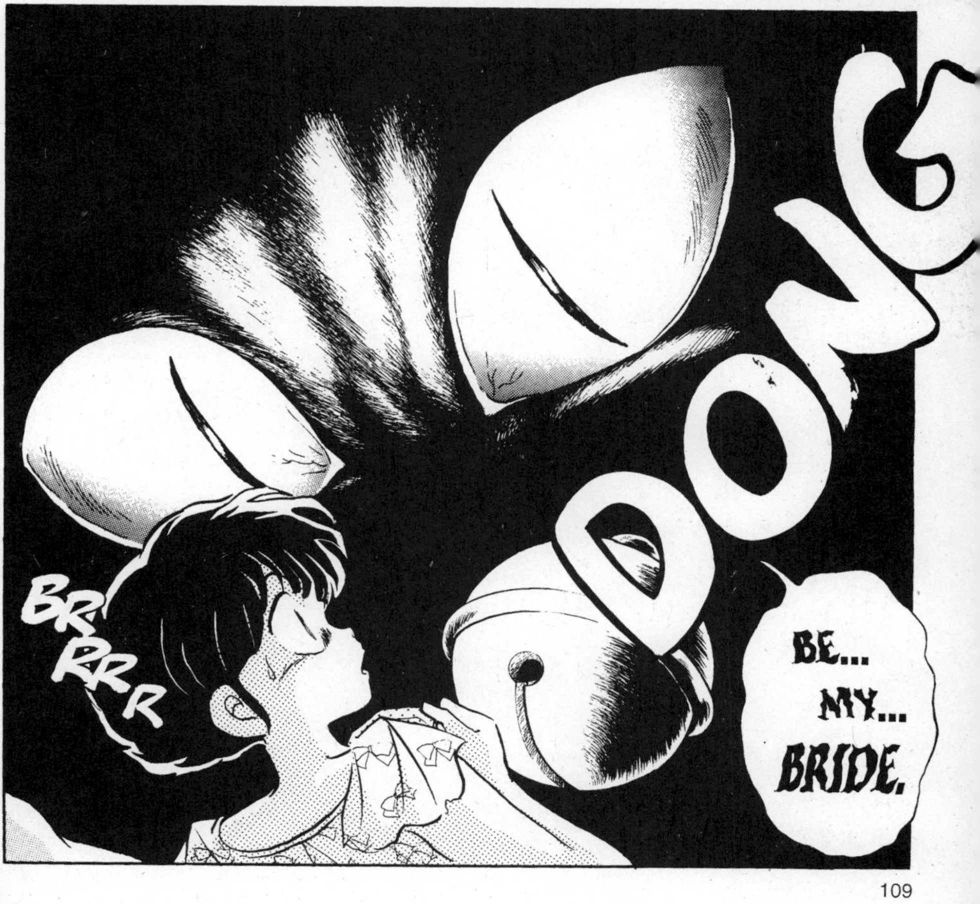
DONG
BRRRR
BE... MY... BRIDE.

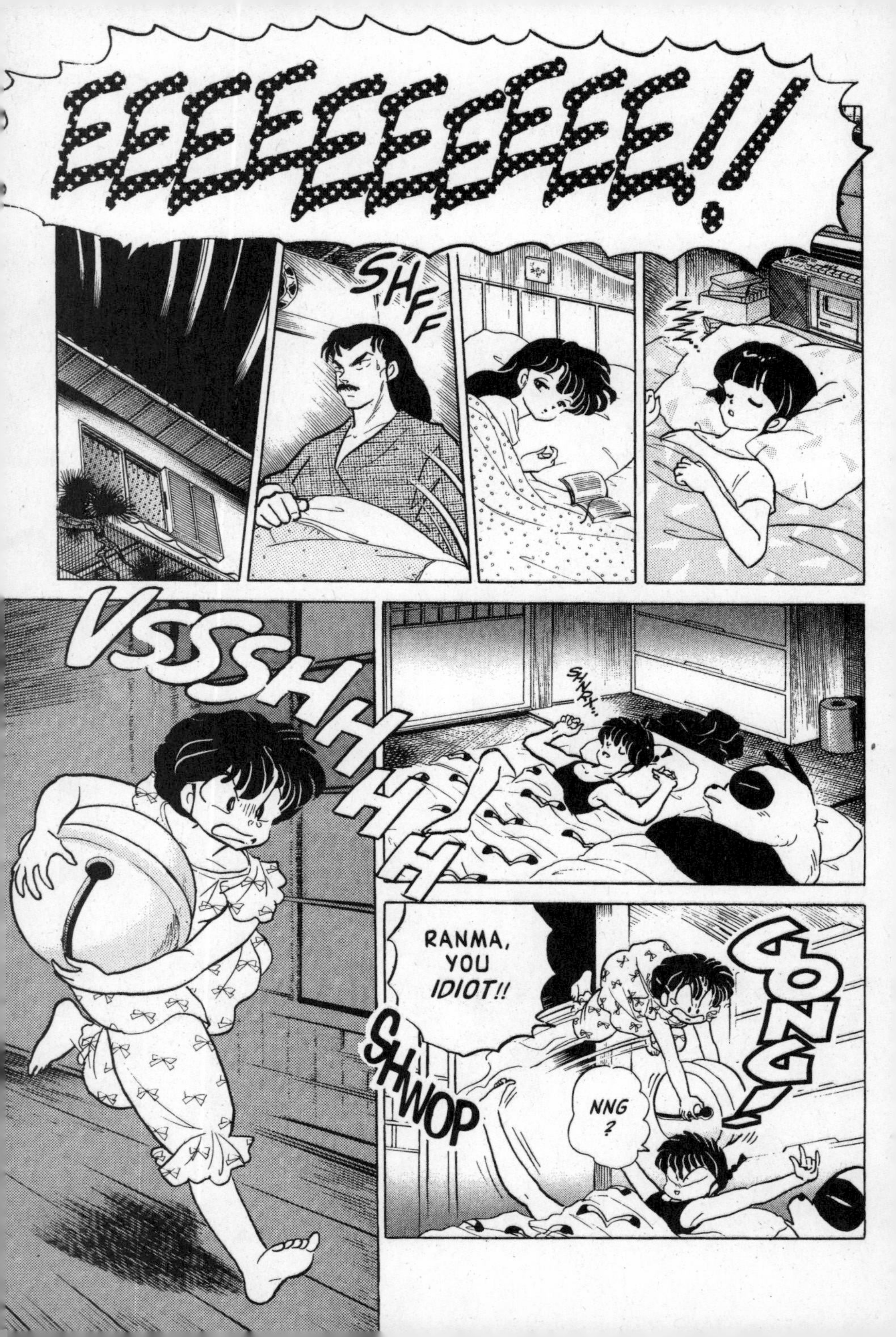
EEEEEEEEEE!!
SHFF
VSSHHHHH
SHNORK...
RANMA, YOU IDIOT!!
SHWOP
GONG!
NNG?

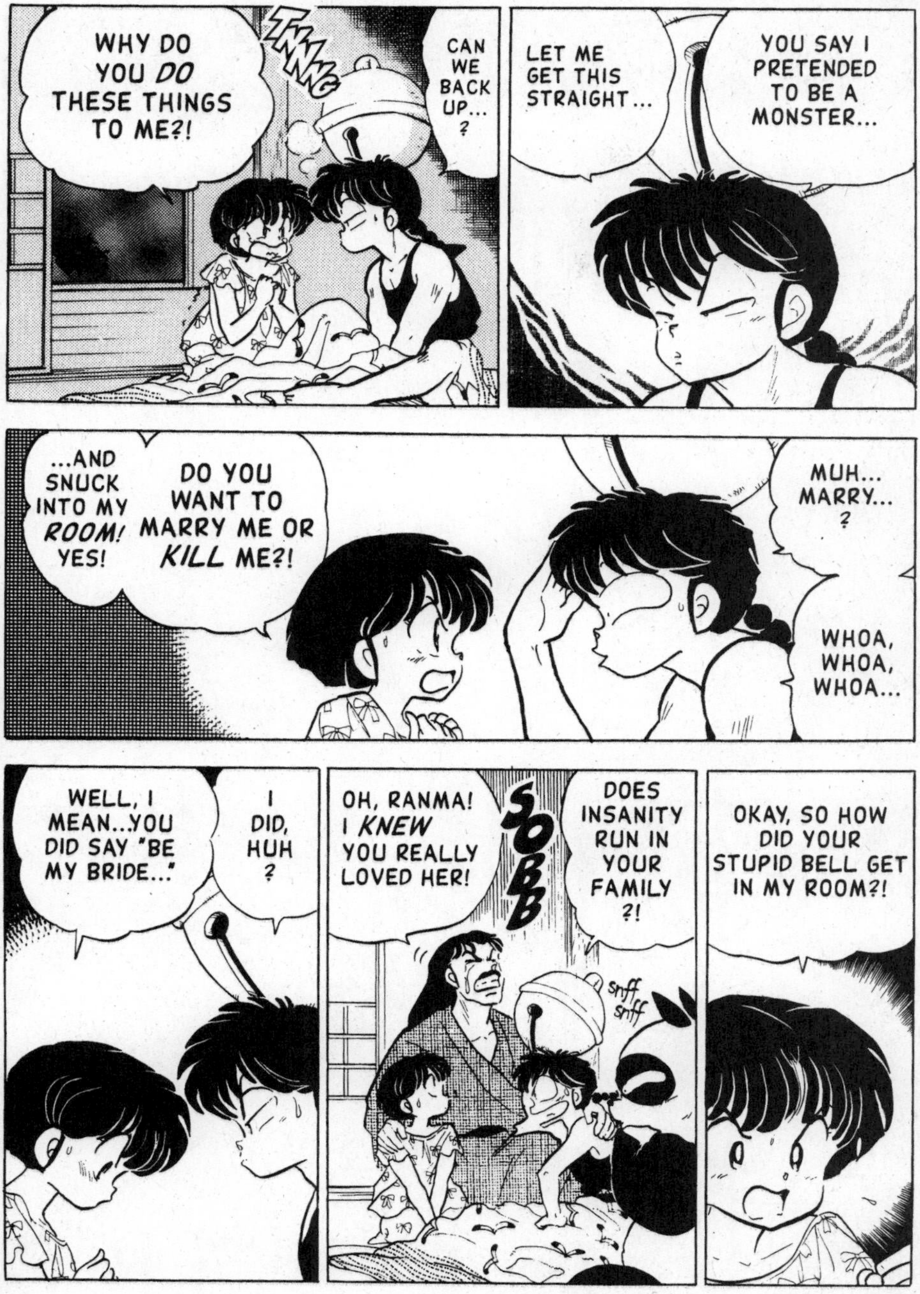
WHY DO YOU DO THESE THINGS TO ME?!
TWANG
CAN WE BACK UP...?
LET ME GET THIS STRAIGHT...
YOU SAY I PRETENDED TO BE A MONSTER...
...AND SNUCK INTO MY ROOM! YES!
DO YOU WANT TO MARRY ME OR KILL ME?!
MUH... MARRY...?
WHOA, WHOA, WHOA...
WELL, I MEAN...YOU DID SAY "BE MY BRIDE..."
I DID, HUH?
OH, RANMA! I KNEW YOU REALLY LOVED HER!
SOBB
DOES INSANITY RUN IN YOUR FAMILY?!
snff snff
OKAY, SO HOW DID YOUR STUPID BELL GET IN MY ROOM?!

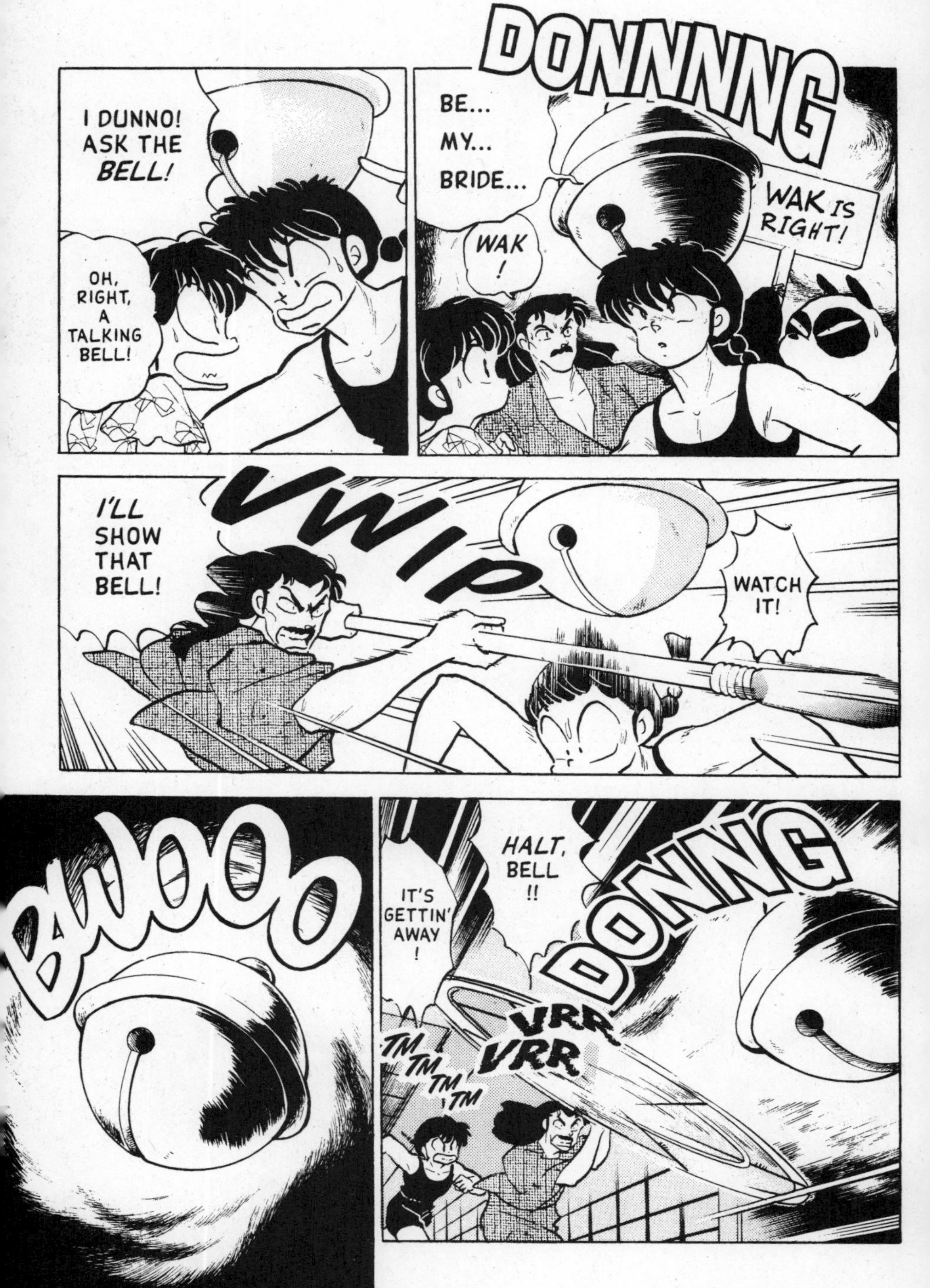
I DUNNO! ASK THE BELL!
OH, RIGHT, A TALKING BELL!
DONNNNG
BE... MY... BRIDE...
WAK!
WAK IS RIGHT!
I'LL SHOW THAT BELL!
VWIP
WATCH IT!
BWOOOO
HALT, BELL!!
IT'S GETTIN' AWAY!
DONNG
VRR VRR
TM TM TM TM

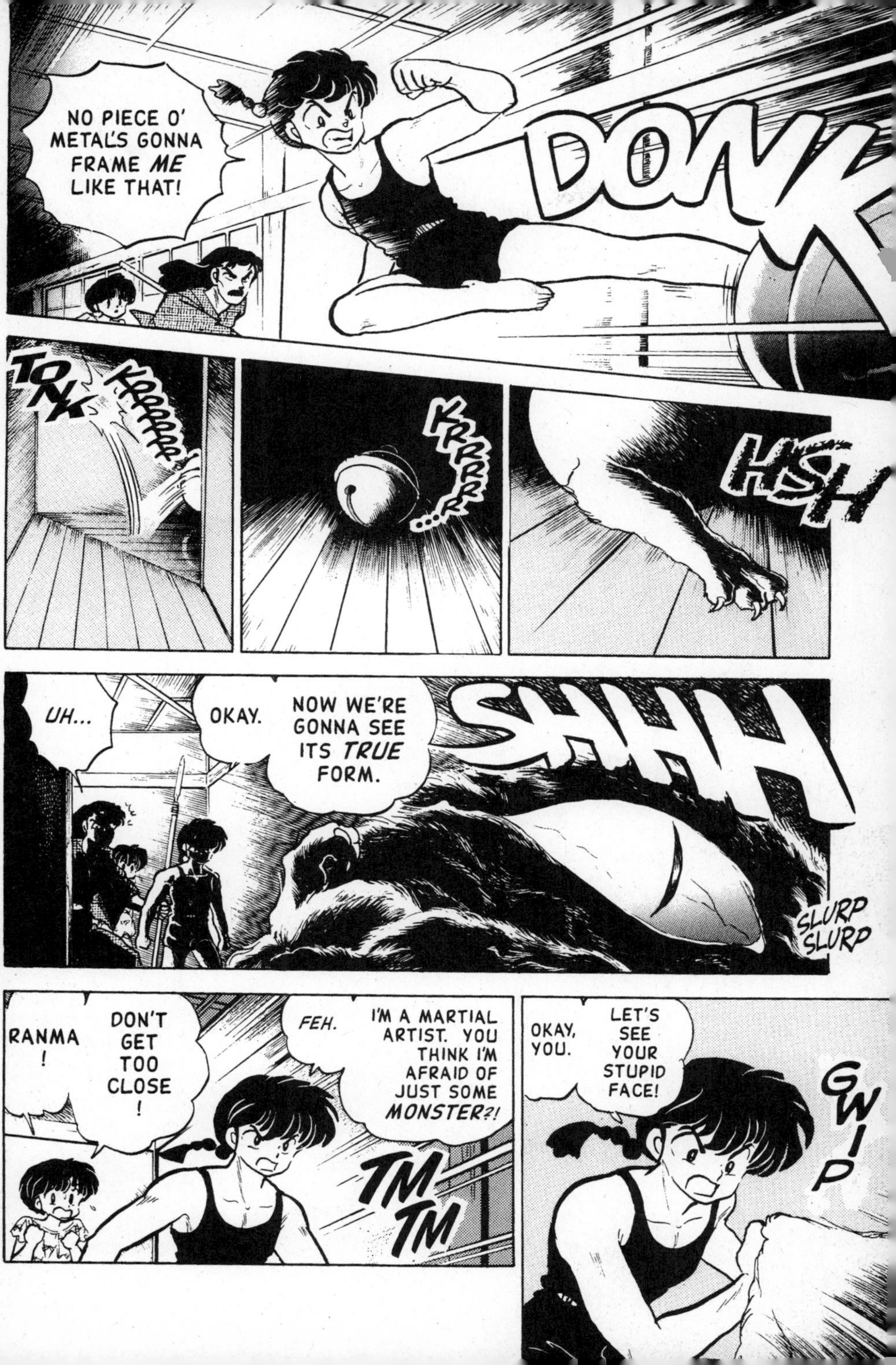
NO PIECE O' METAL'S GONNA FRAME *ME* LIKE THAT!
DONK
TONK
KRRRRRR
KRRRRRR...
HSH
UH...
OKAY.
NOW WE'RE GONNA SEE ITS *TRUE* FORM.
SHHH
SLURP SLURP
RANMA!
DON'T GET TOO CLOSE!
FEH.
I'M A MARTIAL ARTIST. YOU THINK I'M AFRAID OF JUST SOME *MONSTER*?!
TM TM
OKAY, YOU.
LET'S SEE YOUR STUPID FACE!
GWIP

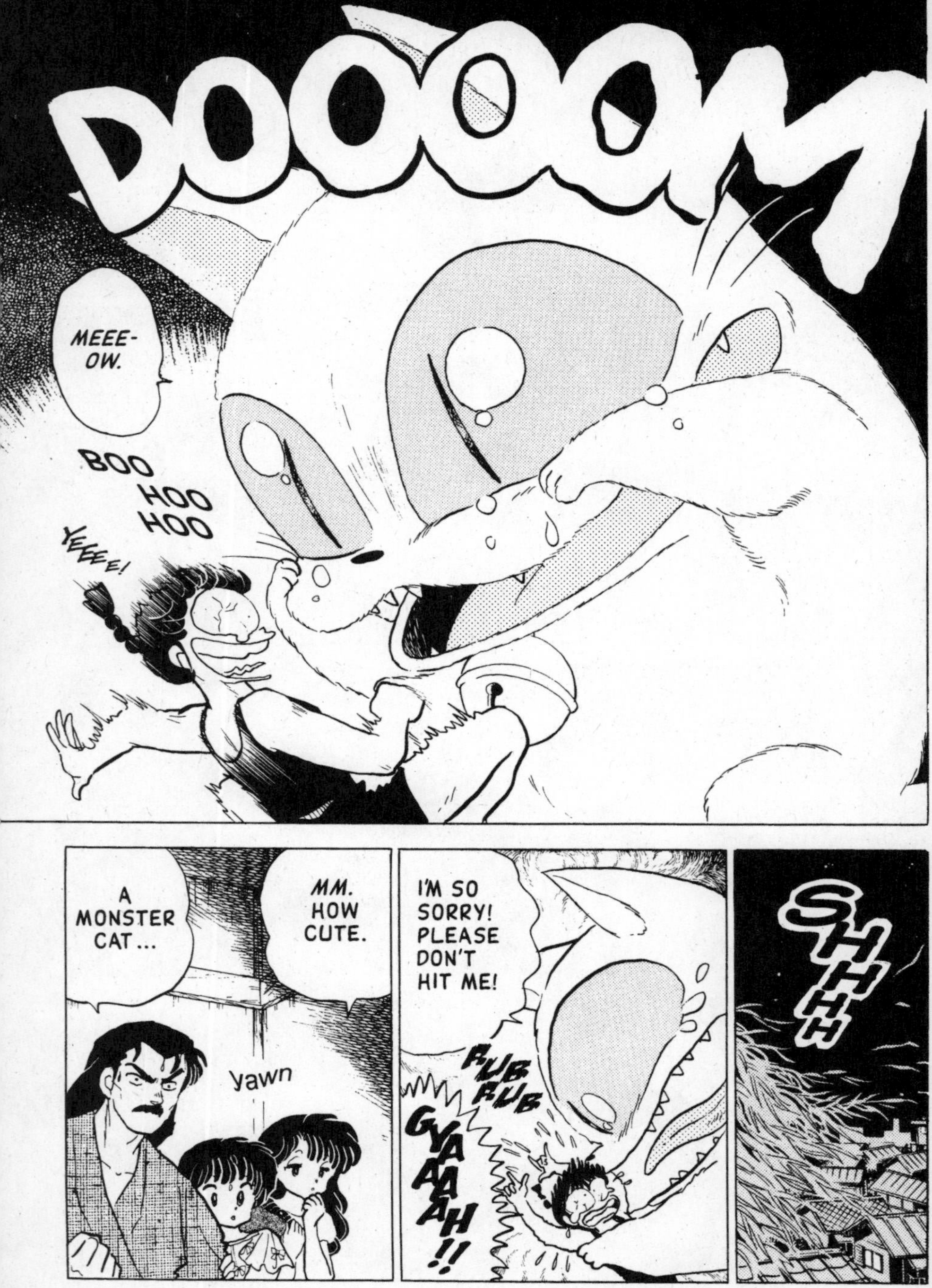
DOOOOM
MEEE-OW.
BOO HOO HOO
YEEEE!
A MONSTER CAT...
MM. HOW CUTE.
Yawn
I'M SO SORRY! PLEASE DON'T HIT ME!
RUB RUB
GYAAAH!!
SHHHH

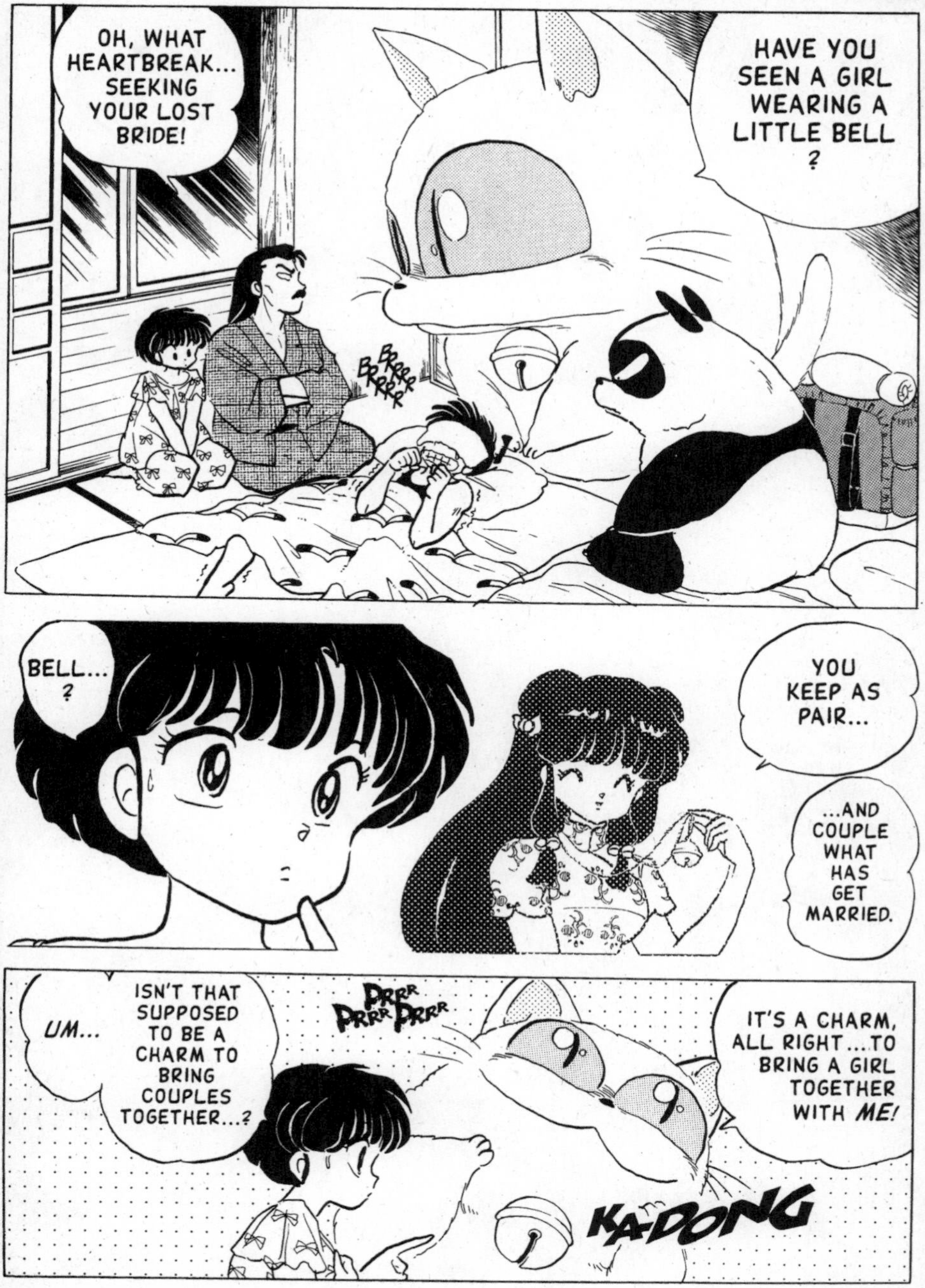
OH, WHAT HEARTBREAK... SEEKING YOUR LOST BRIDE!
HAVE YOU SEEN A GIRL WEARING A LITTLE BELL?
BRRRR BRRRRR
BELL...?
YOU KEEP AS PAIR...
...AND COUPLE WHAT HAS GET MARRIED.
UM...
ISN'T THAT SUPPOSED TO BE A CHARM TO BRING COUPLES TOGETHER...?
PRRR PRRR PRRR
IT'S A CHARM, ALL RIGHT...TO BRING A GIRL TOGETHER WITH *ME!*
KA-DONG

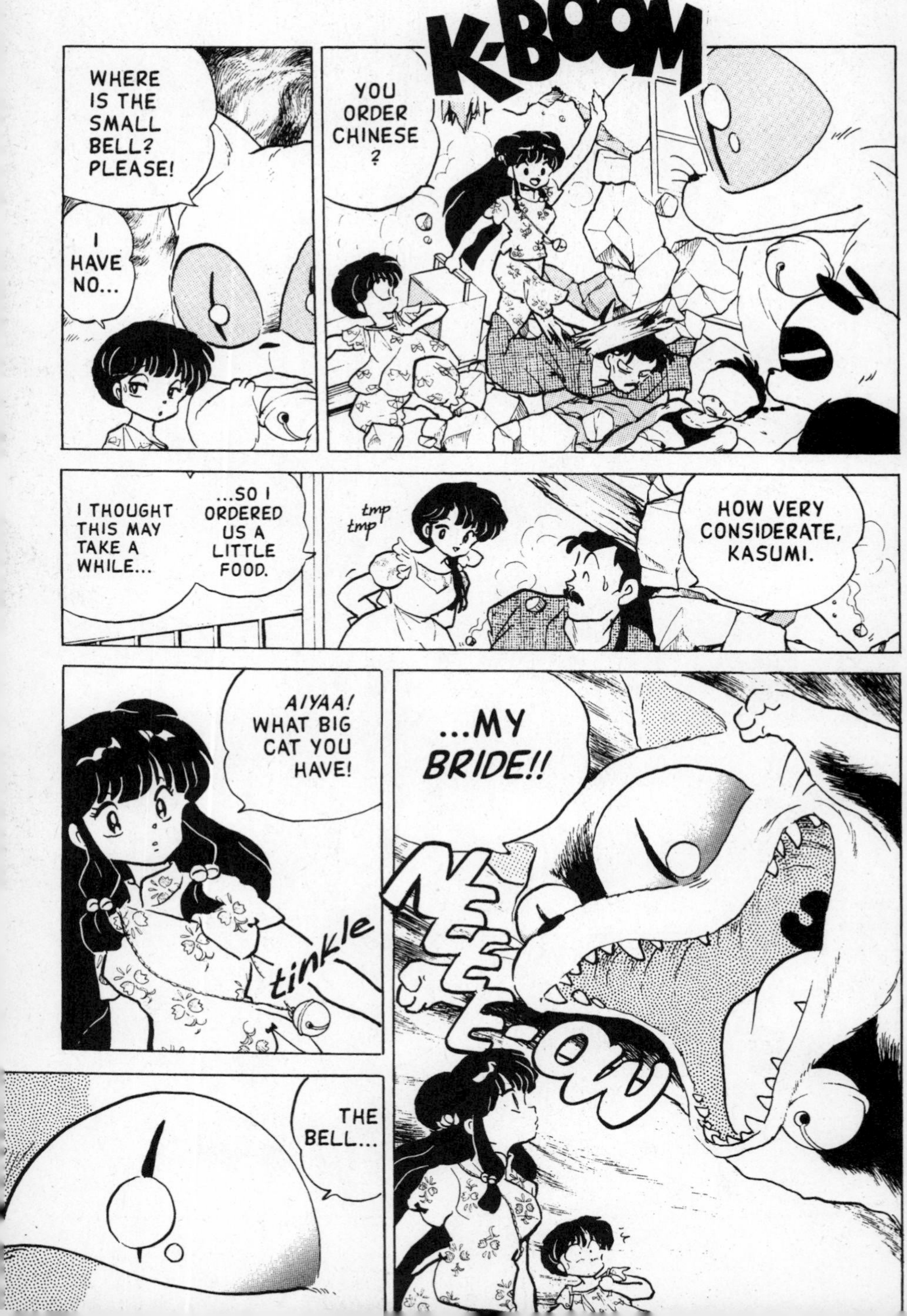
WHERE IS THE SMALL BELL? PLEASE!
I HAVE NO...
K-BOOM
YOU ORDER CHINESE ?
I THOUGHT THIS MAY TAKE A WHILE...
...SO I ORDERED US A LITTLE FOOD.
tmp tmp
HOW VERY CONSIDERATE, KASUMI.
AIYAA! WHAT BIG CAT YOU HAVE!
tinkle
...MY BRIDE!!
NEEE-OW
THE BELL...

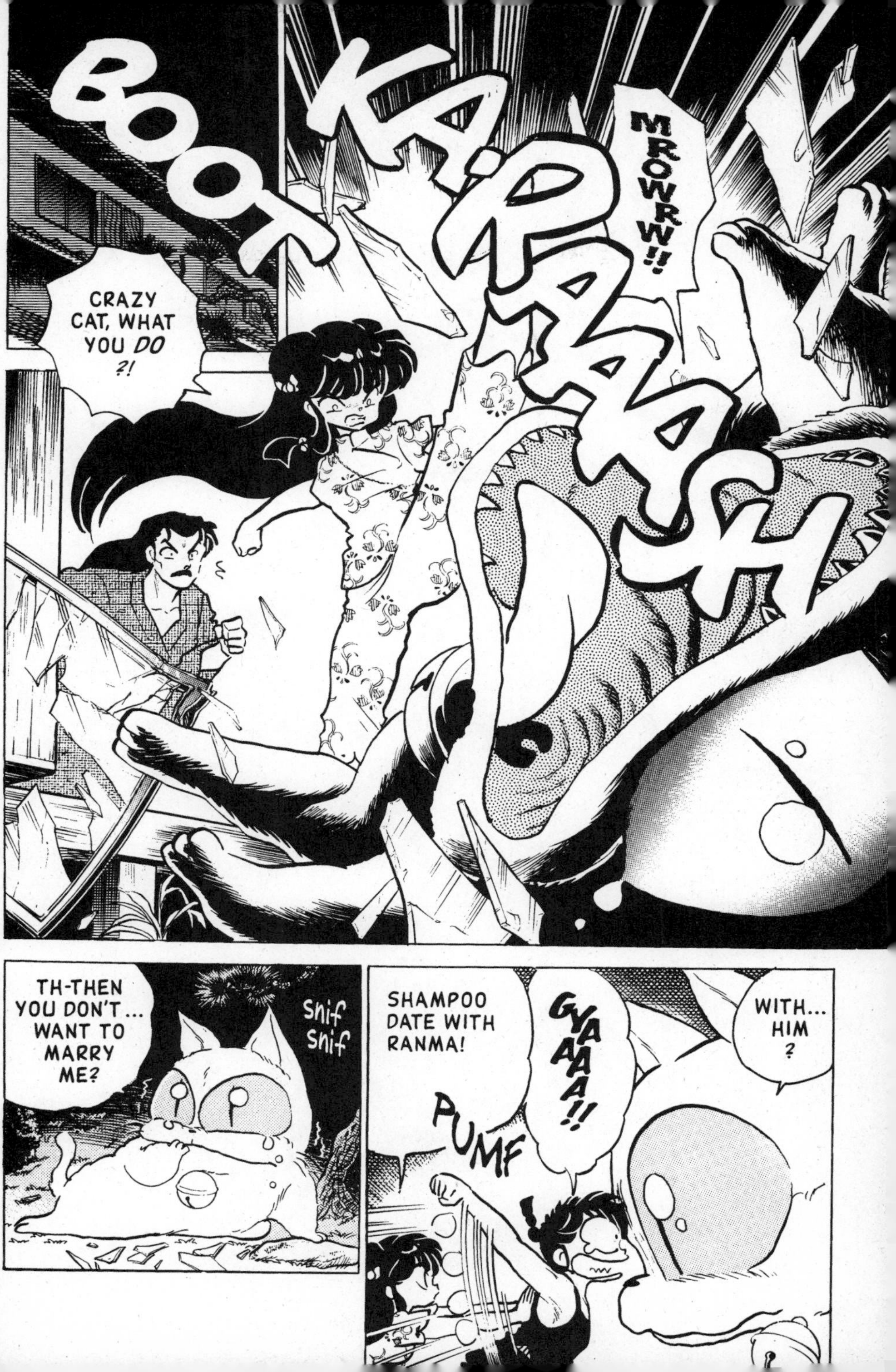
BOOT
KA-RAASH
MROWRW!!
CRAZY CAT, WHAT YOU *DO* ?!
TH-THEN YOU DON'T... WANT TO MARRY ME?
Snif snif
SHAMPOO DATE WITH RANMA!
GYAAAA!!
PUMF
WITH... HIM ?

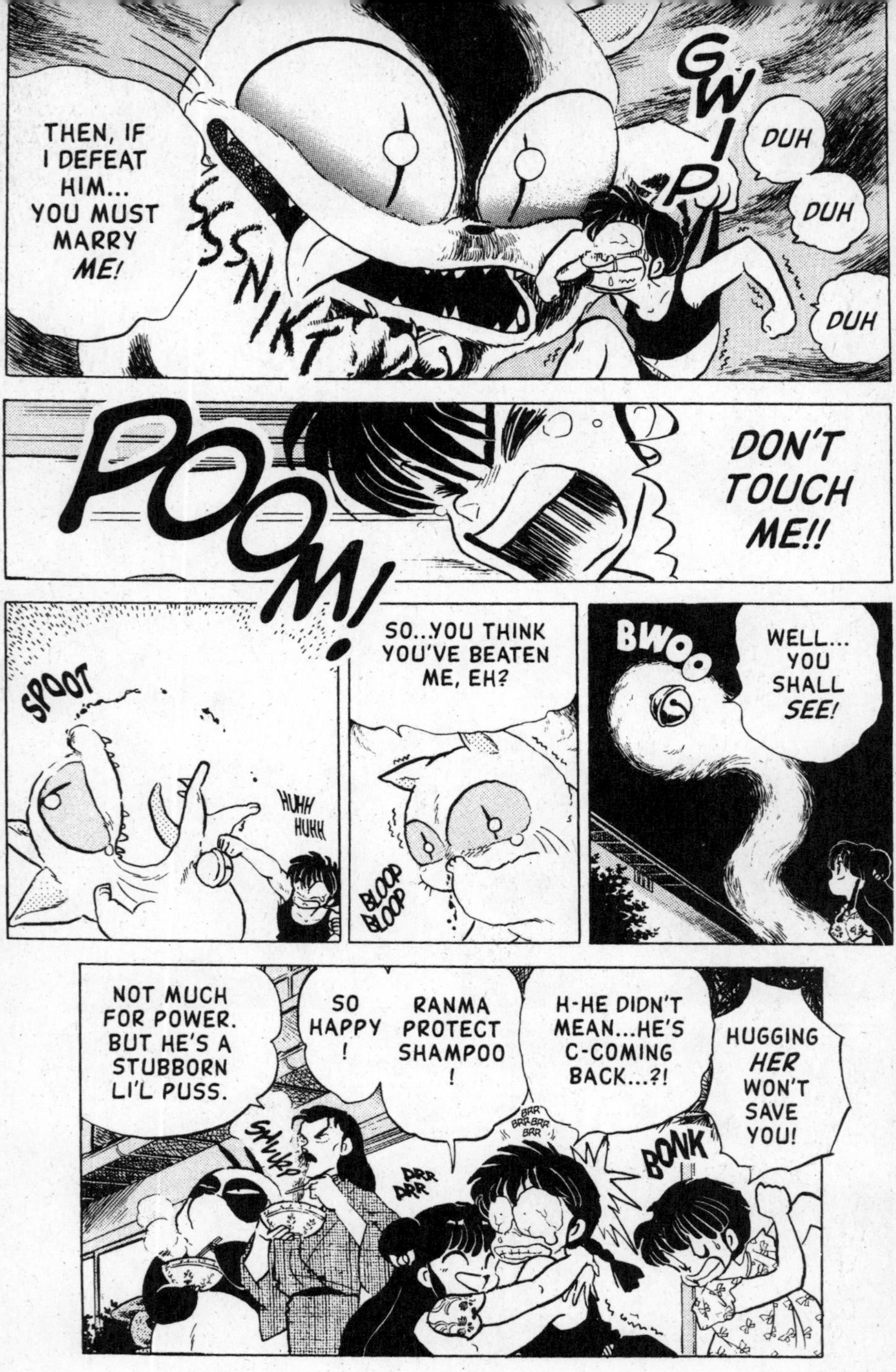
THEN, IF I DEFEAT HIM... YOU MUST MARRY ME!
SSNIKT
GWIP
DUH
DUH
DUH
POOM!
DON'T TOUCH ME!!
SPOOT
HUHH HUHH
SO...YOU THINK YOU'VE BEATEN ME, EH?
BLOOP BLOOP
BWOO
WELL... YOU SHALL SEE!
NOT MUCH FOR POWER. BUT HE'S A STUBBORN LI'L PUSS.
SHLURP
SO HAPPY!
RANMA PROTECT SHAMPOO!
DRR DRR
H-HE DIDN'T MEAN...HE'S C-COMING BACK...?!
BRR BRR BRR BRR
BONK
HUGGING HER WON'T SAVE YOU!

PART 8
KITTY TAKES' A BRIDE

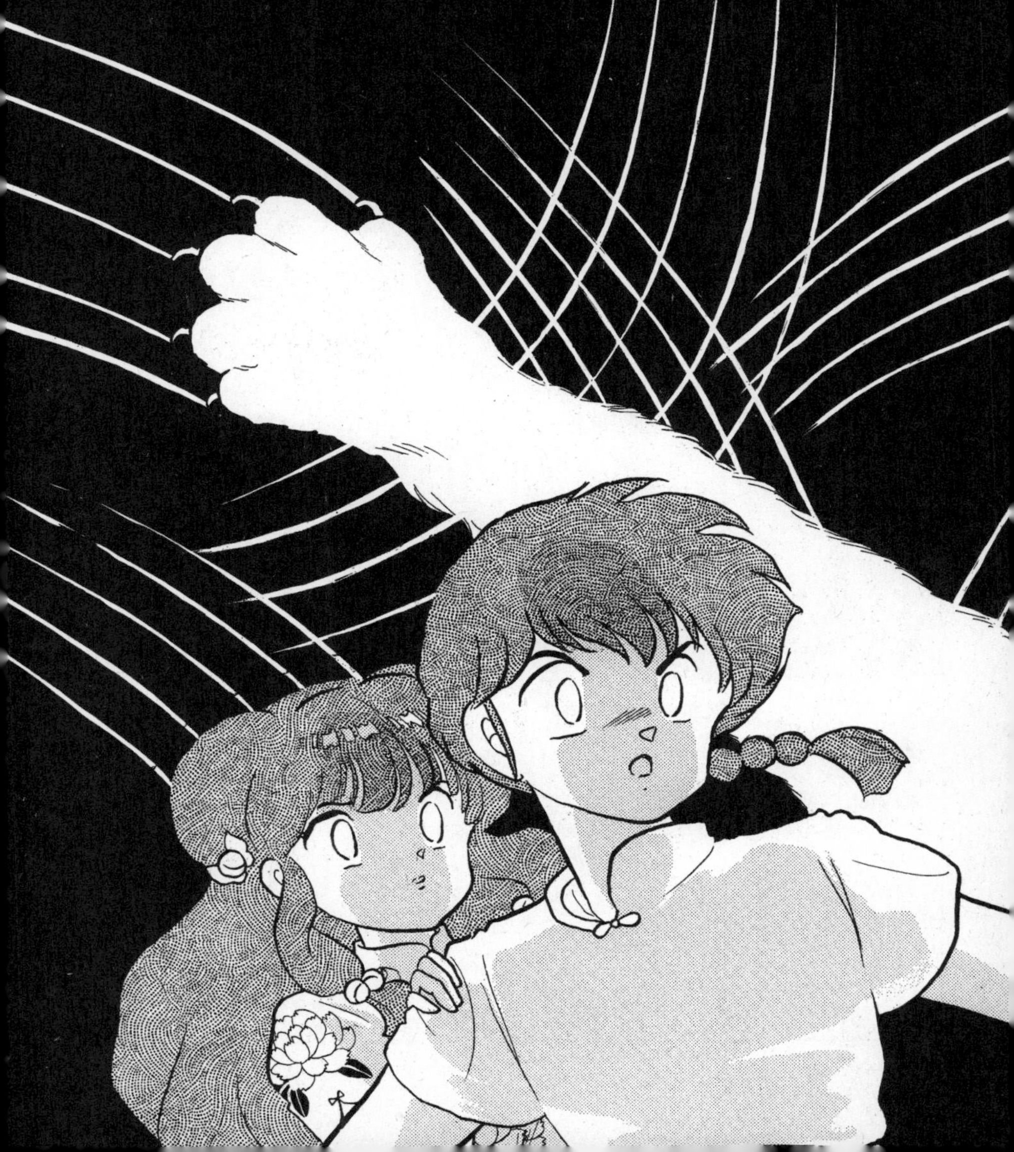

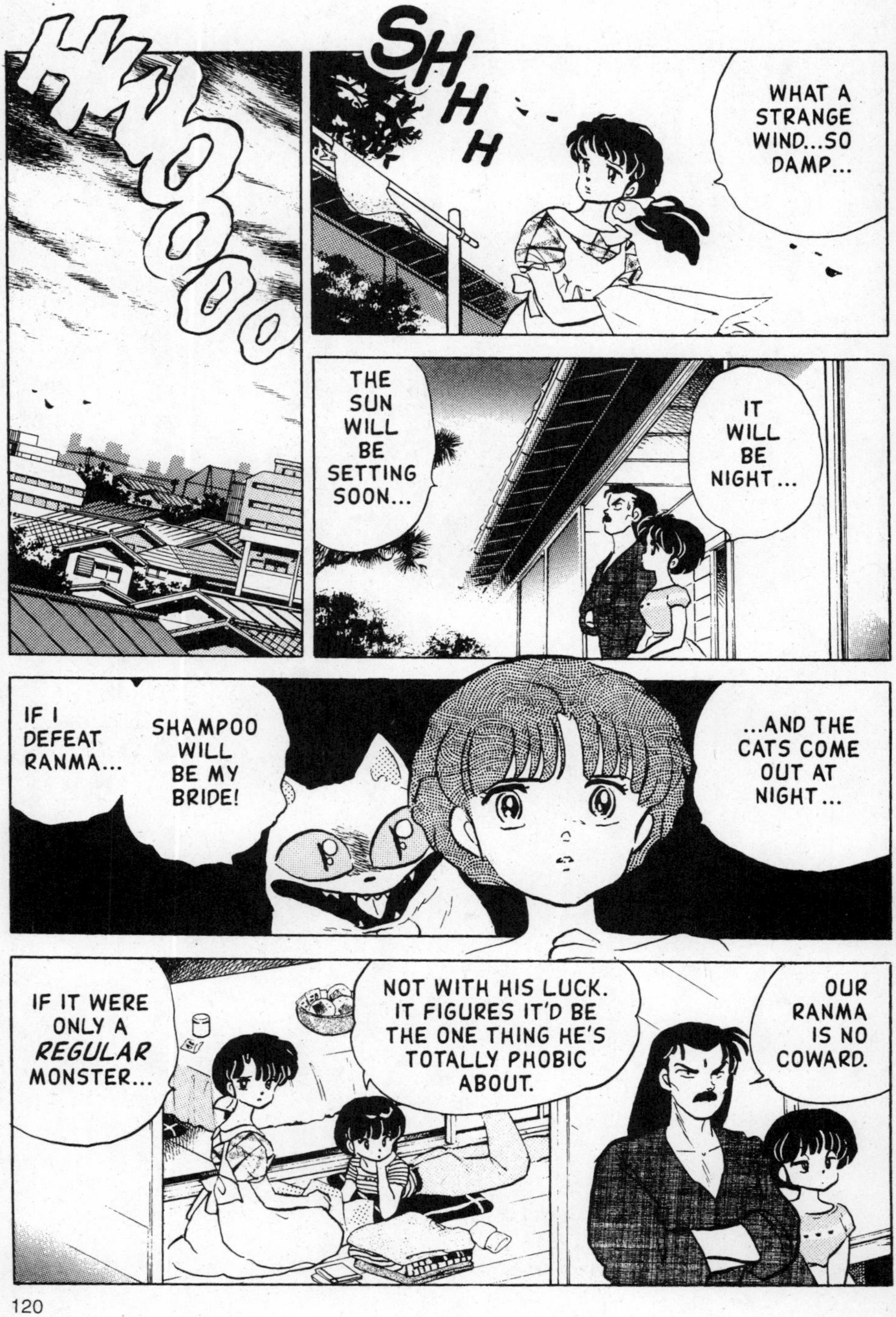
HWOOOOO
SHHH
WHAT A STRANGE WIND...SO DAMP...
THE SUN WILL BE SETTING SOON...
IT WILL BE NIGHT...
IF I DEFEAT RANMA...
SHAMPOO WILL BE MY BRIDE!
...AND THE CATS COME OUT AT NIGHT...
IF IT WERE ONLY A *REGULAR* MONSTER...
NOT WITH HIS LUCK. IT FIGURES IT'D BE THE ONE THING HE'S TOTALLY PHOBIC ABOUT.
OUR RANMA IS NO COWARD.

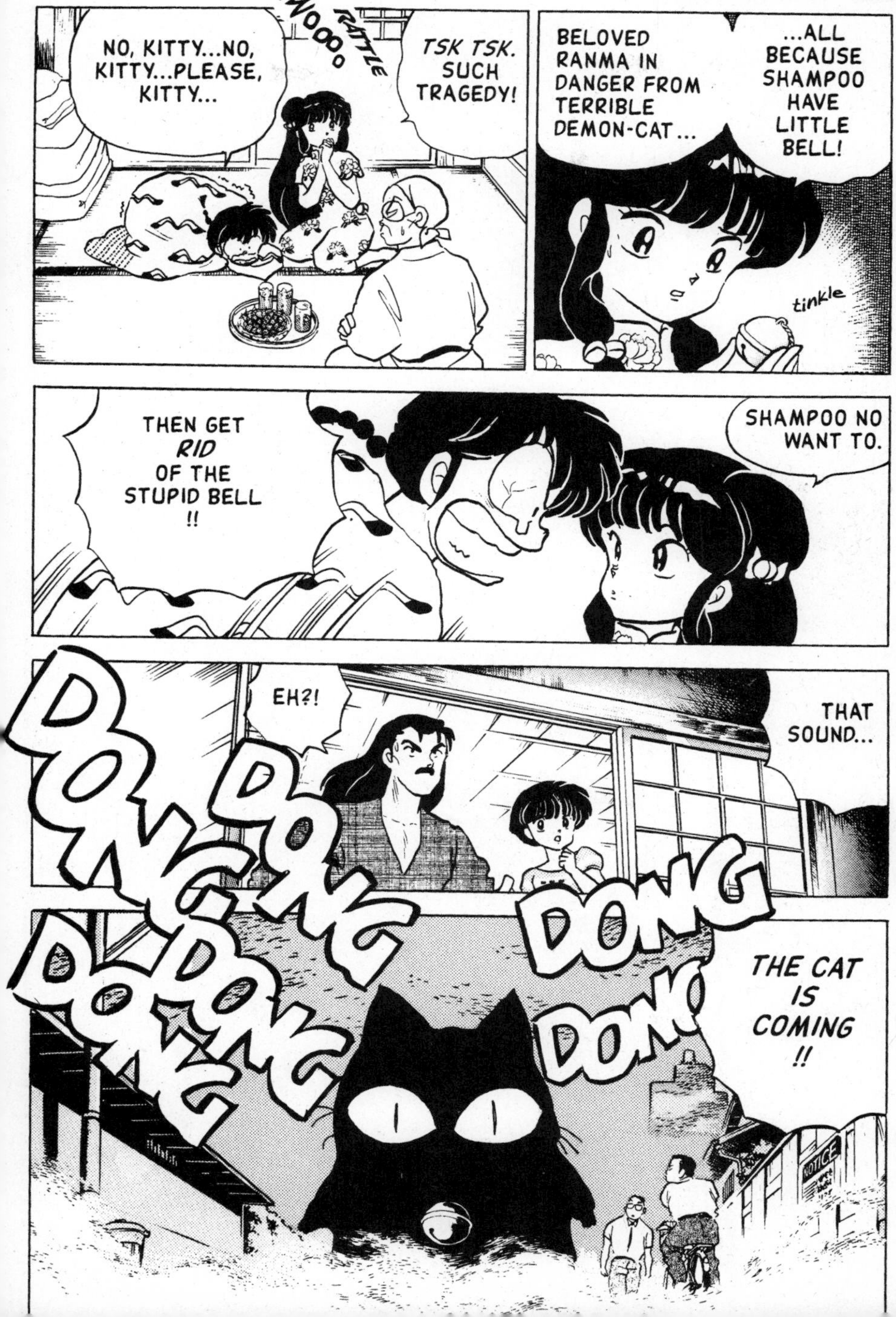
NO, KITTY...NO, KITTY...PLEASE, KITTY...
HWOOOo
RATTLE
TSK TSK. SUCH TRAGEDY!
BELOVED RANMA IN DANGER FROM TERRIBLE DEMON-CAT...
...ALL BECAUSE SHAMPOO HAVE LITTLE BELL!
tinkle
THEN GET RID OF THE STUPID BELL !!
SHAMPOO NO WANT TO.
EH?!
THAT SOUND...
DONG DONG DONG DONG DONG
DONG DONG
THE CAT IS COMING !!
NOTICE

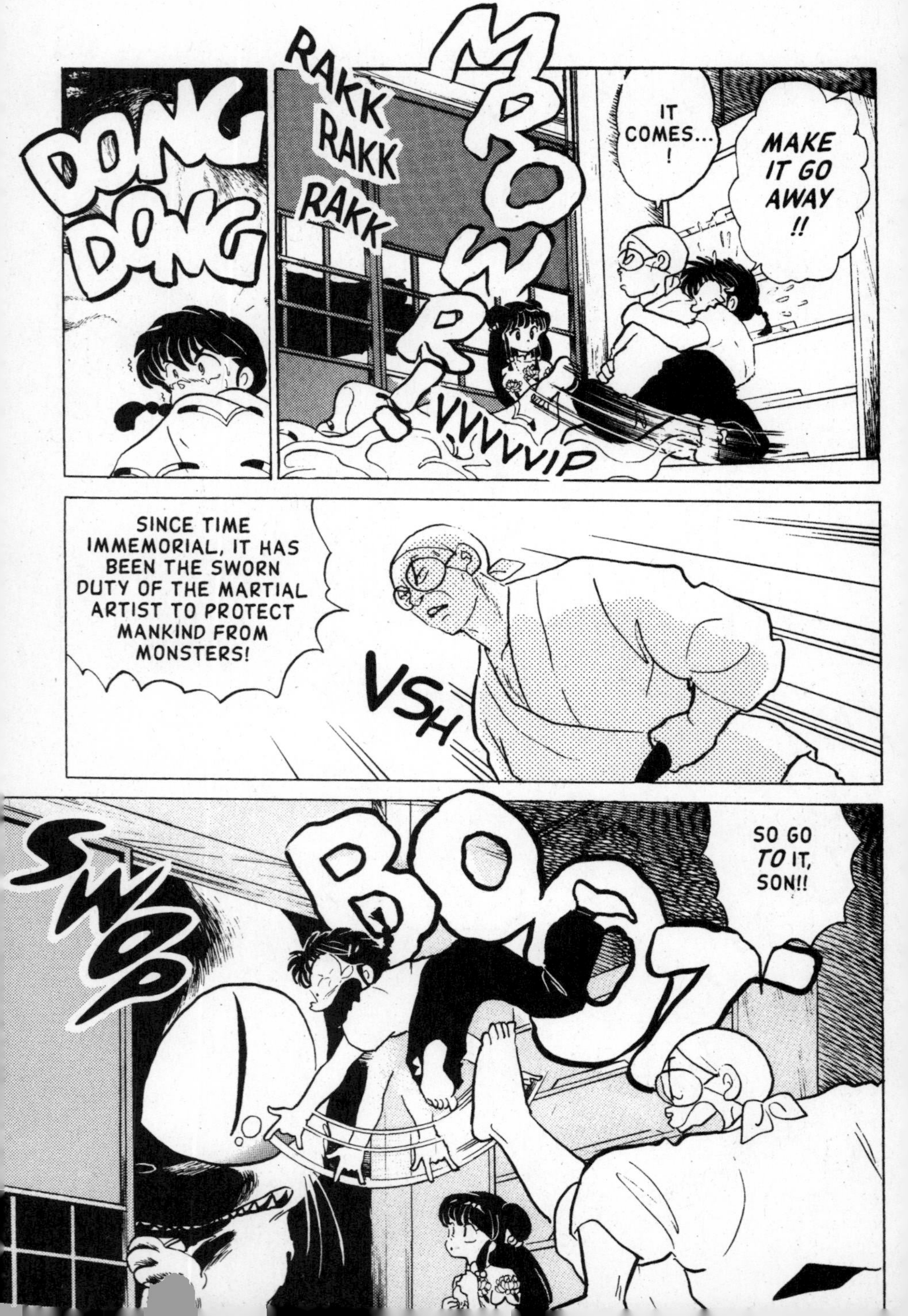
DONG DONG
RAKK RAKK RAKK
MROWR
IT COMES...!
MAKE IT GO AWAY!!
VVVVVVIP
SINCE TIME IMMEMORIAL, IT HAS BEEN THE SWORN DUTY OF THE MARTIAL ARTIST TO PROTECT MANKIND FROM MONSTERS!
VSH
SWOOP
BOOT
SO GO *TO* IT, SON!!

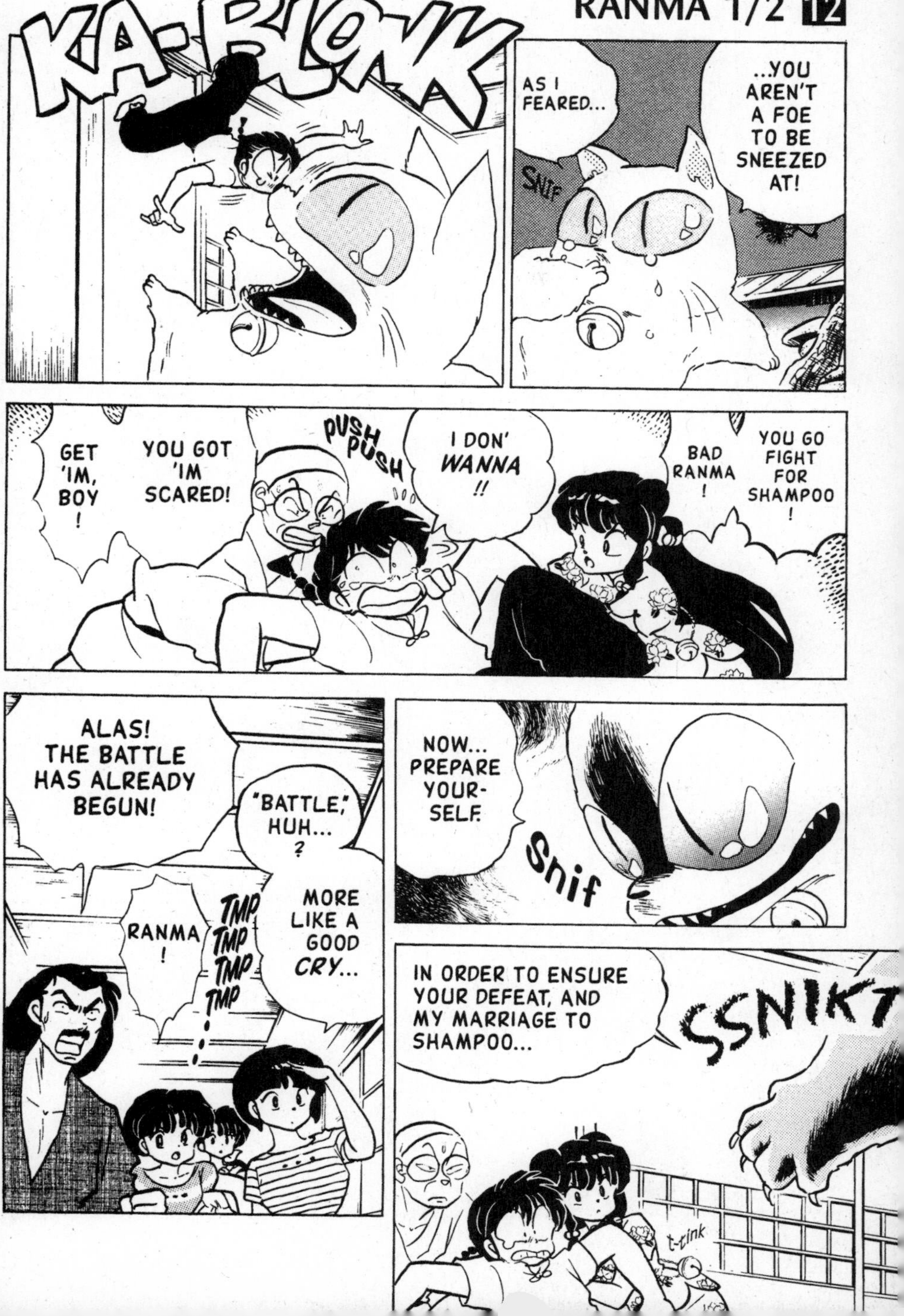
KA-BLONK
AS I FEARED...
...YOU AREN'T A FOE TO BE SNEEZED AT!
SNIF
GET 'IM, BOY!
YOU GOT 'IM SCARED!
PUSH PUSH
I DON' WANNA!!
BAD RANMA!
YOU GO FIGHT FOR SHAMPOO!
ALAS! THE BATTLE HAS ALREADY BEGUN!
"BATTLE," HUH...?
RANMA!
TMP TMP TMP TMP
MORE LIKE A GOOD CRY...
NOW... PREPARE YOURSELF.
Snif
IN ORDER TO ENSURE YOUR DEFEAT, AND MY MARRIAGE TO SHAMPOO...
SSNIKT
t-tink

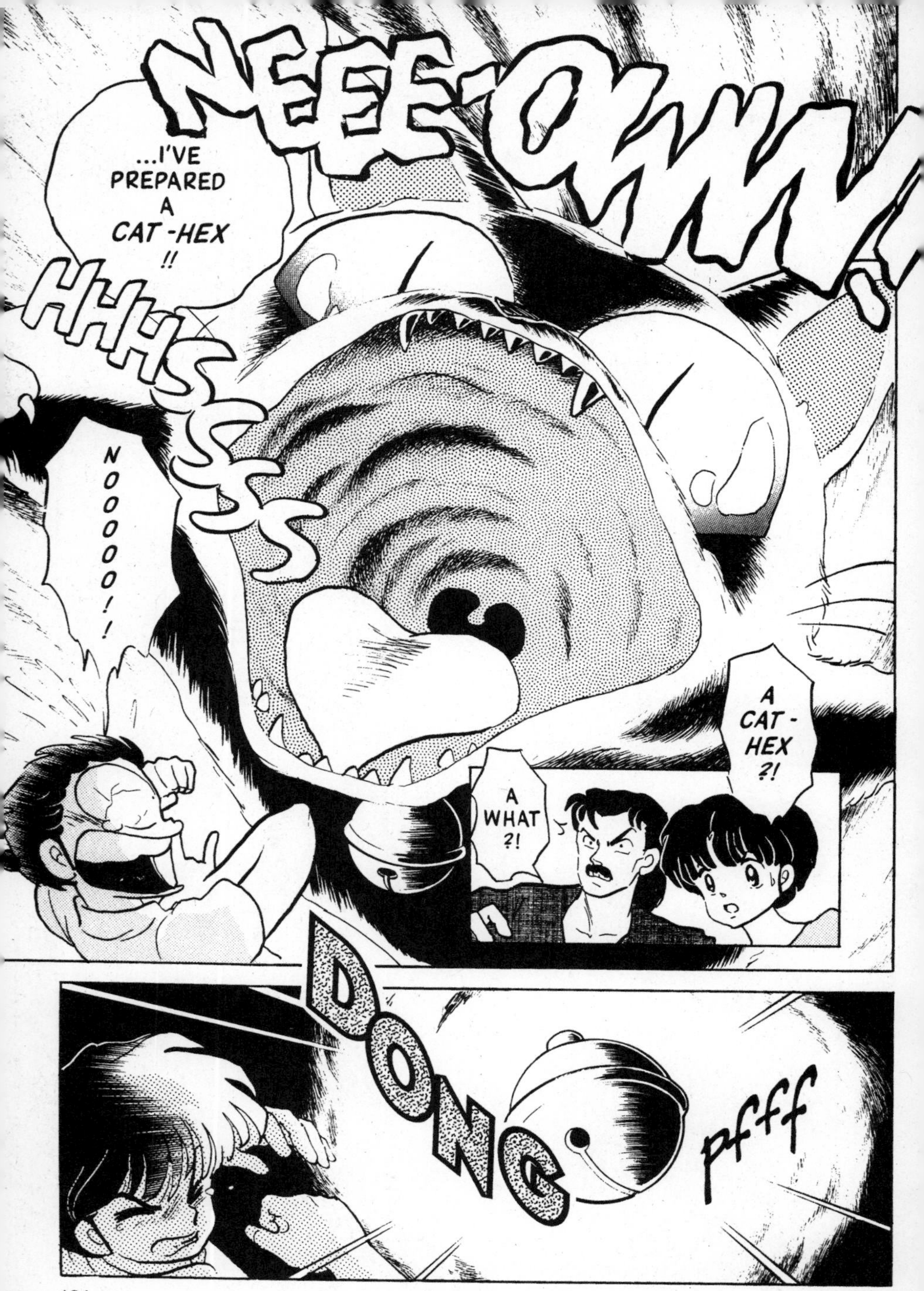

NEEE-OWWW
...I'VE PREPARED A CAT-HEX !!
HHHSSSS
NOOOOOO!!
A CAT-HEX ?!
A WHAT ?!
DONG
pfff

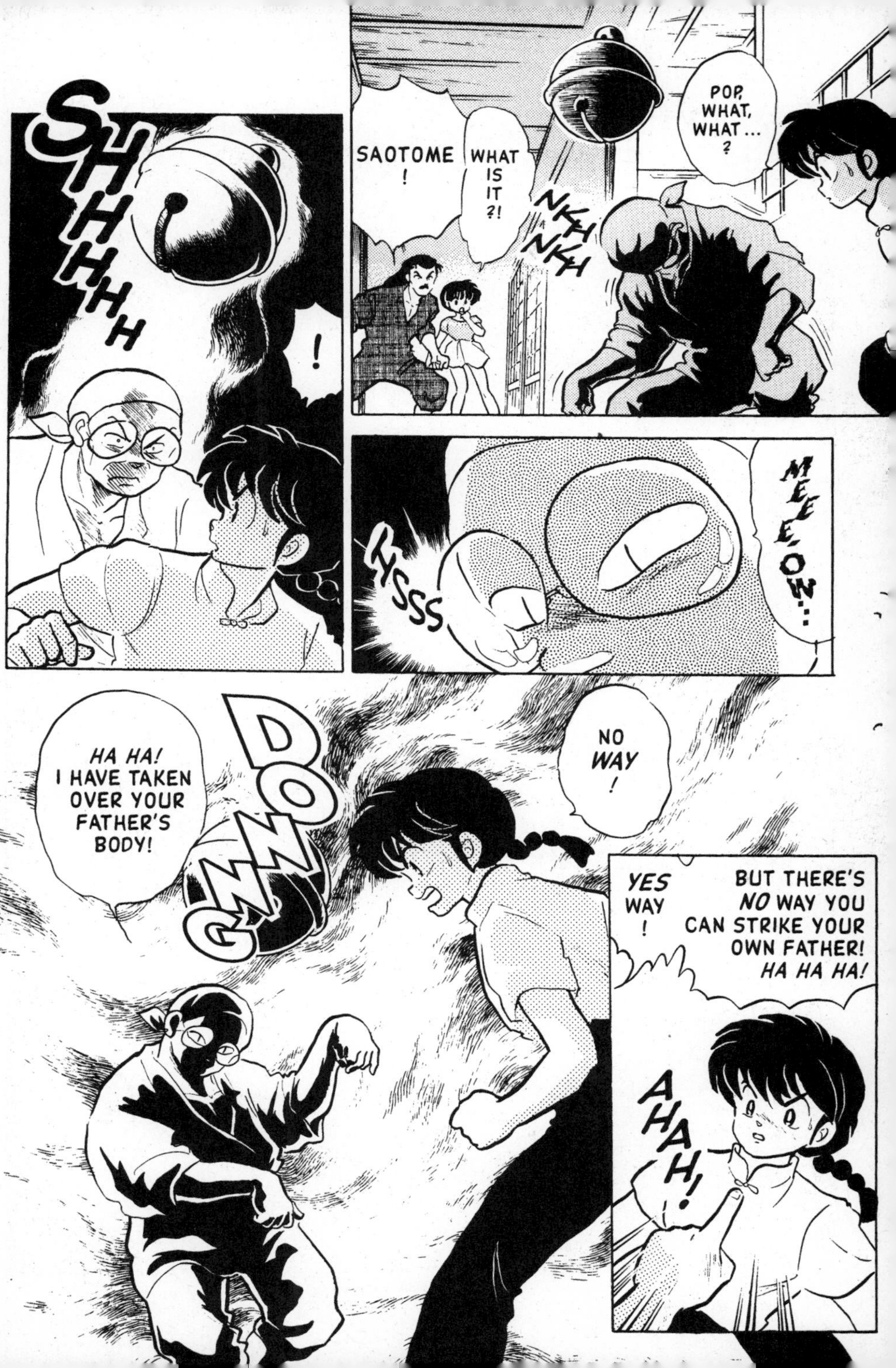
SHHHHHHH
!
SAOTOME!
WHAT IS IT?!
NKH NKH
POP, WHAT, WHAT...?
HSSS
MEEEOW...
HA HA! I HAVE TAKEN OVER YOUR FATHER'S BODY!
DOWNNG
NO WAY!
YES WAY!
BUT THERE'S NO WAY YOU CAN STRIKE YOUR OWN FATHER! HA HA HA!
AHAH!

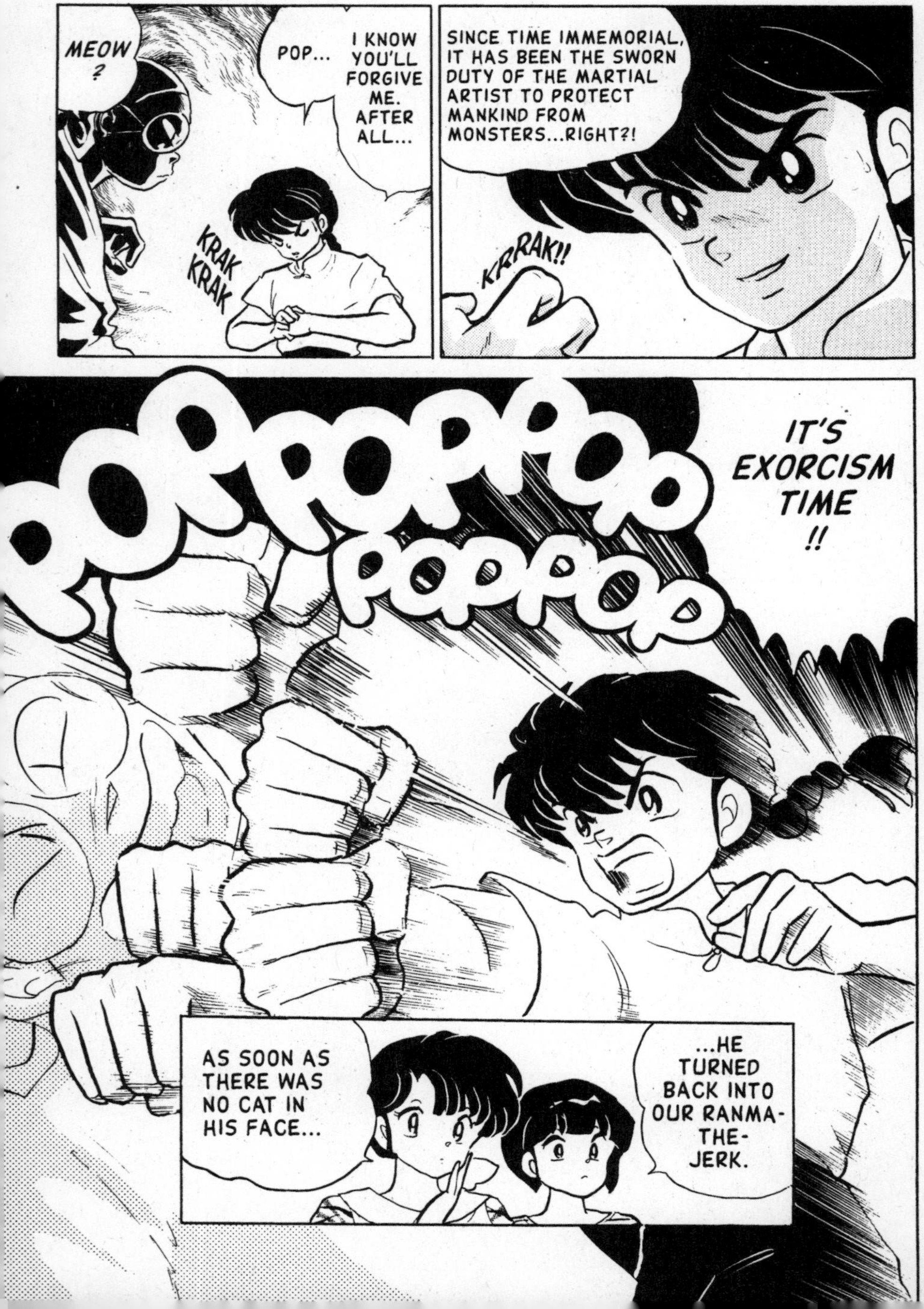
MEOW ?
POP... I KNOW YOU'LL FORGIVE ME. AFTER ALL...
KRAK KRAK
SINCE TIME IMMEMORIAL, IT HAS BEEN THE SWORN DUTY OF THE MARTIAL ARTIST TO PROTECT MANKIND FROM MONSTERS...RIGHT?!
KRRAK!!
POPOPOPOP
POPOPOP
IT'S EXORCISM TIME !!
AS SOON AS THERE WAS NO CAT IN HIS FACE...
...HE TURNED BACK INTO OUR RANMA-THE-JERK.

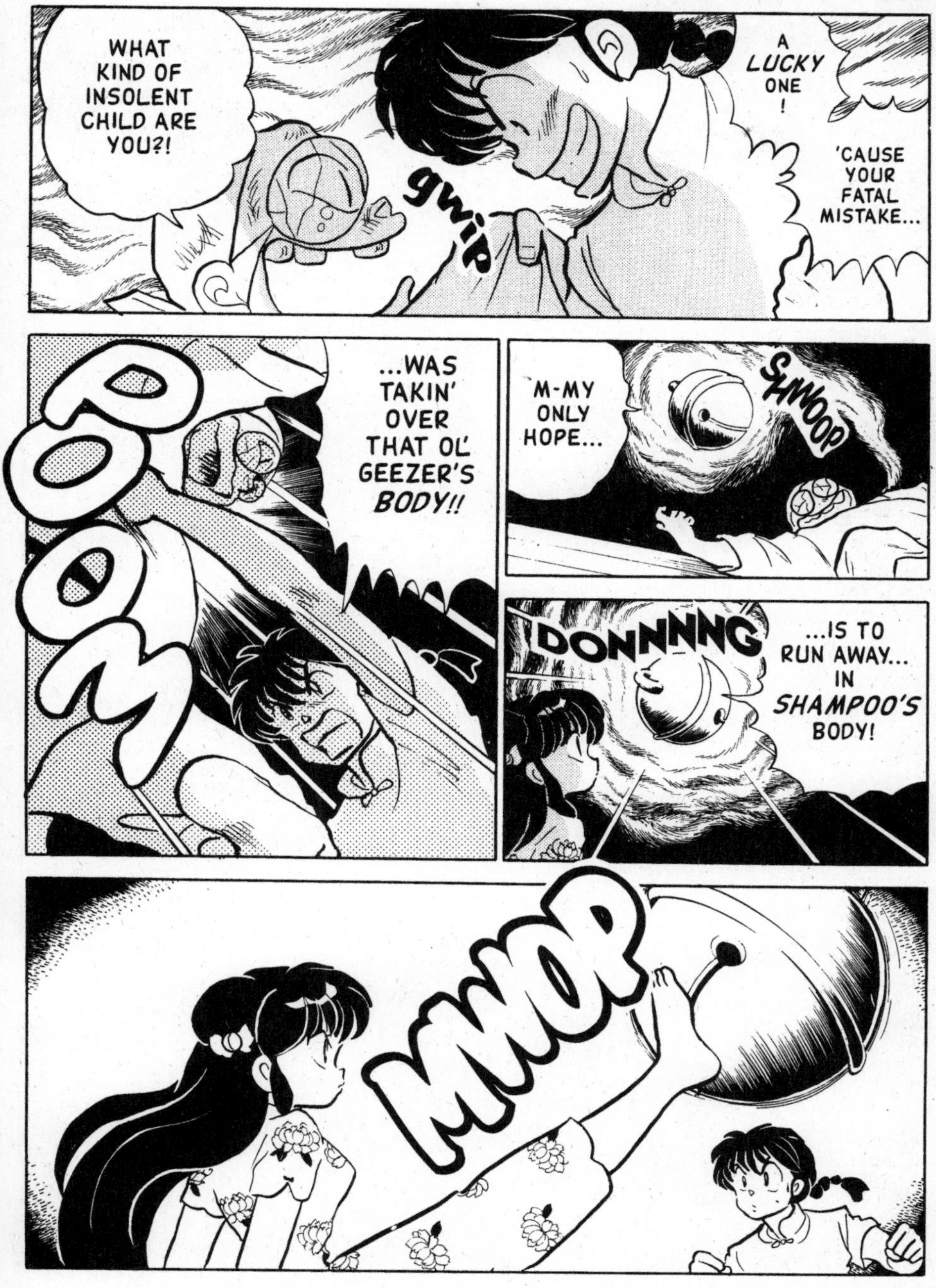
WHAT KIND OF INSOLENT CHILD ARE YOU?!
gwip
A LUCKY ONE!
'CAUSE YOUR FATAL MISTAKE...
POOOM
...WAS TAKIN' OVER THAT OL' GEEZER'S BODY!!
M-MY ONLY HOPE...
SHWOOP
DONNNNG
...IS TO RUN AWAY... IN SHAMPOO'S BODY!
MWOP

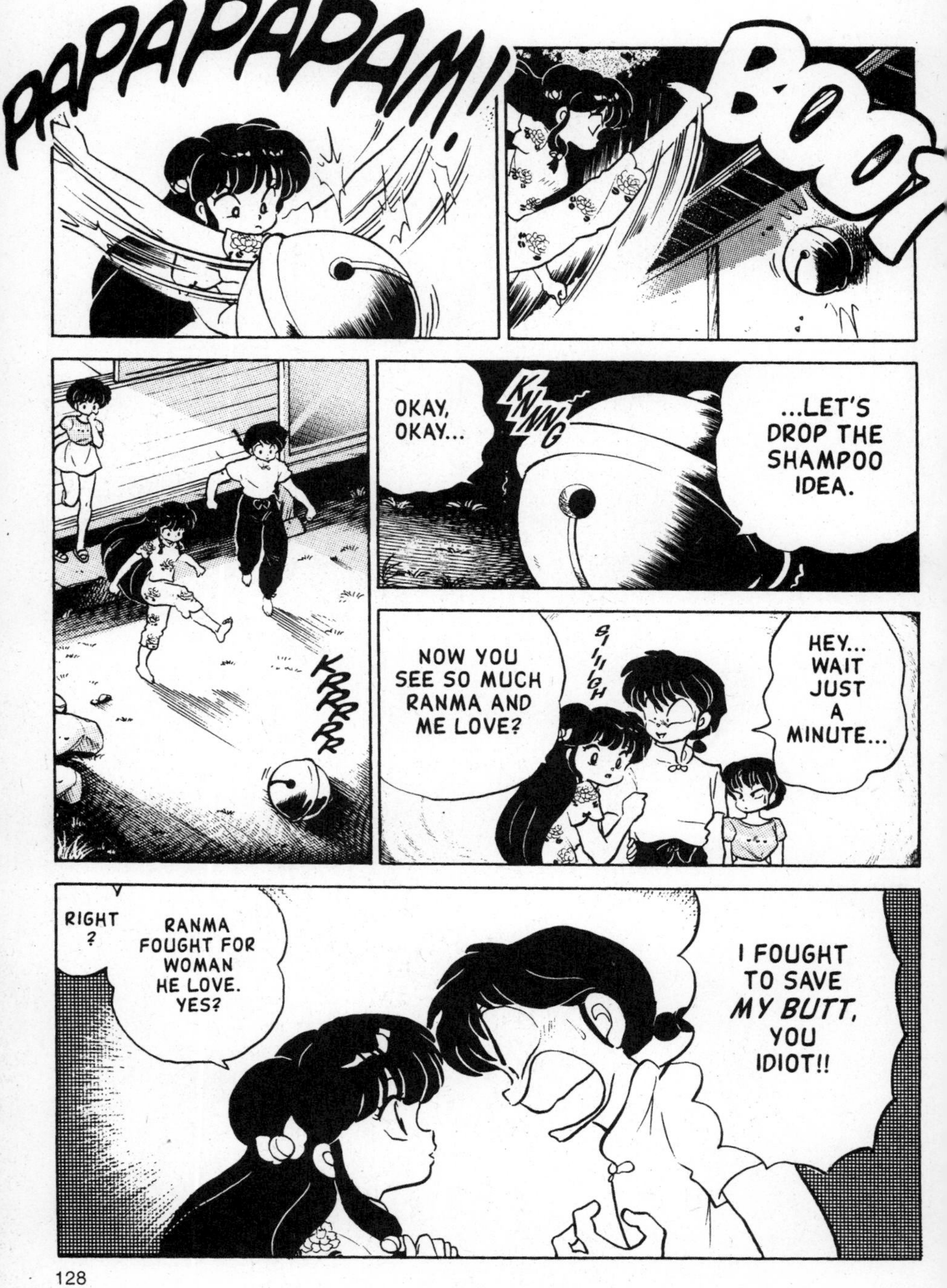
PAPAPAPAM!
BOO
KRRRRR
OKAY, OKAY...
KNNG
...LET'S DROP THE SHAMPOO IDEA.
NOW YOU SEE SO MUCH RANMA AND ME LOVE?
SIIIIGH
HEY... WAIT JUST A MINUTE...
RIGHT?
RANMA FOUGHT FOR WOMAN HE LOVE. YES?
I FOUGHT TO SAVE *MY BUTT*, YOU IDIOT!!

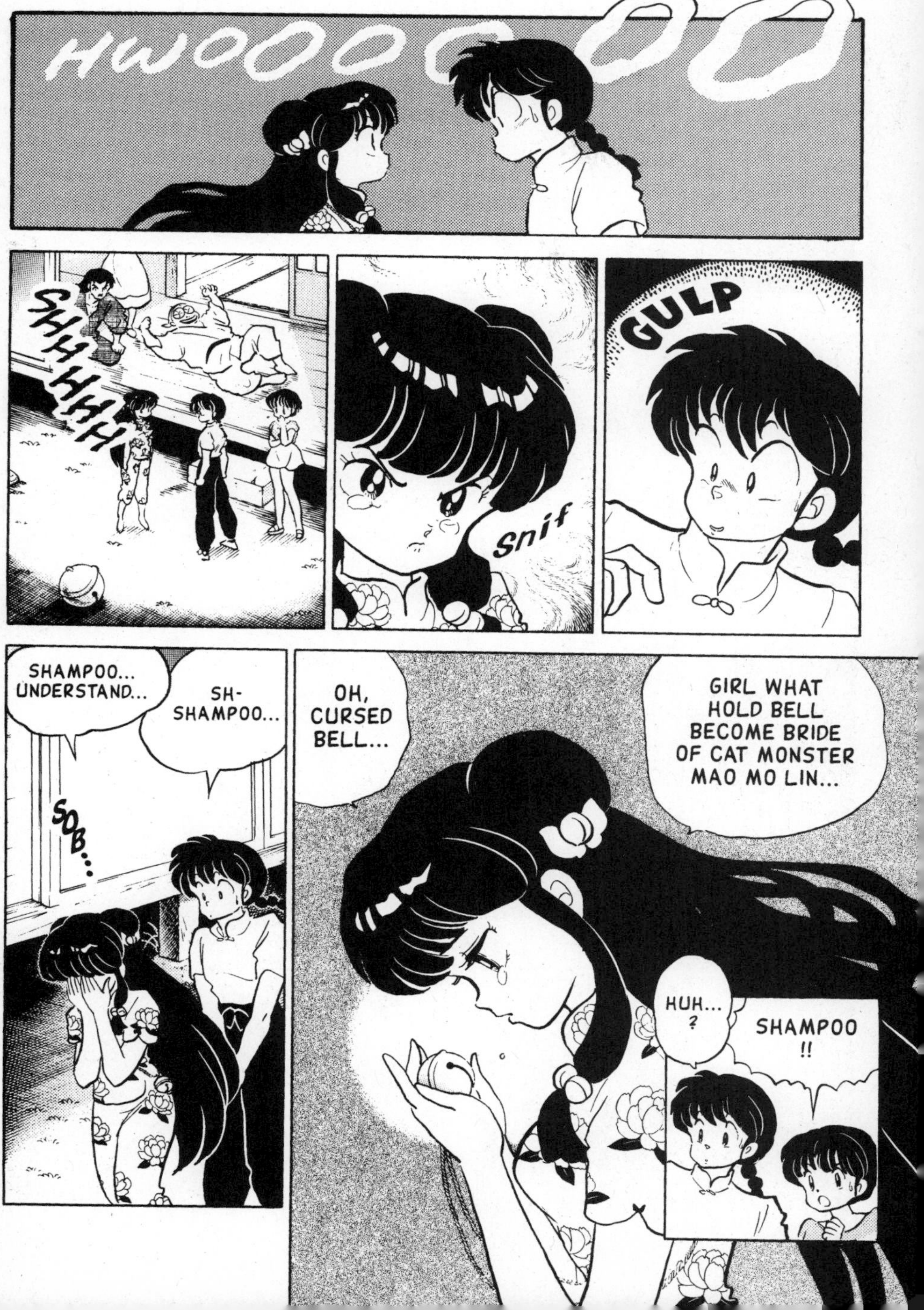
HWOOOOOO
SHHHHHH
Snif
GULP
SHAMPOO... UNDERSTAND...
SH- SHAMPOO...
SOB...
OH, CURSED BELL...
GIRL WHAT HOLD BELL BECOME BRIDE OF CAT MONSTER MAO MO LIN...
HUH... ?
SHAMPOO !!

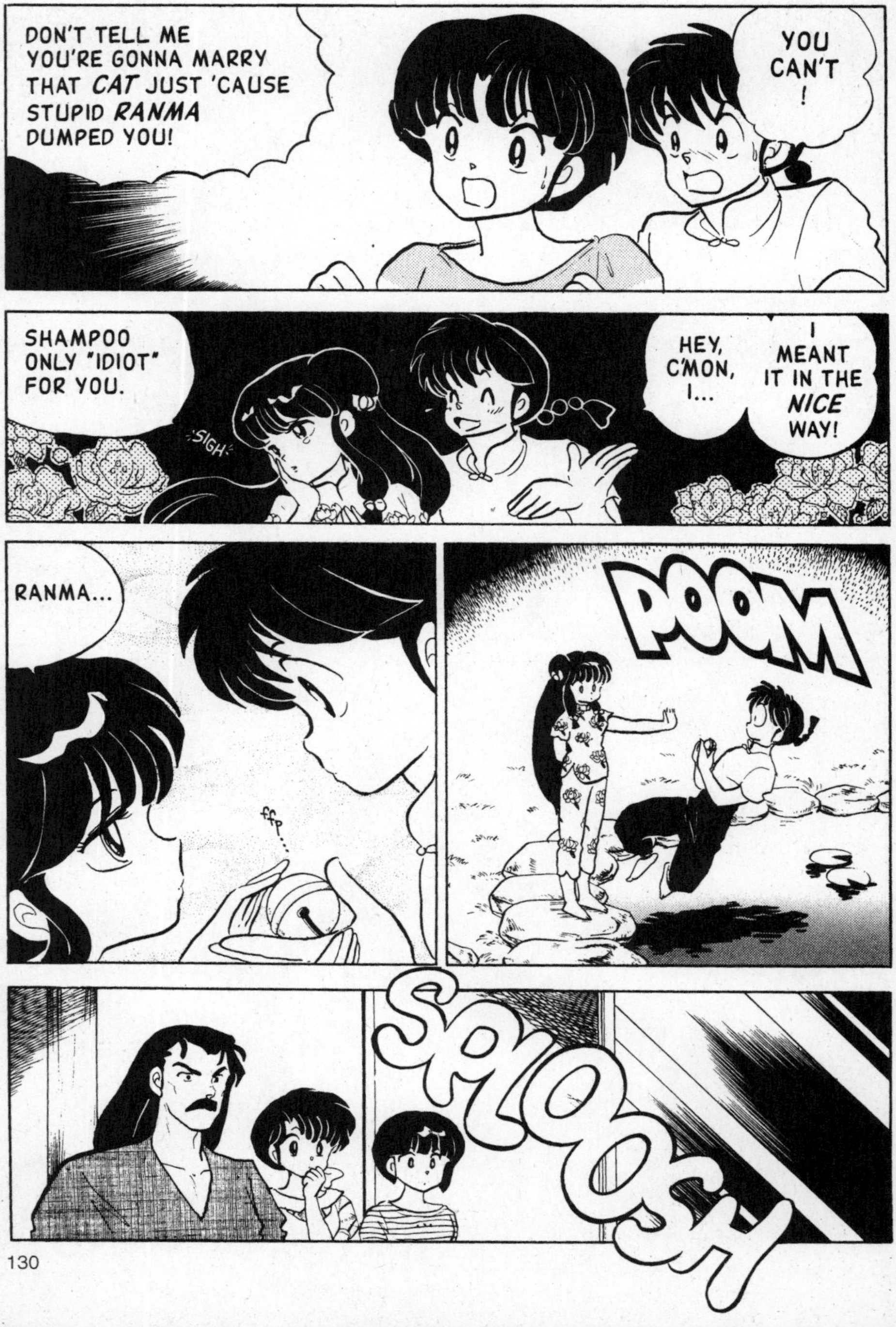
DON'T TELL ME YOU'RE GONNA MARRY THAT CAT JUST 'CAUSE STUPID RANMA DUMPED YOU!
YOU CAN'T !
SHAMPOO ONLY "IDIOT" FOR YOU.
SIGH
HEY, C'MON, I...
I MEANT IT IN THE NICE WAY!
RANMA...
ffp...
POOM
SPLOOSH

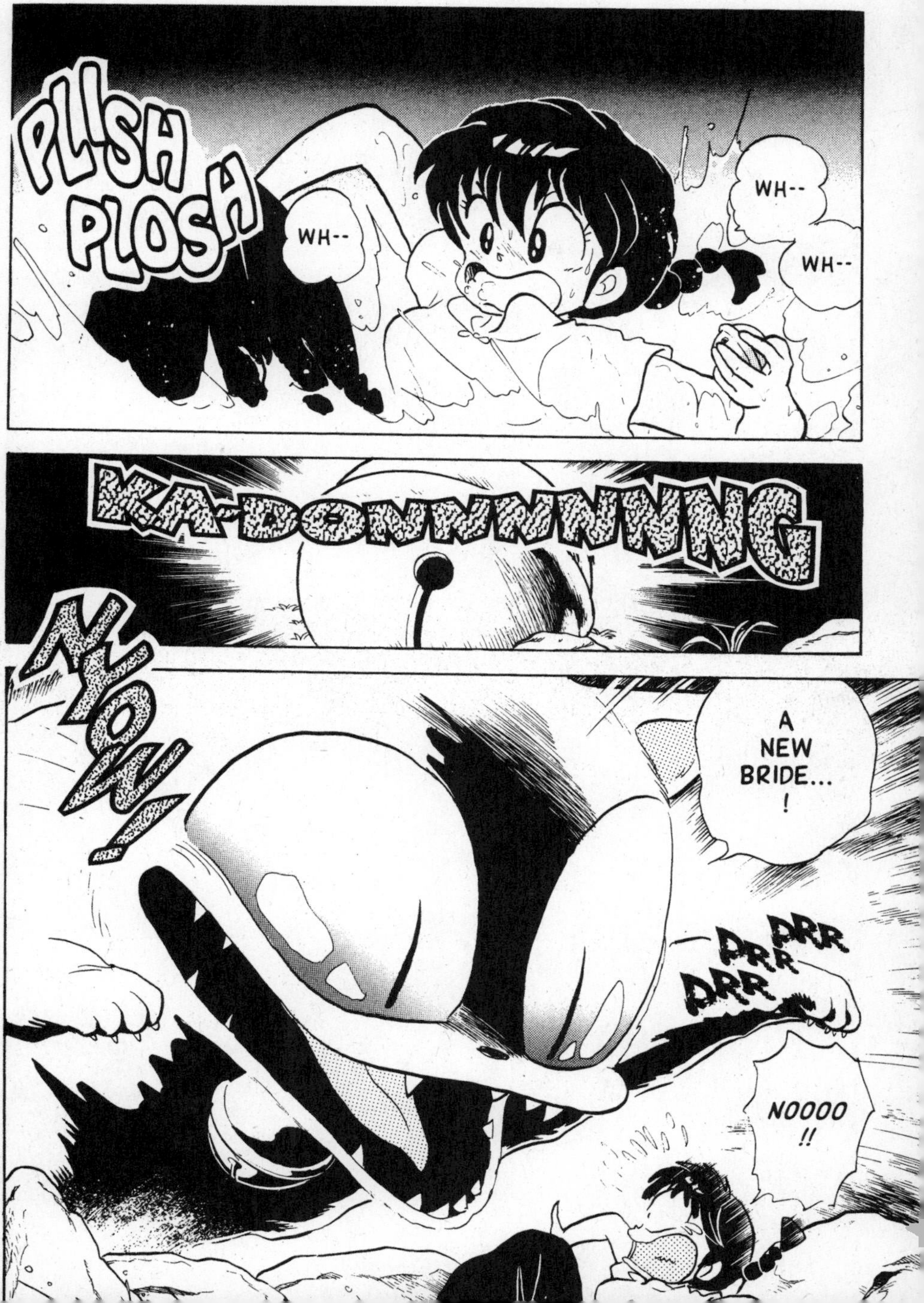
PLISH PLOSH
WH--
WH--
WH--
KA-DONNNNNNG
MYOW!
A NEW BRIDE... !
RRR RRR RRR
NOOOO !!

OOO, SHE'S CUTE!

PRR PRR PRR

LEGGO O' ME!

SS

URK.

SLURP!

BRR BRR BRR

POP!

SHHHHHH

NO!!

THAT SOUND... CAN IT BE !?

RANMA...?

MEE-OW!

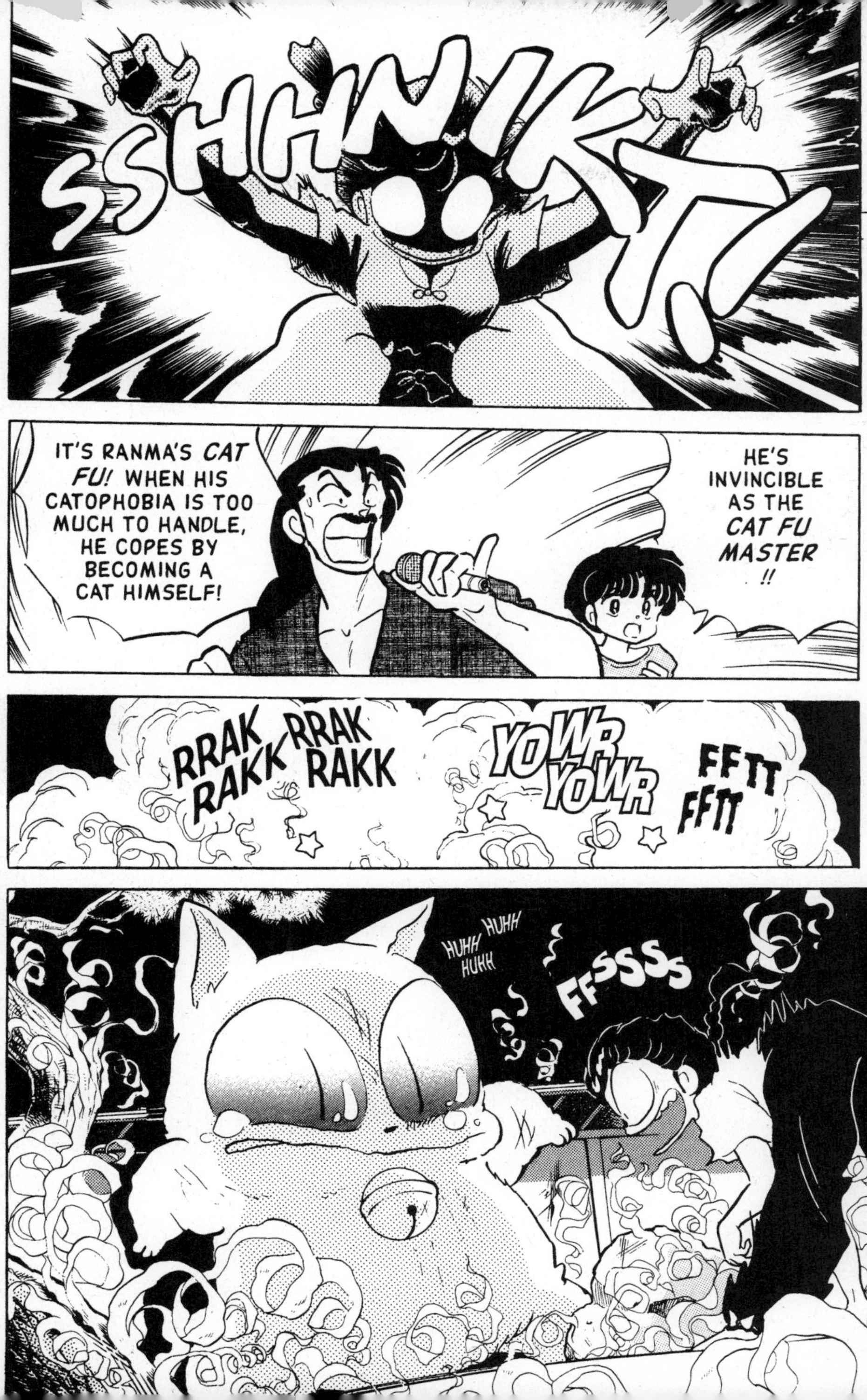
SSHHNIKT!!
IT'S RANMA'S CAT FU! WHEN HIS CATOPHOBIA IS TOO MUCH TO HANDLE, HE COPES BY BECOMING A CAT HIMSELF!
HE'S INVINCIBLE AS THE CAT FU MASTER !!
RRAK RAKK
RRAK RAKK
YOWR YOWR
FFTT FFTT
HUHH HUHH
HUHH
FFSSSS

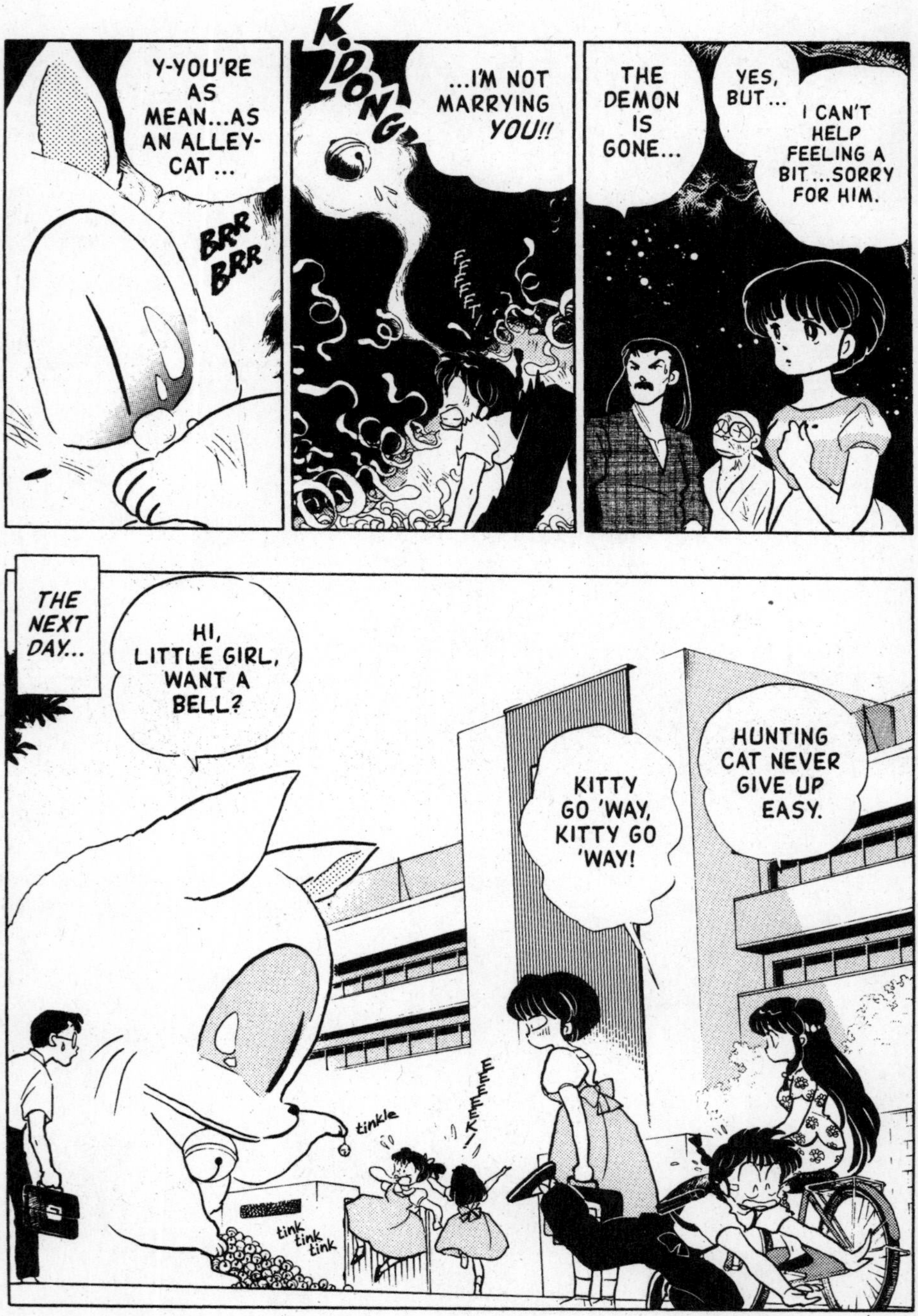
Y-YOU'RE AS MEAN...AS AN ALLEY-CAT...
BRR BRR
K-DONG
...I'M NOT MARRYING *YOU!!*
FFFFT!
THE DEMON IS GONE...
YES, BUT...
I CAN'T HELP FEELING A BIT...SORRY FOR HIM.
THE NEXT DAY...
HI, LITTLE GIRL, WANT A BELL?
KITTY GO 'WAY, KITTY GO 'WAY!
HUNTING CAT NEVER GIVE UP EASY.
tinkle
EEEEK
tink tink tink

PART 9
SWIM LIKE A HAMMER

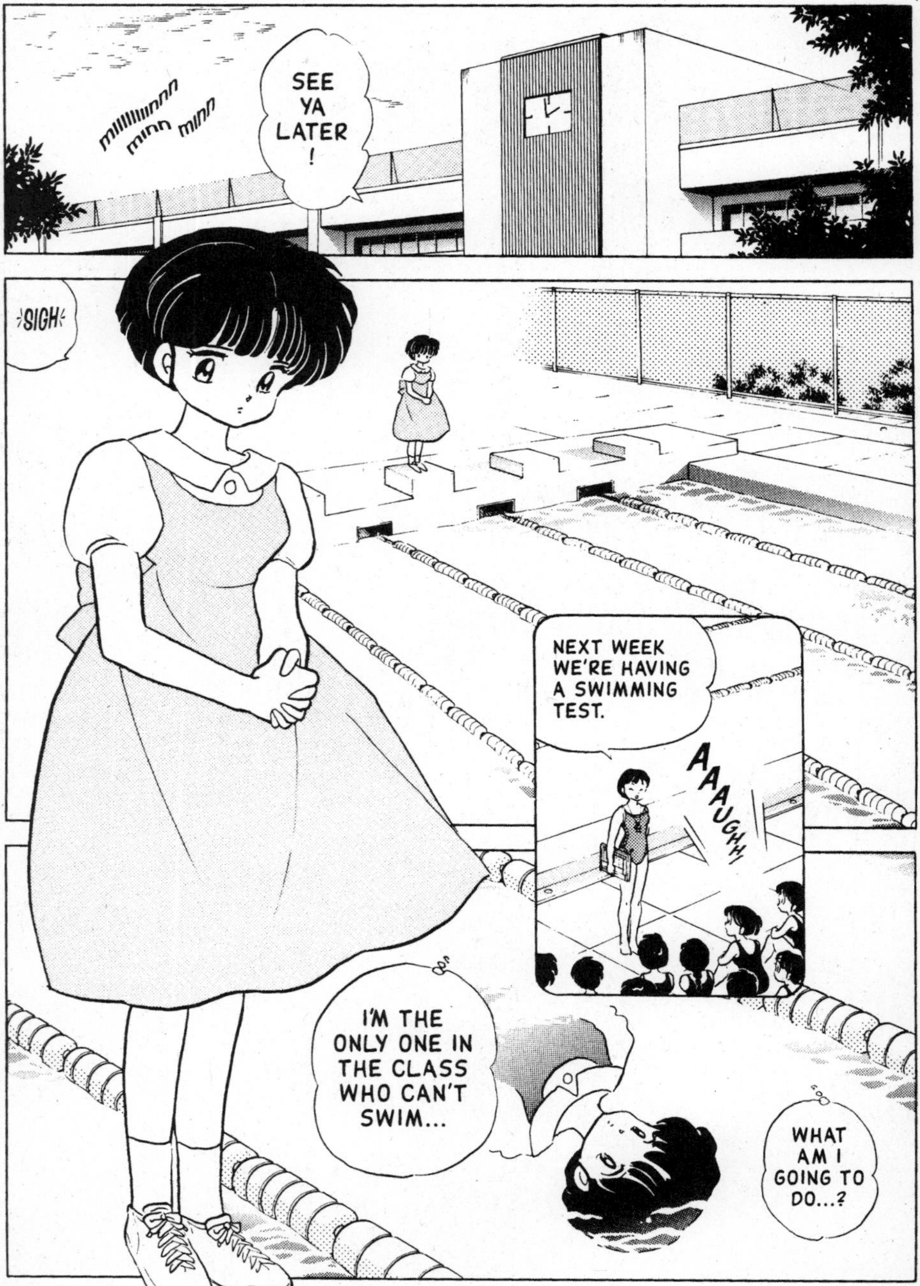

MIIIIIIINNN MINN MINN
SEE YA LATER!
SIGH
NEXT WEEK WE'RE HAVING A SWIMMING TEST.
AAAUGH!
I'M THE ONLY ONE IN THE CLASS WHO CAN'T SWIM...
WHAT AM I GOING TO DO...?

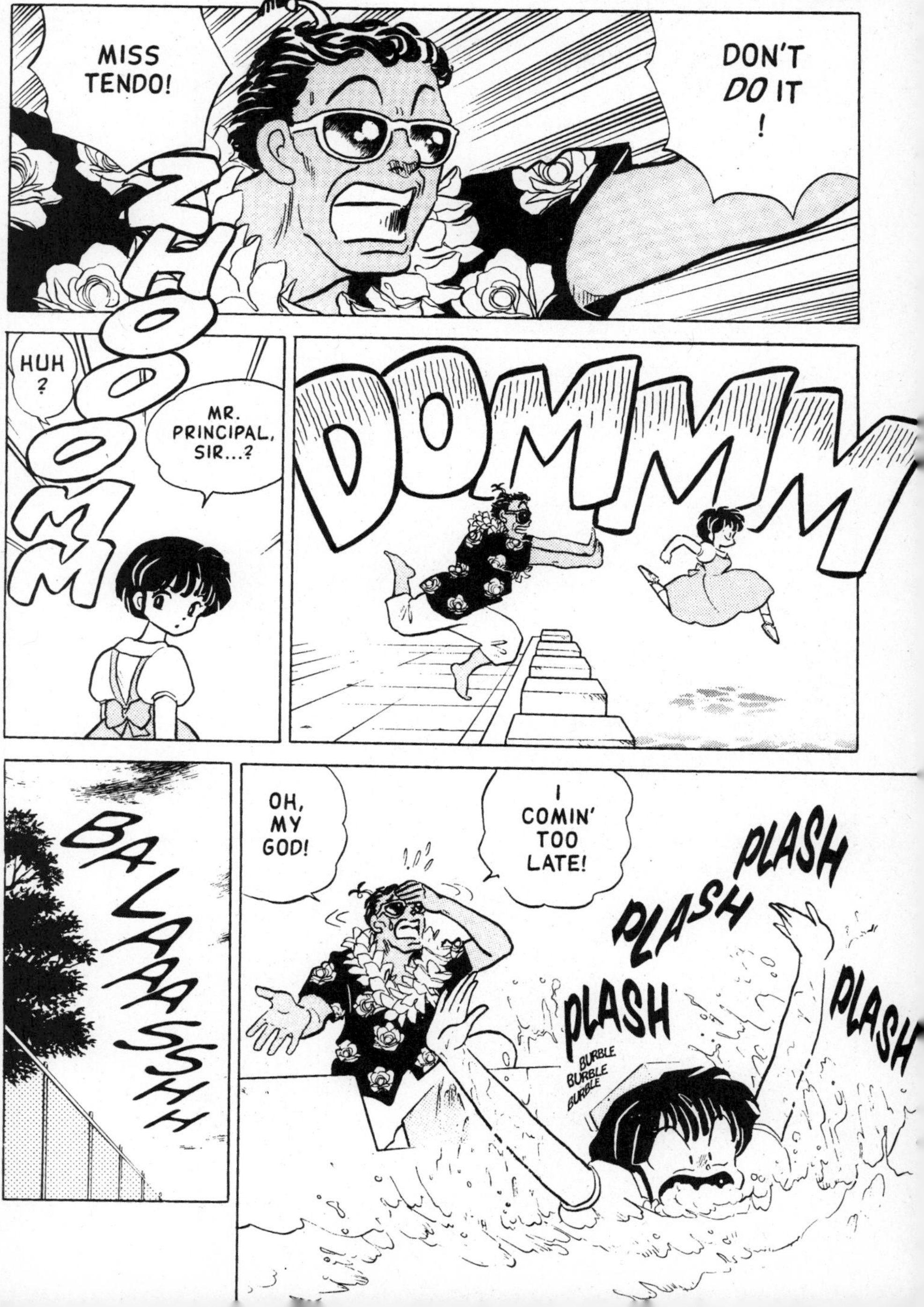
MISS TENDO!
DON'T DO IT !
ZHOOOOOMMM
HUH ?
MR. PRINCIPAL, SIR...?
DOMMM
BA LAAASSHH
OH, MY GOD!
I COMIN' TOO LATE!
PLASH
PLASH
PLASH
PLASH
BURBLE BURBLE BURBLE

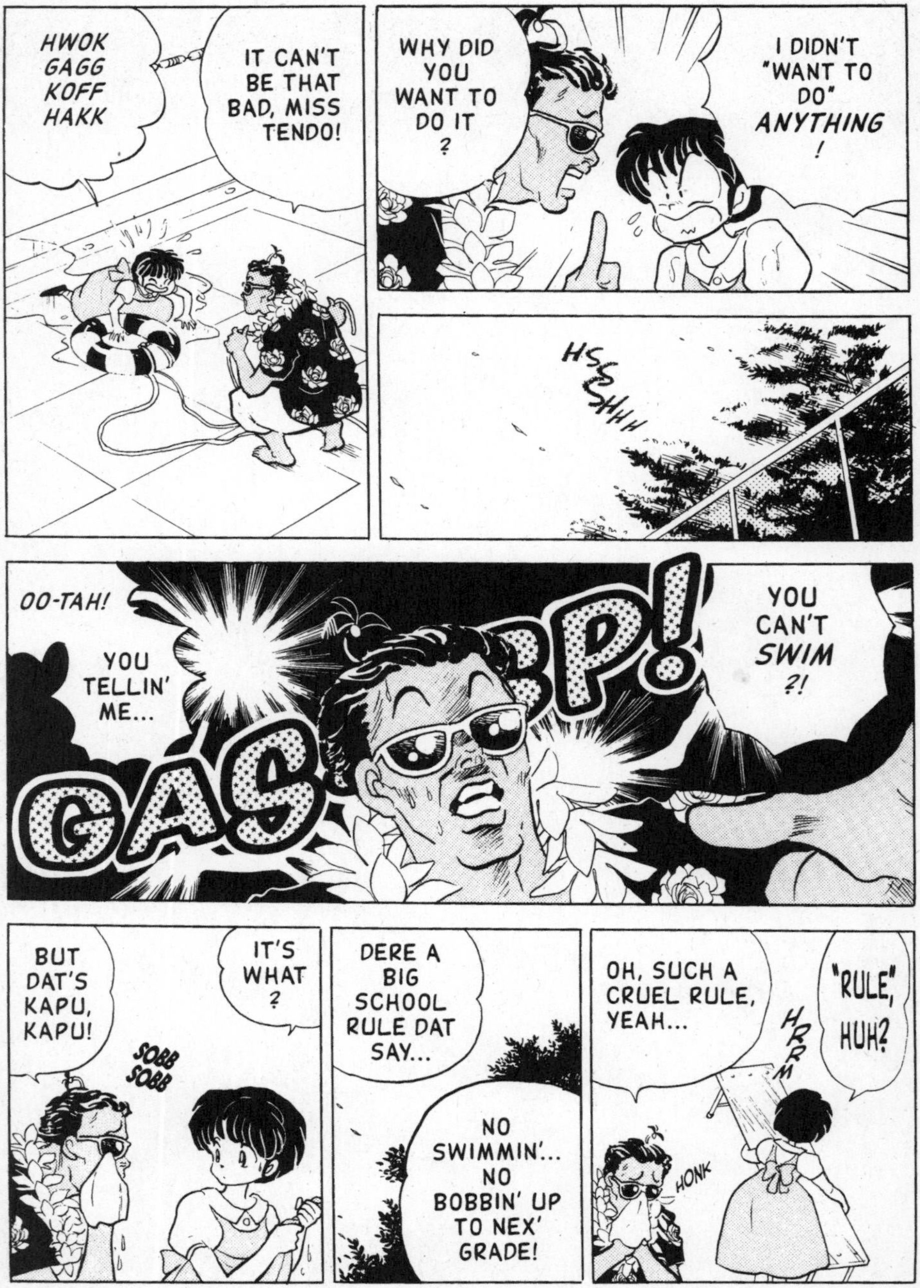
HWOK GAGG KOFF HAKK
IT CAN'T BE THAT BAD, MISS TENDO!
WHY DID YOU WANT TO DO IT ?
I DIDN'T "WANT TO DO" ANYTHING !
HSSSHHH
OO-TAH!
YOU TELLIN' ME...
GAS P!
YOU CAN'T SWIM ?!
BUT DAT'S KAPU, KAPU!
IT'S WHAT ?
SOBB SOBB
DERE A BIG SCHOOL RULE DAT SAY...
NO SWIMMIN'... NO BOBBIN' UP TO NEX' GRADE!
OH, SUCH A CRUEL RULE, YEAH...
HRRM
"RULE," HUH?
HONK

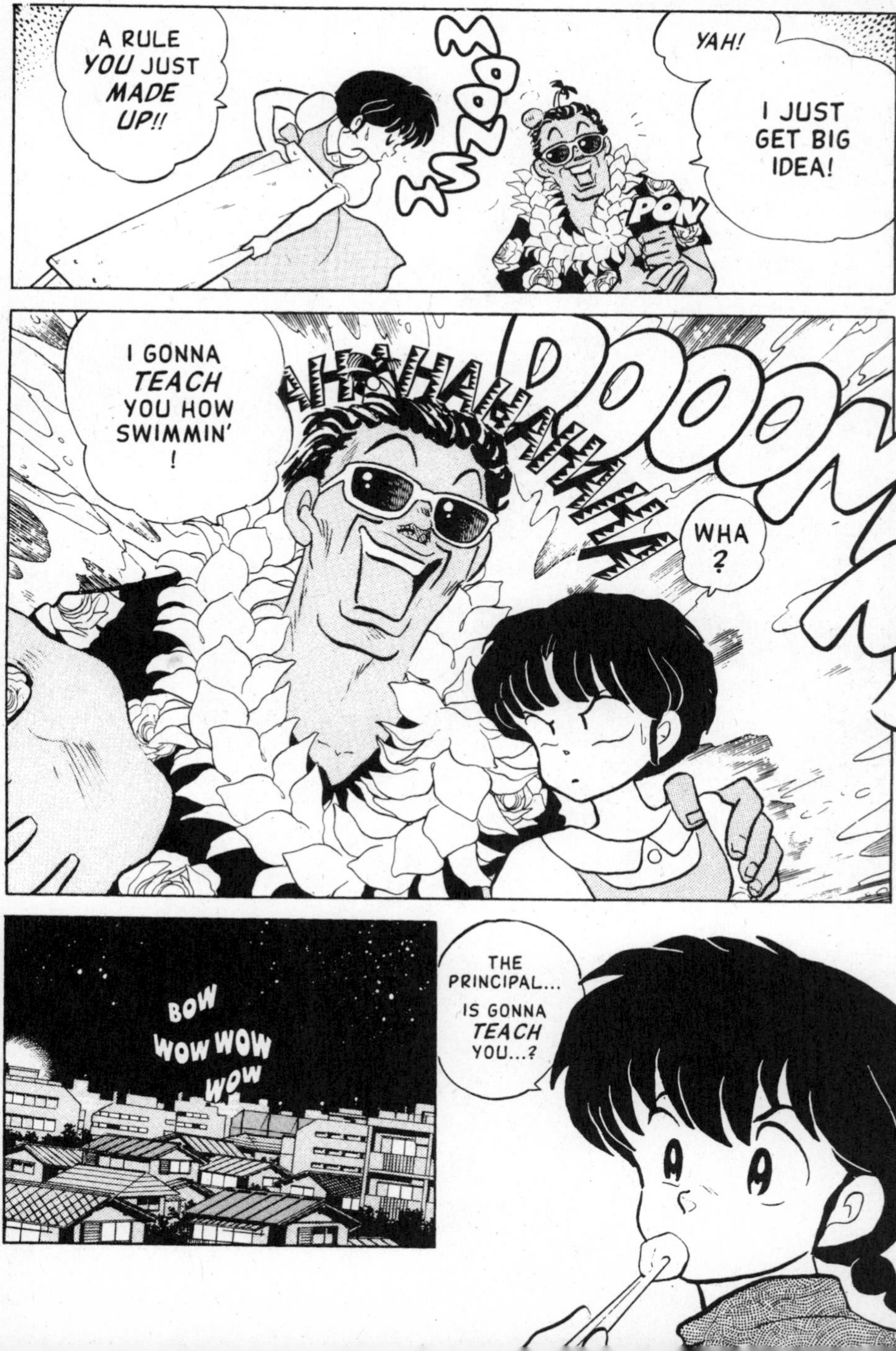
A RULE *YOU* JUST *MADE UP*!!
WOOSH
YAH!
I JUST GET BIG IDEA!
PON
I GONNA *TEACH* YOU HOW SWIMMIN' !
AH HA HA HA HA HA
DOOOMM
WHA ?
BOW WOW WOW WOW
THE PRINCIPAL...
IS GONNA *TEACH* YOU...?

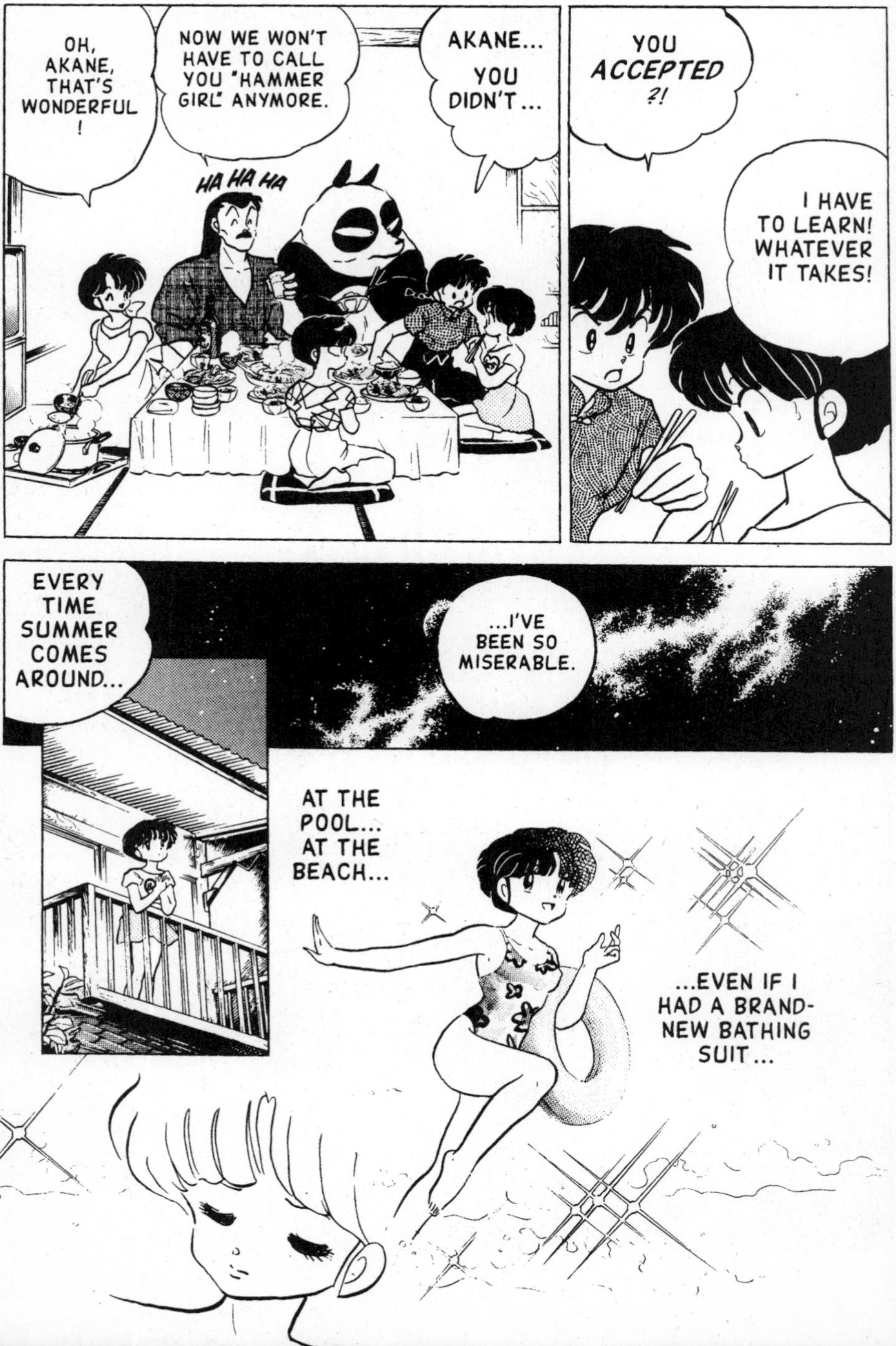
OH, AKANE, THAT'S WONDERFUL!
NOW WE WON'T HAVE TO CALL YOU "HAMMER GIRL" ANYMORE.
HA HA HA
AKANE... YOU DIDN'T...
YOU ACCEPTED ?!
I HAVE TO LEARN! WHATEVER IT TAKES!
EVERY TIME SUMMER COMES AROUND...
...I'VE BEEN SO MISERABLE.
AT THE POOL... AT THE BEACH...
...EVEN IF I HAD A BRAND-NEW BATHING SUIT...

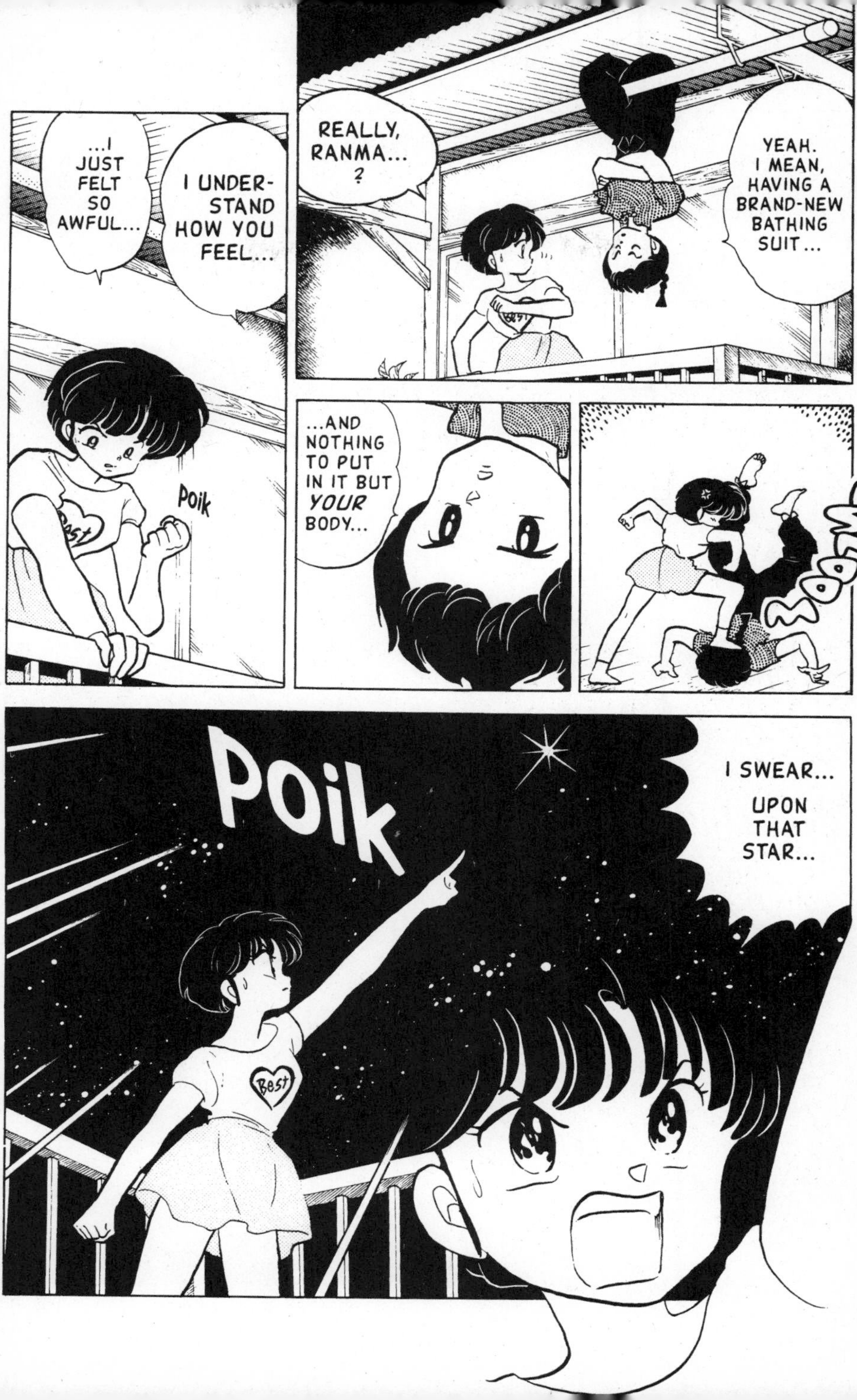
...I JUST FELT SO AWFUL...
I UNDERSTAND HOW YOU FEEL...
Poik
REALLY, RANMA...?
YEAH. I MEAN, HAVING A BRAND-NEW BATHING SUIT...
...AND NOTHING TO PUT IN IT BUT *YOUR* BODY...
WOOMP
Poik
I SWEAR... UPON THAT STAR...

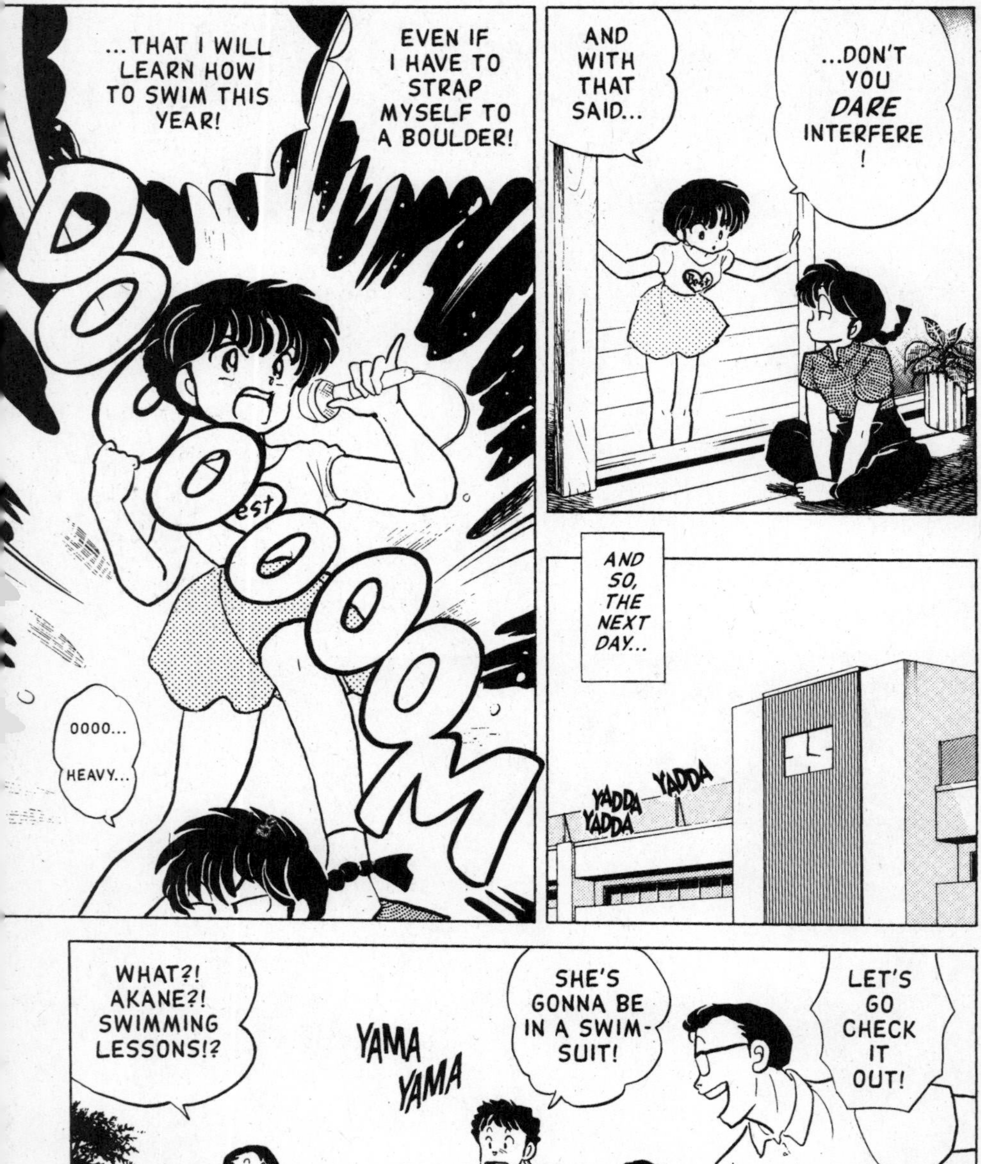
...THAT I WILL LEARN HOW TO SWIM THIS YEAR!
EVEN IF I HAVE TO STRAP MYSELF TO A BOULDER!
DOOOOOOOM
OOOO...
HEAVY...
AND WITH THAT SAID...
...DON'T YOU *DARE* INTERFERE !
AND SO, THE NEXT DAY...
YADDA YADDA
YADDA
WHAT?! AKANE?! SWIMMING LESSONS!?
YAMA YAMA
SHE'S GONNA BE IN A SWIM-SUIT!
LET'S GO CHECK IT OUT!

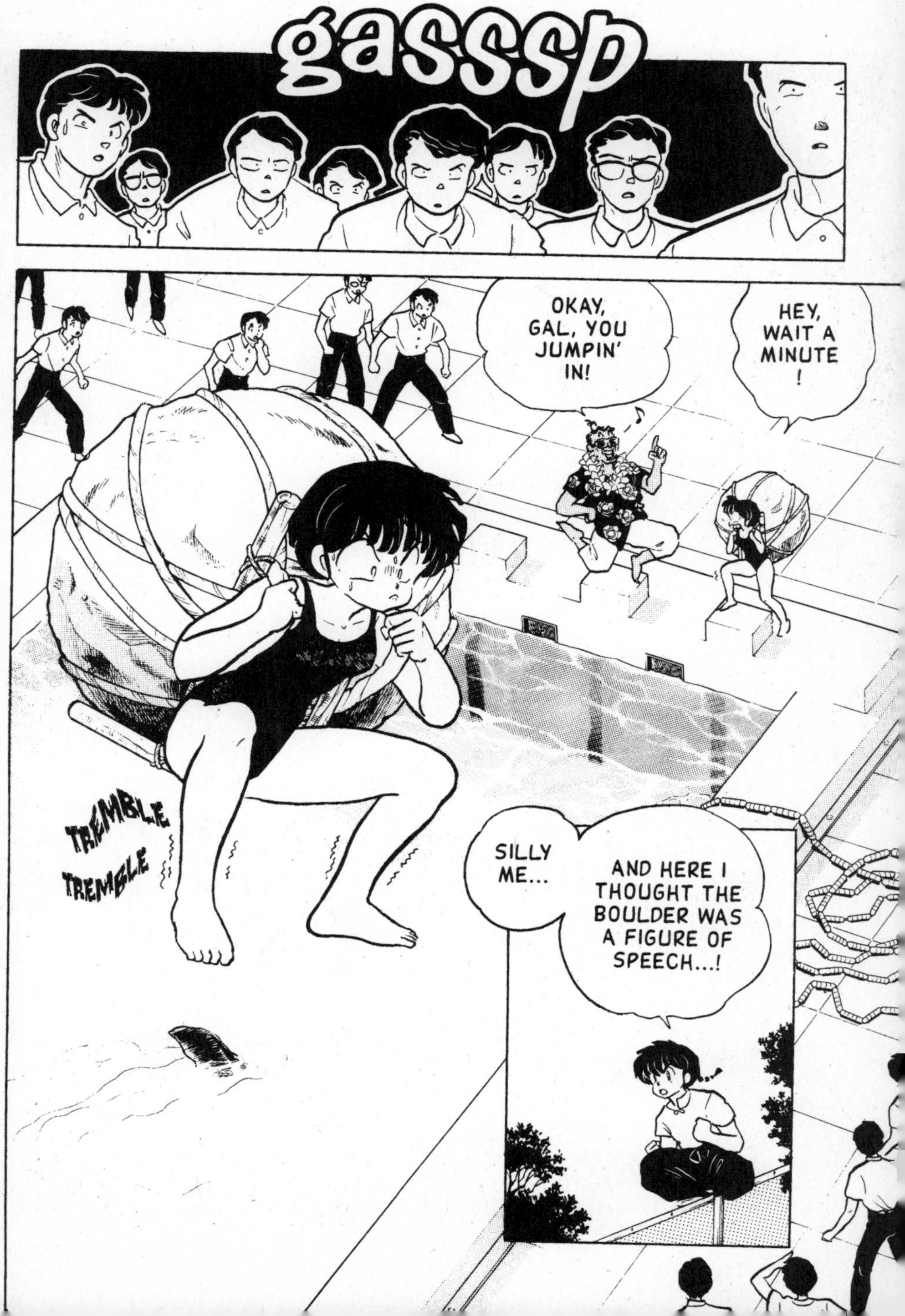
gasssp
OKAY, GAL, YOU JUMPIN' IN!
HEY, WAIT A MINUTE!
TREMBLE TREMBLE
SILLY ME...
AND HERE I THOUGHT THE BOULDER WAS A FIGURE OF SPEECH...!

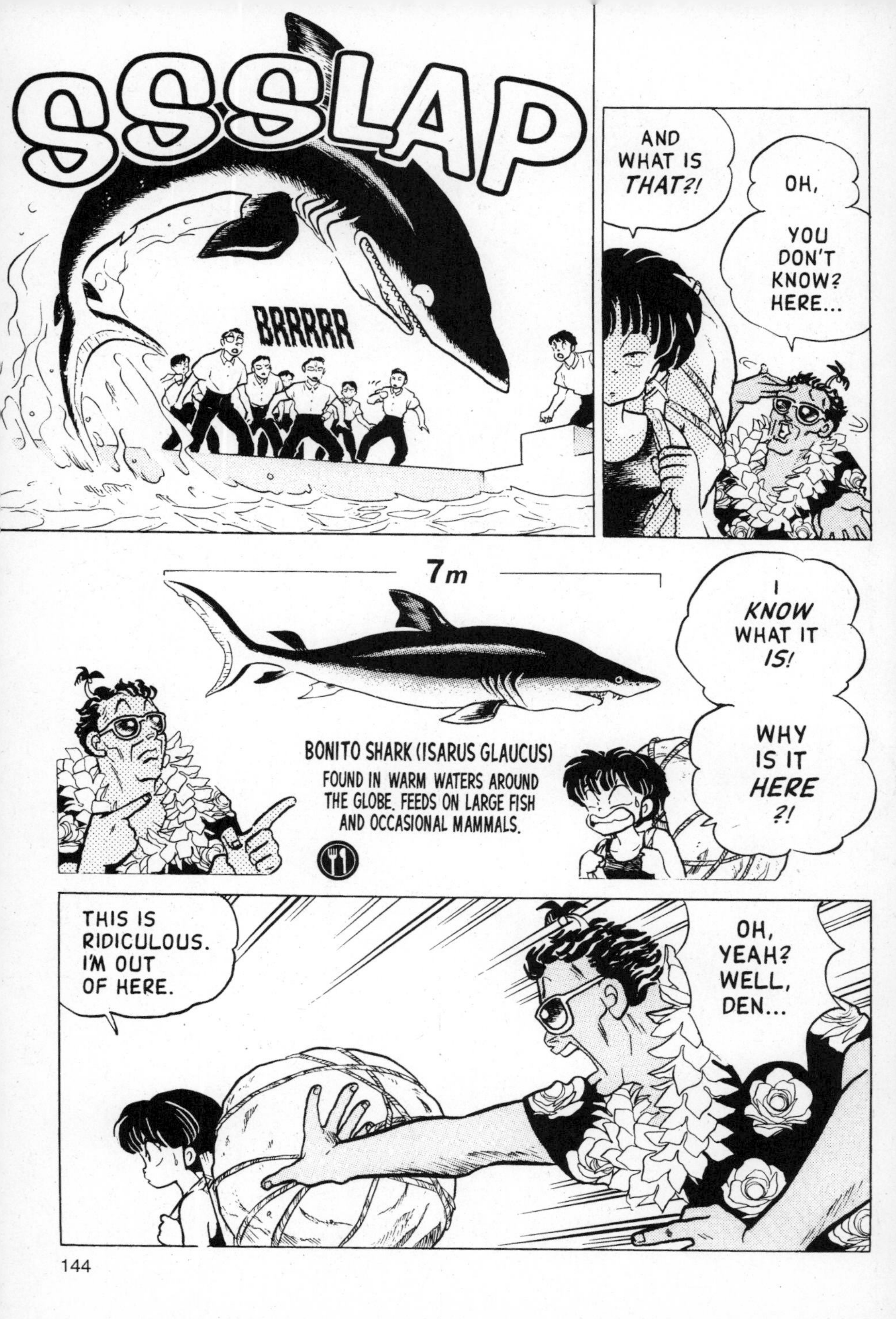
SSSLAP
BRRRRR
AND WHAT IS *THAT?!*
OH,
YOU DON'T KNOW? HERE...
7m
BONITO SHARK (ISARUS GLAUCUS)
FOUND IN WARM WATERS AROUND THE GLOBE. FEEDS ON LARGE FISH AND OCCASIONAL MAMMALS.
I *KNOW* WHAT IT *IS!*
WHY IS IT *HERE ?!*
THIS IS RIDICULOUS. I'M OUT OF HERE.
OH, YEAH? WELL, DEN...

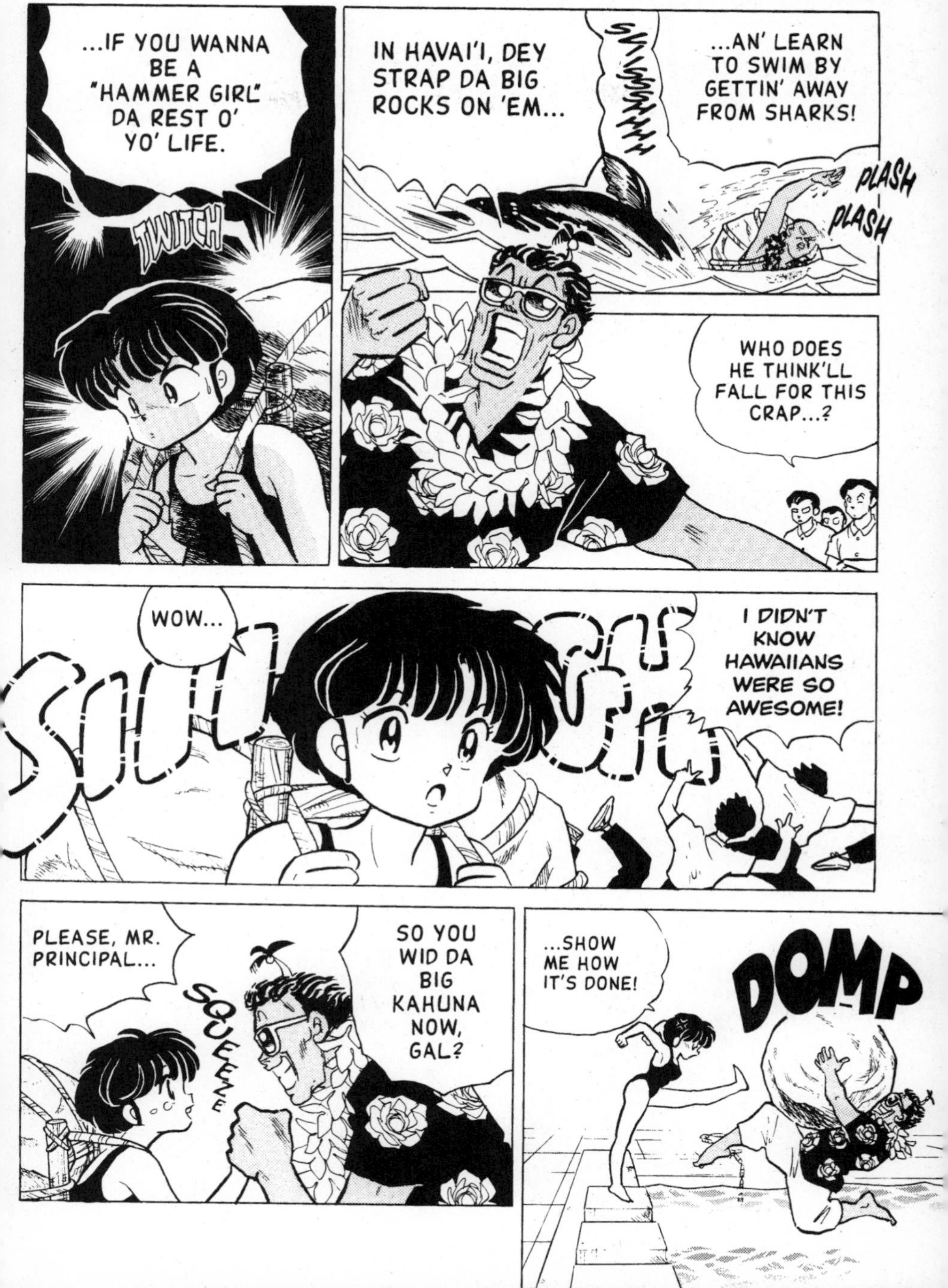
...IF YOU WANNA BE A "HAMMER GIRL" DA REST O' YO' LIFE.
TWITCH
IN HAVAI'I, DEY STRAP DA BIG ROCKS ON 'EM...
...AN' LEARN TO SWIM BY GETTIN' AWAY FROM SHARKS!
PLASH
PLASH
WHO DOES HE THINK'LL FALL FOR THIS CRAP...?
WOW...
I DIDN'T KNOW HAWAIIANS WERE SO AWESOME!
PLEASE, MR. PRINCIPAL...
SO YOU WID DA BIG KAHUNA NOW, GAL?
...SHOW ME HOW IT'S DONE!
DOMP

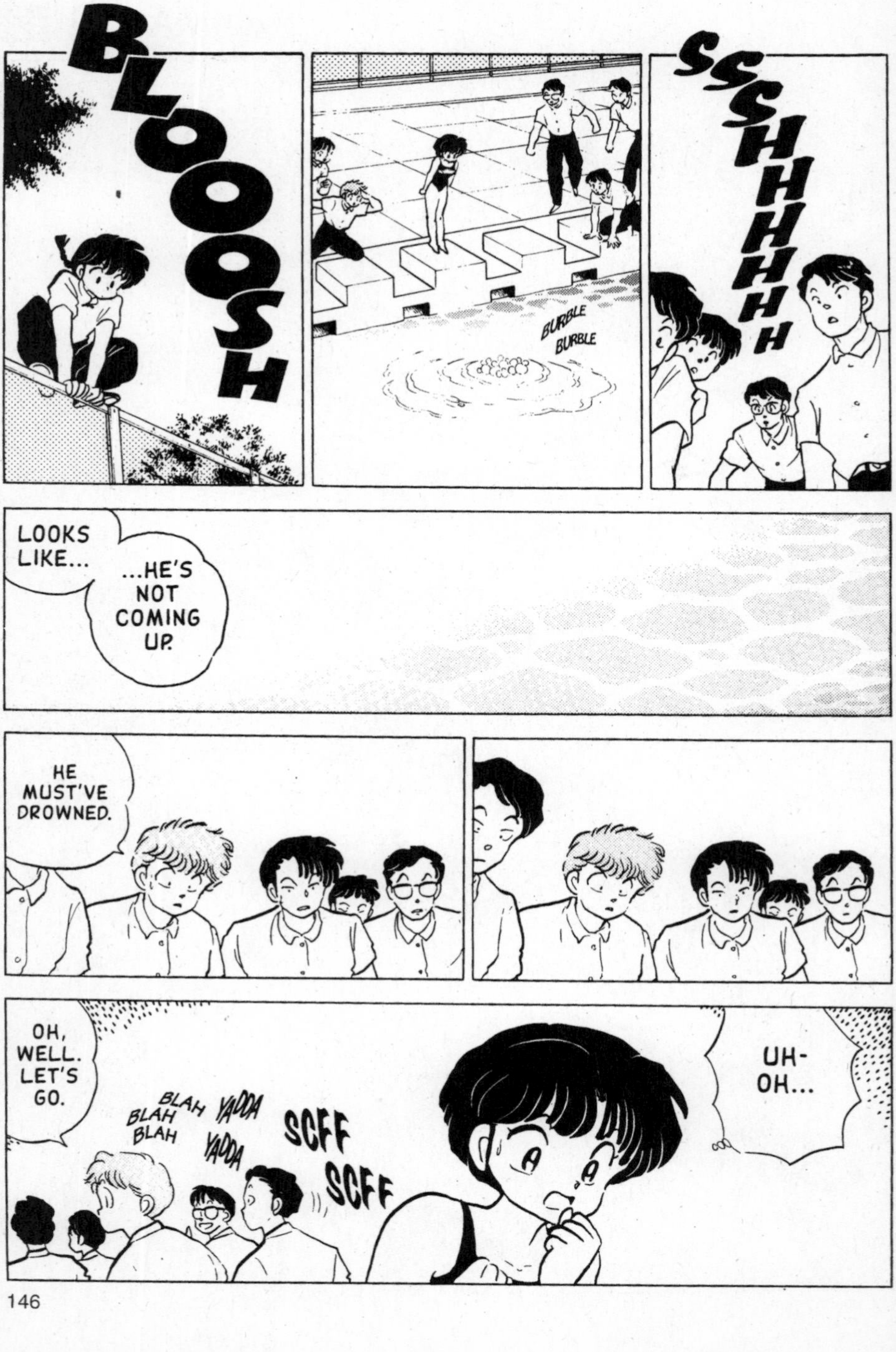
BLOOOOSH
BURBLE
BURBLE
SSSHHHHHH
LOOKS LIKE...
...HE'S NOT COMING UP.
HE MUST'VE DROWNED.
OH, WELL. LET'S GO.
BLAH BLAH BLAH
YADDA YADDA
SCFF SCFF
UH-OH...

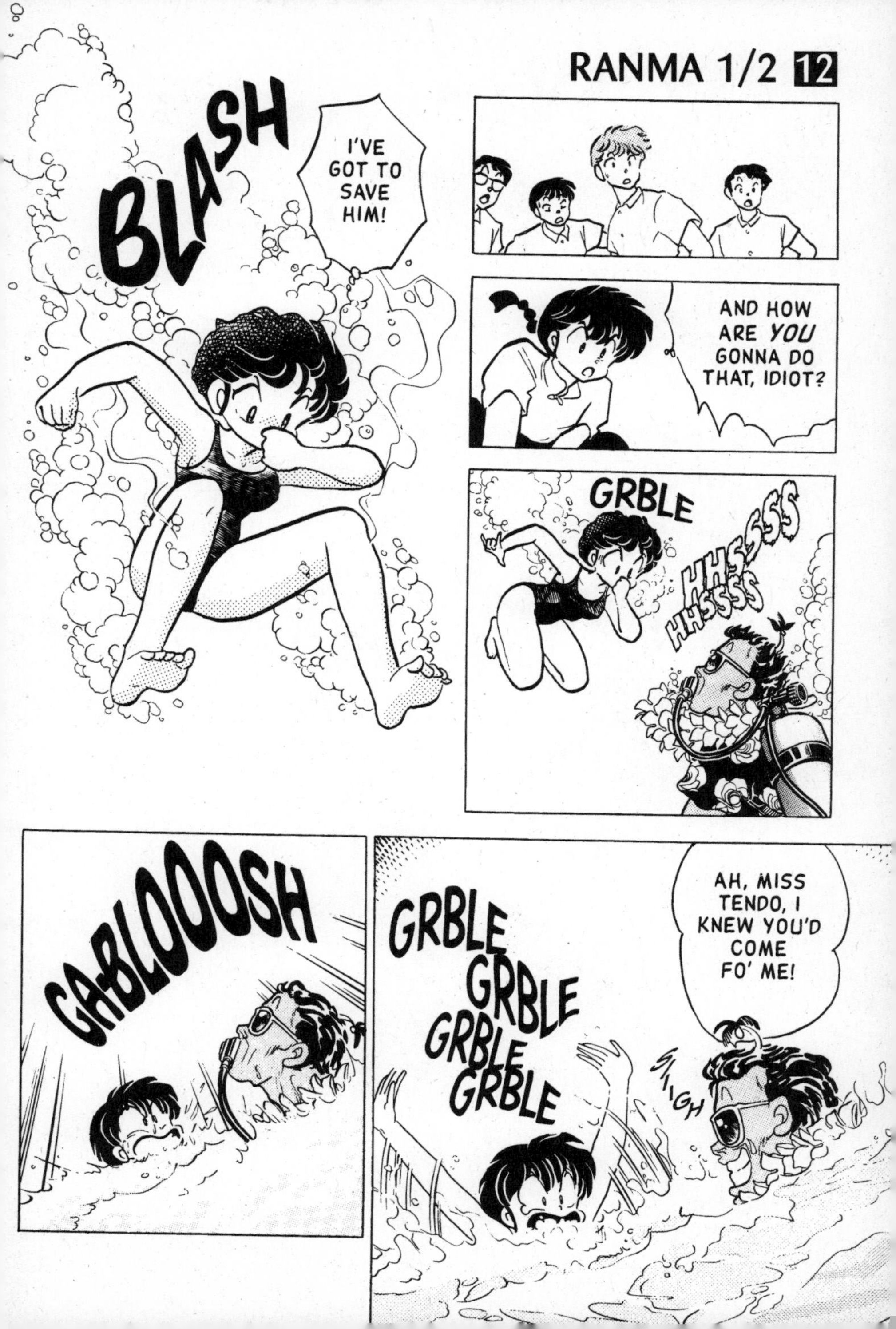
BLASH
I'VE GOT TO SAVE HIM!
AND HOW ARE *YOU* GONNA DO THAT, IDIOT?
GRBLE
HHS-SSSS
HHSSSSS
GA-BLOOOSH
GRBLE GRBLE GRBLE GRBLE
AH, MISS TENDO, I KNEW YOU'D COME FO' ME!

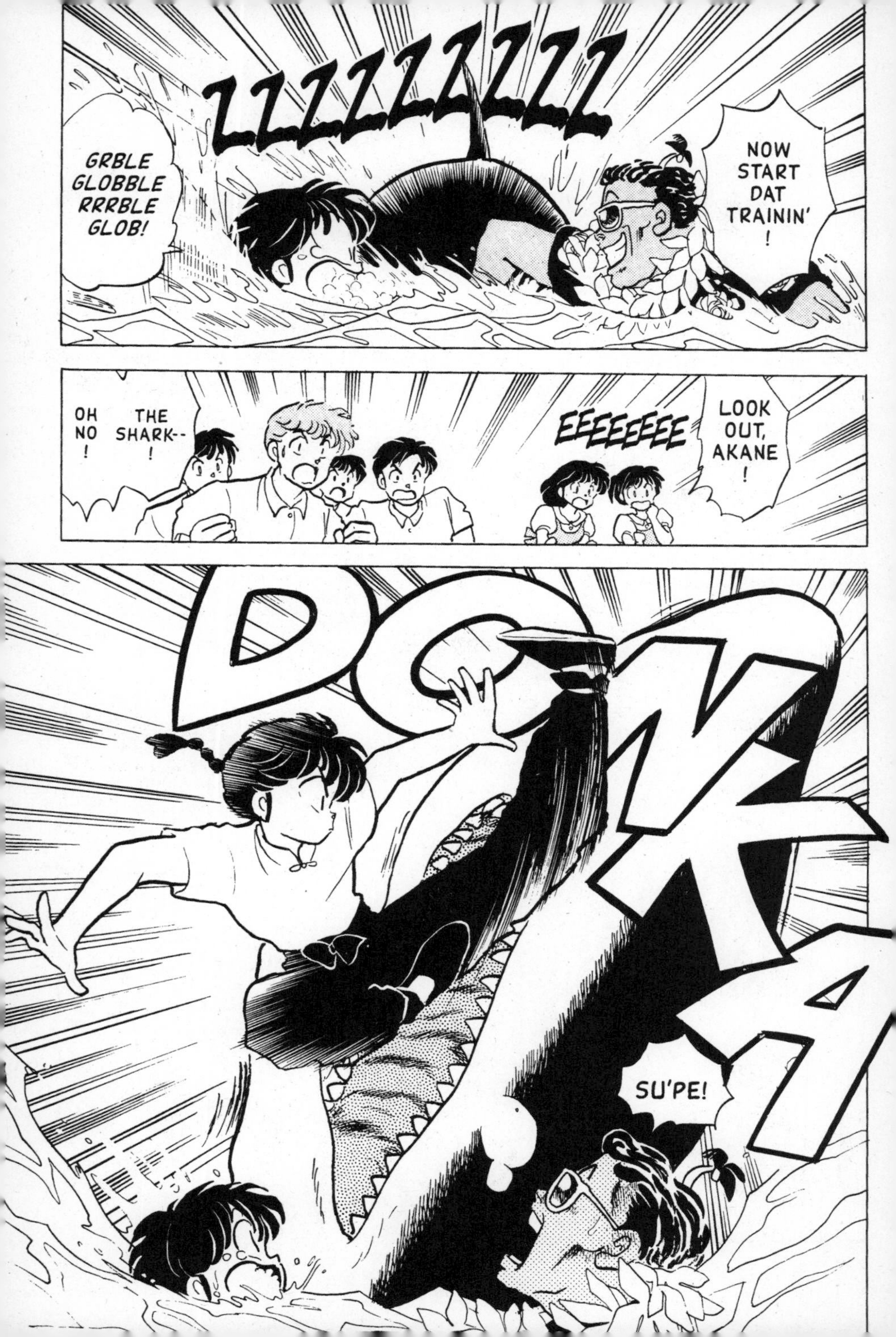
ZZZZZZZZZZ
GRBLE GLOBBLE RRRBLE GLOB!
NOW START DAT TRAININ'!
OH NO!
THE SHARK--!
EEEEEEEEE
LOOK OUT, AKANE!
DOKA
SU'PE!

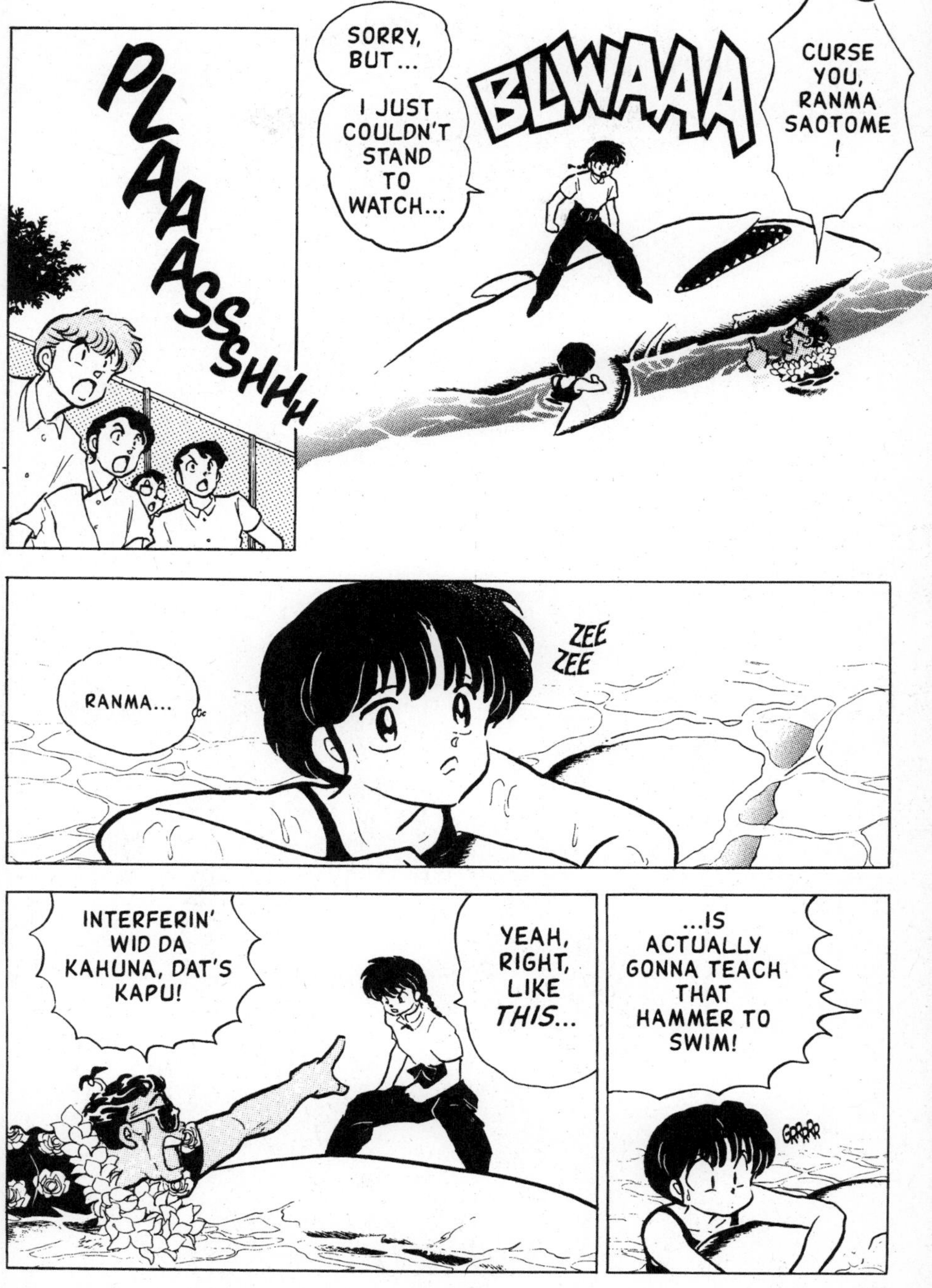
PLAAAASSSHHHH
SORRY, BUT...
I JUST COULDN'T STAND TO WATCH...
BLWAAA
CURSE YOU, RANMA SAOTOME!
RANMA...
ZEE ZEE
INTERFERIN' WID DA KAHUNA, DAT'S KAPU!
YEAH, RIGHT, LIKE *THIS*...
...IS ACTUALLY GONNA TEACH THAT HAMMER TO SWIM!
GRRRRR

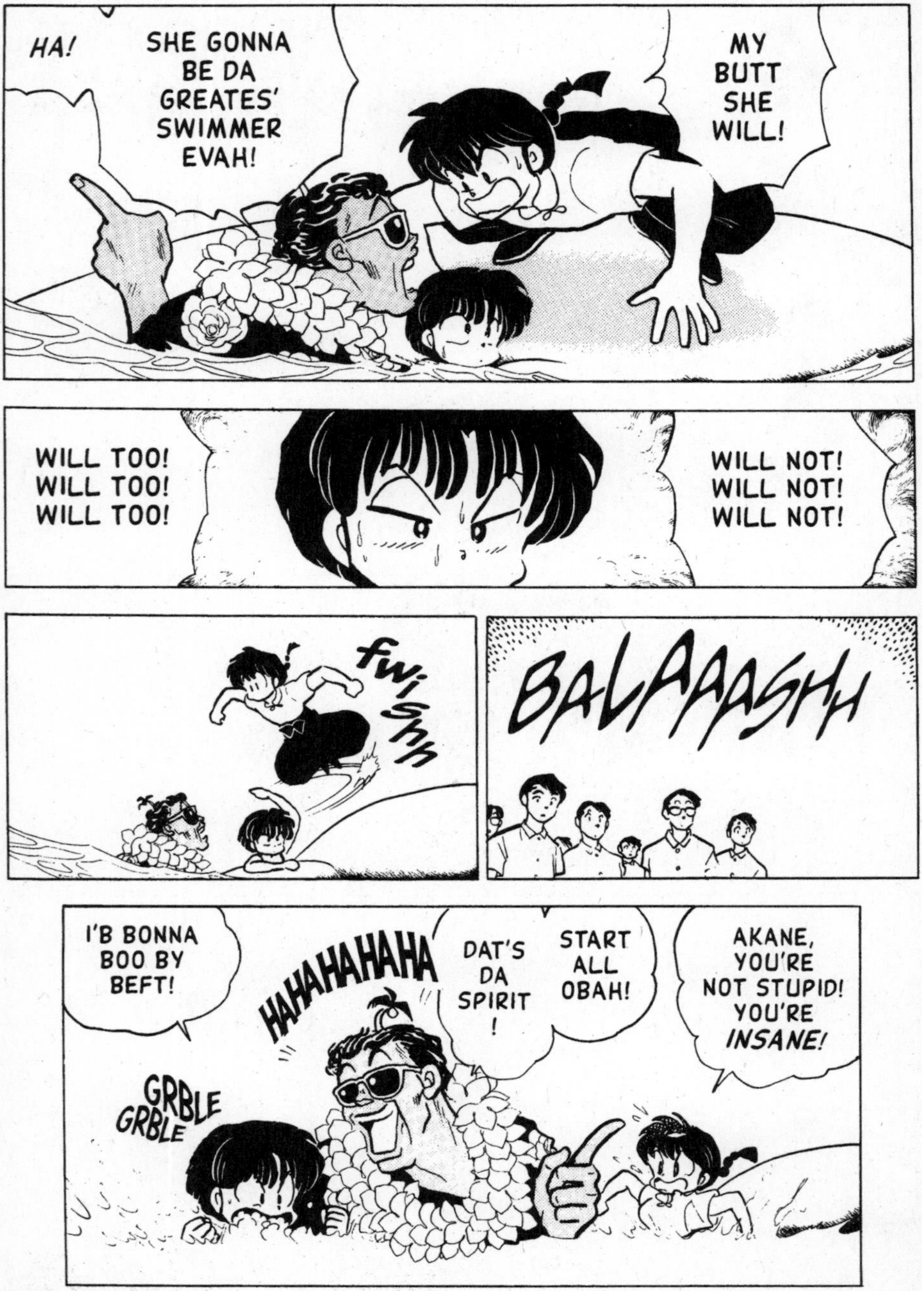
HA!
SHE GONNA BE DA GREATES' SWIMMER EVAH!
MY BUTT SHE WILL!
WILL TOO! WILL TOO! WILL TOO!
WILL NOT! WILL NOT! WILL NOT!
fwishhh
BALAAASHH
I'B BONNA BOO BY BEFT!
HAHAHAHAHA
DAT'S DA SPIRIT!
START ALL OBAH!
AKANE, YOU'RE NOT STUPID! YOU'RE *INSANE!*
GRBLE GRBLE

PART 10
COURAGE UNDER WATER

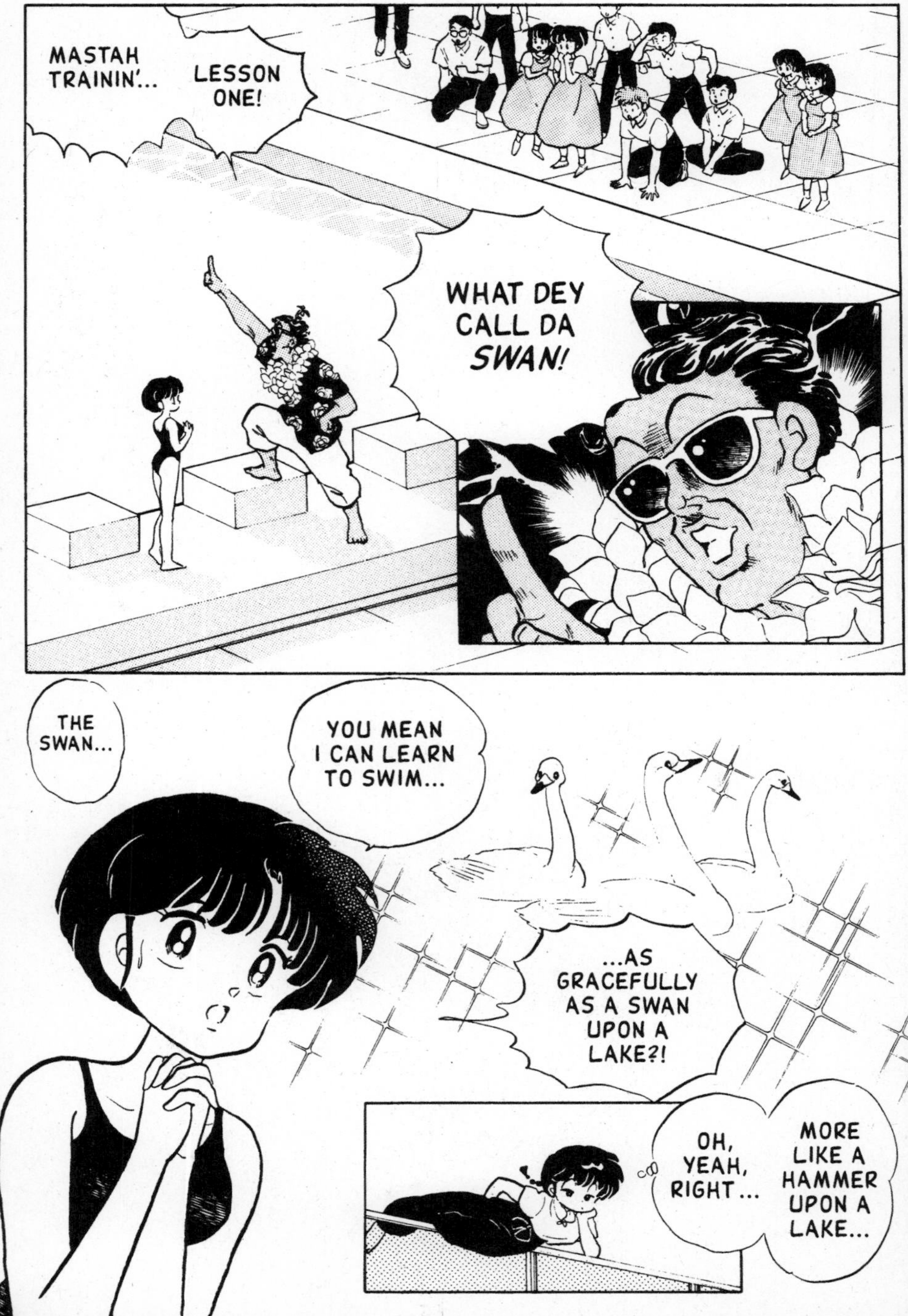
MASTAH TRAININ'...
LESSON ONE!
WHAT DEY CALL DA SWAN!
THE SWAN...
YOU MEAN I CAN LEARN TO SWIM...
...AS GRACEFULLY AS A SWAN UPON A LAKE?!
OH, YEAH, RIGHT...
MORE LIKE A HAMMER UPON A LAKE...

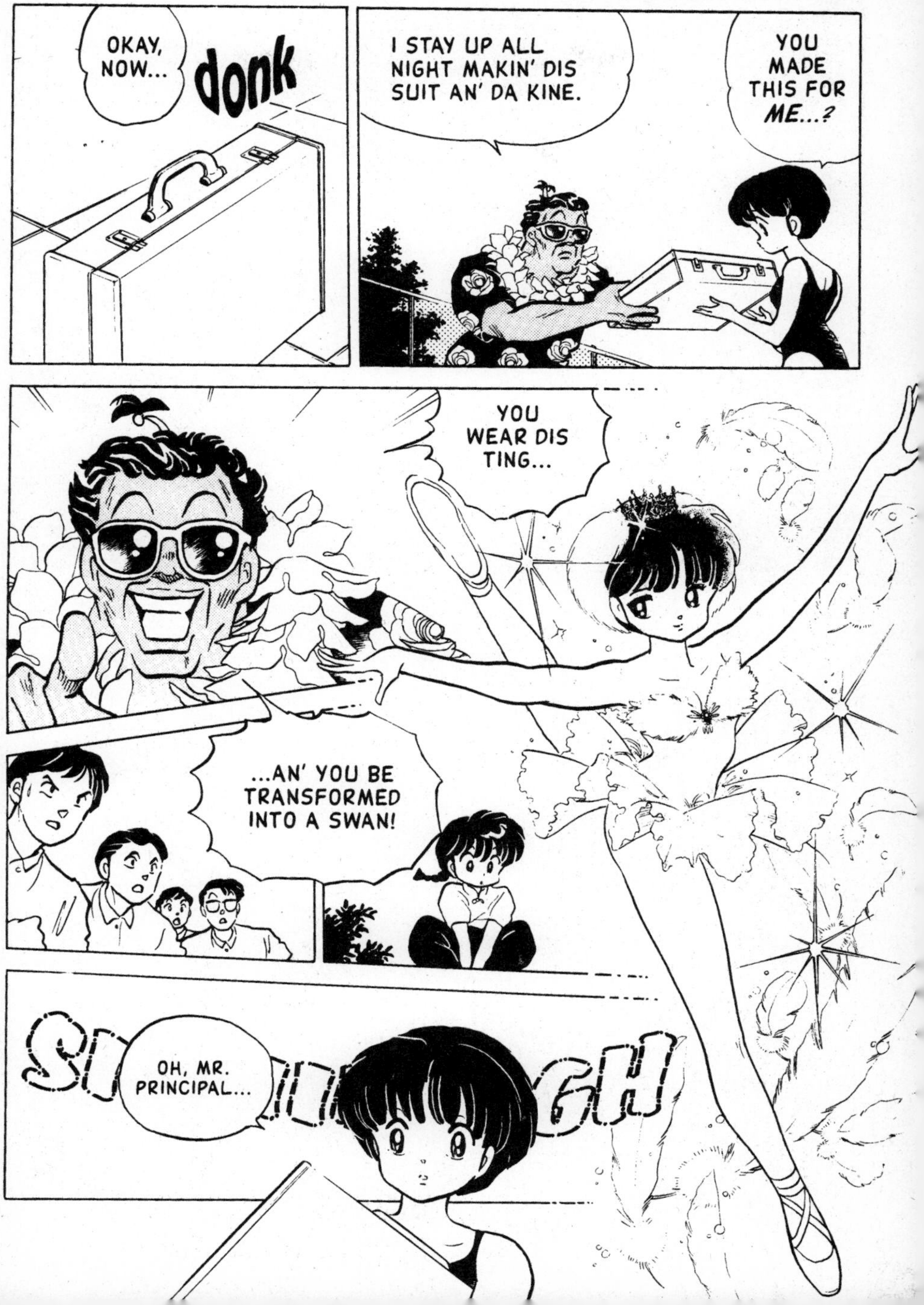
OKAY, NOW...
donk
I STAY UP ALL NIGHT MAKIN' DIS SUIT AN' DA KINE.
YOU MADE THIS FOR *ME*...?
YOU WEAR DIS TING...
...AN' YOU BE TRANSFORMED INTO A SWAN!
OH, MR. PRINCIPAL...

OHHH!
B-BUT THAT'S—
doy-
-Yonnnng
YOU CALL THIS...
GRRRRR RRRR RRRR
...A SWAN ?!
WHAK
OWEE!
YOU'RE MAKING FUN OF ME!
VWAH
NO!
YOU GOTTA HEAR ME, SISTAH !

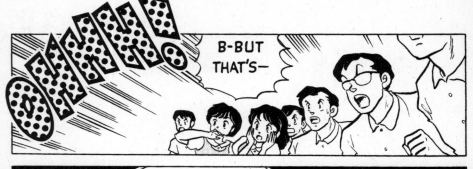

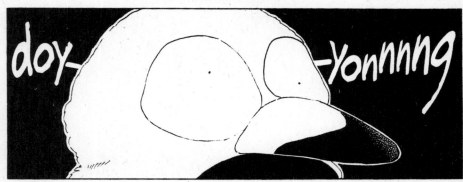

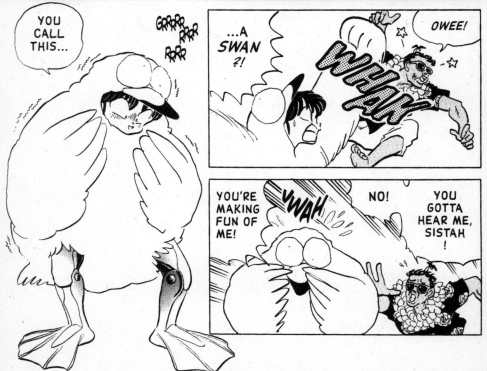

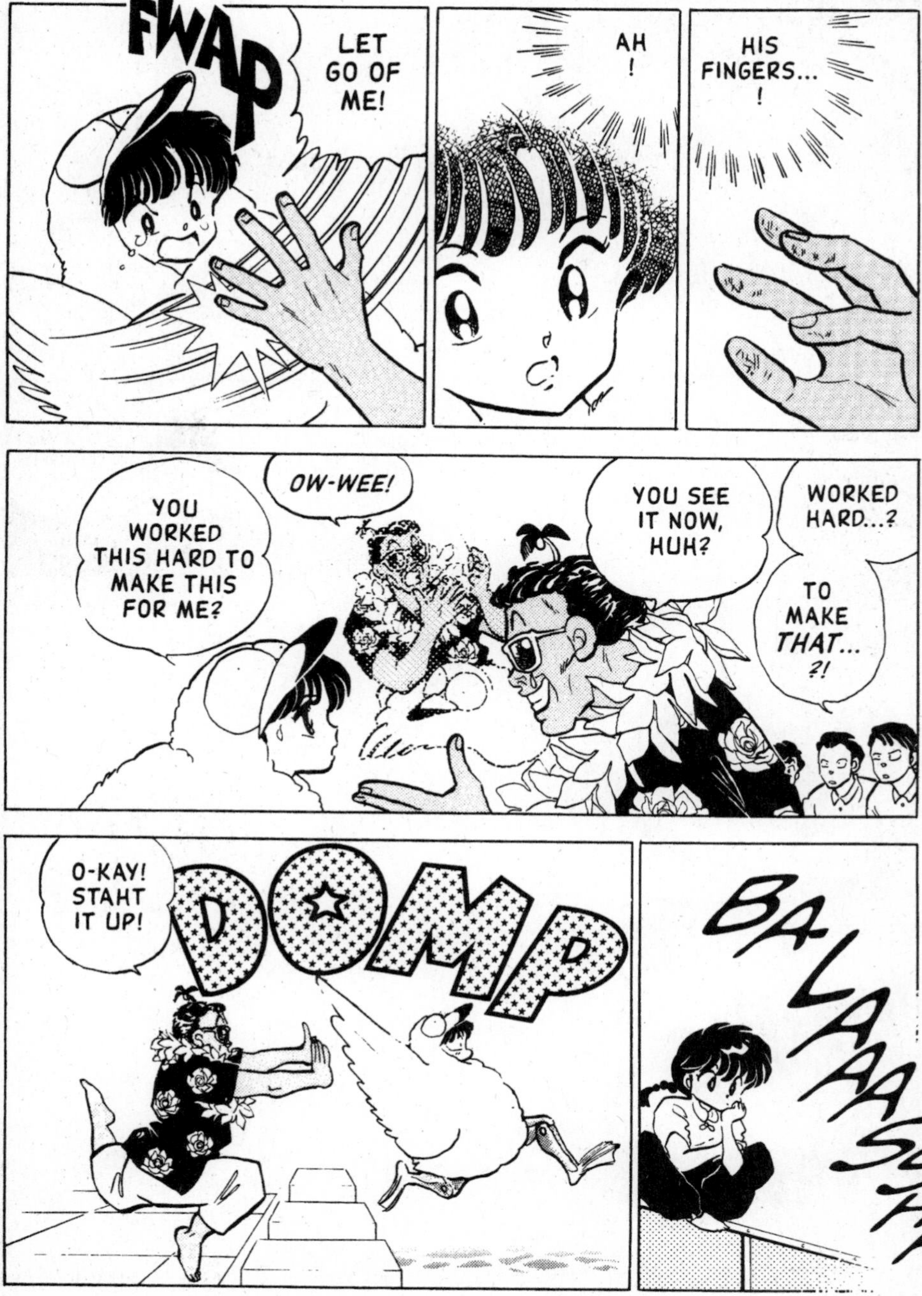
FWAP
LET GO OF ME!
AH !
HIS FINGERS... !
YOU WORKED THIS HARD TO MAKE THIS FOR ME?
OW-WEE!
YOU SEE IT NOW, HUH?
WORKED HARD...?
TO MAKE THAT... ?!
O-KAY! STAHT IT UP!
DOMP
BALAAASSHH

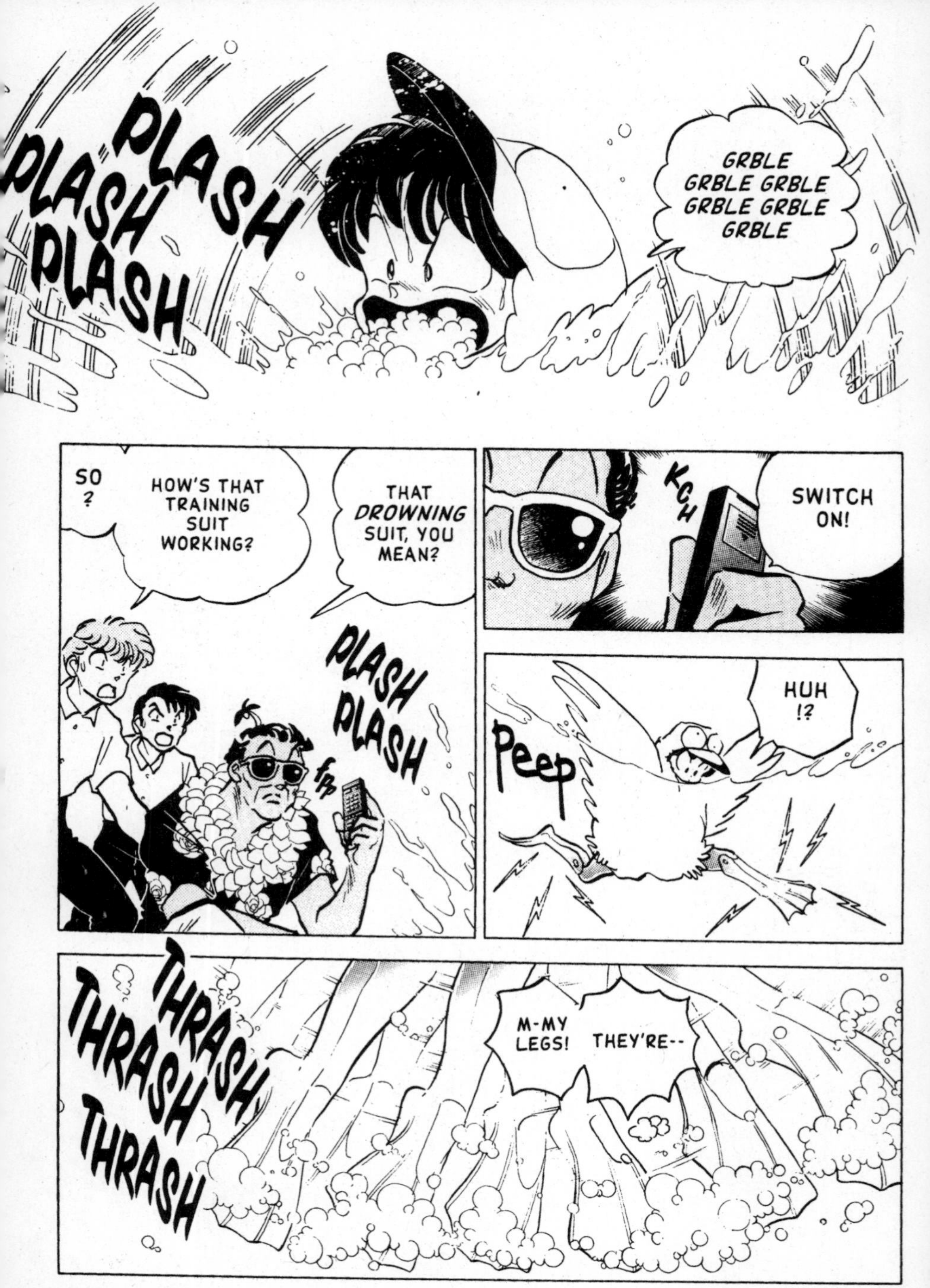
PLASH PLASH PLASH PLASH
GRBLE GRBLE GRBLE GRBLE GRBLE GRBLE
SO?
HOW'S THAT TRAINING SUIT WORKING?
THAT *DROWNING* SUIT, YOU MEAN?
PLASH PLASH
FP
KCH
SWITCH ON!
Peep
HUH !?
THRASH THRASH THRASH
M-MY LEGS! THEY'RE--

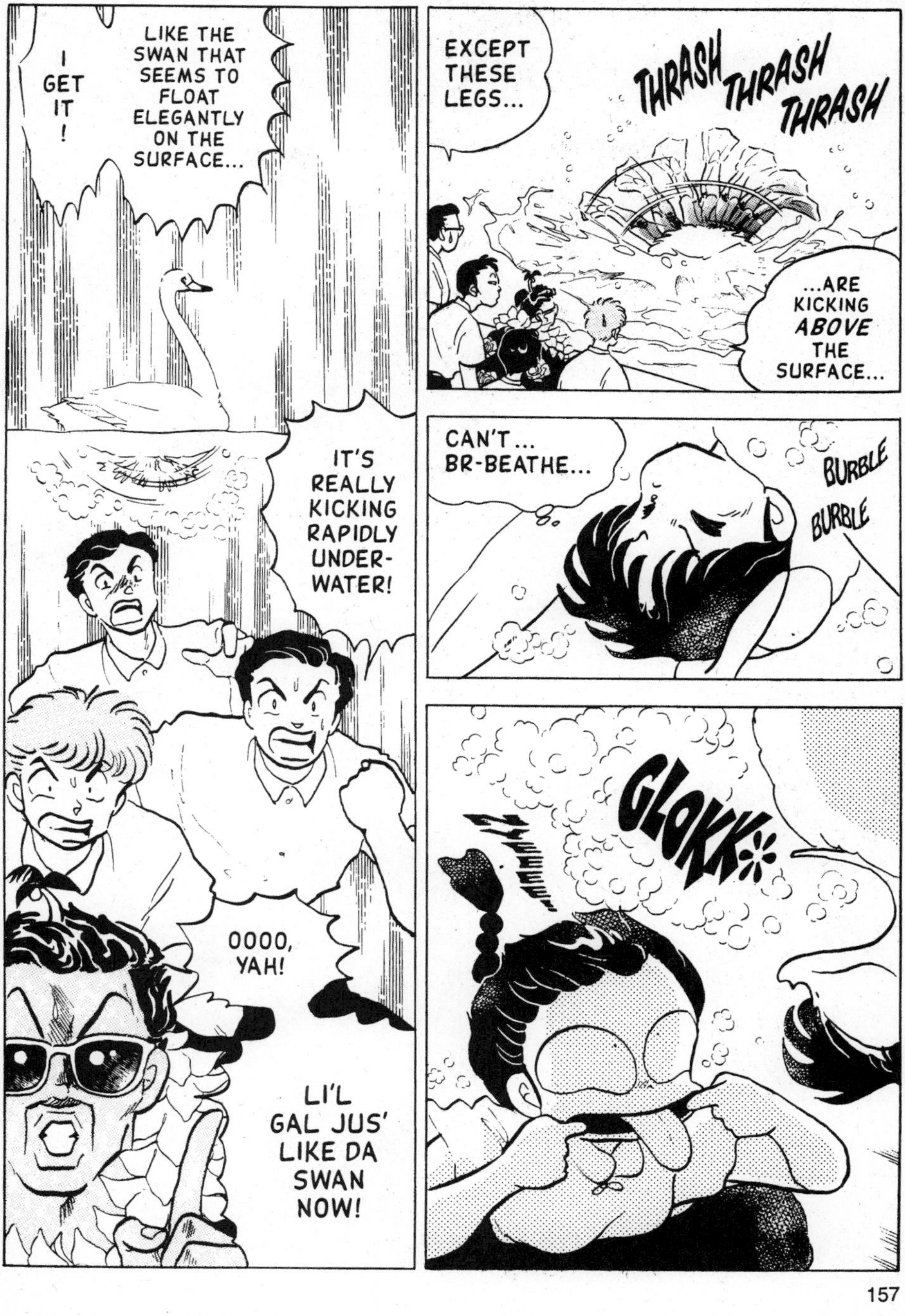
I GET IT!
LIKE THE SWAN THAT SEEMS TO FLOAT ELEGANTLY ON THE SURFACE...
EXCEPT THESE LEGS...
THRASH THRASH THRASH
...ARE KICKING *ABOVE* THE SURFACE...
IT'S REALLY KICKING RAPIDLY UNDER-WATER!
OOOO, YAH!
LI'L GAL JUS' LIKE DA SWAN NOW!
CAN'T... BR-BEATHE...
BURBLE
BURBLE
GLOKK

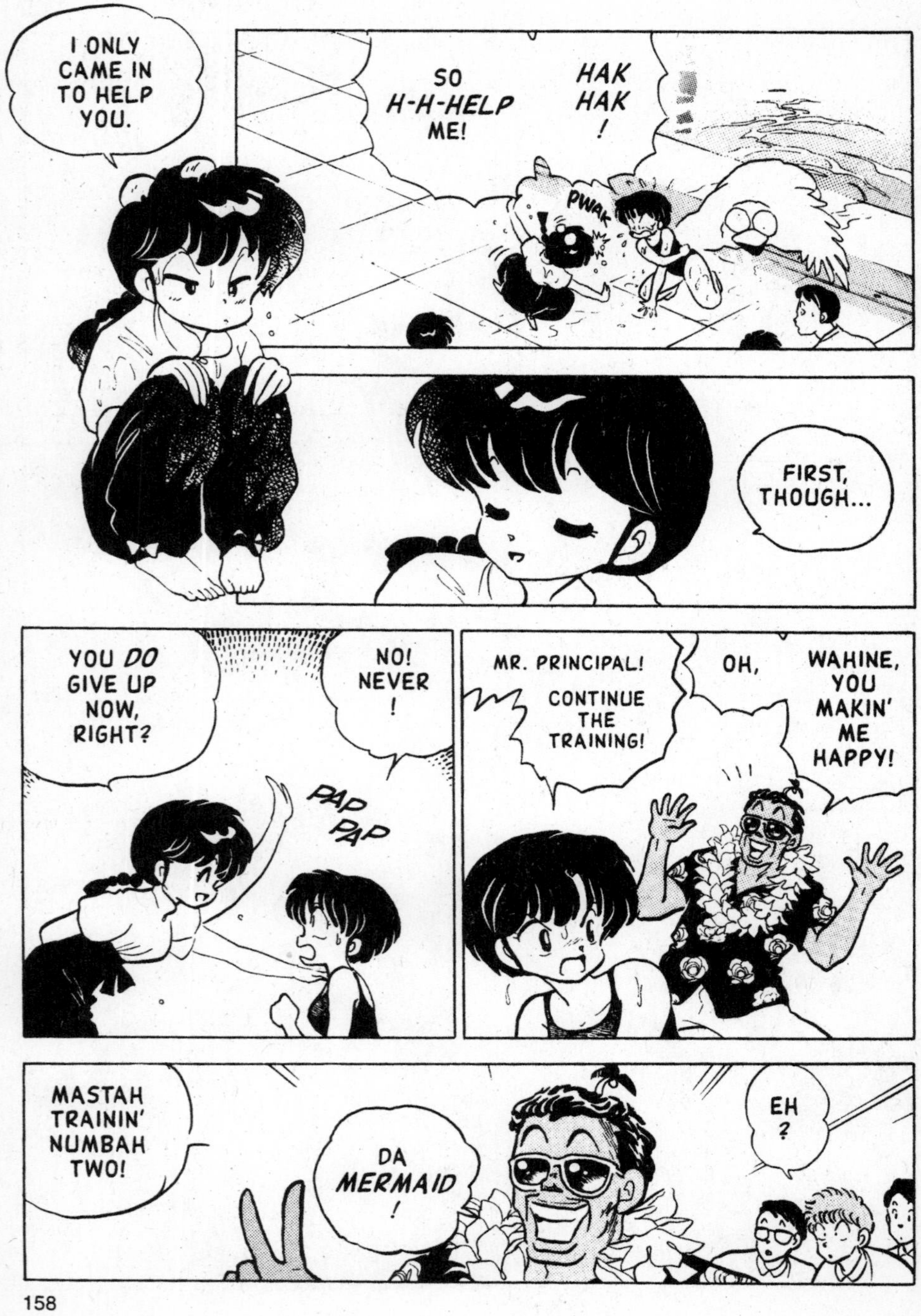
I ONLY CAME IN TO HELP YOU.
SO H-H-HELP ME!
HAK HAK!
PWAK
FIRST, THOUGH...
YOU DO GIVE UP NOW, RIGHT?
NO! NEVER!
PAP PAP
MR. PRINCIPAL!
CONTINUE THE TRAINING!
OH,
WAHINE, YOU MAKIN' ME HAPPY!
MASTAH TRAININ' NUMBAH TWO!
DA MERMAID!
EH?

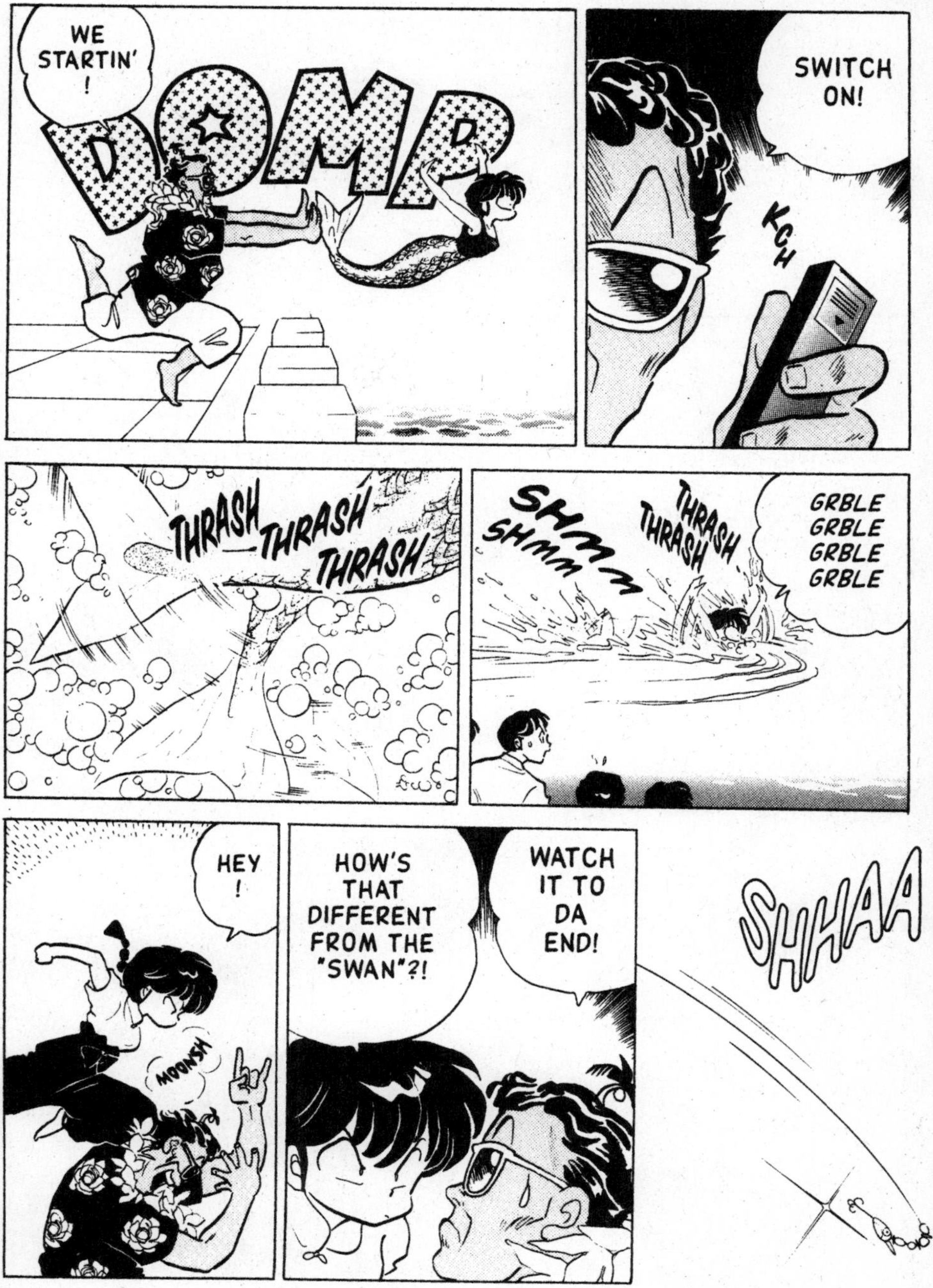
WE STARTIN' !
DOMP
SWITCH ON!
KCH
THRASH THRASH THRASH
SHMMM SHMMM
THRASH THRASH
GRBLE GRBLE GRBLE GRBLE
HEY !
MOONSH
HOW'S THAT DIFFERENT FROM THE "SWAN"?!
WATCH IT TO DA END!
SHHAA

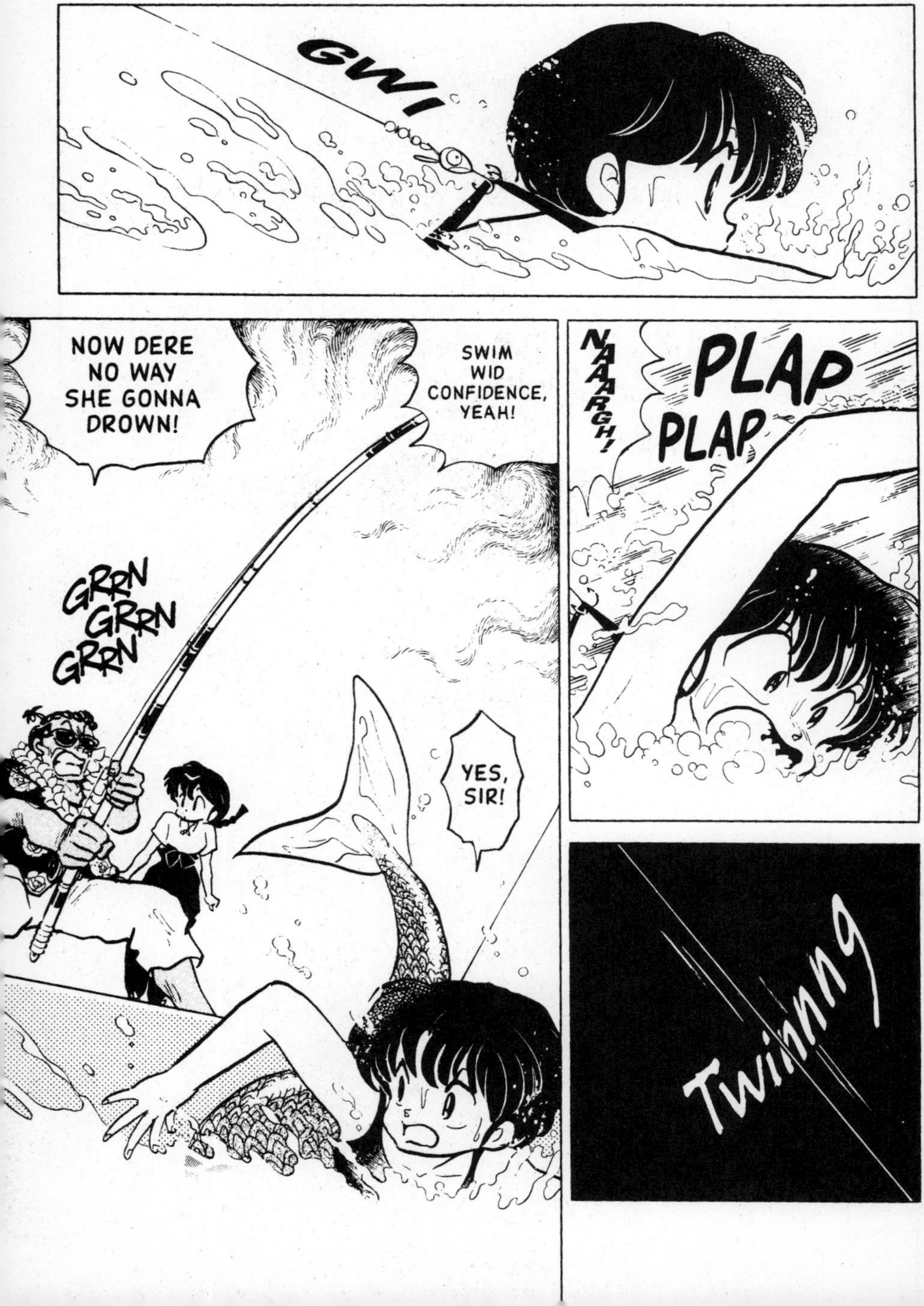
GWI
NOW DERE NO WAY SHE GONNA DROWN!
SWIM WID CONFIDENCE, YEAH!
GRRN GRRN GRRN
YES, SIR!
NAAARGH!
PLAP
PLAP
Twinnng

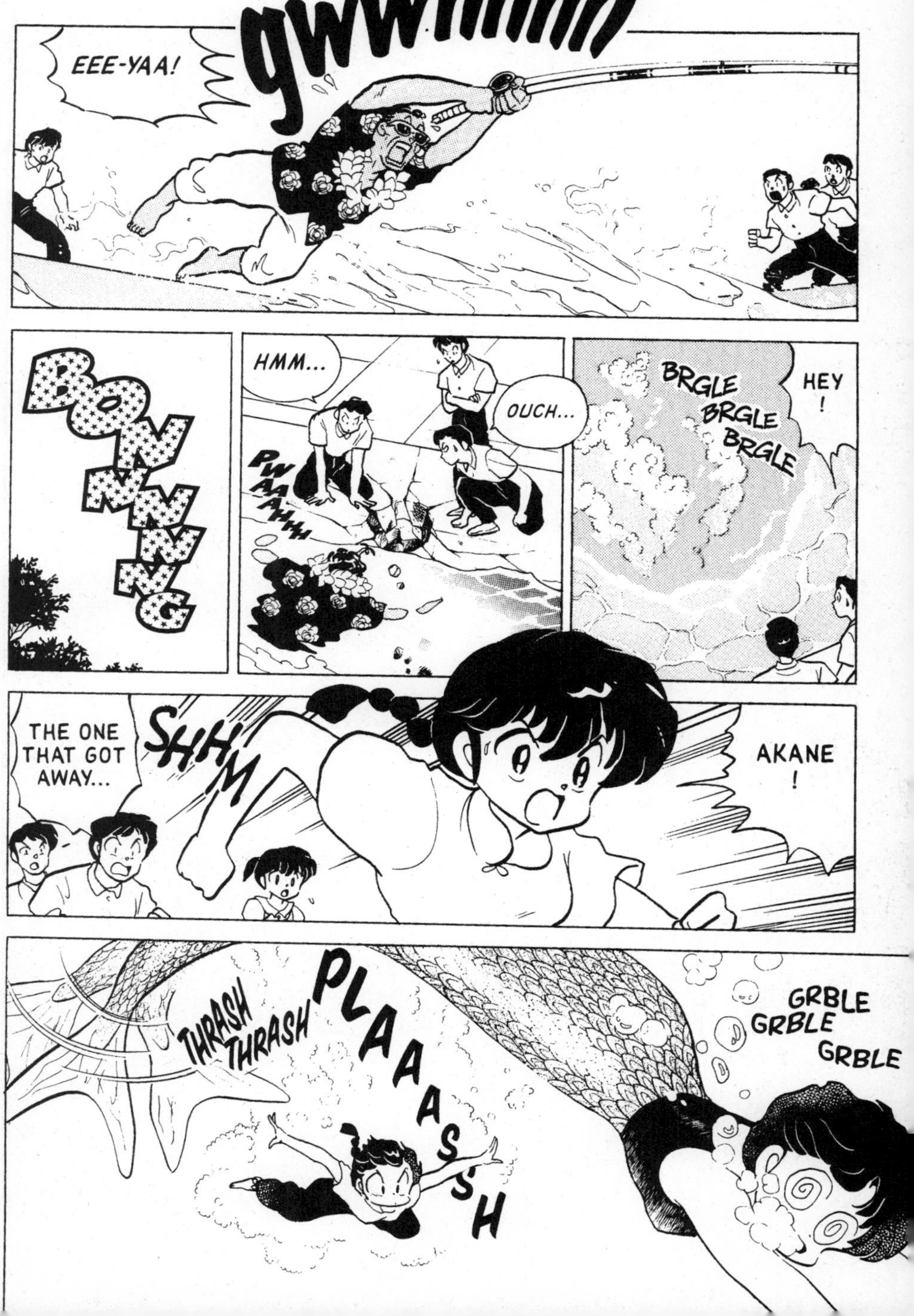
EEE-YAA!
gwwnnnn
BOYNNNNG
HMM...
OUCH...
PWAAAHHH
BRGLE BRGLE BRGLE
HEY!
THE ONE THAT GOT AWAY...
SHHM
AKANE!
THRASH THRASH
PLAAAASSH
GRBLE GRBLE GRBLE

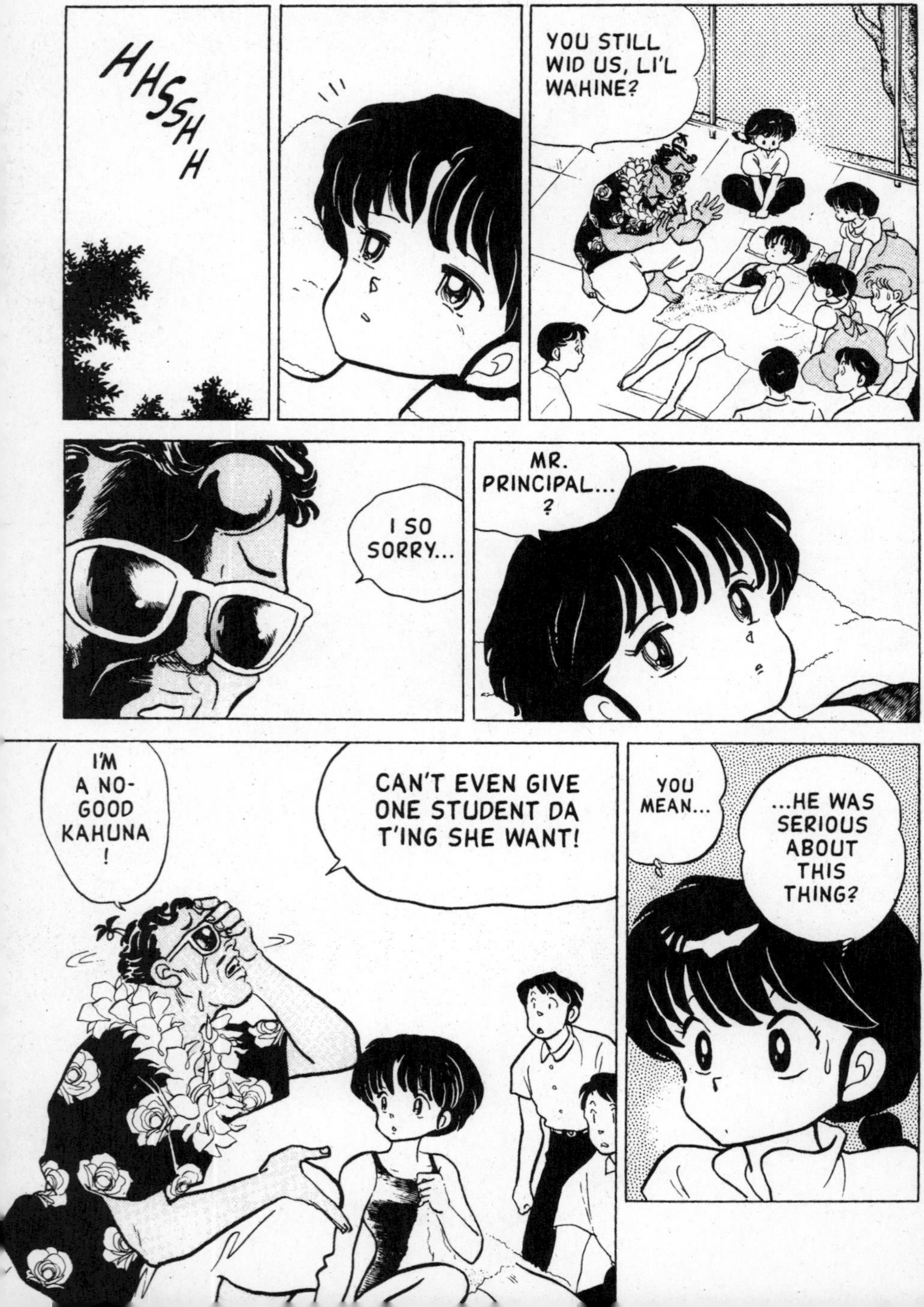
HHSSHH
YOU STILL WID US, LI'L WAHINE?
I SO SORRY...
MR. PRINCIPAL...?
I'M A NO-GOOD KAHUNA!
CAN'T EVEN GIVE ONE STUDENT DA T'ING SHE WANT!
YOU MEAN...
...HE WAS SERIOUS ABOUT THIS THING?

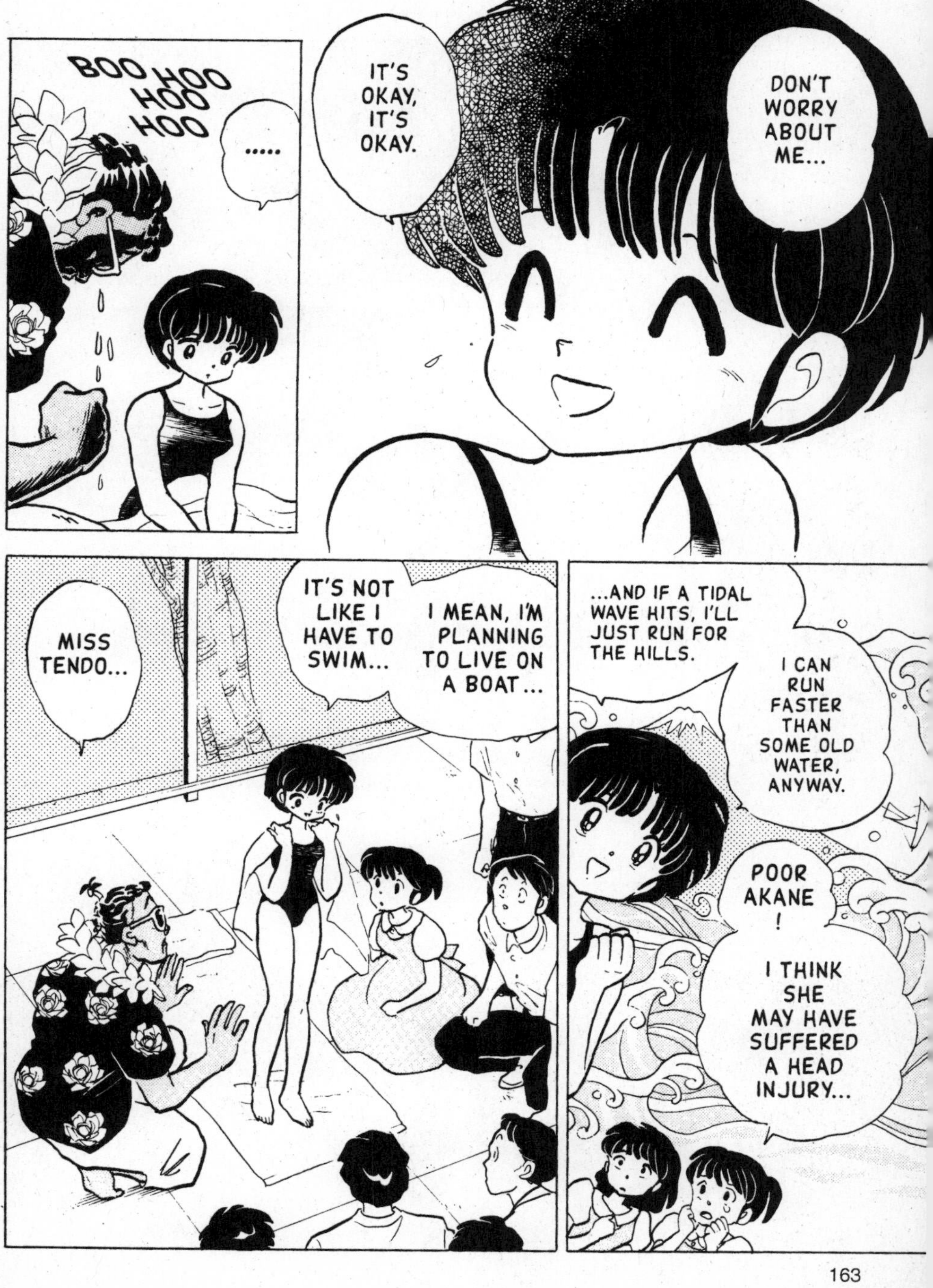
BOO HOO HOO HOO HOO
.....
IT'S OKAY, IT'S OKAY.
DON'T WORRY ABOUT ME...
MISS TENDO...
IT'S NOT LIKE I HAVE TO SWIM...
I MEAN, I'M PLANNING TO LIVE ON A BOAT...
...AND IF A TIDAL WAVE HITS, I'LL JUST RUN FOR THE HILLS.
I CAN RUN FASTER THAN SOME OLD WATER, ANYWAY.
POOR AKANE!
I THINK SHE MAY HAVE SUFFERED A HEAD INJURY...

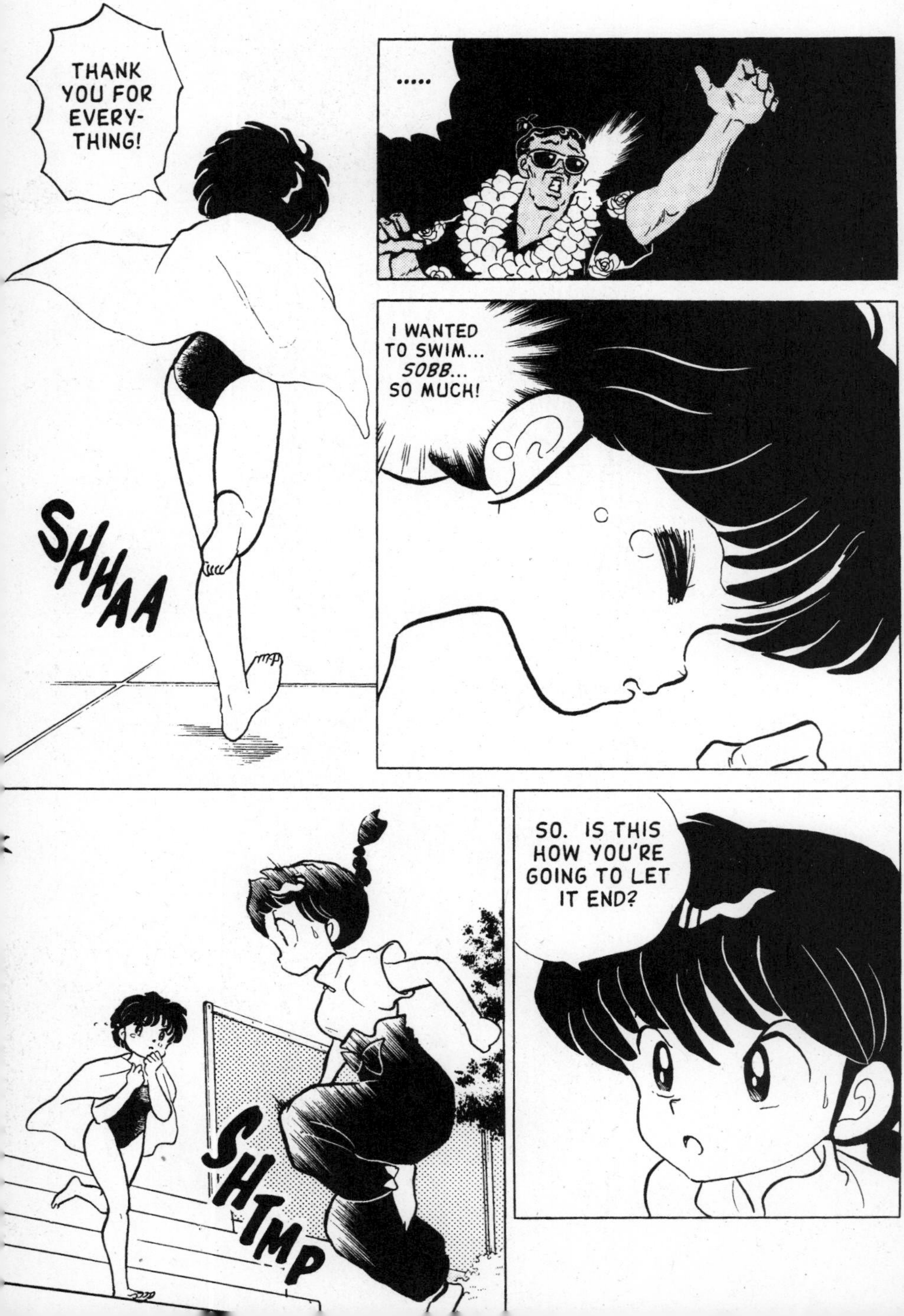
THANK YOU FOR EVERY-THING!
SHHAA
.....
I WANTED TO SWIM... *SOBB*... SO MUCH!
SHTMP
SO. IS THIS HOW YOU'RE GOING TO LET IT END?

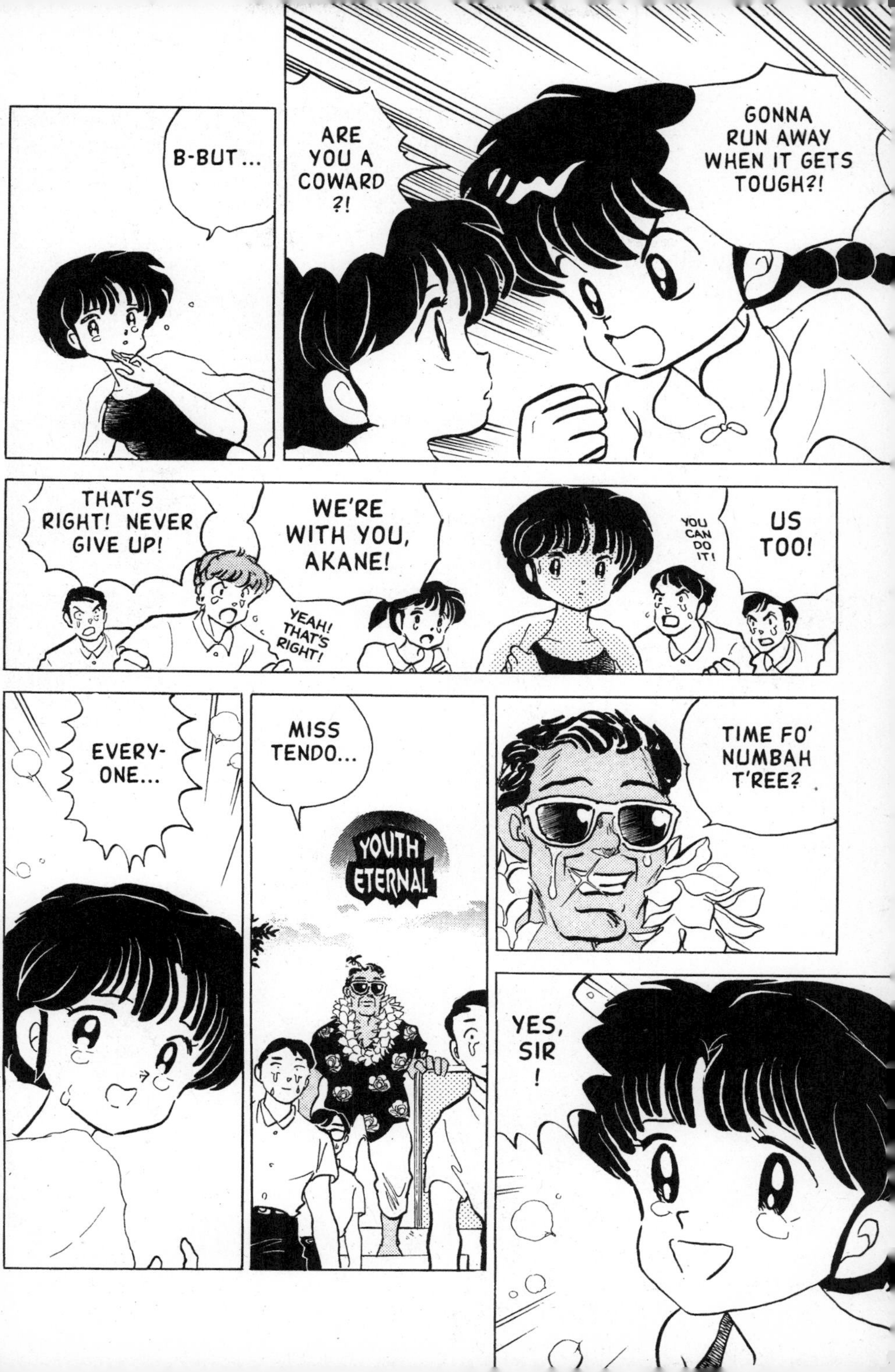
B-BUT...
ARE YOU A COWARD ?!
GONNA RUN AWAY WHEN IT GETS TOUGH?!
THAT'S RIGHT! NEVER GIVE UP!
WE'RE WITH YOU, AKANE!
YEAH! THAT'S RIGHT!
YOU CAN DO IT!
US TOO!
EVERY-ONE...
MISS TENDO...
YOUTH ETERNAL
TIME FO' NUMBAH T'REE?
YES, SIR !

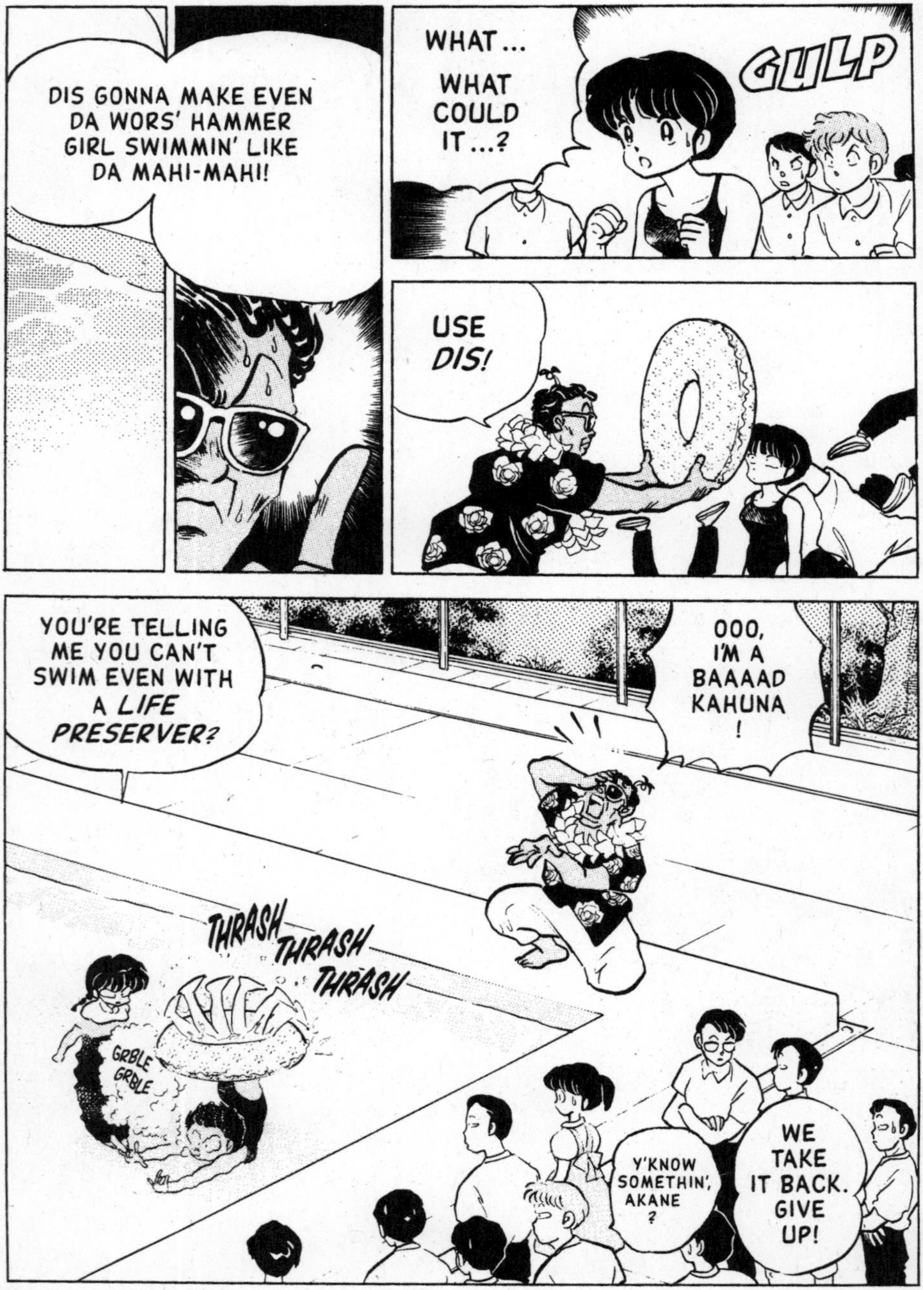
DIS GONNA MAKE EVEN DA WORS' HAMMER GIRL SWIMMIN' LIKE DA MAHI-MAHI!
WHAT ... WHAT COULD IT ...?
GULP
USE DIS!
YOU'RE TELLING ME YOU CAN'T SWIM EVEN WITH A LIFE PRESERVER?
OOO, I'M A BAAAAD KAHUNA!
THRASH THRASH THRASH
GRBLE GRBLE
Y'KNOW SOMETHIN', AKANE?
WE TAKE IT BACK. GIVE UP!

PART 11
STEP OUTSIDE

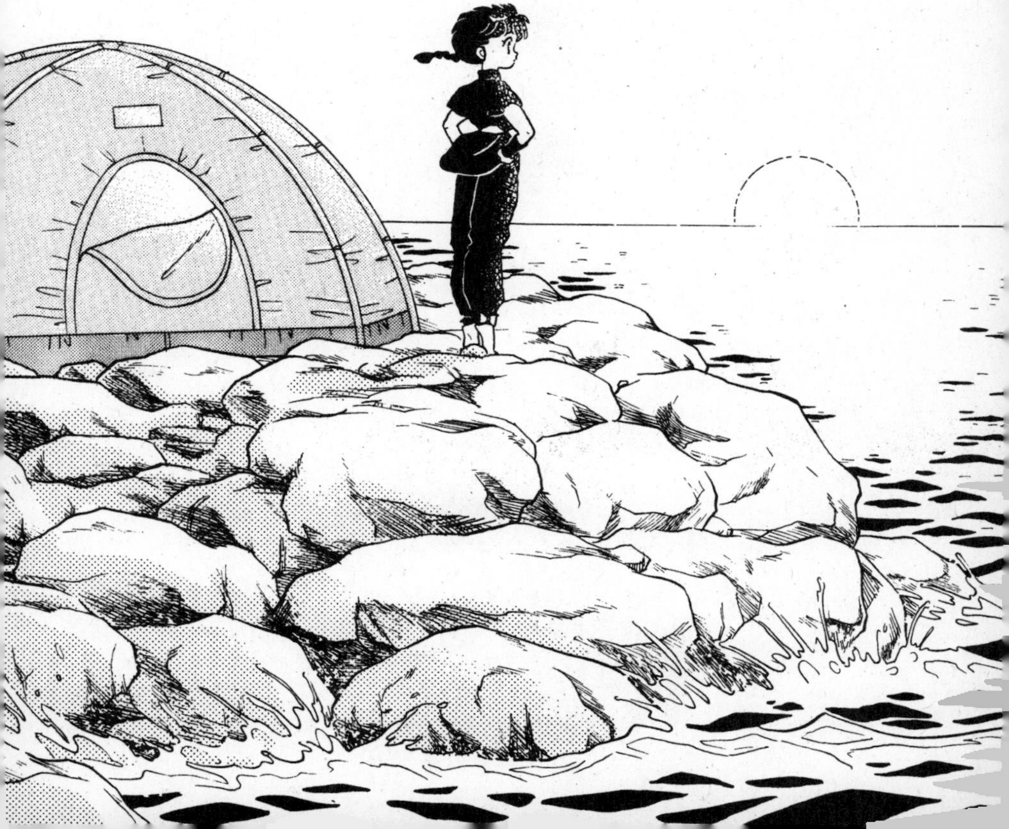

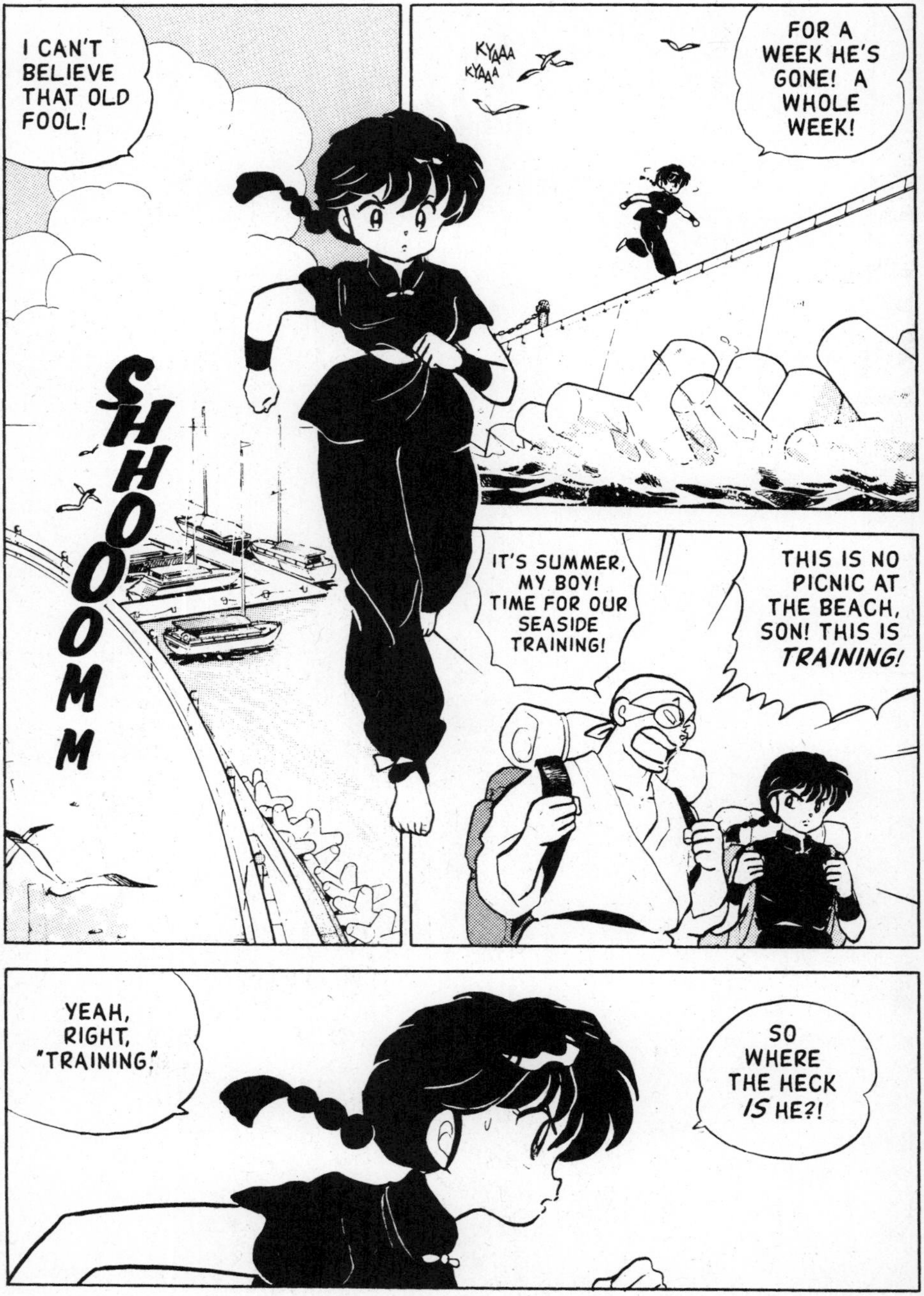
I CAN'T BELIEVE THAT OLD FOOL!
SHHOOOOMM
KYAAA KYAAA
FOR A WEEK HE'S GONE! A WHOLE WEEK!
IT'S SUMMER, MY BOY! TIME FOR OUR SEASIDE TRAINING!
THIS IS NO PICNIC AT THE BEACH, SON! THIS IS TRAINING!
YEAH, RIGHT, "TRAINING."
SO WHERE THE HECK IS HE?!

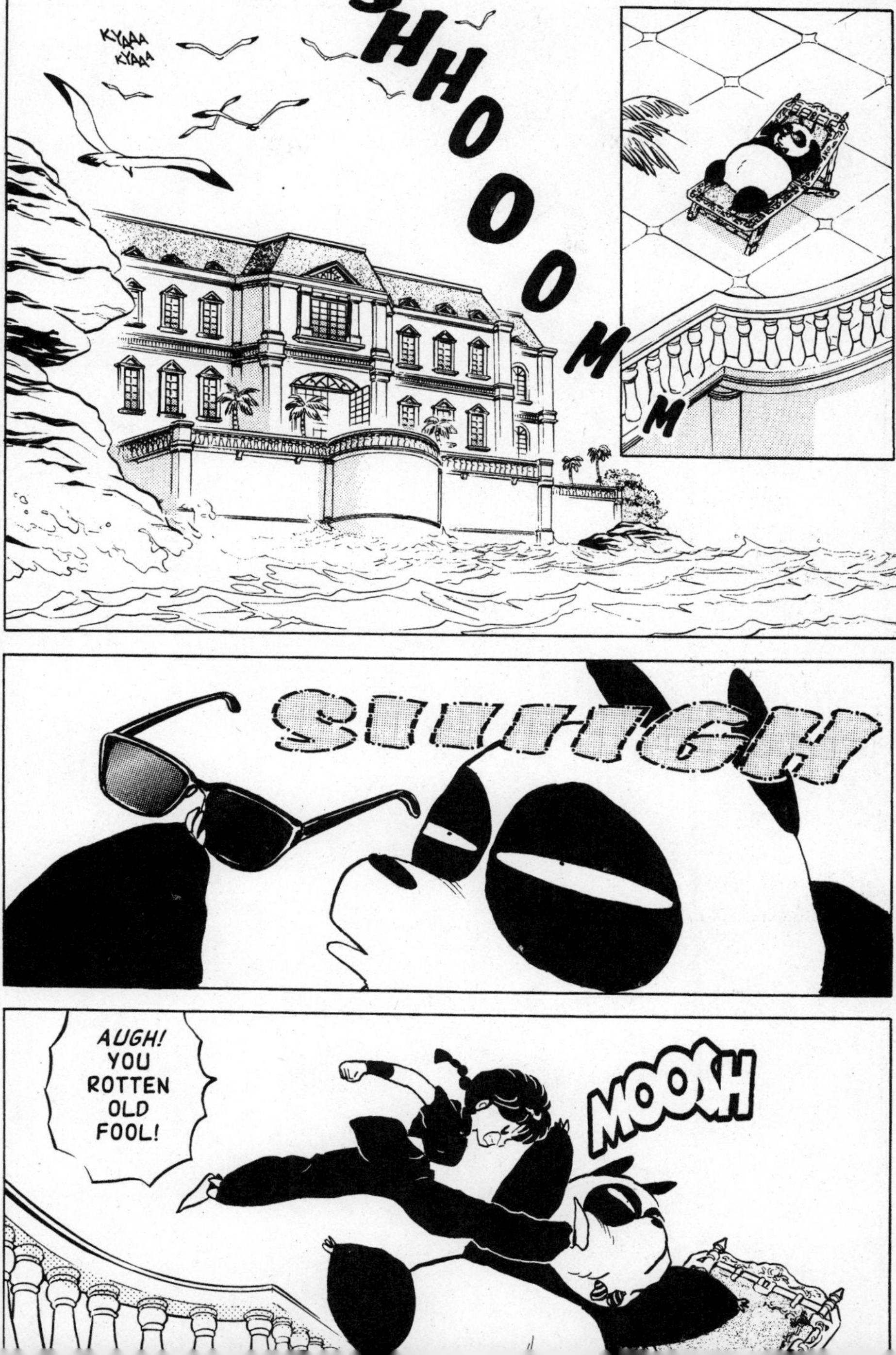
KYAAA
KYAAA
SHHOOOOMMM
SIIIIGH
AUGH! YOU ROTTEN OLD FOOL!
MOOSH

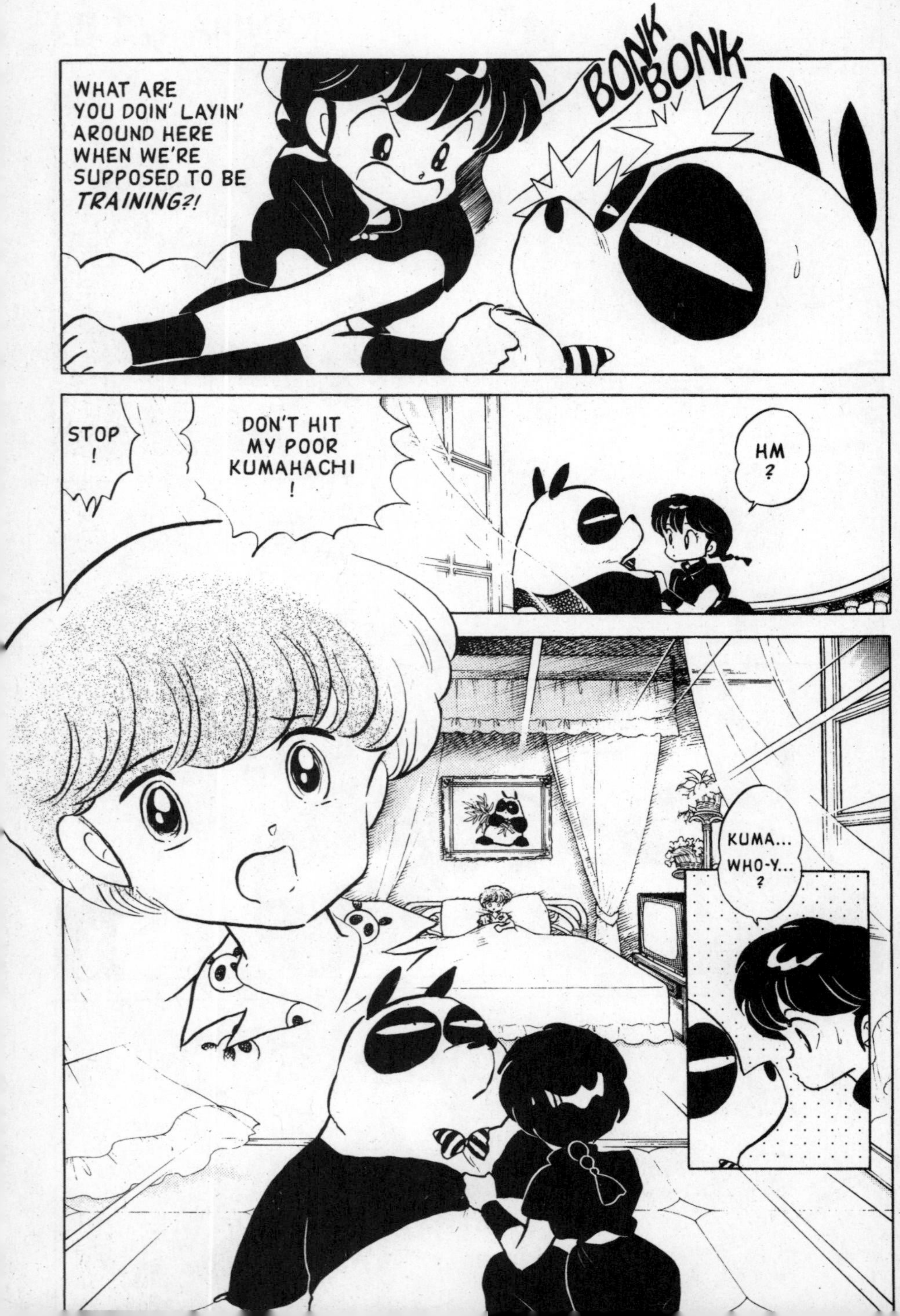
WHAT ARE YOU DOIN' LAYIN' AROUND HERE WHEN WE'RE SUPPOSED TO BE *TRAINING*?!
BONK BONK
STOP!
DON'T HIT MY POOR KUMAHACHI!
HM?
KUMA... WHO-Y...?

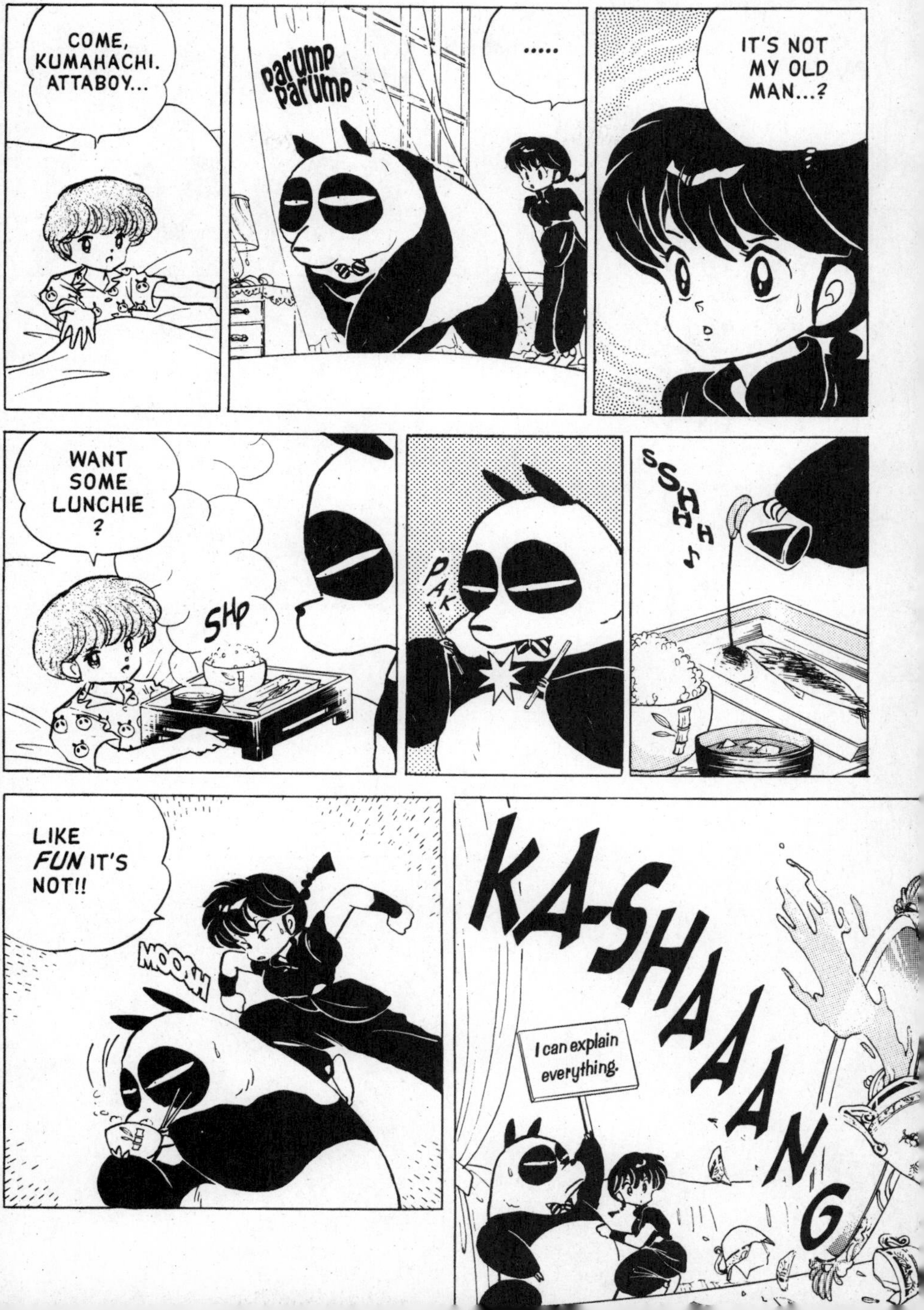
COME, KUMAHACHI. ATTABOY...
PARUMP PARUMP
.....
IT'S NOT MY OLD MAN...?
WANT SOME LUNCHIE ?
SHP
PAK
SSHHHH
LIKE *FUN* IT'S NOT!!
WOOSH
KA-SHAAAANG
I can explain everything.

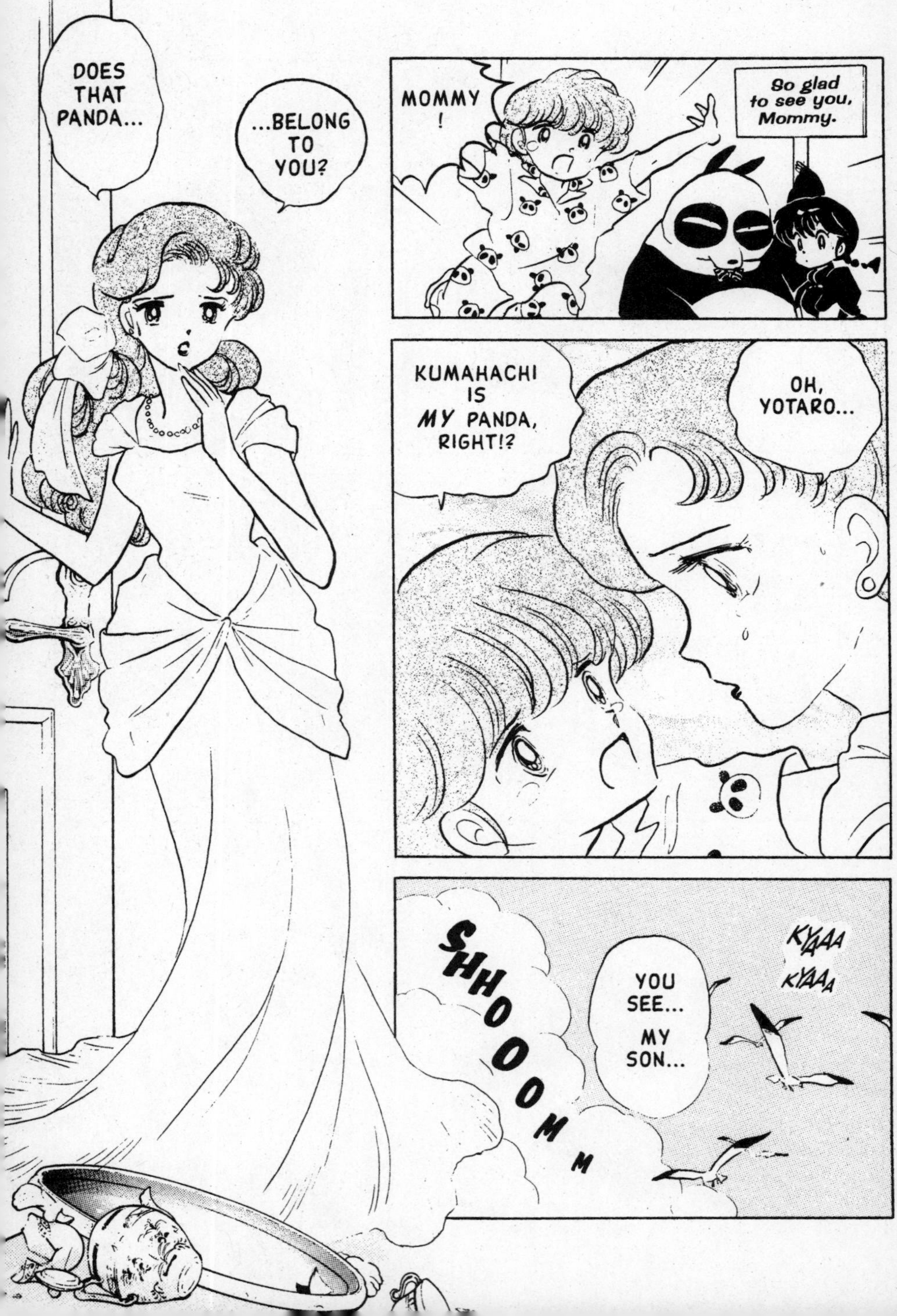
DOES THAT PANDA...
...BELONG TO YOU?
MOMMY !
So glad to see you, Mommy.
KUMAHACHI IS MY PANDA, RIGHT!?
OH, YOTARO...
SHHOOOOMM
YOU SEE... MY SON...
KYAAA KYAAA

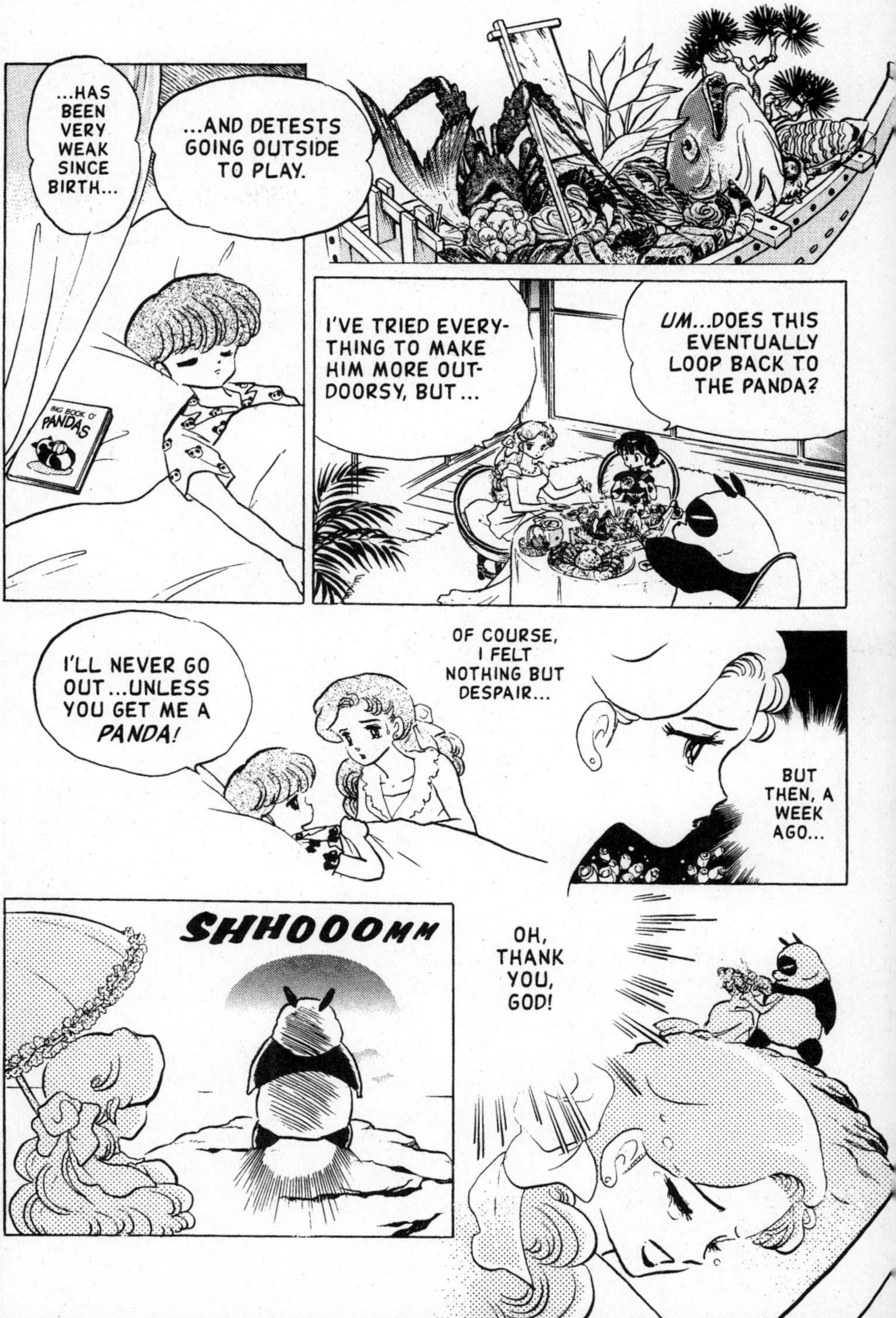

...HAS BEEN VERY WEAK SINCE BIRTH...
...AND DETESTS GOING OUTSIDE TO PLAY.
BIG BOOK O' PANDAS
I'VE TRIED EVERY-THING TO MAKE HIM MORE OUT-DOORSY, BUT ...
UM...DOES THIS EVENTUALLY LOOP BACK TO THE PANDA?
I'LL NEVER GO OUT ...UNLESS YOU GET ME A *PANDA!*
OF COURSE, I FELT NOTHING BUT DESPAIR...
BUT THEN, A WEEK AGO...
SHHOOOMM
OH, THANK YOU, GOD!

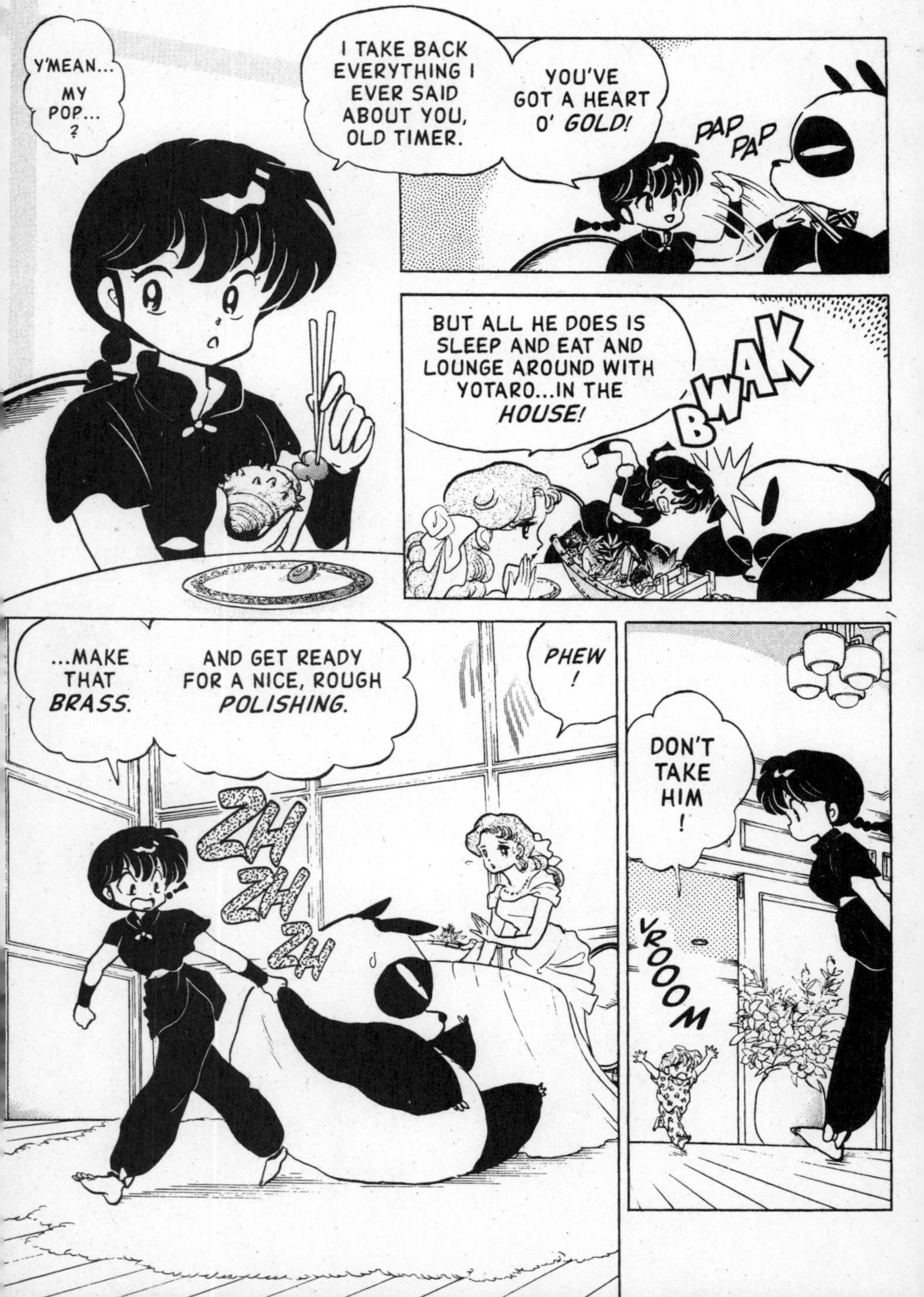
Y'MEAN... MY POP... ?
I TAKE BACK EVERYTHING I EVER SAID ABOUT YOU, OLD TIMER.
YOU'VE GOT A HEART O' *GOLD!*
PAP PAP
BUT ALL HE DOES IS SLEEP AND EAT AND LOUNGE AROUND WITH YOTARO...IN THE *HOUSE!*
BWAK
...MAKE THAT *BRASS.*
AND GET READY FOR A NICE, ROUGH *POLISHING.*
PHEW !
ZH ZH ZH ZH
DON'T TAKE HIM !
VROOOOM

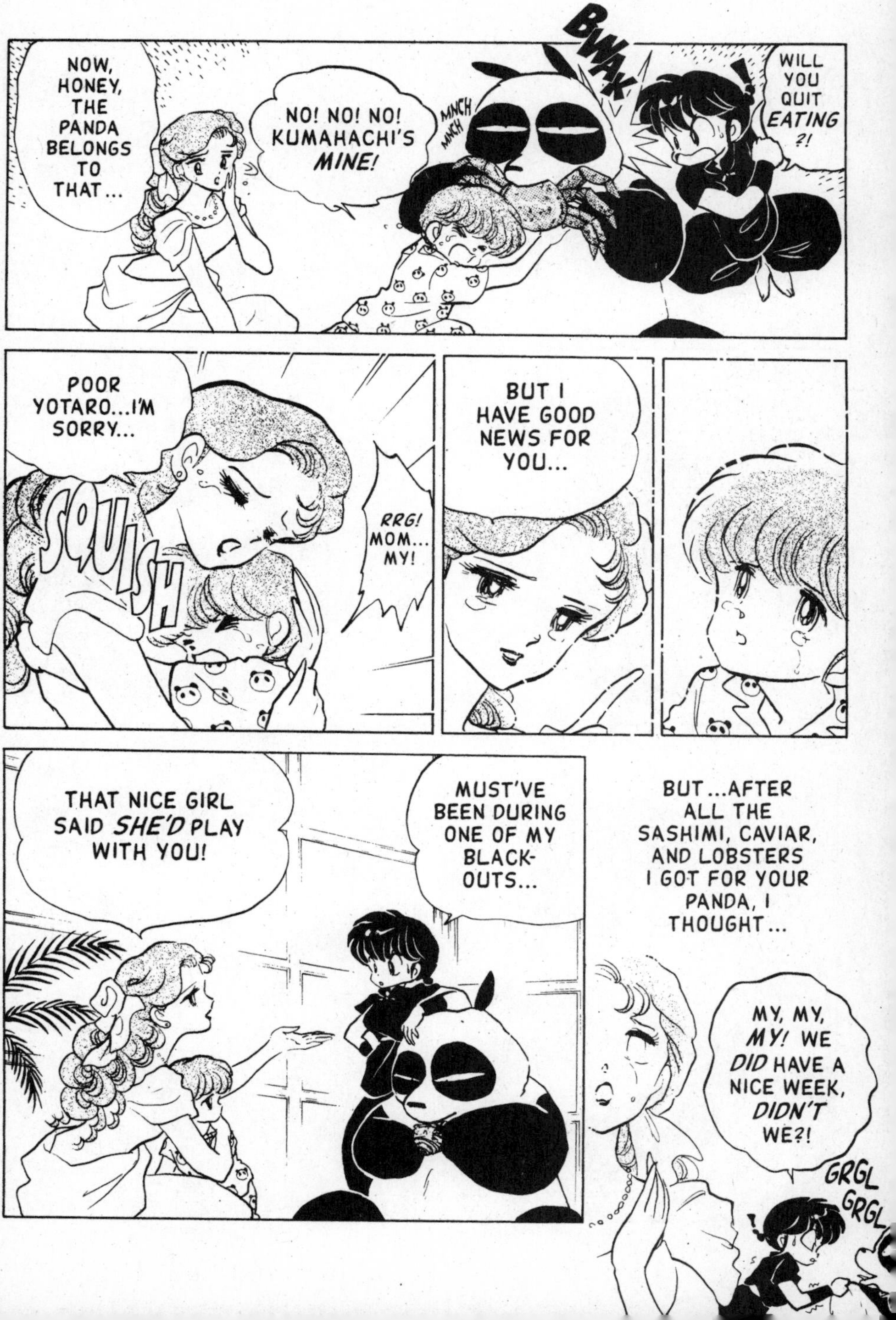
NOW, HONEY, THE PANDA BELONGS TO THAT...
NO! NO! NO! KUMAHACHI'S *MINE!*
MNCH MNCH
BWAK
!
WILL YOU QUIT *EATING* ?!
POOR YOTARO...I'M SORRY...
SQUISH
RRG! MOM... MY!
BUT I HAVE GOOD NEWS FOR YOU...
THAT NICE GIRL SAID *SHE'D* PLAY WITH YOU!
MUST'VE BEEN DURING ONE OF MY BLACK-OUTS...
BUT...AFTER ALL THE SASHIMI, CAVIAR, AND LOBSTERS I GOT FOR YOUR PANDA, I THOUGHT...
MY, MY, *MY!* WE *DID* HAVE A NICE WEEK, *DIDN'T* WE?!
GRGL GRGL

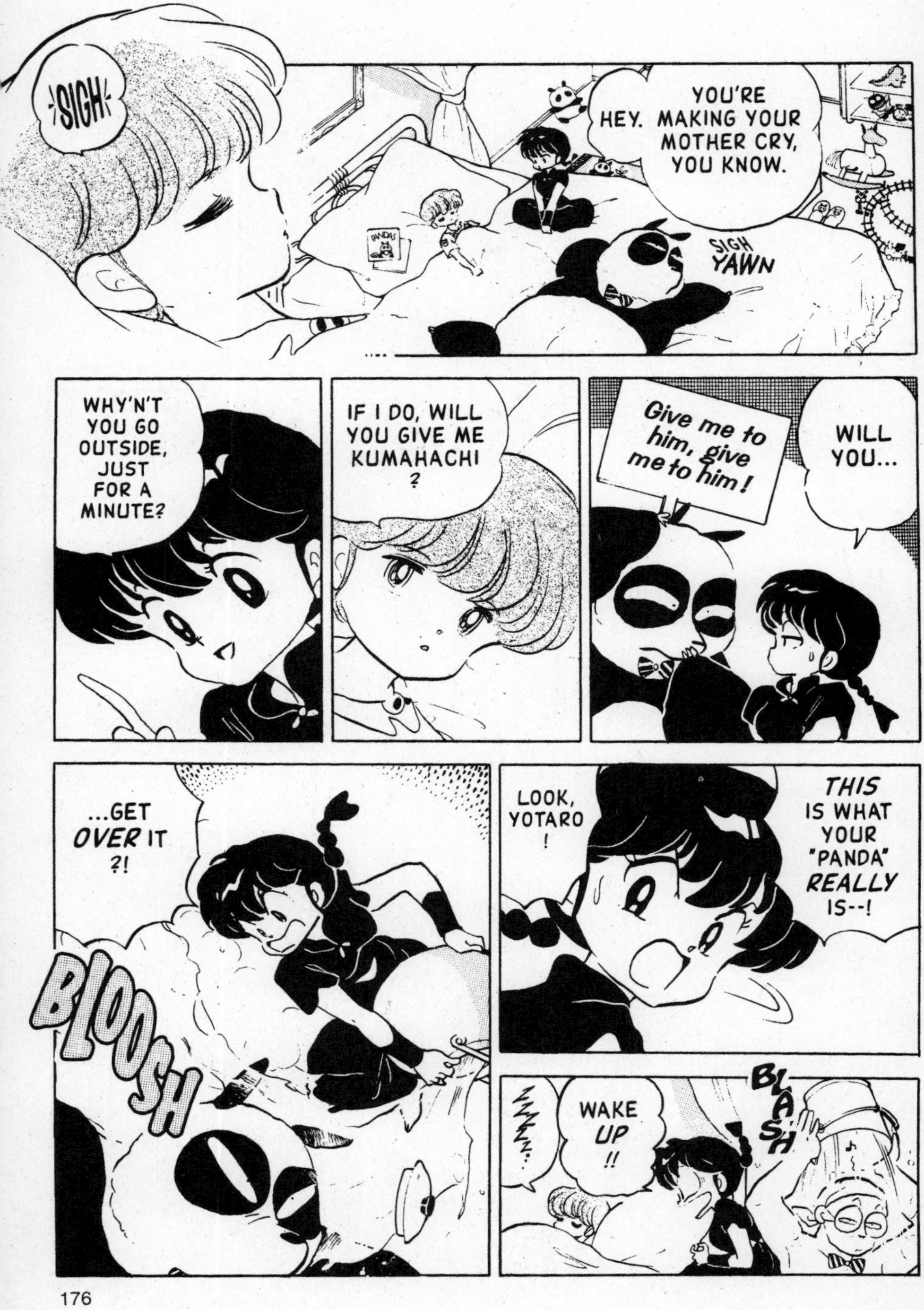

SIGH
HEY. YOU'RE MAKING YOUR MOTHER CRY, YOU KNOW.
SIGH
YAWN
....
WHY'N'T YOU GO OUTSIDE, JUST FOR A MINUTE?
IF I DO, WILL YOU GIVE ME KUMAHACHI?
Give me to him, give me to him!
WILL YOU...
...GET *OVER* IT?!
BLOOSH
LOOK, YOTARO!
THIS IS WHAT YOUR "PANDA" *REALLY* IS--!
ZZZZ...
WAKE *UP*!!
BLASH

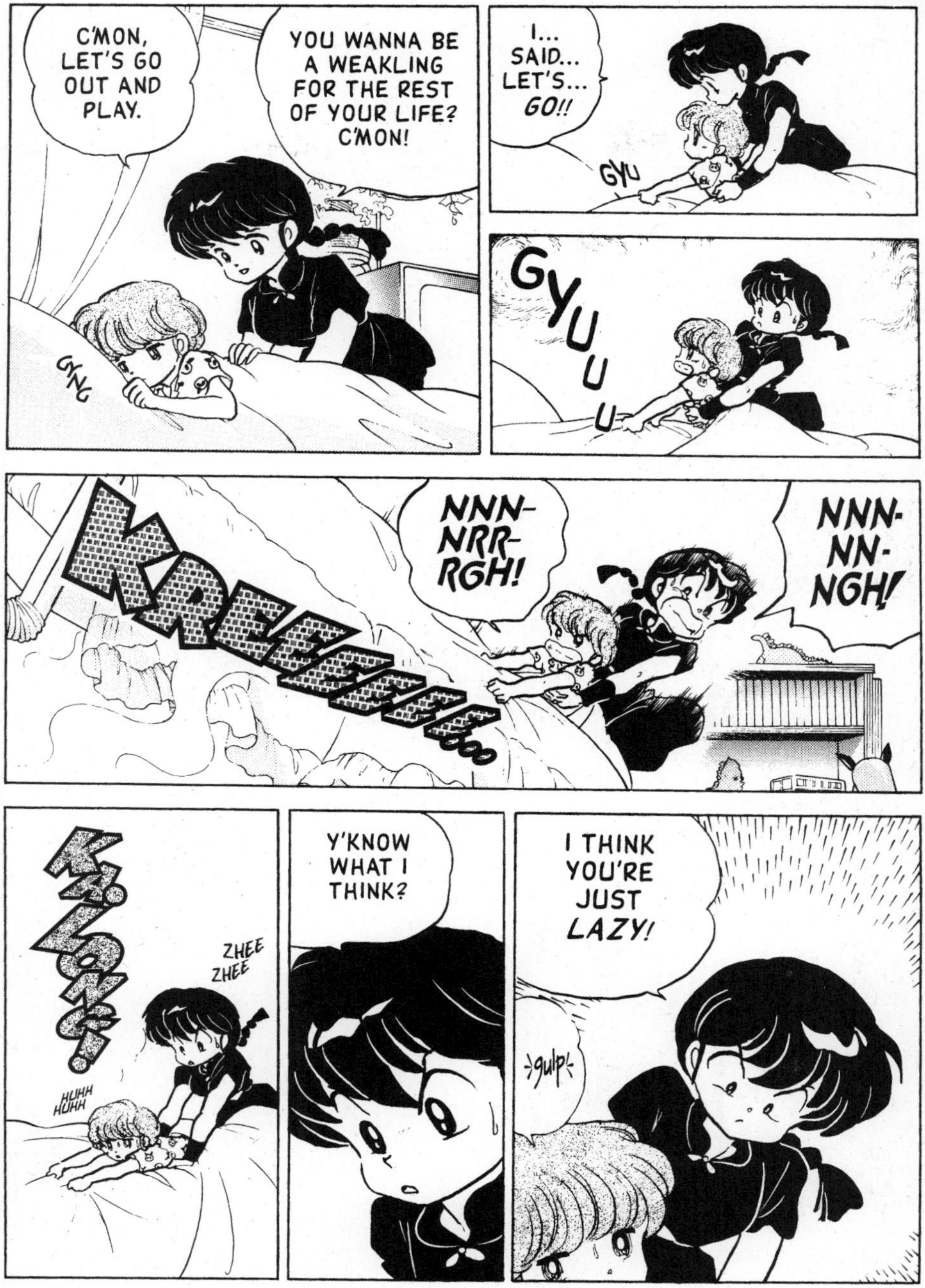
C'MON, LET'S GO OUT AND PLAY.
YOU WANNA BE A WEAKLING FOR THE REST OF YOUR LIFE? C'MON!
GYNG
I... SAID... LET'S... GO!!
GYU
GYUUUU
NNN-NRR-RGH!
NNN-NN-NGH!
K'LONG!
ZHEE ZHEE
HUHH HUHH
Y'KNOW WHAT I THINK?
I THINK YOU'RE JUST LAZY!
gulp

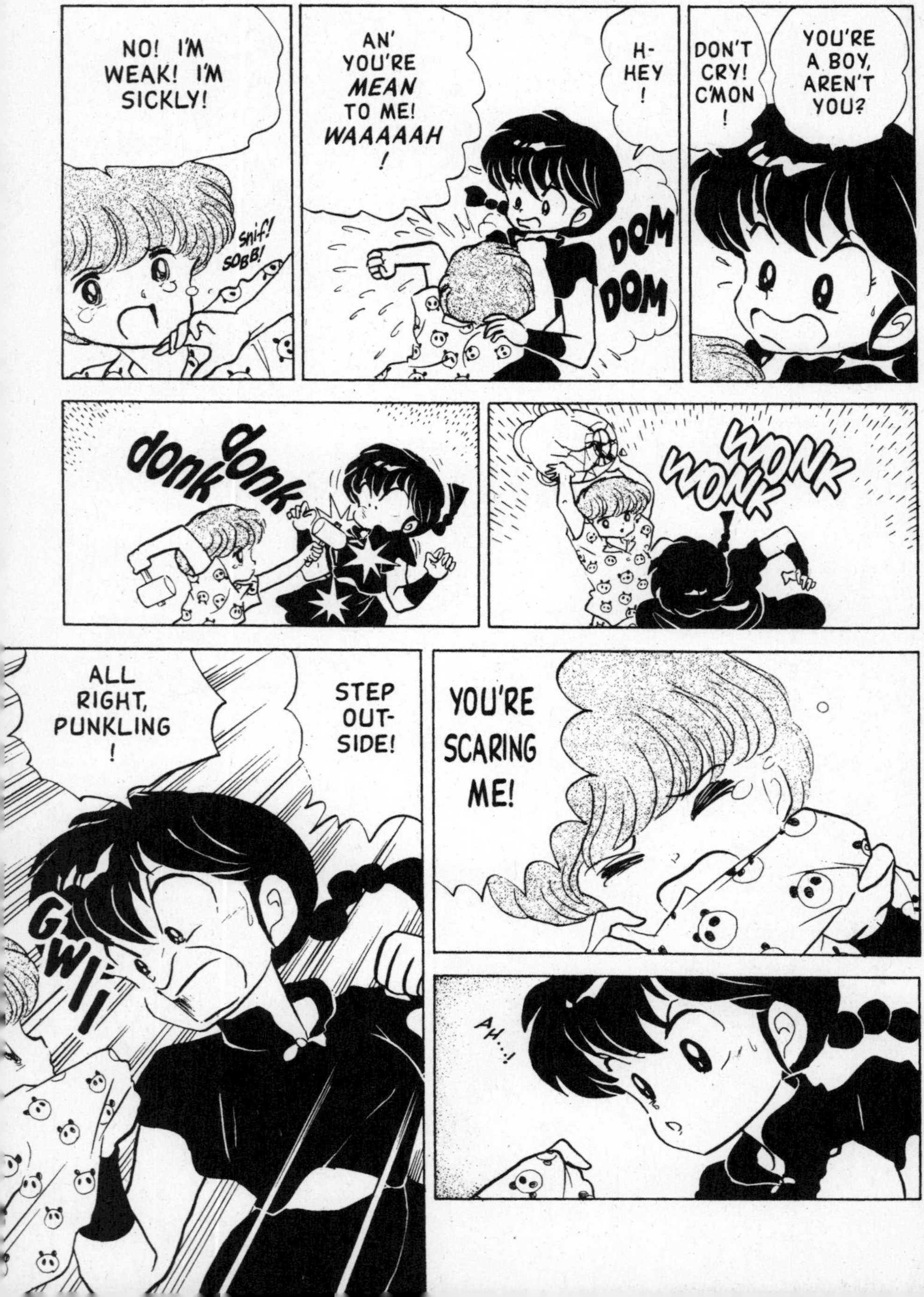
NO! I'M WEAK! I'M SICKLY!
Snif! SOBB!
AN' YOU'RE MEAN TO ME! WAAAAAH!
H-HEY!
DOM DOM
DON'T CRY! C'MON!
YOU'RE A BOY, AREN'T YOU?
donk donk
WONK WONK
ALL RIGHT, PUNKLING!
STEP OUT-SIDE!
GWIII
YOU'RE SCARING ME!
AH...!

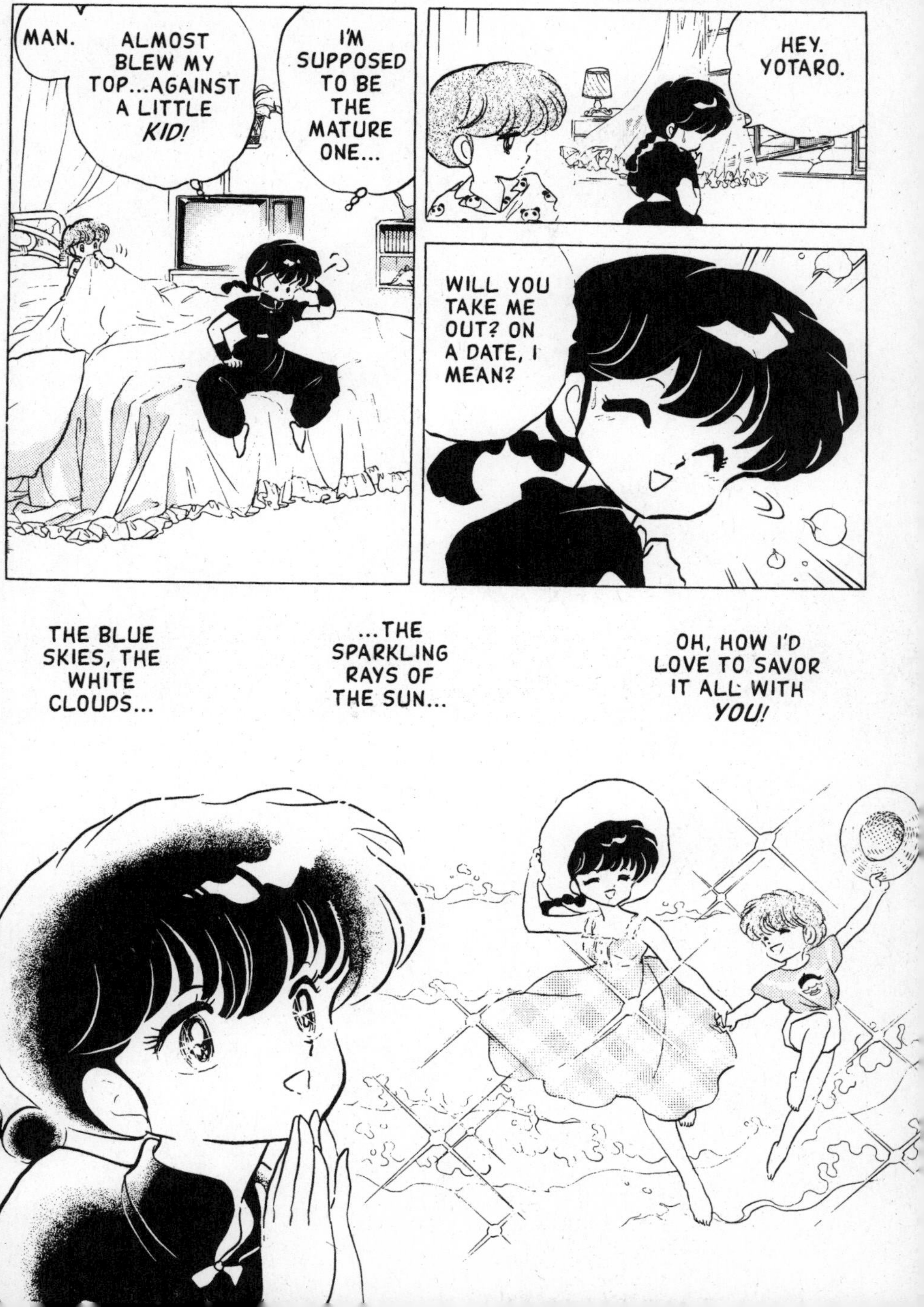
MAN.
ALMOST BLEW MY TOP...AGAINST A LITTLE *KID!*
I'M SUPPOSED TO BE THE MATURE ONE...
HEY. YOTARO.
WILL YOU TAKE ME OUT? ON A DATE, I MEAN?
THE BLUE SKIES, THE WHITE CLOUDS...
...THE SPARKLING RAYS OF THE SUN...
OH, HOW I'D LOVE TO SAVOR IT ALL WITH *YOU!*

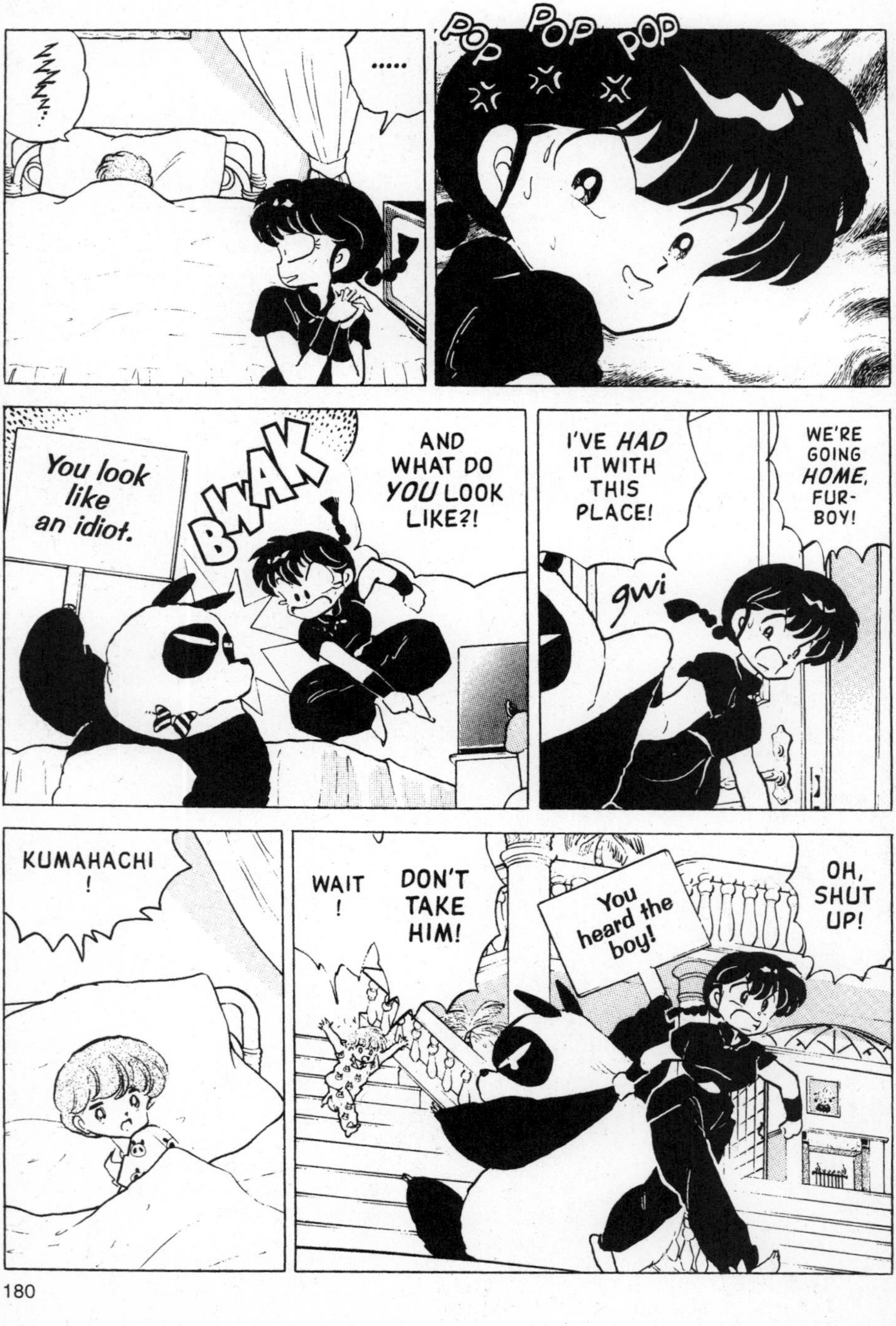
ZZZZZ...
.....
POP POP POP
You look like an idiot.
BWAK
AND WHAT DO YOU LOOK LIKE?!
I'VE HAD IT WITH THIS PLACE!
gwi
WE'RE GOING HOME, FUR-BOY!
KUMAHACHI !
WAIT !
DON'T TAKE HIM!
You heard the boy!
OH, SHUT UP!

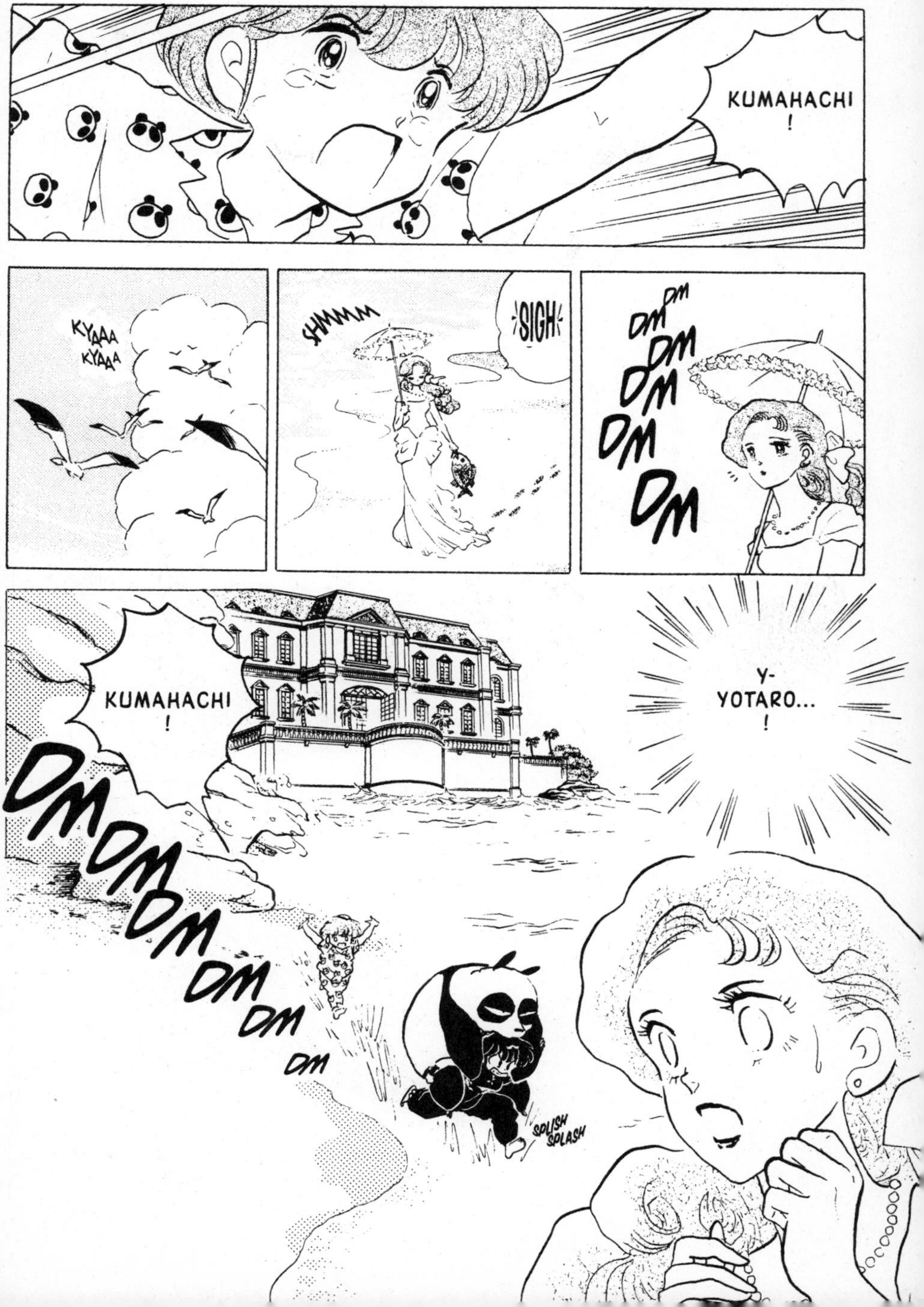
KUMAHACHI
!
KYAAA
KYAAA
SHMMM
SIGH
DM DM
DM
DM
DM
DM
KUMAHACHI
!
Y-
YOTARO...
!
DMDMDMDMDMDM
DM
DM
SPLISH
SPLASH

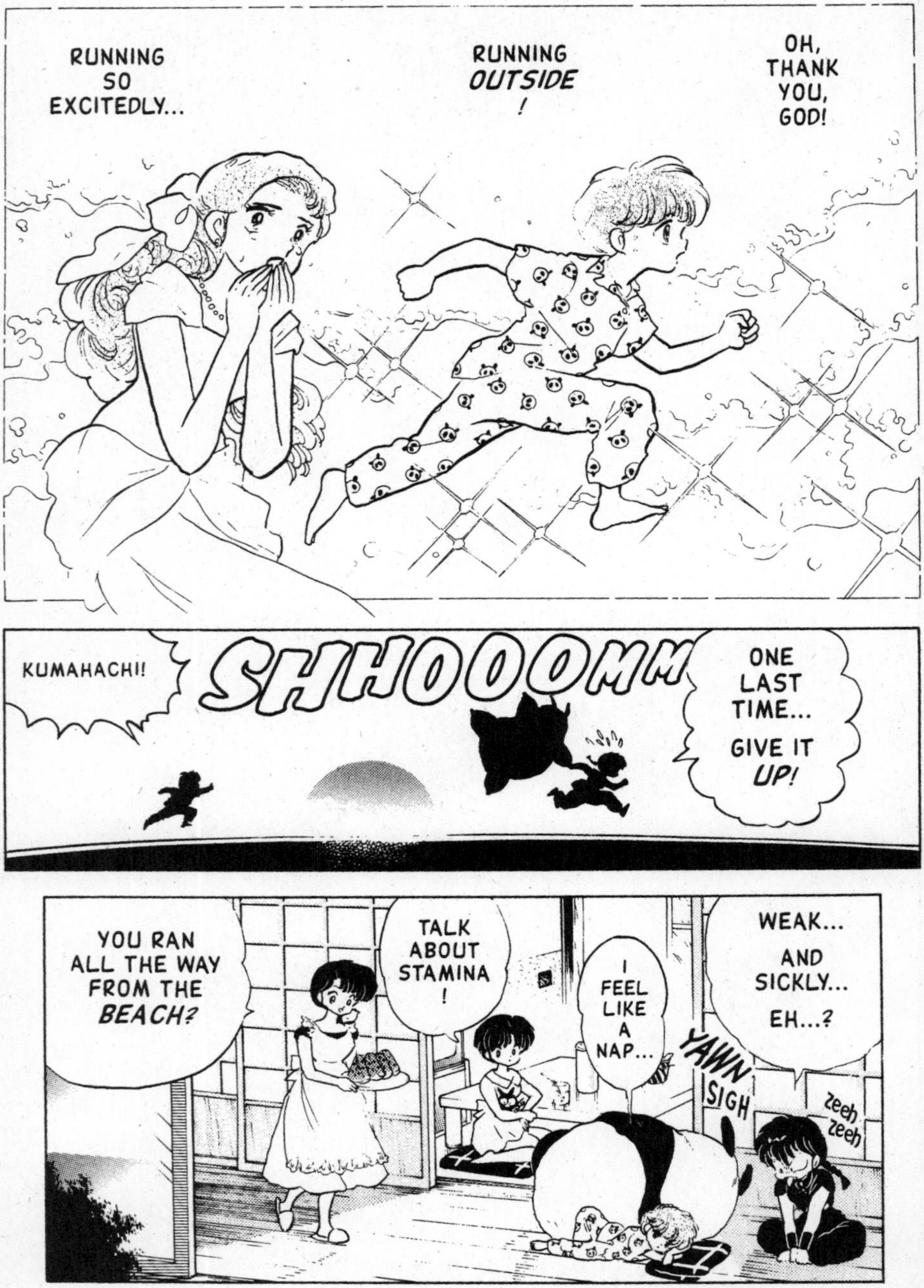
RUNNING SO EXCITEDLY...
RUNNING OUTSIDE!
OH, THANK YOU, GOD!
KUMAHACHI!
SHHOOOMM
ONE LAST TIME... GIVE IT UP!
YOU RAN ALL THE WAY FROM THE BEACH?
TALK ABOUT STAMINA!
I FEEL LIKE A NAP...
WEAK... AND SICKLY... EH...?
YAWN
SIGH
zeeh zeeh

END OF RANMA 1/2 VOLUME 12.